A Misplaced Child

Heather Michelle

Books by Heather Michelle

The Misplaced Children Series

A Misplaced Child

A Misplaced Hope (coming soon)

Late for Dinner Press LLC
P.O. Box 982
Acworth, GA 30101

Edited by Kat Betts of Element Editing Services

Map design by Lizard Ink Maps

Cover Design & Illustration by Rachel George Illustration:
www.rachelgeorgeillustration.com

First Edition: September 2020
ISBN 978-1-952857-00-3

———

To Jesus
For literally everything

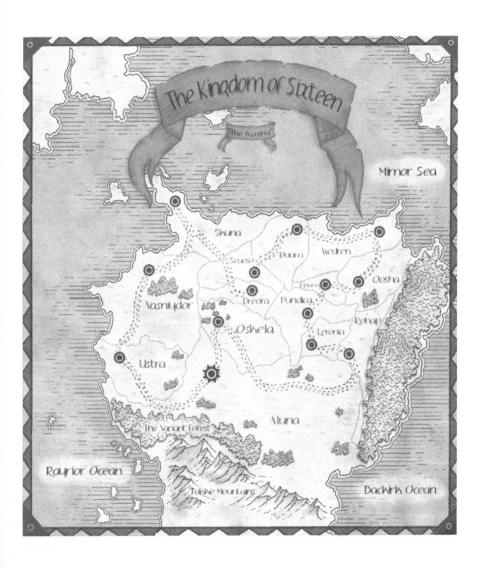

A MISPLACED CHILD

Book One in the Misplaced Children Series

HEATHER MICHELLE

Chapter One

SHE SWORE she would never again tell the truth, at least not when it really mattered.

Telling the truth only hurt her parents and made the kids at school act like jerks. The truth forced her to sit in this room for an hour, three times a week. Defending her actions, thoughts, and emotions was taking its toll. The problem was, if your truth was different from the people around you, didn't it become a lie?

"How was school today?" Doctor Abernathy asked.

"Fine," she lied. She turned from the window to face him.

He sighed and brought his rollie chair around his desk to be close for their 'casual conversation'. Three times a week for four weeks, and you think he would anticipate her preference for the window.

Her head was foggy and she tried to push it away. She needed to be sharp.

Elodie looked back out through the glass to the trees lining the parking lot; hedge maple, amur maple, sweet crabapple. Maple trees symbolized prosperity in many cultures, while an apple tree could be used for regeneration. Bitter rejuvenation. Somewhat fitting for the view. All under-watered from the drought, over-pruned by poor maintenance, and jam-packed into the few feet of space separating the building from the parking lot. She could feel them in her bones, calling out for space, sunlight, and water. The fog flowed through her mind and she closed her eyes trying to focus on her immediate surroundings.

"And yesterday? Was school fine yesterday as well?"

She opened her eyes and tried not to wince. "Yep." She didn't make eye contact, he always got her when she looked him in the eye.

The doctor examined her with one eyebrow raised. She would try the expression later in a mirror to see if she could replicate the look. He dropped his gaze and took off his glasses. Pulling a small cloth out of his pocket, he cleaned each lens slowly as she waited for him to continue. Her parents were paying the bill, not her.

"Well, I'm glad to hear it. Your mother told me about the incident at lunch yesterday, I was worried you would be upset." He put the glasses back on his nose. The cloth went back into his shirt pocket and he leaned back. His chair creaked loudly.

She shrugged, eyes firmly on the wheels of his chair.

"Elodie, what have we agreed about non-verbal responses?"

"It's not helpful," she responded.

"Correct. It is not helpful for what we are trying to accomplish. Now"—the doctor straightened out his arm as if readying the pen in his hand—"would you like to try again and tell me how your day was?"

Elodie sighed to herself. She didn't have to lie, just downplay her feelings, and leave out anything which would make her mom close her eyes and start muttering under her breath.

She could do this.

"They made it into a bigger deal than it was," she began. "Some kids were playing around and trying to get me to tell them another story. I didn't feel like playing, so I told them no. They were pretending like my stories were real and one of the boys was sword fighting a pretend monster and accidentally knocked someone's tray into my table right as Mr. Roberts walked by. He didn't know it was just a game, so he talked to the principal."

Doctor Abernathy shifted in his seat, and the long pause afterward almost made Elodie look up. Maybe he would believe her.

"To clarify, Jackson Gram didn't intentionally drop a plate of spaghetti on your head?" the doctor asked.

No, he definitely didn't believe her.

"I get how it may have seemed like it, but no, it was an accident."

"And these boys were playing a game with you, not making fun of the fantasy world you say you belong in, or about the spell you tell me is trapping you in this world?" His voice dripped with skepticism.

"Exactly."

He was silent again. Was this a thing all doctors did? Leave long pauses in the hopes their victims would crack?

"Up until now, you have been . . . adamant your stories were reality. You said you were living between two worlds, ours and a magical one. Do you no longer feel this way?"

This was it. Time to see if lying really would get her out of trouble. "It was just a game I used to play, but I think I'm done with it. Everyone got so mad at me for pretending my stories were real, it's not fun anymore."

She glanced up at the doctor to see if he was buying it. His eyebrows were raised and his mouth was slightly open. He schooled his features into the quizzical distant look she knew so well and cleared his throat.

"I'm done with all the fairy tales," Elodie lied.

More silence.

She glanced up again. He was examining her closely. She averted her eyes out the window again, watching the sway of the trees in the wind.

Silence.

Doctor Abernathy cleared his throat again and leafed through his notebook. "So to clarify, you are saying you do not believe you are trapped in a spell?"

"Correct."

He peered at her with his eyebrows drawn together. "What planet were you born on?"

"Earth," she said firmly.

"Not Eres?"

"Nope. It was just made up."

More flipping through pages full of tiny scribbled notes. "And you have never been to the Kingdom of Fourteen?"

"Sixteen," she corrected automatically. "And no, it was pretend."

Doctor Abernathy tapped his pen on his notepad, not taking his eyes off of her. "I thought there were only fourteen countries, not sixteen."

Elodie sighed. "No, that was the point. There were originally sixteen but two of them got disassembled. That's why they call it the Twoshy . . . in the stories I created. It doesn't really matter. It was just pretend."

"Right. And so you are saying you do not believe you are a princess and heir to the throne of"—he thumbed through his notes, and tapped a page with the end of his pen—"Aluna. You're not really Princess Elodie of Aluna? The lost princess who was trapped in a spell by an evil wizard?"

"Of course not!" Elodie gave him a look as if to say she thought he was foolish. She thought it was a nice touch, and judging by his flabbergasted look, she counted it as a point to herself.

The doctor broke eye contact first, another point to the crazy girl, and flipped back through his notebook until he looked as if he'd found something good. He nodded slightly to himself, then looked back to Elodie, his eyes narrowed. "So it was all a game? Everything about the Two–shy was made up? All the friends you have told me so much about, even the wizard Gediminas?"

This one was harder for her. The bottom of her stomach was slowly sinking into her shoes. Would it be betraying them to say they weren't real? No. This world wasn't real, she was trapped in it and had to do whatever it took to survive until she was free. While she was here, living in this world where magic made her strange, she could pretend like they didn't exist.

"Nope. They were made up. I made it all up to make myself feel more special," she parroted. The words were familiar to her. So many times she heard her mom say the same to her dad.

He grilled her for a few more minutes as though trying to catch Elodie out on a lie, but she tried to keep her answers short. It was hard. She made sure to use words like *childish* and *immature* a few times with scorn to make it clear this was a decision derived from the enlightenment of her age.

She wasn't sure he believed her, but he seemed satisfied with her answers and moved on to asking her how she felt about going to school the next day.

When her hour was up, Elodie tried not to show her impatience as she said her goodbye, and opened the office door to her mother flipping through magazines in the waiting room.

"Finished already?" Elodie's mother asked in a sugary voice.

Her mother adjusted Elodie's shirt. The movement had become a ritual, her mom pulling the collar of Elodie's shirt higher until the edge of her stark-brown birthmark was hidden.

Her mom had a running theory it wasn't really a birthmark at all, regardless of what the pediatrician said. It must be a tattoo. No birthmark was such a clear and distinct shape. Once or twice Elodie overheard conversations, when her mother said the adoption agency kept Elodie fully clothed during their visits to hide the strange mark. It was a crack in the frame of an expensive TV the salesperson covered up, and now they were past their return policy and couldn't get a perfect model.

"Good afternoon, Mrs. Harper," Doctor Abernathy said. "Before you leave, I wanted a moment to talk about Elodie's prescription."

"I'll be in the car." Elodie picked up her backpack and headed for the door.

"I think we should keep her dosage where it's at for the moment, and see how things . . ."

Elodie walked out into the large, open lobby toward the scent of fresh air. Things had gone well considering this was her first time outright lying to an adult. Still, a knot formed in the pit of her stomach.

Wizard Gediminas always said truth and magic were tied together. If a mage wasn't honest, the fallacy bled into their spells and could cause the spell to break down, backfire, or explode. Gedas was just beginning to teach her what her small plant magic was capable of, but Elodie still felt like not being truthful was a mark against her soul or conscience or whatever was inside of her.

"Hey, Harpy! What are you doing here?"

Elodie stopped, her body cringing at the voice. In the middle of the lobby was a stone fountain, with a wide bench wrapped around. On the bench sat Greg Roberts, Jackson's best friend, pale skin, dirty blond hair and a nasty glint in his shining blue eyes.

Greg looked back toward the office door Elodie had emerged from and squinted as though reading the nameplate and profession on the door.

"Woah, you really are crazy, aren't you?"

Elodie's heart began to pound and the blood rushed into her cheeks. She turned and kept walking toward the exit.

"Hey, wait up!"

Feet pounded behind her as Greg ran up to her. She wanted to run, but he would only make fun of her. She should say something smart or sarcastic to get him to leave her alone.

Her mind went blank, and she gave up on the idea. He would find a way to make her feel dumb for anything she said.

"I knew a kid who used to go to that same office. Doctor Abernathy, right? The kid was so crazy he got locked up in some institution. His parents couldn't deal with him, and the doctors couldn't fix him, so they shipped him off."

Elodie stopped walking. The world tilted for a moment and the blood rushed out of her head. Her parents wouldn't lock her up. It had to be nonsense. They may look sometimes like they regretted adopting her, but they wouldn't lock her up.

Greg was examining her, a small smile on his face. "So how much longer do you think we'll have to deal with you before they send you away?"

A door with a large happy tooth logo opened to their right and a tall beautiful blond woman walked out with a boy who looked like an older version of Greg.

"Greg honey, ready to go?" the woman asked, looking their way.

"Be right there, Mom!" Greg said. He turned back to Elodie. "See you at school, Harpy!" His voice was cheerful and warm and burned against Elodie as he caught up to his family and left the building.

Elodie stood there speechless. She knew her parents were mad at her, but she hadn't imagined they would send her away. She felt sick.

Stepping out of the stuffy building, Elodie saw her mom's SUV parked near the small strip of trees. She made her way to the closest tree, standing in the shade of the yellowing leaves. She put one hand on the gray, black bark, ridged and furrowed under her hand, and let the plant's steady nature seep into her. Reaching into the tree's leaves, she plucked a few of the maple's winged seeds and tucked them into a pocket.

If Elodie became a tree she vowed never to be a hedge maple, and to never be planted in a parking lot. Trees lent peace and protection to their surroundings, while magically they provided strength. Standing there, she had to put the feeling of otherness out of her mind and ignore what she felt from the tree. It was a good way to clear her head and let the anxiety and fear leave her.

Gedas always said trees didn't have feelings, they weren't sentient. While Elodie knew he was probably correct, when her magic made a diagnostic scan of the plants around her it was easier to understand the results by thinking of them as feelings. The plants felt sentient to her.

If her mom overheard, she would say such notions were exactly why she had to take pills, and why she had to talk to Doctor Abernathy, and for goodness sake to get such dangerous ideas out of her mind.

By the time her mom exited the building, Elodie was out from under the tree, and leaning against the locked car. The locks clicked and Elodie opened the door and was buckled in before her mom reached her.

Her mom was silent as they left the parking space and drove to the end of the lot before sitting with the blinker on, waiting for a gap in traffic.

Tick. Tick. Tick. Tick.

Her mother merged into traffic.

"Doctor Abernathy told me you had a great session. He said I should ask you about it," her mom said in her sweetly scripted voice. "So honey, would you like to tell me what you talked about? Did you tell him another story?" The question was posed with a shaky note, and Elodie prepared herself for what she hoped would be a short conversation.

"No, Mom, I didn't tell him any stories. I told him I was done playing that game."

"What game are we talking about exactly, honey?"

Elodie took a deep breath. After years of her mother ordering her to stop making up stories and to quit playing pretend, after years and years of yelling back, pleading, praying, begging for her mother to believe she was telling the truth, Elodie was going to surrender the battle. There was this part of her, deep in her chest that shook with rage at giving up. Her pride wanted to dig in and never back down. Realizing she was clenching her fists, Elodie forced herself to relax and stick her hands in her jacket pockets. She fingered the winged seeds.

"I told him I was done pretending magic and the Twoshy were real. It was a fun game when I was little, but everyone started taking it so seriously, and it's not fun anymore."

Silence reigned again. The car rolled to a stop at the next red light. Elodie threaded the maple seed pod through her fingers and listened for her mother's reaction. Nonverbal communication really did suck when you were trying not to look at someone.

"It was all pretend?" her mother asked, her voice soft and breathy.

Was it disbelief in her voice? Elodie hoped not. "Yeah."

The light turned green. "So, you don't believe it's all real?"

Yep, definitely disbelief.

"I never did, Mom." Her voice wavered, full of defeat. "It was all imagination. Magic, Santa Claus, the Easter Bunny, Hogwarts, God, the Twoshy. Didn't Dad say last week when I lost my molar, twelve was old enough to know the Tooth Fairy isn't real and to grow up and stop playing make-believe?"

She saw her mom flinch out of the corner of her eye. She probably hadn't realized Elodie heard that particular discussion.

"Well I'm stopping now," Elodie said.

The overheard conversation between her parents made its way back through her mind. "Could it be genetic?" her father had asked. The fear of a closed adoption. Maybe her birth mother had been forced to give up Elodie due to mental illness. Maybe Elodie would follow the same path.

Her mom didn't speak, and Elodie resigned herself to looking out the window. She tracked their progress on the familiar route home. When they passed the high school and pulled onto their road, her mom finally spoke.

"Maybe it's for the best, honey. Maybe make-believe and pretending is too dangerous for you. If this whole time you really have been playing a game in your head, it clearly got out of hand. You do see that, right? How your game has hurt people?" There was a realness in her mother's voice Elodie didn't think she'd ever heard.

"What about when you went missing? We searched and searched for so long. The police set up alerts looking for you all over the state, the mall went on lockdown. And then for weeks . . ." Her voice broke, and she took a deep breath as she pulled into the driveway and turned to her daughter. Elodie faced her. "Elodie, we thought you were dead. Do you understand?" A tear fell out of her mother's eye. She'd never seen her mother cry, and the sight was shocking.

Maybe lying really would be for the best.

Her mother wiped away the tear and took a deep breath. When she spoke again, her voice was solid. "I'm not going to ask you right now what you were really doing when you went missing. We can have the conversation another day, but, Elodie, I want you to really think about what you're saying. I want you to decide if admitting it was all a game is true, or . . . Well, just think about why you're saying this now. Why after pretending this fantasy was real, are you suddenly willing to admit you made it up? Why now?"

Elodie looked at her mom with so many questions on the tip of her brain, but only nodded. Satisfied, her mom exited the car.

Elodie hung back, sitting in the car in their shady driveway. The afternoon sun shone through the thick canopy of the old oak tree filling their front yard. She tried to figure out what exactly her mom wanted her to think about. The way she'd asked her 'why now', there was a point she wasn't getting, some fact her mother saw and Elodie hadn't made the connection to. In the end it didn't really matter since she was lying about it all anyway.

The Twoshy was real. Magic was real, even if she could barely feel it in this world. The wizard Gedas, and everyone living in Aluna, her kingdom, they were all real. None of it would change just because of what she told her parents and Doctor Abernathy.

Chapter Two

THE ALARM CLOCK was impossible to ignore. Elodie awoke feeling groggy and switched it off. She reached up a hand and touched the dried herb hanging from her headboard. The tarragon was working, her sleep was again free from nightmares and chaotic dreams.

The plastic stars on her ceiling glowed faintly in the darkness. She'd changed a few of the star patterns over the years without her parents noticing, to make up constellations seen in Eres. Now while she lay in bed, she could see Kellis the Elvman and The Dwarv's Hammer alongside Orion and The Little Dipper. The sight made her homesick.

That was good. When she first traveled back from the Twoshy she missed it so much it hurt, but now the memories had faded like a dream.

After readying for her day, Elodie followed the smell of sizzling bacon downstairs. A table laid with toast and bacon greeted her. Elodie filled a glass with orange juice as her mom added eggs to her plate and set two pills next to her cup.

"Good morning, honey!" her mom declared in a voice sweeter than a glazed doughnut. Elodie wished her mom a slightly less excited morning and swallowed her pills with orange juice before devouring her food. Her father appeared a moment later, summoned by the frying bacon and began shoveling food into his mouth in a similar fashion, pausing for sips of coffee. Her mom set her own plate on the table and sat, taking small, dainty bites.

"Can I have another piece of bacon?" Elodie asked.

"No, you don't need it, honey." Her mom patted her face with a napkin. "I found more leaves and twigs in my washing machine last night. Do you think that's one of the things you can work on next, sweetie?" Her mother's voice was sweet, but the small worry line in her forehead was showing. "Maybe stop picking up every plant you find, and try clearing some of the dead plants out of your room?"

They weren't dead, they were dried. Elodie bit back the words so they didn't escape.

"I mean if they aren't magical to you anymore, why keep them?" her mom asked.

The idea made panic tingle up her spine. She couldn't get rid of her plants. The dried snakeroot for stress and balance, and the toadflax blossoms for peace. Elodie had bad dreams. Gedas said they were prophetic, but she would happily trade that for ignorance and a good night's sleep.

She couldn't imagine her room still being hers if she got rid of her plants.

She had to find an excuse to keep them. Something normal. Something that was the opposite of magic.

When his food was gone, her father leaned back from the table as though just noticing the other people in the room. "Well, isn't it shaping up to be a wonderful day?"

Her mom agreed in the most elegant language, it certainly would be a wonderful day, and her father looked from wife to daughter as though expecting a similar expression from his preteen child. Elodie wasn't feeling particularly conforming at the moment and took her plate to the sink without replying.

Not missing a beat, her father rose from the table. "Alright, well it's that time again, family." He tapped his watch. "I'm off to work some papers."

"Oh, have a wonderful day, my darling," Elodie's mother said, doting on her husband while Elodie turned the water blast stronger on her plate. She grabbed her parents' plates, eating the last piece of bacon off her mom's before rinsing them off.

Her mom ushered her dad out and provided him with bag, keys and wallet. "I love you."

"I love you too, my dear," her father said, grabbing his things and walking out. "Bye, Elodie pumpkin!"

"Bye Dad," Elodie said, loud enough for him to hear.

Once the fanfare of her father's departure was over, Elodie laced up her sneakers and grabbed her backpack. Turning to the door, her mother had keys in hand, their perfectly choreographed morning coming to a close. "Ready, honey?"

Elodie nodded and headed to the SUV.

AS SOON AS her feet hit the pavement outside school, Elodie knew deep down the day was going to suck. What was the point in trying when you already knew how things would end?

The school campus had a combination of old buildings, new buildings still mostly under construction, and random, temporary modules. It all came together in a confused layout. The buildings and cement walkways were painted gray and brick-red, and the new side of the school didn't have any plants or trees in their newly created planter boxes.

The space felt empty and lifeless.

Elodie took a route through the mess of pathways she hoped would pass the fewest students possible. Unfortunately, her first class was in one of the new buildings on the edge of the quad where most students congregated for their last bit of social interaction before the bell.

Head down, she tried to make her way into the quad unseen. No speaking, no sudden movements, and absolutely no eye contact. Walk with your eyes on your feet, but do everything in your power not to bump anyone. If people didn't notice her, they were less likely to start chanting.

Elodie stepped around the corner of the old gym, her first class in sight.

"Crazy girl! Hey, crazy girl!"

"Fatty."

"What's it like in a padded cell?"

A boy ran ahead of her for a moment as though heralding her presence amidst the chants. "Make way for Elodie Harper, princess of the neverworld!"

"Crazy girl, crazy girl!"

"Hey! Is it true your crazy doctor is going to send you away soon?"

"Gonna tell us another story, Harpy?"

Ice ran up her bones and into her stomach. Elodie didn't look up, didn't make eye contact to judge the reactions around her. She felt hot, her cheeks were burning. She just had to make it to the classroom. If she didn't look up, and didn't give them a reaction, they would lose interest faster. She was shaking, every muscle tight and rigid.

Something collided with her shoulder and she flinched.

"El darling, there you are." An arm hooked with hers and pulled her off course. "I really effed up my math homework, can we compare before class?"

A wave of relief and chills ran down her back.

The chanting changed for a moment. "Vanessa and Elodie sitting in a tree, K – I – S – S – I – N – G—"

"What's wrong, Jackson? Jealous you can't get a girl half as hot as me or Elodie? Maybe you should try asking out a trash can. At least *it* won't mind your breath!" Vanessa yelled back before pulling Elodie into the bathroom.

As soon as the bathroom door closed, Elodie dropped her backpack and leaned against the cold brick wall in the dark alcove behind the door. She closed her eyes as the blood pulsed in her head. She tried to breathe out the rage and anger, but her vision wavered black for a moment. Something shockingly cold pressed up against her cheek and Elodie's eyes snapped open. Vanessa's big dark brown eyes peered out of her warm brown face. "Sorry, your cheeks are so red. I thought it would help."

Elodie sighed and took the clump of brown wet paper towels from Vanessa and pressed them against her face. Her cheeks were so hot, she was sure she looked like a talking tomato. "Thanks for the save."

"I thought we agreed you would have your mom drop you down at the end of the road, then we would walk in together?" Vanessa asked, hands on her hips.

Elodie sighed. "Was it as bad as it seemed?"

"No, of course it wasn't as bad as it seemed, El, that's the point. It's never as bad as it feels when you're the one in the middle." Vanessa was rubbing her face as though tired with life. "You just need to learn not to take it so hard so they don't get anything out of it. At least this time you didn't start yelling. GOD that was so bad Monday at lunch, like, you want to know the one thing to make bullies flock to the scene? Start yelling at them to back off like you were doing."

"Nessa," Elodie cut her friend off, before she spent the rest of the day running off with her tirade. "I'm not like you. I'm not as strong as you. When they start in on me, it's like I'm standing in a spotlight and everyone's taking a turn punching. I just can't think."

Vanessa leaned against the wall beside Elodie. "You need to judge the source those words are coming from. If you don't value the person, don't put any value into the words they spew. You are you, and that's perfect." She stepped in close to Elodie, and tapped her on the nose. "You were created for a plan and a reason, so embrace it, and forget anyone who tries to tell you anything else, because this is junior high, and if this was gonna be the pinnacle of life, well, we might as well end it all now."

"Vanessa, if any of the teachers heard you say that, you would be in as much counseling as I am." The earthy wet cardboard smell of the paper towels grounded her and helped regain her focus.

"No, you missed the point, I'm not saying we *should* end it, I'm saying if junior high was what life was all about, *then* we should. But it's not! My dad says the things we experience today may play a small part in who we are someday, but overall, this is just like a tiny blip in our lives. We just have to get through the hellhole that is being a teenager." Vanessa was standing in the middle of the bathroom with her arms out to her sides and finished it all off with a little spin. Elodie couldn't help the small smile making its way onto her face.

"Just promise me you won't move before we graduate, and I think I might survive."

"I promise, but . . ." Vanessa's face fell for a moment, the inner light she radiated dimmed. "I can't follow you into the Twoshy, El. Ultimately, it will be you leaving me when the spell breaks and you go live there forever."

The joy creeping slowly back into Elodie flew out the window. In Eres it was believed this world where Elodie stood right now wasn't real. It was all a spell, an illusion Elodie was trapped in. There were times, like when kids started chanting, where Elodie only got through the moment by knowing none of it was real. But there were moments, like this one, where Elodie couldn't imagine someone as creative and smart and full of life as Vanessa was only a fabrication of the spell.

The bell for the first class rang and Elodie and Vanessa picked up their bags. Elodie tossed the now-warm paper towel in the trash. Opening the door to the glaring morning sun, Vanessa led Elodie to their first-period history class.

"So you still never told me why you didn't meet me before school."

"I didn't ask," Elodie replied. "Don't give me that look, I didn't forget. She's so on edge right now, looking for any reason to pronounce me crazy and report my behavior to the doctor, so I don't want to give her any more ammunition to think anything is out of ordinary."

"What do you mean looking for any reason? Isn't she pretty sold on thinking you're crazy?"

"Hopefully not anymore," Elodie muttered.

"What?"

Elodie stopped and took a deep breath. They didn't have a lot of time, but Vanessa was as invested in Elodie's life as she was. "I lied to them, told them the Twoshy isn't real, and it's a game I made up. But I don't think they believe me yet."

Vanessa was a big believer in honesty. It was one of the reasons Elodie trusted her completely. Elodie hoped Vanessa would understand, and wouldn't hate her for being dishonest.

Honesty, honor, virtue. These were the traits the Twoshy ran on, and were things Elodie worked her hardest to live by.

"Hmmmm." Vanessa tapped her chin with one glittery fingernail. They resumed walking to their classroom and Elodie braced for the worst.

"What?" Elodie asked after a moment. She needed to know if this was the end of their seven-year friendship.

"I was thinking, maybe I could help. Like maybe I could back you up, pretend like it's a game we both played? Like it was something we came up with together and I was in on the whole time. Your mom would believe it, she already thinks I'm weird."

"No, she thinks you're 'odd'."

"Same difference. Well, what do you think? If she asks me I'll play along."

"You mean you're okay with me lying?"

They stopped at the classroom door, the last few students pushed past them. "El, I know you aren't a liar. But desperate times call for desperate measures. You're starting to get into serious trouble over this, all because some stuffy adults refuse to believe in the fantastical. What other choice do we have but to lie?" Vanessa stopped and looked at her pointedly. "Do you think it will help?"

"I'm not sure. She knows I first started talking about the Twoshy a few weeks before we met." The anger drained away, leaving her tired and heavy. Thinking about going to class made Elodie's stomach feel like it was filled with broken glass.

"Yeah, but the day we met you spent all of recess telling me about the cool adventure you went on. Just make it clear we aren't in kindergarten anymore. It was like, our inside joke, the game that brought us together. I mean, your cool stories are why I always hung out with you over the other girls when we were little."

Elodie's eyes narrowed. "Why do you hang out with me now?"

Vanessa sighed like it was obvious. "Because now you're my person, stupid." She tapped Elodie in the middle of her forehead, then ducked into the classroom to find her seat.

The newly constructed classrooms were big and airy with large windows along one side pointing toward the cement quad. In History, Elodie did her best to lose herself in reviewing the next chapter on colonization. Toward the end of the lesson, Elodie's head felt fuzzy and she stared at the board mindlessly.

Suddenly, Vanessa dropped into the desk in front of her, startling the fog away.

"Wow, you okay, El?" Vanessa asked quietly.

Elodie looked around and realized most of the class had broken up into smaller groups. If Mr. Eleon finished early, he let them start on their homework for the remainder of the class, which was code for talk and not get too rowdy. Elodie put her hand on her forehead and closed her eyes briefly. "Yeah, I think I just zoned out for a bit."

"It's not the ruakh, is it?" Vanessa looked around them for the shimmery force Elodie had described many times. In the Twoshy, ruakh was everywhere, like oxygen in the air, it was magic powering the world. But here in the illusion, where magic didn't exist naturally, when a little did slip in it was a visible force in the air. Try as she might, Elodie had never been able to point it out to Vanessa.

"No, ruakh doesn't make me feel like this. Besides, I just traveled six weeks ago, it'll be months before I travel again." Elodie opened her binder and started writing her header on a fresh sheet of paper, copying the homework from the board.

"Yeah, but don't you sometimes see ruakh floating around even when you don't travel? Floating through the air like fine glitter caught in a breeze? God, what I wouldn't give to see magic like you, like, I know it's not perfect and everything, your life being ruled by a magic spell and all, but to be able to use magic . . ."

Elodie looked up at her best friend who was staring into nothing, a look of wistfulness on her face. The ruakh followed Elodie as it found cracks around her existence in the illusion and slipped in, but it usually only showed up in the days before or after she traveled, as though the spell got weaker in those moments allowing magic into this world.

The bell rang, and both girls packed up their bags. Vanessa headed toward the gym for P.E. and Elodie made her way to Math. Her Math classroom was one of four temporary modules clustered together up the small hill on the other side of the library. She headed toward the second building on the left when the bulletin board stretched out between the two classrooms caught her eye.

Regional Science Fair Competition, the heading of one flyer read, followed by information about prizes and awards of extra credit. *Never too early to start building your college resume.*

Elodie didn't care much about college prep, as she hoped to be living in the Twoshy full time by then, but another thought crossed her mind. Her mother definitely cared about her college resume. If Elodie cared about it too, maybe it would make her mother think she was taking this world, this life, more seriously. Science fairs were also a very normal reason for a girl to be interested in plants. It could be the perfect excuse for Elodie to prove keeping plants in her life was normal, practical, and nonmagical.

Elodie ripped a small tab off the flyer with the competition's web address and something glittering and shimmering caught her attention from the corner of her eye. Turning, she saw Jackson and a few of his gang rounding the corner toward her. They were joking and shoving each other, one of them dribbling a basketball, and didn't seem to have noticed her.

The boys were not what had caught her attention. Her eyes refocused and all at once she saw the shimmer rise up, swirling in front of her, between her and the boys. She didn't have a moment to do anything but inhale with a gasp, before the ruakh was around her.

There was a sharp rich odor of freshly tilled earth, and the skin over her whole body tingled. A wind picked up, and she felt a pressure on her bones like something held her tight. She was pulled hard to the left and tumbled through nothing. The nothing moved around her like a raging storm and a gentle breeze. After an extended moment of empty chaos Elodie landed hard on her back. Dirt kicked up around her and she choked on the dust.

With a cough, Elodie said a bad word.

Chapter Three

"ELODIE, that is not very becoming language for a princess."

The voice came from somewhere above her and was followed with a soft chuckle. Elodie rolled onto her side to push herself up. Her backpack, weighed down with half a dozen books and binders, dug painfully into her back and made the maneuver difficult.

It was cold. Bitterly cold.

"I can't be late for class. Gedas, I *can't* be late." Once on her knees, Elodie escaped from her backpack and stood, hands balled into fists looking at her mentor, eyes pleading. She shivered. "If I'm late I'm going to be in so much trouble. Please, isn't there anything you can do to send me back?"

The man leaned on his staff. He looked down at her with his eyebrows pulled together, his gray eyes soft. "My Gull, you know I do not have any control over your emanation from the spell." He used the nickname he'd given her when she was small, not yet the powerful and large albatross of her family emblem, but instead a small seagull, an echo of the woman she would one day be.

Elodie shook her head. "No, that's not good enough. How can you always know when I'm going to show up and when I'm going to leave again if you don't have a way to send me back sooner?"

Her face was getting hot, a sharp contrast to the cold stinging every other part of her. "I can't stay here. If I get into trouble . . . Gedas, my mom wants to commit me! She wants to send me away to some facility where they'll tell me I'm crazy and try to 'cure' me." Tears stung at the corner of her eyes, and she reached up to wipe them away, smearing dirt across her face and into her eyes.

Gedas closed the few feet between them. Pulling a cloth out of an inner pocket he dusted off Elodie's head and carefully worked his way lower to clean her face and eyes. "Now start over, child. Tell me what's changed causing this trouble."

Elodie took a deep breath. "The last time I traveled, when I returned to the illusion, two weeks had passed there." Gedas's eyebrows rose but he didn't say anything. During the time she spent in the Twoshy, little time usually passed within the illusion's timestream. She was usually gone from Earth for minutes, an hour or two at most, regardless of how long she spent in Eres.

"My family thought I was kidnapped. They filled out missing person reports, and it was all over the news. When I finally got back the police found me, and well, they didn't like my explanation for where I was. I told them the truth, I was here in the Twoshy, but they all think this is make-believe and said I was lying. Then doctors got involved, and they started thinking maybe I'm crazy, like maybe I actually believe this is all real, which of course I *do* because it *is*, and now they have me on medication to try to fix me and I have to sit down and talk to this doctor three times a week so he can make sure I'm not going even more crazy."

She was looking down at her dirty sneakers while she talked, and Gedas quietly wiped away each tear as it appeared on her cheeks.

Gedas asked her to turn slowly for him, and he proceeded to beat the dirt off her clothes with his handkerchief. He hit her over the head a few more times than necessary and Elodie chuckled. Pulling a cloak out from under his arm he threw it over Elodie's back. He fastened it around her neck and lowered the soft fur-lined hood over her head.

"I've missed you, child." His smile was soft and his eyes sad.

Elodie held the cloak tight around herself, trying to warm her arms.

She looked the wizard over for the first time since she'd landed. He was wearing well-made breeches and a thick embroidered blue tunic that looked dashing with his olive skin. His boots and the edge of his brown cloak were dusty but of good quality. They must be close to a larger city and didn't plan to sleep in the dirt tonight. Gedas usually made a point to dress appropriately for such occasions, but his current wear looked like any average merchant. His hair was dark brown, streaked through with the beginnings of gray, and he looked like a man in his fifties with finely wrinkled skin, even if he was much older. You would never know he was a man powerful enough to rank as wizard. One of only a handful in the whole of Eres.

The only obvious thing setting Gedas apart from any other person you passed in a market was his long beard, hanging loose down his chest. Most men had beards of a similar length, but wearing a beard loose was not fashionable. Most men wore them braided intricately and neatly close to their chin, rivaling the updo hairstyles worn by women among the elite.

When she'd first met him, Gedas wore his beard in the current fashions, but on learning Gedas was a wizard, Elodie challenged the rank saying all wizards had pointy hats and long beards. Every visit to the Twoshy since, Gedas had worn his beard long, although the pointy hat only lasted a year or two.

"How long have I been gone?"

"About two years." Gedas bent down to pick up her backpack. With a loud groan he lifted the bag nearly high enough to be considered off the ground, and then released it, allowing it to thump back in place. "Reza, Dima, and Cooric!" he prayed. "Are you carrying bricks in here?" Gedas straightened up, a hand on his lower back.

Elodie snorted and picked up the bag. She slipped the scrap of paper from the science fair flyer into her jeans pocket. "I got a lot more classes and books this year. You get used to it." She looked around, suddenly dreading the idea of carrying her books more than the usual distance of one school building to another. There were fields as far as she could see, empty and barren for winter. A small barn, brown and weathered by age sat over a hill half a mile away. She looked at Gedas, disappointment in her heart. "Please don't tell me we have to sleep out here."

"Of course not!" He turned with a huff and a flourish of his cloak and walked toward the barn. "What do you take me for? A young man of eighty or ninety? Sleep outside in the middle of December? Hogwash!"

Elodie adjusted the pack on her shoulder, and followed the old man, praying silently they wouldn't have to sleep in the barn either.

Gedas threw open the rickety door of the barn, nearly taking it off the frame. Familiar horse sounds greeted them, and Elodie relaxed.

"Maybe you should divide up your burdens among the saddle-bags to not off balance the poor sod." Gedas narrowed his eyes as Elodie dropped the bag on the floor with a loud *thunk*.

Elodie shrugged and began hunting around the dark stable for the horse's equipment. Gedas murmured a few words, and a large glowing orb of periwinkle light floated up till it found a nice spot among the rafters. The light shifted in hue and lit up the room like an overcast winter day. The big bay stomped his displeasure and Elodie spotted the saddles and bags sitting in a corner. Dragging a saddle over to the smaller chestnut mare, she straightened the mare's blanket before heaving the saddle onto the horse's back with a groan.

She sighed. She was out of shape.

In the illusion she didn't have any of the daily physical activities life in the Twoshy required. It was hard to find motivation to stay in shape and keep her muscles sharp. She knew how to do something like saddle a horse, but when the spell sucked her back into the illusion she lost all the muscle she'd gained in the Twoshy.

She tightened the straps, and slipped the tack on the chestnut's head. By the weight of the feed bag Gedas had been waiting some time in the cold field. He always knew when and where she would arrive, but sometimes his timing was off.

Securing her books in the saddlebags, Elodie turned to check Gedas's progress, and saw he'd finished before her and was watching her. "And how long for you, my Gull, has it been since you were last with me?"

"Only about six weeks." Elodie grabbed the lead rein and guided the horse out of the barn. Gedas followed her, an inquisitive look she knew well on his face. Once they were both back in the light of day, a small slip of blue light followed them out, and zipped back into Gedas. It took Elodie three tries to mount her horse. Gedas, ever the diplomat, didn't say a word from his perch on the larger horse.

"Which way are we headed?" she asked.

"Hmmmmm." The wizard looked from side to side, and tugged gently on his beard. "You know, I think I have quite forgotten. Perhaps you can use your esteemed knowledge and resources to puzzle out our location." He looked to Elodie with raised eyebrows and a small upturn to his mouth.

"Oh, come on, Gedas, I'm cold and tired. Can't we just go?" Elodie asked with more than a little whine in her voice. Gedas stared unrelentingly at her, dropping one eyebrow and raising the other. Elodie sighed dramatically, knowing her answer, and closed her eyes. She growled a little to herself before she looked around.

She'd spent years of her life out in places like this, forests and fields, learning about the land and the world she was born in and would one day rule. She'd also spent nearly as much time in castles getting etiquette lessons and learning about politics of the kingdom. But Gedas was much fonder of the open empty spaces. He preferred taking her to small villages in the country, or the larger cities and towns around her kingdom where no one was looking for them, and no one knew their rank.

Being just an unknown girl was great, but Elodie didn't particularly like roughing it. Yes, some summer nights there was nothing better than sleeping in the middle of a field of moonseed, the fluffy white glowing seed pods releasing and floating off into the sky in the warm air. Or stretching out on a blanket under an open autumn sky, watching the spark bees fly here and there, buzzing and flashing. She felt connected and safe among the plants and trees, but she didn't enjoy finding insects in her bedroll, and she definitely didn't like sleeping on the frozen ground when Gedas refused to use extra magic for a heat charm. But regardless of the season or weather, Gedas dutifully taught Elodie to survive anywhere in her kingdom, and how to always find her way home.

Looking around, there really wasn't much to see. Lots of empty fields, with a few large barns on the horizon. If she had the right herbs, a little haircap moss or a few sunflower petals, she could use them to magically tell the direction, but in this empty winter field the hibernating seeds and stocks left over from harvest would do no good. She looked up at the sky and the mist hanging low along the hills and decided it was morning. This put the large barns to the west and east with the small tool barn smack in the middle.

This was one of the larger slave farms circling the castles in Aluna. In the correct seasons, those large barns would be filled with people, iron rings glinting around their necks. Her nose wrinkled at the thought but she pushed it away.

It was cold. Bitterly cold, but Gedas said it was December and it wasn't snowing. This put them either north or west of Aluna, closer to the coast. The north didn't have many farms, being so close to the borders of Ustra and Oskela, and the only castle with farms in the country surrounding it was Tross.

Elodie blinked. They were only a few hours from Tross, her castle. If they kept northeast, they would reach the palace road over the next few hills. Elodie tapped the horse's sides with her sneakers and turned the chestnut to the left toward home. Gedas chuckled quietly behind her and brought his horse up till he rode abreast.

"Have you been keeping yourself busy in your last few weeks, my Gull?" Gedas's voice was light and broke the silence between them.

"I guess so." Her eyes still burned after crying and her chest felt heavy. Her legs began to ache at the strain of gripping the saddle as she found her balance and her muscles remembered all the horse training they had endured over the years.

"As I remember, police are the ones who enforce the law within the illusion."

Elodie fiddled with her reins, running her thumb along the edge of the leather. "Yeah."

"And doctors are like healers but without magic. I don't remember you being hurt when you last left my company."

"I wasn't."

"Hmmmm." Gedas tapped his bottom lip with his first two fingers in rhythm.

Gedas weedled more information out of Elodie in his way of not actually asking a direct question, till she was explaining to him about child services and psychiatric care. Before long Elodie was nearly shouting, telling him how unfair it was no one would believe her about the Twoshy.

They found the road a short time later, and Gedas listened attentively as she told him about her decision to start lying. She wiped a tear off of her face and hoped Gedas wouldn't notice.

He always noticed.

"That was very brave of you, my Gull." His arm stretched out, bridging the gap their horses made between them, another clean handkerchief in his hand.

"Brave?" Elodie burst out with a crying gasp. She reached for the cloth and it floated the last few feet between them, a spark of pale blue magic helping it along. "How is lying brave? Doesn't it make me a coward who can't stay strong in what I believe in?"

"The technology of your world, computers, telephones"—he exaggerated each word like it was uncomfortable in his mouth —"why did you stop explaining them and how they work to all the people you meet in the Twoshy?"

"Because they didn't really care about any of it, and they just thought it was weird," she answered, remembering how a messenger had looked at her funny when she tried to explain telephones.

"And do people back in the illusion care about the stories you tell of the Twoshy?"

Elodie thought about Vanessa. "Some."

"What about your parents? Do they care about magic and your time spent with me?"

"No," Elodie declared.

"And does hearing about magic and learning about the Kingdoms of Sixteen add anything to their lives?"

"No."

"Does it hurt them?"

Elodie thought about this one. She thought about the look of worry, fear and dread in her mother's eyes, the broken-adopted-kid look her mother got when she started talking about the Twoshy. Then she thought about her dad's expression, his upturned lip like he smelled something he wished would go away. "Maybe," Elodie decided. "I think so. I'm not sure, but . . . The way it makes them feel hurts me."

Gedas nodded slowly. "And why do you think telling them the truth, even when it may hurt them and yourself, is so important?"

"Because it's the right thing to do," Elodie replied automatically. "Lying is bad, and if I do it, then I have no honor."

"So instead, you believe it would be better to tell the truth and hurt the people around you, all for the sake of your own honor?"

This made Elodie frown, and she thought about it for a few leagues. Honor was important, but at what cost? It was a new thought, one she let sit in her mind while she fell into the steady rhythm of the horse's gait.

The plants lining the road were mostly in hibernation for the winter, save for the occasional spruce or pine. They passed small patches of trees, sheep grazing in the barren fields, and the occasional small creek. The ground was asleep. Filled with seeds and bulbs, all waiting for a break in the cold, for the world to defrost and warm so they could spring to life. Her spine tingled with all the potential life and energy brimming around her.

Before long, traffic began to pick up on the road and they passed men on horses, foot traffic, and carts laden with supplies and goods to sell or trade. A few seagulls flew overhead and they passed a few buildings dotted here and there before the road split.

To the left it would continue on past Tross, following the northern border of Aluna before turning north into Oskela. Elodie and Gedas followed the road to the right. She fell behind to follow in single file as they passed through the large heavy gates and yellow flags hanging limp in the frigid air. The gray stamp of the flag's sigil, a large sea bird in mid flight, a perfect copy to the albatross birthmark on her collarbone, was nearly unseen on the lifeless flags. Elodie ducked her head, trying not to catch the eye of any passersby as she followed Gedas and entered into the Odure District of the city surrounding her castle.

Chapter Four

CARTS CAREENED past as merchants and farmers and travelers wove between traffic in a frenzy of activity. Foot traffic pressed in around Elodie's horse. The buildings around her were not well made, lopsided with patched roofs, uneven stalls propped up in an open market, and traffic casually navigated around a sinkhole in the road. The people wore cloaks much thinner than her own, and the occasional street kid ran by with no shoes.

Then the smell hit her. The air was not pleasant when you first entered Tross.

Her great-grandfather, King Lonan, the first and the last of his name, had made it his life's work to build a proper sewer system through Tross and the outer city, and of course, like every member of her family who'd put their mind to something grand, he had failed. The sewer backed up every winter, and was impossibly vile in the summer.

The companions made their way through the mess till they reached the outer wall of the castle. The wall was barely noticeable, houses and shops built right up against it and sometimes taller in a mismatched patchwork of buildings. Traffic flowed around and past the gateway, with few people crossing through it. Two people stood to either side of the gate, in chain mail and dingy over-washed yellow uniforms, the gray albatross insignia stamped across their chests. The guards looked bored, watching the crowd with blank expressions. The man on the right was nearly half asleep, the tip of his spear dipping with each breath. Brown stains ran down his yellow tunic. The woman on the left had a small white cheer twig in her mouth and her lips were lined with blue marking her addiction to the magical plant.

The guards didn't spare a glance as Wizard Gediminas, and Princess Elodie, heir to the throne, passed under the heavy iron gate into the city's Prole District. The moment they crossed into the outer ring, the atmosphere shifted. The stores and taverns were even and mostly uniform. Paint peeled here and there, debris still in the street, but most of the trash made its way into the thick shallow gutters on either side of the road, flowing down to the outer city. The people who walked here were dressed more appropriately for the weather. And while she still spied the occasional street kid, most of them had shoes. This was where the bulk of the merchant class lived, and Gedas blended in well among those they passed. The foot traffic lessened. While Elodie and Gedas still had to watch out for carriages pulling the wealthy, unwilling to stop for someone on horseback, a clearly defined road through the buildings emerged, winding its way closer to the castle.

At the next wall, twice as high as the first, the men standing on either side held their spears straight and turned up their noses at the people who passed. No spots or stains marked their fading yellow tunics or the gray bird flying across it, but Elodie could see the rust in their chain mail. They eyed Gedas and Elodie suspiciously as they passed.

The Opulent District of the city, was again a clear upgrade. Here the buildings were pristine, each shop clearly displaying the flag of the appropriate guild. Windows shined nearly as brightly as the men and women who walked between them. No beggar would be caught dead in the inner circle. A thief might be caught dead, but beggars preferred to die in the comfort of the outer city. Elodie knew if she turned her horse to the right or the left, she would pass the shops and enter an area thick with beautiful mansions housing the upper class of Tross, and every other lord and lady, baron and duchess of Aluna who felt having a vacation home in the capital was necessary.

The traffic filtered to carriages glinting in the sun, and men and women riding past with armor and knights' shields.

When they made it to the castle wall, taller and thicker than the two previous walls combined, the guards lowered their spears barring entrance to the two travelers riding with no visible crest or emblem. The guards' spears and chain mail glinted in the winter sun, and their tunics were bright yellow and crisp gray as though dyed yesterday.

"Business," the guard on the left stated. No question in her voice.

"The Wizard Gediminas, escorting Her Royal Highness Princess Elodie of Aluna," Gedas answered in the pompous voice he put on when it was expected, or he was being funny. The guards stiffened and Elodie could see the bored disgust melt off the first guard's face. The guards snapped their spears back to their sides, and one of them started to bow before remembering a guard on duty protected, and bowing didn't help with that. Straightening, the guard kicked one of the men just inside the wall, sending him running toward the castle. The two guards parted a respectable distance, leaving room for Gedas and Elodie to pass.

Elodie sighed sadly to herself. Any chance of an incognito arrival was out of the question. She was sure to be whisked away to some boring meeting where the steward and the council would talk till they put themselves to sleep.

The castle was in full view now, at the top of the last hill. Spires positioned randomly around the large frame looked tall from the ground, but in reality the biggest on the west side of the castle made Tross the fifth tallest castle in Aluna. Nesta, the fourth queen of Aluna made it her mission to make Tross the most prestigious capital in the Twoshy. So of course it turned out a mess. Half of the east wing was made of wood, not even stone like a proper castle.

Gedas led them past the guards' barracks and the training fields, toward the stables to unload the horses.

"Elllooooodie! Princess Elllooooodie!"

A small figure in yellow careened down the hill toward her. The boy's arms wove like windmills as he ran, and Elodie got a sinking suspicion she knew exactly who he was. As he grew closer Elodie could tell by the tight curly black hair and goofy smile on his dark face, this running windmill was the slightly older version of a boy she met on her last trip.

Once he was six feet from her, he froze and visibly pulled himself together ending in a deep bow.

Elodie laughed at the sight.

"It's good to see you too, Silas," Elodie said.

A few teens ran up from the stables, bowing and reaching for her and Gedas's reins. Silas stepped in, still bowing, making a point to hold the chestnut's reins while Elodie dismounted. The stable hands took the reins back from him, and Silas sunk lower into his bow. Elodie frowned. She expected Silas to rise from his bow, smile, and maybe embrace her in a hug like he did the last time he saw her, but instead the young boy stayed bowed. "Silas? Silas, why are you still bowing?"

She could hear a soft mutter coming from him and leaned in to hear. "You are supposed to tell me to rise," he said without moving his lips.

Elodie laughed and shook her head. "Rise, Lord Silas of Tate."

Silas lifted himself from his bow in an elegant motion and smiled briefly, then schooled his features again into a professional mask. "It is good to see you, Your Royal Highness, I am glad you could return safely to your castle once again." He greeted Gedas with the same formality, bowing deeply to the wizard, but rising on his own. They continued their hike up the hill to the castle. Gedas led the way and Elodie and Silas trailed behind.

"That was a pretty speech, kid. So how are those decorum lessons treating you?"

His mask broke into a wide grin. "They're an utter nightmare, trust me, Your Highness. We have to sit through an hour of decorum every single day right after horse practice and combat training, which means we're exhausted. If I fall asleep, Master Bernid makes me spend my weekends practicing bows for hours."

"Absolute torture. I can't believe you put up with it, Silas. Really, is it worth it? You should give up and go be a soft lord's son, you'll inherit Tate whether you become a knight or not."

A look of horror slid onto Silas's face. "But I have to be a knight," he said with such conviction. "It's what I'm meant for. Trust me, in a couple of years I will be a squire and then a couple more years I'm going to be a knight. Your knight. I'll defend the realm in your name, and I'll be the best knight there ever was."

"Men will sing ballads in your honor at every tavern?" she asked.

"Naturally."

Elodie laughed, but she knew it would be true, even if his declaration of servitude made her a bit uncomfortable. "Okay, just don't kill yourself in the process. And stop with the 'Your Highness's."

"You know, I don't know if you're allowed to call me a 'kid' anymore, my lady," Silas said, using the slang term Elodie taught him. "I'm almost as tall as you. How old are you, anyways? You don't look any older than the last time I saw you."

"That's because I'm not. I'm only twelve."

"What?" Silas gasped, shock on his face. "The last time I saw you we celebrated your thirteenth birthday at Tate. How are you twelve again?"

"Ask Gedas if you want the complicated answer. The spell gets to choose how old I am when it sucks me back in. I even lost the two inches I grew last summer." She was being short, but the topic frustrated her.

"Wow, that's rotten." Silas thought on this a moment, before turning to Elodie, a very serious look on his face. "My lady, some-day, as soon as I'm able, I am going to find the evil wizard who put this spell on you, and I will find a way to break it." He said those words with such conviction Elodie couldn't help but believe he would.

"You and me both, kid." She wanted to change the subject from the intense moment. "So how old are you now?"

"I'm ten. I just started my page training at the end of summer. Ten is the youngest they take us, and quit calling me a kid. Pretty soon I'm going to be older than you."

"You probably will be," Elodie said darkly. The way the magic was pulling her, Silas would be an old man and she would still be a teenager trying to break the stupid spell.

Two years. For Elodie it had only been a few weeks, for Silas it had been two years since she visited his castle and celebrated her birthday. Gone was the small annoying eight-year-old following her everywhere. Now he seemed more confident in his place in the world than she was.

Elodie groaned at the sight of the welcoming party assembled between the grand double doors. Nearly a dozen men all in fine embroidered tunics and robes stood around looking bored. A round man on the left with a silver beard was first to notice them approaching. He hit the man next to him who hit the person next to him and so on, till all men were standing to attention. They bowed when Elodie approached. Silas bowed a few times to the surrounding people, then ducked to the side.

The man in front was first to approach. He was tall, nearly as tall as Gedas. His skin was light and he had a weak chin and strong nose bringing his face to a point, balanced by the ornate beard braided over his chin and neck. His tunic was a deep purple with what looked like real gold embroidery, matching the gold beads threaded through his beard.

Gedas always said showing wealth by piling sparkly bits onto oneself was a garish form of self-expression.

For the man standing before her, lavish was a representation of more than just his appearance. Duke Oburleck of Comak and Steward of Aluna. He managed Aluna in Elodie's stead, his governing powers falling just short of a proper ruler.

Steward Oburleck stepped forward till he was only a few feet in front of her, and bowed deeply, spreading his arms with an added flourish. Elodie held her breath in anticipation.

"Welcome, Your Highness," he said, raising his bow till he was even with her face. A putrid smell rushed over Elodie as Oburleck's breath reached her. She'd never met someone whose breath was as bad as the steward. She tried not to wince or react noticeably. Eventually he stood straight and smiled wide.

"It's so good to see you safely returned to us again, and such a great surprise," Oburleck said, casting a look at Gedas with a glint in his eyes.

Elodie wasn't sure if this was where she should reply, and the silence stretched. The well-dressed men took the moment to eye up Elodie's jeans and t-shirt. She wrapped the cloak tightly around herself.

Oburleck bowed again, breaking the tension. "As always, Your Highness, we welcome you back to your home. May you find sanctuary from the spell for as long as possible until you can return to your proper place. Your interests are mine, and have you need of anything, you must only ask."

Oburleck was a good man. She didn't particularly enjoy his company and the boring meetings he tried to drag her to, but he did what was right by her and her people. She felt guilty for cringing at his breath.

"Thank you," she said.

"You must be tired after your long journey," Oburleck suggested charitably.

Elodie began to nod emphatically, hoping for the chance to slip away and avoid the status update on all things boring.

"On the contrary, our journey was rather brief," Gedas announced. Elodie shot him a panicked look. "Well, I should see to things in the mage wing, as I cannot neglect my duties all day, but Her Highness, I'm sure, would be happy for a report on the state of the kingdom, having been gone for so long." Gedas had the audacity to smile and wink at Elodie as he nodded to her, and moved past the crowd of stuffed tunics.

Elodie's shoulders dropped in defeat.

"Wonderful. Wonderful, Your Highness, if you will follow me, we shall adjourn to the council room." Oburleck turned and led the men down a hall opposite of Gedas. "We were just having our state planning, but we can catch you up in no time."

Elodie had half a thought to run for it. She spied Silas about to dart off, and caught him by his sleeve. "Oh no you don't. If I have to sit through the boring hours of meetings, then so do you."

"I can't possibly attend a council meeting!" Silas said, eyes wide.

"Why, do you have classes today?"

"No, it's free day," he began, but Elodie cut him off.

"Perfect. You can suffer through it with me. You'll love it, they'll talk about the state of the realm you want to protect so much." Elodie held his arm tight so he wouldn't run off, and prepared to drag him along. Much to her disgust Silas was more than happy to go after his initial hesitation. He quickly caught up to the adults until it was Elodie being dragged like a reluctant lady at a ball.

Chapter Five

THE COUNCIL ROOM was a large room with a low ceiling and one small west-facing window. While snug and warm in the winter, it was sweltering in summer. Maps covered the walls showing regions of Aluna from the Tokke mountains in the south, the coasts to the east and west, and the nations of the Twoshy surrounding Aluna in the north. Chairs lined the walls of the room for assistants and notetakers. In the center of the room was a large rectangular table, with sixteen chairs. Opposite the door one chair in the center of the table was slightly larger and taller than all the others. This was the chair Oburleck aligned himself with. Elodie moved around the table to sit on Oburleck's right, and forced Silas into position next to her. Elodie sat and tried not to laugh or groan as every man followed suit.

"The council recognizes Princess Elodie, heir to the throne in attendance with—uh, her page guest," Oburleck announced.

"Silas of Tate," Elodie filled in.

"Page Silas of Tate," Oburleck repeated. He turned toward Elodie and bowed gracefully, then nodded politely to the boy. A wave of rancid breath rolled over Elodie and she tried not to let it show as she held her next breath. "Before your arrival we were in a discussion of taxes. Gregor, would you please continue?"

They continued. Elodie tried not to look bored. The harvest had been good. Half the room wanted to raise taxes in celebration, the other half wanted to relax them.

Balding red-faced dukes read thick rolls of parchment, and big-nosed lords passed veiled insults. Men rose one by one to interject, agree or speak his own agenda, Oburleck nodded and agreed with points made along the way. Elodie quickly zoned out finding it impossible to think through the fog.

She was hungry.

She'd traveled to Aluna right after first period, and they took roughly four hours to travel to the castle. It was well past lunch for Elodie's schedule. Empty trays, recently picked over by the men, lined the room.

Would it look too bad if she took the last roll and cheese off the tray by the window?

If she stood all the other men would stand too, and it would be weird. Her stomach growled, unnoticed over the near shouting Lord Red Face was producing. Something about wheat prices.

The bacon she'd swiped off her mother's plate felt worlds away. Maybe she could get Silas to grab food for her. No one would pay attention to him getting up from the table.

Elodie looked to her right planning on asking the boy, and her jaw fell. Silas was leaning forward in his chair, a look of intense fascination stamped across his face. His eyes moved from person to person as a different lord or duke took the floor. What could possibly be so interesting? Elodie tuned back into the conversation, then promptly tuned back out. They were still talking about grain. What was wrong with this kid?

Elodie's new plan for the remainder of the meeting was to watch Silas watch the meeting. He was way more interesting, nodding softly or frowning when someone spoke their opinion.

Elodie's attention faltered again and a foggy inattention drifted into her mind.

A knock sounded and Elodie snapped back to clarity. A man in the gray-and-yellow servants' livery opened the door and carried in a large platter of food. Elodie's eyes bulged and she swallowed the saliva forming in her mouth. Several other servants followed the man in, one scooping up the empty trays, and the others carried fresh trays stacked with gleaming pastries and tarts. Elodie spotted a small pile of orange preserve turnovers on the nearest tray and it was as if a spotlight flipped on above them and small birds began singing in the distance.

The lords in the room stood or sat patiently, waiting for the servants to leave before resuming their discussion. Elodie folded her hands in her lap and tried not to look too pathetic as she exerted her willpower.

Once the servants left, and the men resumed their debate, she waited till the third lord made his way to a snack table before she jumped from her seat. The men still seated followed, standing respectfully as she walked to a table and made her selection. Loading eight of the different pastries onto a silver trimmed plate, she tried not to drool before she reached the table. Once she sat, the majority of the men took their seats while a half dozen or so took the opportunity to grab their own refreshments.

Elodie shoved the first bun into her mouth, dates pecans and cinnamon danced over her tongue. A teacup and matching saucer landed softly on the table in front of her. Silas smiled at her, and set his own teacup down next to hers.

"Did Gediminas forget to feed you again?" he whispered. Elodie nodded and tried to swallow as Silas returned to load up his plate. Once she managed to clear her mouth of the fruit bun, Elodie patted her face politely with the napkin Silas bought her, proving she still knew at least some of her etiquette lessons.

With her hunger less sharp, Elodie picked up her teacup gracefully, and brought it to her face, inhaling deeply. A black tea with strong ginger and cloves. There was an underlying flavor of mint, myrrh and tea tree, three ingredients proven to cure bad breath. Elodie wondered if Oburleck knew the tea wasn't the standard blend from the castle kitchens, or if the servants were trying to privately remedy a problem they knew existed. Smiling into her cup, Elodie took a sip. The myrrh was a little over steeped, not surprising as it needed a shorter steeping time than black tea leaves, but Silas had added a good deal of sugar.

Silas munched on a biscuit smeared with jam, his attention back on the duke currently talking about inflation. The talk went on and on. Elodie had a harder time paying attention once her stomach was full and her fog rolled back in.

At last Oburleck rose from his chair. With a long hard sigh, his breath rolled over Elodie and brought her to attention. Before he stood the room had been silent, as the men had talked themselves out. Oburleck's actions brought movement as the men around the room adjusted their postures and refocused.

"Thank you all for that lively and thorough debate." Oburleck met each man's eyes. "This subject is important to our kingdom, and it is fitting for each of you to care for it in turn. This year has been fruitful, and I agree it is time the people felt the relief for their hard work. Lightening taxes is not a decision we make easily, as we do not raise taxes easily or in haste. That being said, we must find a place taxes can be lowered to benefit the entirety of Aluna while strengthening the economy and increasing the crown's benefits." Each man nodded to one point or another, and the steward took a deep breath. He looked down at the rolls of parchment spread out before him and selected one, placing small weights at the top and bottom to keep it expanded.

"Now, let us look at the gains for each line of revenue and tax intake from the last few years." Oburleck then proceeded to launch into figures, occasionally asking a different noble to explain or expand on a number. Elodie allowed her attention to wander and willingly let the fog drift in like a familiar friend.

"There!"

A hand landed hard on the table and Elodie jumped.

"I believe we have it," Oburleck announced. "We shall reduce taxes for a few key industries, reducing the immediate returns to the kingdom, but providing the hard-working people a break for the new year. Based on the figures we have studied, the best places to lower tax and reap benefit to the people will be over the bound-servant and bordello trade."

Each man began to pack up their scrolls and papers as Oburleck spouted off a few last-minute instructions on who would do what to implement the decision.

Elodie wiggled in her seat. This was it, she would soon be free.

As the men rose and left the table, Elodie noticed some looked pleased, others smug, and a few frustrated yet resigned.

Elodie stood and stretched. Looking to her side she saw Silas watch the men go, the excitement still present in his eyes. He looked at her, then his eyes moved over her shoulder and he nodded. Elodie turned to face Oburleck. The older man kissed her hand as he bowed over it. Elodie tried not to wince.

"Your Highness," he said, meeting Elodie's eyes. He was way too close for her nose's comfort. "Thank you for joining our meeting, I hope it was insightful for the current state of the kingdom."

Elodie nodded. "Yes, it was great. Thank you, Steward Oburleck."

"Wonderful," he said with a wide grin.

She was surprised to see his teeth were perfectly white. She always expected them to be rotten.

"Tell me, will you do me the honor of dining with us tonight?" he asked.

Elodie smiled politely. "Thank you, Steward Oburleck, you do me an honor. Although I was expecting to dine with Wizard Gediminas tonight." Elodie hoped the steward didn't press the issue.

"How unfortunate indeed. Another night perhaps," Oburleck said. Elodie made a noncommittal reply as was expected, and Oburleck bowed with ceremony and flourish, leaving the room. Once he was gone, Elodie sunk into a chair.

"Well you sure enjoyed yourself," she said to Silas.

"And how could you not?" he asked, a wistful grin on his face. "The way Steward Oburleck commanded the room, amazing."

"I mean it seemed like he just sat and listened, then summarized everything at the end."

"No! Are you kidding me? He had the other nobles eating out of his hand! My lady, he had a clear set agenda, then he directed the conversation and brought every noble to agreement on his point of view. I can't imagine the planning, persuasion and manipulation that takes!"

"Silas, none of those sound like good things."

"Depends on how you use them."

"Wait, I'm lost. Start over." Elodie rubbed her face.

The ten-year-old sighed like someone much older. "Those men were arguing, each person wanting something different. Steward Oburleck listened to each person state their case, making each one feel heard and validated. Then at the end he posed an ambiguous solution only half of the room agreed with. Then they dove into the numbers."

"Don't remind me."

"But that's where he did it," Silas said, pounding a fist into his hand to underscore the point. "He used facts, and made each person explain or get involved with the figures, then he twisted the interpretation to reach his end goal." Silas was staring at her, as though she should get this. Elodie stared back blankly, her brain not up to critical thinking. "My lady, what was the end decision?"

Elodie thought. "They decided to lower taxes on boundservants and bordellos. Slaves," she interpreted with a grimace.

"Yes, exactly. The whole point of lowering taxes would be to help the working class, but instead he lowered taxes on industries that benefit the upper class. That's why my uncle was so angry. Only a few key councilmen will benefit. He just passed a law to make his biggest supporters rich by playing every person in the room into agreeing with him. He's brilliant."

Elodie laughed at Silas's excitement.

As they slipped out of the room, Elodie grabbed the last orange turnover off a tray. "So now what?" she asked before taking a bite.

Silas sighed and the excitement bled out of him. "I have class-work to complete before tomorrow."

Elodie winced. He could have been doing his work, but instead she insisted on dragging him to a boring meeting. The pages didn't get much free time. "Why don't you come back to my rooms and I can help? I'm good with math, and I bet Gedas will turn up and can help with history."

Silas made a face. "I don't think it would be proper."

Elodie made a rude noise. "Oh please. We will be in my sitting room, and we can keep the door open or something. I'm sure the maids are still fluttering through getting everything cleaned up."

"Oh alright. I'll go get my books from the pages' wing and meet you at your rooms." The boy turned and took off down a hall to the left.

Elodie looked around the stone hallways to reorient herself. The light globes lit the walls illuminating familiar tapestries. She turned right.

A few passages later Elodie spotted the hall leading to the throne room. She paused. This was the wrong direction, but she turned from her course and walked toward the large ornate doors. Elodie had to peer through the fading light to examine the portraits lining each wall. Kings and queens of the last few genera-tions looked back at her. Each man or woman of the royal line displayed their albatross birthmark in the oil paints, the mark shown with greater honor than the crown on their heads. At the end of the hall, just before the heavy doors, was a portrait of her father and mother, standing side by side. Crowns sat on both their heads, but the birthmark on her father's arm was highlighted, becoming the focus of the painting.

She brushed a cobweb off the corner and examined her mother, her features so delicate and soft. She didn't think she saw much of herself in the elegant woman. She'd never met her mother and wondered what type of woman she'd been. Would her voice be sweet and brittle? Or would she be soft and gentle, generous with hugs and smiles?

She'd met her father the first time she traveled to the Twoshy. She'd been five and found the ruakh for the first time under the table in the ice-cream shop. She'd fallen through the nothing and landed in the leaves and sticks of a forest floor. Her legs got scraped up by a peppermintsteel bush, and the hem of her dress was stained blue by the decaying cheer leaves. Her love of plants started that day, as the spark of her magic bloomed inside of her.

Her father waited for her in the shadow of a cheer tree, the sun filtering through the leaves casting a magical blue light on his face. She'd thought he was a knight, and he didn't correct her.

It wasn't until her next trip she'd seen a portrait and understood the man who'd sat beside her on a log at the edge of the forest and told her all about her birth world and the spell that held her had been her father. Both her father and mother had grown old, and passed on before her return, but Gedas had been there the next time when she fell through the shimmer into the middle of a courtyard in Tross. He took her on an adventure to the coast after life at the palace and the chaos and novelty of the princess's return became too much.

After that, her travels fell into a pattern of monotonous life in the castle, smothered with courtesy, mixed with exciting journeys to forests, or villages, or some other remote location where Elodie would meet people and learn things about her world.

Over the years the oddity of her random appearances and disappearances wore off. The people of Aluna knew and accepted their princess was trapped in a spell by an evil wizard, and now, instead of a queen they had a steward.

Life went on.

She was starting to lose track of how many times she'd traveled since then. Maybe five? Maybe eight?

Elodie didn't bother trying the door handle to the throne room. She knew it was locked and would remain so until the *someday* when the spell would be broken, and she'd become queen.

Queen.

It was one of those things people always referred to as being inevitable for Elodie. When Elodie was pulled into etiquette lessons and protested at learning another curtsy, whatever mistress or lady who deemed it necessary would remind her someday when she was queen, she would appreciate the knowledge. Someday when she was queen she would need to know the formal greetings for every title and rank of person within all fourteen kingdoms. Someday when she was queen she would look back and thank her teachers for shaping her into the woman she would become.

When she asked when their someday would come, they always got a look of curiosity followed by disinterest and a change of subject. It was for greater minds than themselves to know the workings of magic and the world, they would say.

Elodie would let it go, leave the questions and mystery for later and for someone who would know the answer. Most of the etiquette lessons faded to the background of her mind until she needed them. Someday she would have responsibilities and a destiny, but for now she was just an unexpected complication in the day.

The only one who didn't see her as a complication and didn't wait for a faraway someday to teach her, was Gedas. He didn't answer every question, but he also never pushed knowledge or responsibilities away with an excuse of a later date. He didn't speak about when she would be queen, or when the spell would be broken, and Elodie didn't ask. He focused on the here and now, and on lessons of the past and how they shaped the future.

It was enough.

Chapter Six

SHE ONLY GOT LOST ONCE on the way to her rooms, ending up near the wooden wing of the castle. The wood was not a good insulator and the air was musty and cold. Her footsteps thumped on the loose boards. Tapestries covered the walls, but where the wood was visible the boards were beginning to warp and crumble as moisture and bugs ate away at the old wood. This wing would need to be renovated again in the next few years. If only it could be renovated with higher-quality materials, it would last longer and look better. If Aluna had prospered so much in the last season as the council meeting indicated, the kingdom should have enough finances to make the castle, the face of the land, at least somewhat presentable.

Backtracking her path, Elodie used a servant's staircase to find her rooms. Swinging the door wide, she startled a few maids carrying folded linens, the clean fabric tumbling down a few dirty steps.

"Watch where you be going, girl!" the older maid scolded Elodie. Elodie started apologizing profusely. They would have to rewash everything by hand. "What's your name girl, and where do you work? I'll be reporting you, see if I don't!"

"Uhhh," Elodie stammered. Remembering where she was and

who she was, if she told the maid her name, they would start apologizing to Elodie, and it was her fault. She didn't want to make things awkward for the maid who chastised her.

Elodie assessed her surroundings and ran for it.

Thundering down the tight spiral staircase Elodie used the banister to propel herself faster. She could feel the nails in the banister pulling, no longer anchored well in the stone walls. She heard footsteps pounding behind her.

"Get back here, you little chit!" a voice echoed. She skipped a few steps on her way and nearly fell down the stairs. The small landing signifying the next floor was upon Elodie before she realized it, and she stumbled on the suddenly flat ground. She ripped open the door and raced out into the hallway. Running as fast as she could past a few men who looked important and rich, relief flooded Elodie. No maid would chase her past the men. She rounded a corner and stopped in time not to plow into a footman walking toward her.

Elodie, red faced and desperately trying to pull a breath into her heaving lungs, stood tall with what she hoped looked like a regal pose so the man would hesitate before questioning her.

"Apologies, my good man," she gasped in the most arrogant and noble-sounding voice she could muster through her staggered breathing.

Elodie wandered a few hallways before recognizing a tapestry of her great-great-great-uncle and the prized war horses he was famed for breeding. His entire stock had of course died from a rare plague shortly after the tapestry was completed.

If she continued down this hall then went left when it ended, then took her second right, her rooms would be down the hall. She spent the walk trying to regain her breath, and work out the sharp pain developing in her side.

Silas was standing with a small stack of books outside of the door of her rooms.

"Are you alright?" His eyebrows knit together in a frown.

Elodie nodded, her face was bright red from the run, as was her life every day after P.E. "I took the long way around."

Silas laughed. "Did you get lost?"

"Hey, don't laugh at me."

"This is your castle, my lady."

Elodie punched his shoulder lightly then moved past the boy, stopping dead in the doorway.

"I wasn't sure if I should have gone in without you or not," the page replied.

Elodie let her head hang. She'd been hoping for a nice quiet evening, but in her sitting room were a half-dozen servants sweeping and dusting and organizing. Gray-and-yellow-clad people were fluffing cushions and shaking out curtains. To Elodie's horror she could see a maid through the door to her dressing room setting up a stool for fittings next to a rack filled with garments.

Someone must have cleaned out the large hearth in Elodie's room for a small pack of cindix, small burnt orange mouse-like creatures who lived off ash, fled from the inner rooms. A maid rushed out of the bedroom, arms full of dusty white sheets. She spotted the cindix a moment before she stepped on them, and overcorrecting, stumbled and dropped the linens at Elodie's feet. The cindix escaped into a gap between the wall and the bookcases and the maid froze at the sight of Elodie. She looked around as if pleading for someone to come to her rescue.

Mistress Piera came out of the dressing room and barked an order at the maid to keep moving. The maid jumped and scurried to pick up the dropped cloth. Spotting Elodie, Mistress Piera clapped her hands once. "Your Highness, how wonderful to see you again."

Every person in the room froze, the brave peeking toward the door to see Elodie. "Alright, the lot of you, finish up with your tasks, and you are dismissed," Piera directed.

Elodie quickly stepped to the side as, with a flurry of activity, maids and servants began scooping up cleaning supplies and fleeing the room. The cleaning detail gone, Elodie motioned for

Silas and stepped inside. She sat down in one of the overstuffed cushions.

"Princess, as you are newly arrived, we have prepared the castle's head seamstress to get you properly outfitted," the stern woman said, her eyes on Elodie's jeans and sneakers.

Elodie winced. The head seamstress, Madam Beulah, was a gruff old woman who liked to poke Elodie's belly and make small comments about how her garments usually had a better silhouette.

"There's no way we could delay until tomorrow, is there? I promised Page Silas I would assist him with a task, after he so graciously allowed me to take up a huge portion of his time." Elodie crossed her fingers under her cloak.

"No, there most certainly is not."

Elodie had known the older woman for years and Piera was quite familiar with Elodie's ways of getting out of anything involving corsets or ladylike responsibilities. It was strange the way time flowed for Elodie, popping in and out of people's lives in the Twoshy, seemingly never changing while they changed before her eyes. Mistress Piera had been much younger when Elodie first met her. Her copper eyes had held a lightness and joy which had slowly disappeared over the years. Her thick dark brown hair was now mostly gray, and her warm brown face was growing creased and wrinkled.

"How about the young lord gets started on his task, and you can allow the head seamstress to check the fit of some of your older gowns? This way you will have something appropriate to wear in the morning." Mistress Piera gave Elodie's jeans one more stern look then turned back toward the dressing room, knowing Elodie would follow.

"I'll be back in a few minutes," Elodie said with a sigh.

"Why don't I just let you go? I can work on this myself. You don't need to help me," Silas said, his books still in hand.

"Silas?"

"Yes, my lady?"

"Park it."

"Excuse me?"

"Sit down. I'm going to help whether it's proper or not so relax and let me help." Silas bowed and Elodie turned back toward the fitting room. "Oh, and one more thing," she called over her shoulder. "Stop with the 'my lady,' okay?"

Her dressing room was larger than her bedroom back home but felt cramped with racks of clothing and bolts of fabric spread about, and the half-dozen seamstress assistants running around.

"Charmaine!" Elodie smiled as she spotted a familiar face.

Tall and elegant, her bright red hair coiffed into a twisted updo, the woman turned to Elodie with a brilliant smile. "My lady." She gave an elegant curtsy using the full range of her long limbs to make the movement powerful yet artistic. She rose with a flourish before her serene face broke and the freckles on her nose crinkled as she smiled and let out a deep chuckle.

Elodie laughed and crossed the room. Charmaine closed the distance between them and bent down to give Elodie a long and firm hug. "That was beautiful, Charmaine, a curtsy fit for a throne-room introduction. How many hours have you spent practicing in a mirror?"

"Only a few hours a week," Charmaine said, pulling back and holding Elodie at arm's length. "Now, let me look at you. Oh, it's so good to have you back. You haven't aged a day. Don't give me that look. Yes, I know you find it quite annoying, but what I wouldn't do for such young skin once again." Charmaine leaned back and pressed the back of her hand to her forehead in lament.

Elodie stomped on her self-pity and smiled. She'd known Charmaine for years, since the woman was much younger, mending Elodie's clothes and working under the head seamstress. As Elodie dropped in and out of Aluna the bright blue eyes became framed with wrinkles and the pale freckled face grew long as her youth faded.

"Now, how about we get started on these gowns?" Charmaine asked, gesturing to the stool in the center of the room.

Elodie sighed as she moved toward the stool. "Are we waiting for Madam Beulah?"

"No, my dear, the crone has retired at last. Don't worry, this will go much faster than the usual fittings."

Elodie turned back to her friend. "Who took over as head seamstress?"

"I was graced with the honor, my lady," Charmaine said with a small bow and a wicked smile.

Elodie laughed. "You mean I never have to get poked by Beulah again? Oh Char, this is the best news I've had for weeks."

"Don't get too excited, I'm still going to make you stand and twirl for me." She laughed and pushed Elodie toward the stool.

It became clear almost immediately that the fitting would not be completed that night. The dresses from her last trip no longer fit. She'd spent nearly a year and a half, turned thirteen, grew several inches and ended up quite a few pounds lighter. Unfortunately, her old body was one of the things the spell decided she should have back when it sucked her back into the illusion.

Charmaine winked at Elodie and let her know it was a relief, as the fashions changed so much. It would be a travesty to force a princess to wear two-year-old dresses.

It wasn't her fault, but it still felt terrible when they attempted to pry the fabric over her body.

Embarrassed and feeling low, Elodie returned to the sitting room where Silas had his books open over a table. She ordered him to sit when he jumped to stand for her, and then again when he tried to help her drag a chair closer to the table. One way or another she was determined to get Silas to relax.

"So what are we working on?" she asked, settling into the chair and looking over the books and tools before him. He had a large slate tablet with a few dozen math problems scribbled over it, only two of them looked worked on.

Charmaine and her assistants moved quietly in the background removing the ill-fitting gowns and their equipment. Elodie thanked them again as they left and gave her friend one more hug.

"I have a number of problems Lord Riyan gave us to solve. I'm not very good at all this. I like the history and strategy lessons better." He glanced away from Elodie, back to his slate. "It's not hard, but it takes forever."

Elodie looked down at the slate. "Do you know your times tables yet? What each number times the other comes out to from one to ten?"

"I don't have them memorized." Silas pulled a face. "Lord Riyan says we should, but I haven't had the time. I can figure them all out eventually."

"Okay." Elodie took the slate and grabbed his chalk. "You work on something else, and I'll write these all out, leaving enough space so you can rewrite them and go over them. Sound good?"

"It's really no different from when I get together with the other pages." He propped a large book open and got a piece of paper. "Most of us had tutors for the last few years, but Ralf and Nic are the best at figures. I'm the best with strategy, so we all work together."

Silas pulled out a quill and his belt knife and set to work sharpening the end of his spare pen. Elodie stared down at the slate and started solving each one.

"So Lord Riyan teaches your math?" Elodie knew the men on the council had other duties, but she couldn't imagine the old wrinkled man teaching a room full of young boys. In the council meeting he rose to stand on shaky legs. He was sharp and direct with his views, and terrified Elodie a little.

Silas laughed. "Yes, he's about as good of a teacher as you can imagine. Impatient and a complete—" Silas trailed off abruptly as Mistress Piera returned carrying a tray with tea. She set it on a side table and began preparing a few cups.

"Thank you, Mistress Piera, but you don't have to do that," Elodie said.

"Nonsense." Mistress Piera laid two cups of tea next to the children, then moved to a chair in the corner of the room. Settling herself, she pulled out a bag with a soft blue linen garment and set to sewing. Elodie thought about protesting her need for a chaperone but sighed instead. Silas was only ten, but being a page added another level of rules and formality Elodie, try as she might, wouldn't be able to argue away from Mistress Piera.

She turned back to the slate, and continued solving the problems, listening to the occasional scratch of Silas's quill, or the long pauses as he read from the book before him. As she worked on the routine math problems, Elodie's mind began to grow fuzzy around the edges as the fog rolled into her head and found a place to rest. Billowing up every now and then as a thought tried to stir it, the hazy clouds drifted and fell mutely back into place.

A hand rested on Elodie's arm. The fog surrounded her with an embrace.

"Elodie." The word had no meaning in the echoless fog. Muted, it stopped dead in the air.

As though a strong wind blew through her mind, the fog left her all at once, and she jumped in surprise. Gedas's clear gray eyes were inches from her own and both his hands rested on her shoulders, holding her rather tight.

Had he been shaking her?

She blinked and looked down. The slate was gone, with only a slight dusting of chalk still on her fingers. She looked to her side. Silas sat with concern etched deep in his browline. He held the slate in his hands.

Had she fallen asleep?

"Are you back with me now, my Gull?" Gedas asked softly. Concern was written in the crinkled corners of his eyes. He was kneeling in front of her, the table had been moved to the side and a few books lay on the ground.

"Sorry." Elodie blinked a few times and shook her head. "I've been zoning out a lot lately. I think I'm just tired."

Gedas looked her over from top to bottom, the same look he used when trying to puzzle out something complex with a little concern mixed in around the edges. Then he nodded once, and stood as if dismissing the question. "Have you eaten dinner yet?" he asked as though nothing else had happened.

"No, but I had a rather large tea time since we skipped lunch."

"Well then, we will have to remedy that. Mistress Piera, would you be so kind as to arrange for a small meal to be brought up?"

Mistress Piera stood nearby, watching Elodie, but snapped back to the present at the order. "Of course, Wizard Gediminas." She straightened up her sewing on the chair before leaving.

Gedas groaned as he sat in an overstuffed chair. Silas moved the table back in place and picked up the books. Elodie grabbed the slate and looked over her work. She'd only made it about halfway through the problems before she'd spaced.

"Now, tell me what you are working on there, dear boy," Gedas said.

Silas straightened out his books and papers, trying to find his place again. "I'm supposed to write four pages on the founding of Aluna."

Elodie felt guilty again for stealing the boy's afternoon.

"Ahhhh." Gedas smiled softly and leaned forward. "And what is the focus of the essay? The militaristic approach of the founding?"

"No, that would actually be fun." Silas frowned. "Duke Devoss wants us to focus on the political aspects of it."

"And where are you so far?"

"That's my problem. There doesn't seem to be much here about the governing or public affairs of the founding." Silas flipped a few chapters in the book before closing it harshly.

Gedas reached across the table and lifted the book to read the cover. "That is because there isn't in this book. You managed to find the most militaristic book on the founding of Aluna from the palace library. Honestly, it's quite impressive how much this book will be of no help."

Silas set the book down hard on the table. "But this is supposed to be the best book! It details all of the major battles, even the ones between the Elvmen and Wulfram's forces. I had to promise a second year I would do his stable duty last weekend so I could get it." Silas ran a hand over his face before he fell back.

"And so you know the how of the battle, but does the book cover *why* Wulfram decided to gather leaders from the prominent countries of his time, and set sail to a continent already occupied by a magically strong people, and invade?"

The question made Elodie uncomfortable. This was her many-times great-grandfather they were talking about, but she'd never heard the founding of Aluna and the Twoshy referred to as an invasion before.

Silas was frowning as well. "No."

"Tell me what you know of Wulfram's choices and life before he was known as our first king." Gedas settled back in his chair.

Silas leaned forward. "Well, I know he had seven brothers, and he was the youngest. His father was the ruler of Laridae, and his family was known for living good long lives, so there was no way he would ever be king." Silas's eyes grew narrow. "So he came here so he could be?"

Gedas nodded. "Not quite enough to write four pages on, even while using rather expressive handwriting. I suppose I will need to remedy that."

Elodie smiled in delight and set down the tablet. Gedas was her favorite storyteller, and this sounded like one she hadn't heard before.

Chapter Seven

GEDAS SETTLED in his seat and took a deep breath. Elodie and Silas shifted, excitement moving through them.

"Gather in close and I'll tell you his tale," Gedas began.

The words washed over Elodie and Silas forming a tangible bond over the small group. The words were magic, steeped with tradition, expectation, and anticipation. Storytelling was nearly sacred in the Twoshy, and the opening lines built a space where the magic of a story could exist uninterrupted.

"A few hundred years ago, Prince Wulfram of Laridae decided to make a mark upon our world. The youngest of eight brothers, he was small in stature and short in influence. The world was before him and yet it refused to look up and take notice."

A man walked into Elodie's mind as though it was a stage. Strong blue eyes and pale skin. He stood in a throne room, a head shorter than the woman standing to his right. A pensive wistful expression crossed his face as he looked on to an older man, crown on his head. Desire radiated from the man. A desire to be seen, to have a place in the world his own, and yes, a desire to rule.

The magic of the tale passed images, memories, and emotions from Gedas to Silas and Elodie. Silas gasped and Elodie let out her own breath of surprise. The face was not one of a portrait or tapestry, but one of the actual man, of Wulfram in his home in Laridae. Most tellers wouldn't have a true memory from so long ago. Only someone who had been there, passing on the tale from teller to teller would have such a clear image. Now, Elodie and Silas had the face. They could share it with others through a tale.

A young boy, the same blue eyes, watched as an older boy, gold circlet on his head, walked beside a king. Flags with red tern sea birds flapped in the distance. He wanted the king to look his way, just for a moment.

Please, just look.

"As a young child he watched and observed as his eldest brother learned what it took to rule the kingdom, then watched as each brother before him came of age and found a place in the world, until there seemed to be no place left for him. He took a knight's path to adulthood, believing the career would provide him direction and means to live his dreams, and took the symbol of an albatross for his shield to set himself apart from his family."

The boy grew, sword in hand, fighting opponent after opponent, each one taller than the last. He fought for himself and for his future. Pride swelled in his chest with every battle. He fought a man two feet taller than himself and won quickly. The young man stood before a crowd. He knelt and the king spoke over him, addressing him at last. He stood before the kingdom and held a shield with the albatross crest.

"As a youngest son must have something to occupy his time, Wulfram was given an ambassadorial role for his kingdom, and sent among the neighboring lands to broker deals and good faith with their neighbors. This is how his sphere of influence grew. His first post in the land of Pecraetho he met Franz, the brother of the elected ruler, and the two men grew a bond that would change their world. While Wulfram was a visionary, an influential and persuasive leader at heart, Franz was ambitious. He had the resources at his disposal to get what he wanted, but he lacked the understanding of Human nature that enabled people to find power. Living in a land that elected their leaders, and being not particularly likable, Franz knew he'd reached the pinnacle of advancement in his country. While on their own, each man would spend the rest of their days grumbling in the background of parties with no action, together the two heretical men hatched a plan. They would gather as many like themselves as they could find, those with power and resources, and those with ideas, and they would use the lure of a new future. They would set out for a new land they could rule."

A bronze-skinned man with sharp features plotted over dinner with Wulfram. They disagreed and argued before they patted each other on the arm and went their separate ways.

"Over the years he found others like himself. Outliers on the fringes of their world with nothing to inherit. Younger sons, nephews of lords, bastards and daughters who would be passed over for their relatives. He found them and created his own circle of influence."

Faces crossed Elodie's mind. Red-gold skin surrounded by pale hair. Blue eyes in a tan face. A bald man with fiery gray eyes.

Wulfram appeared. He approached a well-dressed dark-skinned man and whispered in his ear. Wulfram approached a beautiful woman who was busy in a workshop, clay over her arms and smeared across her face. Whispers across a throne room. Meetings in a market. Faces appeared one after the other. Some real, others living portraits, or rough images from a tapestry. In the eyes of each was a spark, a light of hope. Hope radiated from each of them.

We can create anew. We can have something all our own. We can do it better. We can do it right.

"Highborn and low. Man and woman. Magical, intellectual, cunning or influential. It started in his own kingdom as a whispered idea: if you had every resource available to you, and no fear of failure, what would you do with it?

"The dreamers. The rebellious. The ambitious. They adopted his ideas of a different path. This wasn't treason, they said, they didn't want to kill or usurp their own people, they wanted to find another way to prove their destiny and fulfill that one thing that drove them forward."

Meetings in dark corners and in tavern rooms. Visionaries dreaming and planning. Plotting and scheming. Deals for finances, trade agreements for sponsorships.

"To the southeast, across the sea, was a continent not often visited by Human feet. After the great Human wars of several centuries before, the other races, tired of the Hu way of bickering and fighting had separated their cultures and governments from Hu life, and chose to live apart. There were still small nations or groups of each of the races all over the world, but the land to the south was known to belong wholly to the Elvman, Dwarvman and Aviman. Having lived apart from the other races for so long, and having only their own dreams in their eyes, it was easy for the Hu to see the races of men and women as only an obstacle to their own ends."

A small girl with green swirls on her skin ran to a man, who lifted her and spun her in circles. Their laughing faces covered in green markings shining with joy. A man with golden red feathers running along his head and down his arms greeting an orange feathered woman as they passed. Two children laughing and running through a tunnel being chased by a short woman with a bath towel.

"Wulfram and Franz spent several years proselytizing. They found leaders who joined their way of thinking and worked to grow their own faction within their nations. They convinced existing leaders to appoint and create their own colonies. Slowly but inevitably the plan began to take shape, until one day they had sixteen partially formed nations, all looking for land to plant their roots.

"The first time the leaders of each budding nation sat together, Wizard Sayormough, the leader of what would one day be known as Pundica, declared their meet magically strong and powerfully binding. They spent months drafting the Constitution of Sixteen, setting broad rules that would enable each nation to function wholly independently, yet bind them all together. They pored over old maps of the continent and set borders for each nation. Our continent is not evenly divided as you well know, and those years of politics and planning determined what each nation would receive."

Maps stretched out on tables with weights and markers spread about. Men and women argued and drew lines through rivers and forests and mountains. They drew red slashes through cities and villages and wrote new names above them.

"The battles that proceeded, you both know quite well," Gedas continued.

Men and women in shining armor lined the ridge of a valley as carts were packed in a village below, and then the image faded.

The old man nodded to the two children in turn, a sad smile on his face. "To our great fortune, the Dwarvman and Aviman did not stay to fight the expansion. The Avi disappeared south into the mountain range that creates a natural barrier to the southern half of the continent. The Dwarv disappeared from the land completely. But the Elvmen stayed and fought for their land. The settlement of the Kingdom of Sixteen cost many more lives than originally estimated. So many so, two of the original Sixteen nations were not able to form and Aluna absorbed the land originally set aside for the lost nations."

The memories were back, flowing through her mind; a man in a gold helmet falling in battle with an arrow through his neck. A woman with glittering blue magic wrapped around herself clutching her heart and falling to her knees as her magic contracted before blasting out and felling the warriors around her.

"We won in the end, if destroying a people can ever be considered winning. After being mortally wounded, the Elvman king gave up his life to place a final curse onto Wulfram's crest."

His ears were long and ended in a point. His face, pale with green whirls and streaked with sweat and pain. He clutched at a sword in his chest. Wulfram stood on the other end of the sword, blood streaked across his face as he pushed the blade through the Elvman king. The king gasped as he inhaled each breath and stretched out an arm, crossing the distance to Wulfram. He placed a long finger on the albatross crest. A flash of green flew from the Elvman king, down his arm and through his finger,

into the crest and Wulfram's chest. Wulfram's face filled with shock and a
pulse flooded through him into Elodie making her collarbone tingle.

"Wulfram gained a throne all his own, where he could rule and
leave his half-cursed legacy to his children."

Elodie pulled at her collar, revealing the birthmark in the shape
of the albatross sigil first belonging to Wulfram, and then to all of
Aluna.

Seeing her movement, Gedas nodded and continued. "Yes,
with his dying breath the Elvman king pressed his finger into the
Sigil on Wulfram's chest, burning the mark into his flesh. A mark
passed down to each of his heirs to represent the curse infecting
the ambition of each of the line so their life's pursuit would always
end in toil."

She shook off the pulse of energy she felt from the tale and
rubbed at her mark. The battle was still around her, the dead
laying in the grass, but Elodie tried to push it out of her mind.

Elodie had never felt very ambitious toward anything and
hoped she didn't need to worry too much over the curse of her
family. Sadly, she reflected, it must have been her father's life
pursuit to see his family and children grow into adulthood. That
would account for Elodie being ripped out of their lives at such a
young age. Between her family's generational curse and the spell
trapping her in an illusion, it was hard to become invested in
anything or anyone when it would only be taken away by magic.

Before she realized it, the story was over, and the world
around her came back into focus. The smell was the first thing to
hit her.

Dinner.

The servants had returned during the story and set out two
small tables with covered trays. Mistress Piera sat in her chair with
her sewing.

"So that's it then? He did it all just for the sake of being king?"
Silas asked.

Elodie turned to him and saw he'd pulled out a scrap of paper
and was scribbling notes across it. He paused and looked up, first

at Gedas, and then to Elodie when Gedas didn't immediately respond.

Elodie looked at Gedas. The older man was leaning back in his chair as though deep in thought, staring off to the side. One hand held his chin through the thick beard, while the other drummed on the chair's armrest. At last, he shook his head and turned back to the children. "It is unimaginable the lengths a man will take to cement the place in the world he believes should be his." Gedas rose from his chair with a groan and stretched like a cat, his frown gone. "Now, shall we eat?"

Gedas made his way to the trays of food, and Elodie followed, leaving Silas behind to scribble his notes. She wasn't sure how she felt about the story Gedas told. While she knew the Elv had met her ancestors in battle, she'd never thought of the cost to the people who'd been all but eliminated. She only ever thought of the curse and the cost to her own life.

As Gedas uncovered the trays, the aroma of rich food hit Elodie and her mouth watered. He scooped up one of the gold-lined china plates and passed it to her.

Elodie piled roasted pink potatoes seasoned with rosemary and a little dill onto her plate. Her favorite. She would have left with only potatoes had Gedas not added a few slices of what looked like turkey, and a few green things.

"Will you join us, Mistress Piera?" Gedas turned to the older woman still in her chair in the far corner of the room.

"No no, Wizard Gediminas, you are very gracious, but I'll be fine to grab something in the kitchen later on." Her stern face said the thought alone was a violation of decorum.

"Oh please, we have so much more food than we actually need," Elodie said. "You may as well eat now before it gets cold. You know I don't care about formality."

Mistress Piera's eyes softened. "Maybe once I am through with my task." She lifted her sewing back to her attention.

Elodie nodded, figuring it was as good an answer as she would likely get, and poured herself a glass of lime water. She ate her food with reckless abandonment as Gedas returned to the table with two plates in hand. He set one next to Silas's elbow and tapped the boy's paper with one long finger. Silas looked up startled.

"Eat before your food grows cold, my boy, all the academics of the world cannot replace the need for nourishment."

"That sounds like one of those lessons learned from experience," Elodie said smiling to Gedas.

"In fact it was, my Gull." Two water goblets floated to the table, helped along by small blue sparks. One rested itself next to Gedas, and the second in front of Silas. Elodie saw Silas's eyes widen at the sight and tried not to smile. Gedas would spout odious lectures on wasting magic if he caught anyone in the act, but kept himself far above those rules. "I spent many meals during my time at the academy hidden away in the library trying to add to my knowledge."

"The Magical Academy in Pundica?" Silas asked through a mouthful of turkey.

"Of course, my boy, it's the only place of learning on this continent equipped to train and accredit wizard-level magic users."

Silas asked another question, and Elodie yawned, trying not to let the half-chewed potatoes fall out of her mouth. The fog started to roll in at the edges of her mind, and she took another bite of potatoes, willing the starch to vanquish the clouds. The potato helped, and as her mind cleared she pushed the plate away and pulled the slate in front of her again to finish the last few problems. She looked up to find the piece of chalk and saw Gedas examining her closely while Silas asked him a question about the differences between an enchanter and a sorcerer certificate. Elodie blinked, and Gedas turned back to Silas, answering his question as though nothing had drawn his attention.

Elodie found the chalk and returned to the slate. She fought the fog a few more times as she finished the simple problems, and after a particularly hard push against the fog, slapped the piece of chalk to the table in triumph. Silas looked up from his writing and

Gedas peered at her over the top of a book. Clearly more time had passed than she realized.

Gedas set the book down, and Elodie smiled when she realized he'd been reading her Earth science book. She noticed her books and binders had been added to one of the bookcases by a helpful servant. No doubt her backpack was in the back of a wardrobe, and the gum and other odd bits were organized in a drawer somewhere.

"You've had a longer day than us I'm afraid, we should let you get to bed," Gedas said, raising from the overstuffed chair.

It was true, Elodie had already started her day when she fell into the early morning of the Twoshy, so it was definitely close if not past her bedtime.

Silas rose and bowed low. "I should have realized." He began packing up his things.

Elodie shook her head. "This was fun. Maybe you could bring the other pages sometime, and I can help with the math." She smiled at the thought of the assorted pages crowded in her sitting room. If she could get them past being too scared to talk to her, it might actually be fun.

"Maybe," Silas said. "I don't think we would get much work done."

Elodie laughed and it turned into a yawn. "You're probably right."

Mistress Piera appeared, summoned by the yawn.

"Now, Her Highness needs to get to bed," she said, clucking and ushering Elodie to the dressing room. Elodie passed through the room, not sparing a glance for the lavishly decorated walls or ornate mirrors now visible with the racks of gowns removed. She reached her large bedroom and Elodie flopped backward onto the bed, sinking into the feather-stuffed mattress and blankets.

"Now now, let's get those garments you believe pass as clothes off before you get too comfortable."

Elodie groaned and sat up. Mistress Piera was there in a moment pulling off Elodie's cloak, and Elodie stood and undressed herself so Mistress Piera didn't have to. She wasn't particularly fond of being treated like a doll. She kicked off her sneakers and Mistress Piera held out the soft blue fabric she'd been sewing. Reaching out, Elodie realized it was a nightgown, soft to the touch. The neckline was covered in embroidery a few shades darker blue than the fabric. She recognized the symbols for health and peace in the design.

"Your old night clothes were moth-eaten."

Warm affection filled Elodie's chest. She'd spent her evening sewing the gown so Elodie would be comfortable. The embroidery was careful detailed work that would have taken time Mistress Piera could have spent doing anything else.

"Thank you," Elodie said with sincerity.

Mistress Piera muttered an 'it's my duty' before bending down and picking up Elodie's discarded shoes. Elodie undressed and pulled the nightgown over her head. She unbuttoned her jeans and kicked them off with her socks.

Picking up the jeans quickly, she folded them nicely on top of her shirt so Mistress Piera wouldn't have to. "If we could not throw out my jeans," Elodie started, then began stuttering at the stern look from the mistress. "The–the pants. I can still wear them around my rooms when I don't need to be in a dress."

The mistress nodded and scooped up Elodie's discarded clothes and tapped off each light globe around the room. "Now in bed. You need rest and will likely have a full day ahead of you, my lady."

Elodie nodded and peeled back the covers before Mistress Piera reached them. She slid between the soft sheets and was asleep as soon as her head hit the pillow.

Chapter Eight

THE PILLOW WAS soft against her face. Something was off, but she couldn't place it. She didn't have to pee bad enough to wake, and the room was light, but not bright enough to wake her. Her alarm hadn't gone off. Curtains rustled and light flooded the room.

Elodie jumped up and tried to stand, but the ground was farther than expected. A gasp sounded as she teetered to the side and fell onto the plush woven carpet.

This definitely wasn't her carpet.

The memories came flooding back. She was in the Twoshy, in her room in the castle.

"Your Majesty, I'm so sorry," a soft voice said from above her somewhere. She turned her head and saw a girl a few years older than herself cowering by the thick curtains.

"Highness," Elodie said with a groan.

"Wh–what?" The maid covered her face in terror.

"I'm a highness, not a majesty. I don't get majesty till I take the throne." Elodie made to sit up, then thought better of it. Her muscles ached fiercely and she decided maybe the floor would be fine.

"Wait, let me help, Your Highness." The maid rushed to her

side and Elodie found the motivation to get off the floor before the older girl helped.

"Really, I'm fine." A wave of dizziness washed over her as she sat on the bed. "And you don't need to address me by any title. I actually kind of hate it."

"I'm so sorry, Your High—I'm sorry." The girl bowed.

"Seriously, it's not your fault." She tried to calm the girl. "I'm totally fine, I just forgot where I was for a minute. Happens all the time, trust me. I don't even think you woke me up, I just woke myself up and thought I was gonna be late to school or something. Really, please stop looking so scared, you aren't in trouble."

The girl's lip trembled while she tried to smooth her face. Elodie pushed away her own irritation as she realized this wasn't the type of servant who was going to trust her when she tried to be nice.

"Would you mind getting me a glass of water?" Elodie asked, switching tactics.

The maid bowed and darted out of the room, relief painted on her face. Elodie sighed and climbed back into her feather-soft bed, pausing as another wave of dizziness hit her. Had she really stayed up so late the night before? She hurt all over, like she'd spent the last two days riding from sunup till sundown, pausing only for combat lessons or something equally tiring. She'd only ridden a few hours the day before, and shouldn't feel *this* sore.

The maid returned and bowed, holding out the glass.

"Thank you so much." Elodie reached to take the glass, and her arm trembled, nearly spilling the water. Luckily the maid was on edge, and steadied it.

"Sorry." Elodie tried again, this time gripping the glass with both hands. She took a quick sip, then tried to set the glass on her bedside table. Her arms felt weak, and the maid caught the glass before it dropped.

"Are you alright, Your Highness?" the maid asked, setting the water on the table.

"Yeah, I think I just need more rest." Elodie sunk back into the pillows, her muscles spasmed in her arms with the effort. The change of position made her head swim, and she lost consciousness in a wave of black.

ELODIE AWOKE, something cold and damp on her forehead. She was surrounded by a blanket of fog, warm and humid on her skin. The cold was a relief. She opened her eyes and saw only fog.

The cold dampness moved slowly and softly around her face, warming with the contact of her skin, till it disappeared all together and she heard a soft splash and gentle dripping. Then the cold softness was back on her face and neck. Her muscles tightened repeatedly in her back and shoulders, then in her legs, over and over again. Her heart was racing, and she fought until she had nothing left and fell again into the thick sweet fog.

Chapter Nine

THERE WAS something annoying tapping her face. She tried to shake it off, but it continued. She tried to wipe it away, but the fog caught and held her hand.

"Come on, girl, cooperate with me here," the fog said. Goosebumps ran over her back as the air reached the hot sweat sticking the nightgown to her skin.

She was sitting up in the fog. This was vaguely confusing, and the wave of dizziness came over her again. Her body tried to roll back into the pillows but she was held tight. Something cold was pressed to her lips and a pressure on her jaw opened her mouth. A cool thick liquid touched her tongue and she swallowed.

Dandelion, peppermintsteel, and a number of others. The flavors mingled in her mouth, joined by the sharp tingle of someone's magical gift. This alone nearly caught her attention. It wasn't safe to drink something magic she hadn't examined, but then she couldn't remember why it was unsafe, and the magic felt familiar, and she started to sink back into the fog.

Something tapped her face again. More of the thick liquid came in, and Elodie chewed before swallowing. Chia seeds, thickening the polyjuice into a near gel. The patting and tapping on her face kept her attention long enough for her to keep drinking.

Before she knew it, she was being lowered back into a wave of fog and clouds, swept around by the dizziness and sank back to sleep.

Chapter Ten

SHE SMELLED the breath of a dragon, and it nearly rose her from her sleep before the beast backed away. "Poison?" the dragon asked.

"No," answered a voice. "Something else."

Back into the fog Elodie fell, and in the fog she saw the dragon again. A huge dragon with gleaming gold and purple scales. Silas arrived with a sword made out of words.

Elodie tried to cry out, to warn the boy of the dragon, but Silas was a knight now, and though he was still the boy of ten, Elodie felt the man he would become and knew he carried the wit and courage of twenty.

The dragon breathed his fire, and Elodie gasped. Silas dodged the flames and swept his sword across the dragon's neck. Elodie turned away from the sight as the head rolled, thumping down the executioner's block. She tried not to vomit as the copper smell of a life draining away hit her nose.

In a moment she was saved, whisked away again by a feeble wave of fog.

Chapter Eleven

THE SOFT SOUND of a page turning reached Elodie's ears. Familiar breathing patterns accompanied the rustling and a calm peace washed over her. The fireplace crackled, spreading warmth into the air.

She turned toward the sound of her mentor and smiled at Gedas, the greatest wizard of their age, sitting in an armchair next to her bed. His legs were crossed, and her seventh-grade science book was propped open against one knee.

"You know, this Earth is not so dissimilar from our own, aside from the lack of ruakh in the atmosphere." Gedas looked up to meet Elodie's eyes.

"Isn't that expected though?" she asked. "If the world of the illusion was framed or shaped after this world, it makes sense they have the same gravity, seasons, length of day, and all that other sciency stuff." She yawned. They even had many plants, animals and insects the same. Only the species who required the ruakh to exist and survive could only be found in Eres. The land masses were different shapes, and the water-to-land ratio was a little different, but near the equator it was still hot, and near the poles it was still cold. Fundamentally, the two worlds were the same, supporting the same Human race.

"Indeed." Gedas closed the book, keeping a finger in the pages to mark his place. "And how are you feeling, my Gull?"

She was achy all over, like she'd spent several days doing pushups and running laps, but her head was clear. Very clear. She felt more alert than she had in a long time.

"I feel awake. Like really awake. Still really achy, but some willow bark tea will probably help."

"Drink this first," Gedas ordered, leaning forward to grab a large goblet of something off the bedside table and handing it to her. Leery of a repeat performance with the water glass, Elodie grasped the large cup with both hands and found, although sore, her muscles were doing as she asked. She took a sip to prepare herself for the possible taste, but it wasn't bad. Crisp and refreshing with a side of bitter. Thistle bright, burdock root, greyglove, sage, dandelion, chia seeds, and a number of other herbs, all known for their detoxifying properties either naturally or magically. She drank it all down. When a magic user told you to drink something for your health, you did it.

When it was gone, Gedas took the empty goblet from her and handed over the water glass. Her lips felt dry and cracked and she drank half the water in one go.

"How long have I been out of it?"

"You arrived in the Twoshy three days ago."

"What?!" Elodie spilled a little water down her front. Gedas handed her a handkerchief to dry herself with, a frown on his face. "What exactly happened?" she asked.

"It would appear something in your system was incompatible with your magic, and reacted. No, you weren't poisoned, although we should think about starting more in depth lessons on poison detection now you are getting older."

"I'm not getting older, I'm getting younger. I was thirteen last time I saw you remember?" The spell affecting her age and body was an endless frustration.

"Hush, you know well what I mean. You may be in the body of

your twelfth year, but your magic and mind continue to grow. Believing yourself to be younger than you are only lessens the potential you allow yourself to reach. If you believe you are nothing more than a twelve-year-old girl, then it will be so."

"So you're saying you don't know what's wrong with me?"

"No, not yet."

"You don't like not knowing things."

"No, I do not," Gedas said with a scowl not directed at anything in particular.

"So what's on the schedule for today?" Elodie set the empty cup on the table. She felt alive and alert like she hadn't in a while. She wanted to go out exploring or collect herbs or something. She felt achey, but knew stretching and moving would be the best fix to keep her from stiffening. Energy budded inside of her.

"I believe Seamstress Charmaine has a rack of gowns she needs you for pinning." A small smile lifted the corners of his mustache.

Elodie fell back into her pillows. "On second thought, I think I might need another day of bed rest to get back on my feet."

"Nonsense. After one of my tonics, lying about unnecessarily would only be a stain on my reputation. I will announce to your maid, a rather skittish young lady I may add, that you are awake, and ready for a bath. I'm sure you will feel tip-top after a nice warm soak."

"Tell 'em to make it super hot," Elodie said to Gedas's back as he left the room. "I'm so sore." She stood from her bed and was incredibly relieved when she didn't feel dizzy or weak. She had no clue what could have been wrong with her, but trusted Gedas to give more care to her health than she ever could. The idea of more advanced poisons training was definitely an ideal outcome.

Someone brought her lunch while she waited for a warm bath to be drawn. Many of the castles and richer homes of Aluna had excellent plumbing, cold and hot water, heated magically, and pumped through pipes creating running baths and showers, sinks and toilets. But in the palace, the upgrades had not gone well.

It had been part of the advancements her grandfather, King Zonel, tried to install after his father King Lonan attempted to upgrade the city's sewer system. Sometimes Elodie felt gypped being a princess of a magical land, where anything her family tried to accomplish ended up being spoiled by a generational curse.

As she ate her lunch in her sitting room, she listened to the sounds of servants one after another enter the dressing room and fill up the gleaming copper tub. Elodie tried not to let the guilt of the effort involved make her feel anxious. She could have gone down to the larger communal baths below the castle like all but the most pigheaded nobles tended to do, but she'd forgotten how much work went into drawing a bath when your ancestors were failures at doing anything grand.

By the time the bath was ready, most of the servants were gone. All but a few stayed behind to help. Elodie thanked them profusely for preparing everything, and then asked them to let her bathe herself. The maid who'd been there when Elodie fell out of bed approached with a paper packet.

"My lady, Wizard Gediminas asked us to give this to you." She curtsied, not meeting Elodie's eye.

"Thank you so much. And thanks for your help the other morning."

The maid bowed out of the room, and at last Elodie was alone.

She opened the packet and sniffed tentatively. The sharp scent of rosemary and peppermintsteel reached her. She took another sniff. Chamomile, lavender, eucalyptus, comfrey, and a strong touch of cayenne.

She smiled. Healing, strength, and muscle relaxers. This would definitely help with her soreness. She reached into the packet and scooped up the majority of the herbs and held them. Closing her eyes, she took a deep breath. As she slowly exhaled she looked inward, down into her own essence, following a path she'd learned to follow long ago, until she found a small blue spark of something wholly her. It felt warm and familiar like a friend, yet strange and awesome like seeing fireworks for the first time.

Following the familiar path back out, she brought a small strand of something invisible and remarkable with her and nudged it into the herbs. She didn't ask the ruakh to change the herbs or to make them something they weren't, she asked only for them to be all of what they could be, and gave them a little strength.

When she was done she wiped a small bead of sweat off her forehead and sprinkled the herbs and salts evenly through the water. Next she picked up the big wooden spoon near the side of the tub and stirred till the salt dissolved. The smell filled her nose, soothing her mind. The water was hot as Elodie sunk in. She gave herself a few minutes to acclimate to the heat, soaking in the warmth, then washed her hair.

The soap and oils she used always made her hair feel somehow dry, tangly and greasy at the same time for a few days or weeks until her hair grew used to the more natural process and became lavishly soft. Once washed, Elodie balled her hair up in a loose bun, and leaned back so it would fall out of the tub. She sunk into the water, up to her ears and stayed like that for a long time. Eyes closed in a restful doze, she let her muscles soak up the healing properties of the herbs. The soothing presence of her magic flowed around her. She liked the world like this, muffled yet amplified in that wonderful underwater way.

The sound and vibrations of footfalls reached her through the water as someone approached. Cracking an eye, Mistress Piera stood arms crossed staring down at her, a thin smile on her wrinkled face. Mistress Piera held out one hand and Elodie put her dripping hand in the maid's.

She examined Elodie's water-wrinkled fingers and nodded. "Quite beyond pruned. I would say you are done cooking, Your Highness." She turned and grabbed a large length of drying cloth, and spread it out in her arms. Elodie sighed and climbed out of the water, shaking slightly as the rush of cold air hit her body. Mistress Piera chuckled and wrapped her in the cloth. Elodie held the fabric tightly to herself and rushed to the fireplace in her bedroom.

Mistress Piera followed Elodie with a few lengths of cloth, and wrapped one around her hair, and used another to dry her arms and legs. The towel was traded for a thick robe, and she provided Elodie with underthings. As Elodie rubbed lotion into her skin, Mistress Piera insisted on her sitting in a chair before the fire so she could properly brush out and dry her hair. "I won't allow you to fall ill again on my account."

Elodie tried to relax and watch the cindix playing in the embers of the fire. This treatment wasn't strange to someone who'd grown up in this world, and she shouldn't feel guilty for the attention or for the servants draining her bath one pot at a time in the other room.

Her hair was dried, and the bathtub emptied and removed. Rustles and thumps came from the dressing room as Charmaine set up. Elodie took a deep breath. Fittings with Charmaine had been much less painful than with the old head seamstress. The dynamic of their relationship shifted as Charmaine aged and Elodie did not, but Charmaine still treated Elodie like a dear little sister who she would protect and always enable to shine. And shine Elodie had in so many beautiful gowns over the years. Charmaine deserved the head seamstress position. She was brilliant and talented.

For every gown she made, Charmaine always made breeches and tunics for Elodie. She ignored the complaints of whoever was supposed to be in charge of the princess's image, and argued a person should be free to wear what made her comfortable.

It wasn't unheard of for a woman to wear breeches in Aluna, depending on her class, rank or position. Yes, for anything official Elodie would don a dress, but when she went out riding, or adventuring with Gedas, breeches were perfectly acceptable. Elodie didn't dislike wearing dresses, or the elegant gowns, but she did like variety, and there were many activities where the flowing garments got in the way.

The fittings on the other hand, were something she detested. Standing like a doll while others moved around her made her feel self-conscious and oddly isolated.

"Let us get the worst of the lot out of the way first, shall we?" Charmaine suggested, grabbing up the clothes typically worn under a corset.

Elodie smoothed out her face, trying not to let her feelings make the experience miserable for anyone else in the room. She hoped the dresses wouldn't need to be taken out anymore, making her feel like a balloon among streamers. The underclothes were dropped over her head, and the corset was fastened around her waist. Charmaine took notes where anything needed to be adjusted.

Corsets really weren't as bad as everyone always made them out to be in history class. They were uncomfortable purely because they limited the range of motion and prevented slouching, which Elodie was quite fond of. But once tightened into a well-made corset, Elodie felt snug and safe. Being twelve she was wearing a slightly less shapely corset than she would wear when she came of age, but even with the sporadic waist training that came with being forced into and out of the spell, the binding was not painful.

Luckily extensive hoop skirts had gone out of fashion before Elodie was old enough to be put in one, and instead, several petticoats were dropped over her head and fastened into place.

"Blue is the color of the season," Charmaine announced as she swept up a light sky-blue satin gown, and dropped it over Elodie with the help of her assistant.

Elodie shouldn't have been worried about the initial fit, Charmaine was brilliant. Very little pinning was needed to make the dress hang properly. It was beautiful. The dress itself was light blue, but the neckline was bordered by rich blue embroidery, depicting what looked like a sky full of clouds. An ocean view lined the hem in matching embroidery.

They pinned two more gowns nearly as elegant as the first, one creamy purple and the second bright yellow. Next they moved on to more casual dresses. These didn't require a corset and served well for when she didn't need to be stately, or wanted to slouch.

When they reached a darker burgundy dress, Charmaine

paused with a sigh. "I thought this color would be perfect for your complexion. I've never been able to wear it with hair as red as mine."

Elodie laughed. "Maybe when you're old and gray you can make yourself an elegant burgundy gown."

Charmaine's eyes lit with excitement. "Yes, that's genius! I will wear nothing but burgundy and red as an old timer. I will shock everyone I pass in the streets with my daring use of orange and yellow."

They giggled together as they lowered the gown over Elodie. The dress had white lace around the wrists of the long sleeves and the hem line.

Elodie pulled at the neckline, cut several inches below her collarbone. "It's beautiful. Perfect for winter, but couldn't we make the necklines on all of these a little higher? I'm going to freeze if I don't wear a cape everywhere I go."

"Nonsense. It would be a disgrace for you to wear anything that didn't show your birthmark," Charmaine said with a tap on the mark on Elodie's collarbone.

It had long since been tradition for the fashions of the Twoshy to follow the placement of the current king's or queen's birthmark. It was thought to be an honor for anyone of the royal line to display their mark at all times. This had been rather unfortunate for her great great great-Uncle Garyt whose mark had been just to the left of his navel. The plump man had tried for most of his life, unsuccessfully of course, to make crop tops a thing in Aluna. There was an unfortunate portrait of him hanging somewhere in the wooden wing of the castle where it would not frequently be encountered.

When the fitting was done, Charmaine had one of the basic dresses set to fit her well, and Elodie was freed from the room in a green smock dress with long thick skirts and matching slippers. She promised to have tea with Charmaine in a few days.

She exited her rooms at full speed, not wanting anyone to

change their mind over her freedom. Elodie didn't have many friends left in the castle, but she could always bug Gedas.

The mage hall was on the fifth floor of the castle. Gedas had said once, the best of mages preferred to be far apart from the rest of civilization, as there were fewer interruptions to their experiments. Gedas even insisted the maids not enter his workroom to clean. This wasn't done for the sake of Gedas's experiments, but was to make sure nothing disastrous befell the maids. For a child like Elodie, one who would be around magic her entire life, Gedas believed in trial by fire and taught her early on how to detect and avoid the dangerous magics. She was ten the first time Gedas allowed her to be alone in his workshop to work on her own project. She made a syrup for a maid with a sore throat. The syrup worked, and the maid later reported the disappearance of a chronic toothache she'd been the owner of for years.

Gedas made her spend three months recreating the syrup and every step of the process until Elodie figured out what had healed the tooth.

"Isn't healing more things a good thing?" she'd asked over and over again, but Gedas insisted. Any unpredicted result of a magical working was a bad and dangerous thing. Something going unexpected, even when the results were positive, was a sign of a sloppy plan. If Elodie wanted to practice sloppy magic, Gedas wouldn't teach her a moment longer. Elodie had sighed and got back to work in diagnosing her mistake. It turned out the moonseed and elderflower had reacted unexpectedly together with the specific heat temperature used. It was an easy fix once she found it.

She spent the following months creating a proper cure for a toothache, writing the recipe and magical process down in her personal potion book she'd started when she was seven.

She knocked four times on the last door at the end of the hall.

The voice boomed from within the room.

"Confounded mortals!"

The walls shook, the metal fittings on the door rattled against the wood as though about to come to pieces.

"Let the gods curse the unworthy who so dare to interrupt a great and powerful wizard at his work!"

Dust, knocked loose from the mortar in the walls, fell slowly to the ground.

Elodie knocked again.

The door swung open with a glint of blue fire around the handle, and Elodie stepped into the sitting room dusting off her dress.

The walls were lined with bookcases, packed full of books and scrolls so it resembled less a library and more so the discount shelves of a thrift shop in an illiterate town. The floors were covered in a thick brown carpet, and a few plush armchairs and scattered end tables, all piled with books, were dotted around the room. In the corner by the only section of wall not covered with bookcases was a fireplace with two red tall-backed chairs facing it. Elodie made for the unoccupied chair and began unloading books from the seat. She dumped them on a table already overflowing with books. "Are you trying to scare off anyone in particular?" she asked, setting a heavy leather-bound tome on the floor.

"Maids, messengers, colleagues. They are all the same to me in the end. Frivolous distractions wanting only to take from me a precious portion of the time I have left in this world," Gedas said, not looking up from his book.

Elodie dropped into the chair once it was empty. "Because American history is so important?" she asked, eyeing her history book in his hands. He must have finished the science book some-time earlier in the day.

"I expected you to take much longer in your fitting."

"Nope," Elodie said. "Charmaine is awesome. Half of the things she made fit me on the first try."

"Well then, what are your plans for the rest of the evening?"

Elodie blinked. "Isn't that what you usually tell me?"

"You are getting older, my Gull, and I believe it is nearly time for you to start making those choices for yourself."

"I'm not getting older, I'm aging painfully slow. At this rate by the time the spell is broken everyone I know now will be dead and you will be five hundred years old." Gedas raised one eyebrow at her. "Are you already five hundred?" Elodie asked, unsure.

Gedas said nothing, but instead closed a bookmark into her history book and tucked it into the crevice of the armchair. Bracing on the armrests he lifted himself shakily with an exaggerated groan. He limped slightly toward the door leading to his work-shop and Elodie followed rolling her eyes. With a subtle twitch of his finger Elodie would have missed had she not known it was coming, the candles and lamps in the room fizzled to life.

"Now," he said with a look around the room. "As you are apparently not yet self-reliant enough to direct your own life, how about you instead replicate this for me." He picked up a wide-mouthed jar from one of the shelves and placed it on the worktable in front of Elodie. The jar was dark amber and she could tell nothing about the contents. Remembering Gedas's comment about teaching her more of poisons, Elodie decided not to open the jar right off and take a big whiff as she would usually do.

"How long do I have?" she asked, peering tentatively at the jar.

"As long as you remain in the Twoshy."

"And how long will that be?" She looked at him out of the corner of her eye. It was another frequent conversation of theirs. Everyone knew Gedas could somehow predict the exact time and day Elodie would be sucked in and out of the spell, and yet Gedas never admitted to it openly.

"Do you truly wish to know your future, my Gull? Leave nothing to the imagination or to surprise you down the road?"

Elodie thought about it and peered at the jar. "I don't know."

A tentative knock sounded from the door to the hallway.

"Gods above! Who dares knock upon the door of a most busy wizard? Be gone!" Gedas bellowed, the magic infusing his voice with power. On this side of the door nothing shook or trembled as Elodie had experienced when knocking.

"That should do it. Continue," Gedas said calmly, turning back to Elodie and gesturing toward the jar.

Elodie took a deep breath and focused on the jar. She decided touching the outside would be safe enough, as Gedas had done the same, and she didn't think he'd magically protected himself. She reached out her hand, and another soft almost indistinguishable knock reached their ears. Elodie looked up, surprised. Gedas's eyebrows were also raised, and he turned to head back toward the sitting room. "Hm. Must be important."

Elodie followed behind so she could see when he opened the door. A kid a few years older than her stood on the other side of the door frame. He shook where he stood. "P–p–please, Lord—Wizard Gediminas, sir."

Gedas stood ungraciously, arms crossed, peering down at the boy with menace.

"Is—is Her Highness here perhaps? I have a message." He held up a small roll of paper like a shield. The messenger's eyes landed on Elodie further in the room, and he relaxed slightly. Gedas took the letter and closed the door in the boy's face.

"You know, I don't get nearly as many interruptions when you're not in town." Gedas handed the message to Elodie with a grin. "It smells like it's from Oburleck."

Elodie grabbed the small note. It was on thick heavy parchment, not the readily available sheet paper, and unrolled it. The writing was in a glittering amethyst ink.

The Lord Steward of Aluna, Duke of Comak, does humbly invite Her Royal Highness Princess Elodie of Aluna and Tross to dine with them in an informal setting of their personal dining room. Dinner will commence at Her Highness's convenience.

"Dinner," Gedas announced reading the note over her shoulder. Elodie grimaced.

"You know, you didn't need to be so mean to the messenger." Elodie looked up at her mentor with her eyebrows furrowed.

"I do what I must to live the life that I wish," he said, his face unapologetic. He crossed the room back to the fireplace and picked up her history book before flopping back into his red chair. "Have fun at dinner."

Elodie walked out the door and slammed it behind her, a little harder than her mood called for.

Chapter Twelve

A MAN in the purple and gold livery of Comak, Oburleck's holdings, stood outside of Oburleck's suite of rooms. He announced her inside with a deep bow. The crown provided guards and servants to all guests staying in the castle, but it was a show of wealth to bring additional guards or servers. Oburleck had gone a step further and dismissed all palace servants in his rooms in place of his own.

Elodie straightened her posture before walking through the door. She pushed back her shoulders, and lifted her chin into the disposition so familiar in the aristocracy.

"Ah, Your Highness, I'm so glad to see you on your feet." Oburleck emerged from a side room and Elodie held her breath. He took her hands and held them firmly. "I was so distraught when Gedas told me you were ill, and I am endlessly relieved to see you've made such an abrupt and miraculous recovery."

"Thank you." She carefully turned her head away from his direction before inhaling. It didn't lessen the smell. "I'm honored by your prompt invitation to dinner."

"No, no, my dear child, the honor is mine. Please, make yourself comfortable, dinner will be ready in a few moments." He bowed and extended his arm toward a small parlor and Elodie walked toward the glow of the fire in the next room. "I hope you don't mind, I also invited Duke Devoss to join us."

Devoss stood from his chair and bowed to Elodie. "Your Highness, I'm glad to hear you're feeling better." Elodie nodded in return and muttered her thanks. She found an elegant and uncomfortable chair and sat, the men following her example.

Devoss's presence was a relief. With both men in company she wouldn't be expected to carry the conversation.

Elodie visited this room frequently when the previous steward occupied them. His granddaughter had been a dear friend to Elodie before she died. Then, the sitting room had been homey and comfortable with overstuffed chairs and family portraits. Now, the room was lavish and stiff. The leather furnishings shone, and the carpets looked new. Two large bookcases covered one wall and each book was ornate and decorated with gold.

"Yes," Oburleck agreed. "It's a relief knowing we have such a competent wizard on staff who was able to uncover the root of your illness and find a remedy so quickly when the rest of the palace mage staff and healers were so stumped over your condition."

Elodie asked Devoss how his family was as the servant in the purple livery announced the meal. The three aristocrats made their way into the dining room.

"So kind of you to ask," Devoss replied. The servant helped her into her chair and the two men sat, Oburleck at the head of the table, and Devoss to his left, across from Elodie. She hoped the angle would help prevent Oburleck's conversation from ruining her appetite.

"The Duchess and I have been lucky enough to announce she is burdened with our fifth child, due in early spring." Devoss took a few large gulps of wine before gesturing for the glass to be refilled. "I say burdened mind, but it truly only applies if this will be our fifth daughter. Cooric willing, this one will be a boy at last."

Elodie offered her congratulations and was rewarded by Devoss continuing his lament on the curse of daughters and the strain they weighed on his coffers as the first course of tomato bisque was delivered.

Elodie's mouth watered at the wonderful aroma. Remembering her etiquette training, she picked up her soup spoon and dug in gracefully. It was creamy with the rich floral and aromatic flavor of basil.

Oburleck ate carefully, preparing each spoonful with consideration before bringing it to his mouth during a polite pause in the conversation. Duke Devoss on the other hand ate with single-minded ambition between draining his wine glass.

"Do you know how long you will be in residence?" Devoss asked through a mouth full of salad. "I have a mind to send for my oldest daughter, she is about your age and would make a fine lady in waiting."

"No, Your Grace, I don't know how long I will be here. It depends on how long the spell lets me stay, and if Wizard Gediminas has any other plans while I'm here."

"If you wish to stay in residence you only need to make it known," Oburleck interjected, a frown across his face. "Command Wizard Gediminas if you wish not to be taken on such excursions. Your well-being has too long been left in one man's hands if you ask me, but while I have no authority over the relationship, you outrank him in every way. If you set the order for your care, I will put the full weight of my support behind you, Your Highness."

Elodie thanked the servant who set a plate of steaming lamb in front of her. She took a slow deep breath and let the mint and rosemary flood her senses. "Thank you, Steward. I enjoy the lessons and trips Gediminas takes me on. It's not something I want to change." She picked up her meat fork and knife and cut a small piece off her lamb, focusing on the meal and pointedly not making eye contact with either man. The lamb was delicious, smothered with a rich mint sauce

"How old are you now, child?" Devoss asked.

"Twelve."

"How on Eres are you now twelve? I was certain we celebrated your thirteenth birthday when last you were in residence. I know the mages of Pundica have talked theoretically of time travel in the past, but tell me, have they perfected the skill? I'm sure the ladies of the court will be ecstatic for the opportunity to reverse a few years."

"No, Your Grace, the spell controls my age."

"Oh, I hadn't realized. Is this commonly known?" he asked, turning to Oburleck, with a look on his face Elodie didn't recognize.

"No, Your Grace, as with most aspects of the spell, the secrets of its inner workings are a mystery to all it would seem but Wizard Gediminas. I have asked him if he would be willing to explain the phenomenon in the past, but he has always been unwilling," Oburleck said, frowning.

"That is rather strange, you being his interim ruling sovereign, for him to refuse a request. Especially when the request pertains to the well-being of our beloved princess." Devoss turned to Elodie with a doting smile. Elodie sighed and tried to provide a weak smile in return.

"Well of course he never refuses a request," Oburleck clarified. "No, he explained quite readily, in colorful language no man on Eres could ever decipher. It is understandable one of his rank and skill as Wizard would have a hard time communicating to the general populous. This is why I think it wise the castle employ more magic users of competent but less prestigious rank. There is definite value in the council of many over one man who believes himself smarter than the rest."

"Well said, my good man." Devoss raised his wine glass in salute and tipped it to his mouth before realizing it was empty. Frowning, he gestured to a servant who dutifully poured his fourth glass. "Our poor Elodie here deserves the most sympathy on the matter. I often feel sorry you are forced to spend so much time in his crotchety company. You should be here in the castle among your people, not forced to rough it in the woods or wherever he takes you. I can't imagine you learn much. Does he often explain things with riddles?

"No." Elodie kept her face neutral toward Devoss. His expression made it clear he expected her to elaborate. He frowned when she didn't.

Gedas only answered with riddles and magic babble with people he didn't like, or who he believed were below his worth to care about. He always explained things to Elodie if she asked. It was his way of challenging her curiosity. Yes, pride and arrogance probably fueled a large part of his rudeness, but if someone was smart enough to understand him, or wasn't willing to plead ignorance, he didn't bother to translate.

"No?" Oburleck asked, surprised. "So then he did explain your age affliction to you or were you just satisfied in knowing it was all a part of the spell?"

Elodie's ears grew hot at the implied naïvety. She took a cooling sip from her water goblet. "What Wizard Gediminas knows of the spell has all been gained through his observations and research. There isn't a simple answer to any of this. We don't know exactly why time runs slower in the spell than it does in the Twoshy or why sometimes my age reverts when the spell reclaims me, but Gedas—Wizard Gediminas does have theories and he's explained these to me in a satisfactory manner."

"I don't particularly like the idea of these theories we have no concept of," Devoss said before he took a large mouthful of lamb. He continued, talking around the cooked meat. "Your well-being is so important to all of us, you understand. One man shouldn't have absolute knowledge and authority over you."

"If his explanations have been so satisfactory to you, please, would you do me the honor, Your Highness, to explain his theory on your age?" Oburleck asked, his face open and kind as though ruled by nothing more than curiosity and concern for her.

Elodie sighed. "Sure." She thought for a moment trying to keep the frown off her face. "It's like a bucket of mud." Oburleck frowned and Elodie sighed again. Gedas was a much better teacher than Elodie ever hoped to be. "The spell is like a bucket of mud, and ruakh is like a big flood of clean water. When I am pulled into the Twoshy, it's as if the mud is stripped away and I am free to live here as I am. Living and growing and using my magic. When the spell takes me back, it's like I'm shoved back in the mud, and I'm coated again in the illusion. Only the smallest traces of ruakh follow me, so I can barely feel any of my magic when I'm there."

"And what of breaking the spell? Does Wizard Gediminas have any *theories* on this?" Oburleck took a polite bite of his food.

Elodie's shoulders tensed, and she tried not to frown. "No."

"Ah, I see." Oburleck stroked the grain of his neatly braided beard. "Well I know Wizard Gediminas does focus more on the intellectual side of his craft than the practical. Maybe I can reach out to the mages of Pundica to see if they have made any progress on the matter. I do so hate to see you trapped, Princess. It is time you were with your own people again, ruling your own nation. I would happily step down as Steward if only it meant you were free from this curse."

"Not sure that will help in the end, Oburleck," Devoss said. "With that whole prophecy business says our girl here will be the one to break the curse, it would likely be futile to enlist more help outside of making sure she has a proper teacher."

Elodie frowned. She didn't know what Devoss was talking about.

"Ah, yes of course." Oburleck looked to Elodie. "I'm sorry, Your Highness, are you not familiar with the prophecy?"

Elodie tensed, she didn't like admitting a lack of knowledge, especially when she was sure it would end with Gedas being accused of something. "I've heard a few prophecies over the years, which one are you referring to?"

The corner of Oburleck's mouth rose in the slightest smirk, but the rest of his face stayed in his kind and gracious mask. "The one Wizard Gediminas spoke of to your father when you and the other Misplaced Children were first taken. The prophecy that stated *you* would be the one to ultimately break the curse which binds you and the other Misplaced Children in the illusion."

The room disappeared. Her stomach flipped, and the hair stood up on her arms. The spell was temporary, always spoken of as though it would come to an end. But the how of it, how it would break, she'd never really questioned.

She wouldn't be queen until the spell was broken, she'd never heard of a prophecy identifying her as the one who would be responsible for the spell's demise. This opened up a new world of possibility if Oburleck was to be believed, and really, why would he lie?

She tried to mask the emotions running through her head. She didn't think she could lie outright about her knowledge of the spell, but she also didn't want to admit ignorance. Her silence turned out to be answer enough as Oburleck smiled apologetically. "I know it can be hard to believe someone we trust doesn't have our best interests at heart, but truly, Princess Elodie, if you have need of me, or need any assistance in managing your relationship with Wizard Gediminas, I am at your service. Don't allow fear of his supposed power or rank allow you to be taken advantage of. Not all of us are scared of such a man."

Elodie shook her head. Oburleck had it wrong. Gedas did have her best interest at heart, even if she was the only one he cared for. She trusted him emphatically. "I appreciate your concern, Steward Oburleck, but I do trust Gediminas."

"Of course," Oburleck said charitably before changing the subject. Elodie took another bite of food.

She'd been losing focus so easily lately, her mind drifting into the clouds at the lightest touch of distraction. As the two men continued on with explaining their plans and the benefits to the realm, Elodie prayed for the loss of focus to return so she could blink and find the meal over. Instead she found her focus and attention sharp. She couldn't will herself to fade out as she sat through the excruciatingly dull conversation.

Elodie covered a large yawn as she placed her spoon into her now-empty pudding bowl. Catching her yawn, Devoss nodded and drained his last glass of wine. "What brutes we are, keeping you awake, my girl, so soon after you've recovered. We should allow you to retire."

Elodie didn't argue as she folded her napkin and placed it next to her plate. They said their long goodbyes before Elodie left the steward's rooms and started the trek back to Gedas.

The older man greeted her as she entered the small library.

"Devoss addressed me improperly ninety-three out of ninety-six times," she informed him, flopping into her chair.

"Devoss was there? That warthog," Gedas remarked as he shifted in his seat, closing her history book around his thumb.

"He's not a warthog, his family crest is a fox."

"No, a fox is too great a compliment for that man. Foxes are known for being cunning and sly, his father was a fox. He is a warthog."

"They're planning on lowering taxes for key businesses like bordellos since the crops were so good."

"Like I said, warthog." Her book cracked as Gedas opened it and examined the page.

"They asked me about the spell," Elodie began, unsure how she should broach the subject. "They asked if I knew how the spell would be broken and said it was prophesied I would be the one to break it."

Gedas looked up at this, a disgusted look on his face. "Imbeciles. They don't know what they speak of. Put it out of your mind, my Gull. Such things will only cause you grief to think on."

"So there is a prophecy then?" Excitement ran through her chest.

Gedas was silent as he read her book. Elodie knew better than to prompt him. He heard her and would answer in his own time. It was several minutes before he did. "Prophecies are something not to be relied on when planning the future. Translations are too easily skewed or misinterpreted. It is not healthy to treat a prophecy as directional."

"So if that's the case, you should tell me the original prophecy so I can make sure I'm not following some interpretation."

"It's best if you forget it." He turned the page.

"Please Gedas, I just want to have a normal life. To grow up in this world where I belong. I'm so tired of flipping back and forth. I would almost wish the illusion was real, if only it meant I would stop being shoved from one to another."

"Now, my Gull, you know better than to make wishes the gods may hear and follow up on to their own ends." He stood and moved to her chair, placing a hand on her shoulder. "I know how this is never an easy answer to hear, but truly child, this is a conversation best left till you are older."

"Older? Gedas, aren't you the one always telling me I am older than my age and need to act accordingly?" Elodie stood up, knocking off the old man's hand, her hands balled at her sides. "Saying you will tell me when I'm older is just your way of saying you won't tell me at all. Not at this rate." Feelings bubbled in her chest making her breath ragged. Her cheeks felt hot. "Tell me then, you somehow are the only one able to tell when I will appear and disappear so you must know. How many times am I going to end up celebrating my thirteenth birthday before it finally sticks?"

"Yes, girl, when you are **older**. For despite your age and maturity, **you still insist on acting like the child you look**."

Gedas's face looked like a storm was brewing. Elodie had rarely ever seen him truly angry before, and never at her. The lightning forming on his brow was not metaphorical. The thunder building in his voice caused Elodie to pause and her anger started to drip away, diluted by shock and hurt. Pressure built in the back of her throat and in her eyes. Her nose started to sting.

"**When you can prove yourself a responsible adult Human being I will treat you as such. Until then, BEGONE.**" The last word billowed out of him, catching in Elodie's hair and the edges of her dress like a sudden wind.

She turned on her heel and fled from the room before the tears started pouring.

Chapter Thirteen

THE HEAVY CURTAINS rattled as a maid threw them open. The sun poured into the room and Elodie threw her thick down blanket over her head and tried to burrow into the mattress. The previous day's worries still felt like an ache on the back of her spirit, sapping any desire for society from her. She ignored the subtle sounds of activity around her room. The clinking of metal on ceramic. The soft rasp of metal sliding along wood. Light steps fading away, and the *thunk* of a door being closed. Elodie didn't care if her morning tea got cold, she tucked the blankets tighter around herself and let the distant muffled sounds of the castle lull her into the light dose of a lazy morning.

Heavy footsteps registered at the edge of Elodie's consciousness, like a drumbeat warning of danger. Though her subconscious tried to bring her to urgent wakefulness, it took the door banging open for Elodie to jerk awake. She sat up confused.

"That's quite enough of that, my lady. Do you plan to sleep through lunch as well?" Mistress Piera said from the edge of the bed.

"Am I late?" Elodie asked stupidly, looking around for the alarm clock that didn't exist in this world.

"Late? Late for what? No, my lady, you have nowhere to be and no time to be there. Apparently, them who decide such things don't think any tutors should be appointed while you are in residence." Mistress Piera started muttering to herself about legal guardians and a lack of direction and structure as she pulled the blankets away from Elodie, breaking the bubble of warmth she'd sunk into. Elodie held in a shriek as her skin attempted to flee from the cold. "Don't go giving me that look, my lady. The longer you sit there the colder your bathwater gets."

Mistress Piera picked up the tray of cold tea and left the room without a word. Elodie peered over her bed at the thick carpet ending three feet from the door leading to her washroom. Taking a deep breath, she stood and rushed as fast as she could over the cold tile.

Undressing as fast as possible, she stepped into the warm water. It burned slightly against her icy toes. She sunk into the warmth, and let it ease the chill off her spine. The steam and lavender rose around her.

Elodie tried to relax in the water, as she felt all baths deserved someone to lounge lavishly, but guilt creeped in, ruining the effect. Like the tea cooling while she snoozed, the bath must have cooled and gone to waste. The servants would have drawn a second bath for her, bringing the warm water in from the pump on the south side of the castle a bucket at a time.

She vowed to trek down to the rooms under the castle for her next bath.

The state of the palace was a mess. Even some lower class homes a few miles outside of the palace walls had better plumbing.

Elodie ran her hand through the warm water stirring up the dried lavender buds floating on the surface. Lavender, lavandula. A part of the mint family, it could be used for anxiety, insomnia, pain, healing, hair loss, or as an antifungal.

She didn't feel soothed or relaxed.

Instead she felt guilty and anxious. Not just over the water, but also over how things ended with Gedas. She needed to apologize for how she'd acted. He was the one person, aside from Vanessa, who'd always been on her side, no matter what. If he felt there was something she didn't need to know, she would trust him. His anger had surprised and scared her, but here in the water and the lavender she could push it away.

She splayed her fingers in the water and felt the lavender buds brush up against the edge of her magical consciousness. She gave them a sharp nudge and the dried buds bloomed in the bath. The light-purple flowers danced through the water, releasing a fresh and beautiful fragrance.

Another trickle of guilt bloomed deep inside of Elodie. She took her eyes from the water and grabbed the thick soap next to the tub and began the task of cleaning. To revive a plant just so it could be poached in a tub, then dropped down a drain. Useless. The magic had been utterly useless. She had power to do something no one back home in the illusion could do, and she used it to make her bath more pretty. It was a tasteless action and a waste of magic.

Mistress Piera entered with drying cloths, underthings and a gown, and helped Elodie wash her hair.

Thick stockings. A warm woolen moss-green dress. Leather boots, a little too big. Soft kid gloves. A deep brown wool cloak to button it all in.

Once outfitted for the weather, Elodie ventured through the castle using a combination of the less-used corridors and servant paths to avoid as many of the higher rank as possible. On previous trips she'd sometimes dress in plain clothes and try to pass herself off as a servant, just to avoid the stares, the bows, and the titles. She gritted her teeth whenever she passed a servant or courtier who wasn't too busy to notice her presence. She entered the kitchens, only startling one maid scouring a large burned-out pot, and slipped through the back door to the palace grounds quick enough not to be spied by the head cook.

The cold crisp air, a contrast to the overly warm kitchen, smacked her face with a refreshing chill. She pulled the cloak tight around herself and headed off to the east end of the castle toward the more industrial buildings. She would go see Gedas and apologize for her attitude eventually, but for now she wanted to remember this world, feel it around her. Hear it, smell it, and see it. All of it. The old and elegant tapestries and furnishings of the castle, the stink of the lower city. This world was real and was the only reality. Her life back in the illusion was counterfeit and fake, dreamed up by some wizard long ago.

As she stood near the open door to the palace smith, feeling the blaze of the forge on her face, smelling the hot metal and burning coal, and feeling the repetitive pounding nearly in her bones followed by the rush of air and roar of the fire as an apprentice pumped the billows, it became harder and harder to remember the small details of home. The illusion. She couldn't remember the color of her pillowcase, or the smell of the detergent in a freshly washed towel.

As she watched the glowing metal reshape into something new, the memory of her mother's fake sugary voice, the memory of the confused and disappointed look in her father's eyes, it all started to disappear deep into her, like a dream. Not gone, just forgotten for a time.

The blacksmith was a short wide man, with muscles bulging and stretching with each pound of the hammer. Elodie had tried once to lift one of the large hammers and hadn't been able to get it an inch off the ground. This man wasn't much taller than Elodie, shorter than his assistant, a boy maybe a few years older than her. But while the assistant had height, the blacksmith had strength. His arms were nearly as thick as the scrawny boy's waist. He wore an undyed tunic and thick, worn breeches. The shirt was soaked through with sweat from the fire and heat, clinging to his powerful muscles and showing his dark skin through the wet fabric.

The man stopped his rhythmic swings and set the hammer

lightly on a bench before shoving the glowing pole into a vat of water. The water hissed and bubbled to an immediate boil. He wiped the back of a sooty glove across his forehead before turning and picking up a waterskin. Spying Elodie at the door he nodded before lifting the waterskin to his mouth and draining it. Some of the water escaped the edges of his mouth and ran down into his intricately braided black beard.

Elodie's face grew hot as she smiled and ducked out of the doorway back into the cold air. He hadn't recognized her, so she left before he or someone else did. It was common enough for small children and passersby to stop and watch, but the castle would likely be buzzing with the news she was in residence. Elodie wanted to watch, but she didn't want to make the craftsman stop his work to pay respect.

Wandering back toward the stables, Elodie ventured over to the practice grounds where a spattering of clacks and clangs made it clear the field was in use. The swordsmen were young, swinging clunky, ugly-looking swords. Elodie spied Silas on the edge of the chaos. The kids were spread out over the field, paired up. One sword wielder would swing their sword while another blocked, and then they would switch roles. The sword master stood watch over it all, eyeing the kids with deadly focus and calling out sharp orders now and then. He was a tall lean man with thin graying hair pulled back to show the harsh lines of his pale face.

Before long the sword master called a halt and began to pair off half the kids, while the rest stood watch. There were twenty or so kids, a mix of boys and girls, all of different ages. Most were around Silas's age, but a few nearer to fourteen or fifteen. Silas, Elodie noticed, was faced off with a boy nearly a foot taller than him. The boy looked timid, hunched over and a step farther back than the others in his row. Silas looked relaxed and ready, a small smile on his face.

The sword master called a sharp word, and the kids moved to action.

The pages started in on each other. For the most part they followed the same attack-and-defend pattern as though stuck in the rhythm until one or the other would take the offensive. Silas and his partner hadn't yet moved. The taller boy stood ridged. Sword up in the air and in front of himself, both hands gripped tightly to the hilt. Silas stood grounded, his feet apart, and sword crossing in front of his chest. He seemed to be waiting, although Elodie wasn't sure for what. His body relaxed, the point of his sword dropping to the ground as though heavy. The taller boy moved then. He stepped forward, lifting his sword even higher as if to hit Silas over the top of the head.

When it was over Elodie wasn't quite sure she'd seen it all. Silas tucked in his sword and darted under the taller boy's reach. The boy's blow missed, and Silas attacked. He hesitated long enough for the taller boy to get his sword in the way and block the attack. As their swords clashed, Silas did a little something with his wrist, and a sword went flying. Elodie blinked. The taller boy slouched and walked away to pick up his fallen blade. When all five matches were complete, the winners and losers moved away and the remaining ten pages paired off.

Of course. Of course Silas was amazing at this. Silas was amazing at everything he did. Silas was ten and small for his age, and he just bested a boy several years older and several inches taller.

The weeks she spent in Tate when they first met had been interesting and lovely. Tate was one of those cities in Aluna not lacking due to poor city planning or cursed construction. The castle had real plumbing in the guestrooms and was made entirely of strong sturdy stone. It wasn't at risk of collapsing into the ground at any moment. Tate was on the edge of the north western border of Aluna, only a day's ride from the capital of Rohap. This put it in a great place for Gedas to expand Elodie's familiarity with regional plants and their magic.

While Elodie resided in the castle of Tate, Silas was a constant shadow. He was smart for his age, confident and outgoing like only an eight-year-old could be.

Elodie had found him completely annoying.

If it was daylight and Elodie was not in her rooms, Silas was following her and Gedas. At first he'd been in awe of the wizard, as most were, but soon Gedas's easy-going ways allowed Silas to open up. Gedas usually tried to scare away anyone but Elodie. People chattered and Gedas didn't like chatter. But Silas proved to be one of the rare exceptions.

She'd always been the only one Gedas focused on or tried to teach, but for those months she spent in Tate, he taught Silas right along with Elodie. He made a point to expand topics away from the natural and strayed into politics and the thinking arts. Silas loved it, but Elodie found it boring.

A more self-aware person would realize she'd been jealous of Silas, and Gedas's attention on him. He'd been fascinated with everything about her, stories of the illusion, the language differences and slang she used, even the way she held her arms.

Meeting him again now, those memories felt far away. She was glad for someone to talk to who wouldn't bow after every third word, and while he was still only ten, in many ways Silas felt older than she did. He knew how to navigate the politics of her kingdom and was brave enough to attempt it. She wanted to hide and avoid it all.

His second match, Silas was paired with a blond girl, maybe a year or so older than Silas. This girl had a wicked gleam in her eyes and when the sword master called the start, she attacked Silas with brutal force. Silas won, but it was a closer thing and they were the last match of five to finish.

Elodie climbed up the railing outlining the practice yard for a seat and a better view.

In the spring more people would be surrounding the yards watching the pages practice as the second or third year pages prepared to graduate to their squire years. For now, Elodie was the only one braving the cold to watch the newly minted pages. In a few months knights and other nobility could take a new squire into their service. For those squires of noble birth, this was an opportunity to apprentice and learn the ins-and-outs of knighthood before they themselves were knighted. For the squires of common birth, they could still be taken into the service, but not with the hopes of becoming a knight. Instead squiredom was their chosen career path.

While a first-born lord's son like Silas could become a page at ten and need only spend the required two years as a page before graduating to a squire, common-born pages had to be sponsored by a lord of the realm, and were typically older. They also spent three or more years as a page before being granted a place as a squire. For a common-born, having the skill or knowledge to pass the page tests and graduate was not enough to grant them a squire's place.

The rhythm and clattering cacophony of their blows was peaceful in a way. Before long each match and the winners of each match battled until only two remained. Silas and a sandy-brown-haired boy with olive skin. This boy looked to be good, but not as good as the girl Silas fought earlier.

Elodie began to hear whispers of her name and title. Looking around she realized several of the pages noticed her and were spreading the news. Silas was mid block when he looked up, barely blocking a blow crashing down toward his hand. When he saw her, he started to wave with a big smile then dodged a swing from his opponent. He had to take a few big steps back and made himself refocus.

He won again.

When the training master called their practice for the morning, Silas turned to a lanky boy around Elodie's age, and gestured him to follow as he headed to Elodie on the fence. The other boy was a few inches taller than Silas, his skin was warm brown and he had short curly chestnut hair. His page's uniform was not as fine as Silas's. The hem on his pants was too high and badly sewn and his tunic's embroidery of the Aluna crest was beginning to unravel. The castle only offered so much to its less-distinguished pages.

When the boys reached Elodie they paused a few feet away and bowed properly.

"Your Highness, may I introduce Page Eyvindur of Tate. Eyvi, I present Her Royal Highness, Princess Elodie of Tross and Aluna."

Eyvi bowed a second time, his eyes were wide and he didn't look at Elodie. She gave a nodding bow in return, not about to attempt a curtsy while sitting on the fence.

"That was quite pretty, Silas, thanks for the intro." She shared a wide grin with Silas. "You know, you boys sure look fierce out there swinging around your big pointy swords."

Silas held up his sword showing it to Elodie. "Not as pointy as you think. They're quite blunt."

Elodie looked at the sword. The edge was as thick and wide as the center of the blade as though only a heavy strip of metal. More a swordlike object then an actual sword. The edges of the steel were notched and dented from the abuse of the pages.

"Well, in your hands it sure looked like some legendary sword with a grand name. Remind me to tell you the story of a sword named Excalibur sometime."

Silas's eyes lit with interest. He would remember.

"Tell me, how is it you're a first year and the best swordsman in your class at *ten*?" she asked.

Silas bowed his head in false modesty. "Because I've been copying the men at arms in Tate at their sword drills since I was five, and practicing with father's best squire since I was seven." His smile dropped and he looked away. "Really I'm not all that good. I'm weak and small and have short arms. I just know a few good tricks and how to use an inexperienced fighter's moves against him."

"Oh that's all?" Elodie asked with a chuckle. "Well I guess it's good you're only *ten* and have time to grow longer arms and build your strength and get all big and bulky." She turned to the other boy, who tried to smooth his expression of shock at Elodie and

Silas's conversation. Did he think she was too forward or not proper enough? "So Eyvi, how long have you had to put up with Lord Humility over here?"

Eyvi's eyes widened and he stammered before looking at his feet. "You—Your Highness, I have known Silas—Page Silas all my life, my lady. That is, all his life, beg your pardon, him being two years younger." He met her eyes for the briefest moment before looking back down.

"Page Eyvindur, will you do me a favor?" Elodie asked.

"Ye—yes, Your Highness. Of course."

"Will you please, whenever it's just us, call me Elodie? Just drop the titles." Eyvi looked up at her full in the face, shocked out of his nerves. "I don't want you to get in trouble since I know you're supposed to follow decorum as a page, so in public I totally get needing to use titles. But you're Silas's friend, so that makes you my friend. And I really hate friends calling me by titles. Cool?"

Silas nudged his friend. "Cool means okay."

Eyvi dropped into another low bow. "Yes, my—Elodie. I will do as you ask."

Elodie nodded over the boys' heads. The sword master stopped his conversation with an assistant pushing a large heavy wheel-barrow filled with the thick practice swords and was looking their way.

The man and wheelbarrow left the field toward some storage sheds, and the training master turned and stalked toward Elodie and the boys. Elodie saw him coming, and shot an intentional look at Silas, a flick of eyes behind him to warn of the man approaching. Silas and Eyvi turned as one and straightened, their posture improving in an instant.

They both gave the older man a bow and Silas again took the introductions. Master Driard, gave an elegant bow.

"It's a pleasure to make your acquaintance at last, Your High-ness. I believe we were in Jach at the same time two years ago, but I wasn't lucky enough to meet you at the time. We were most worried to hear your health took a turn, but I am glad to see you are back on your feet. Are you enjoying your stay in the capital?"

Elodie took a deep breath and pulled back on the proper mask she liked to discard. "Thank you, Master Driard, for your care. I find the capital quite well, thank you."

"That brings me happiness, my lady," he said, bowing again. "If you will excuse me, I see two of my students have quite forgotten their places. Page Silas, Page Eyvindur, I do believe you are holding up the supplies manager by not promptly returning your practice blades. For the inconvenience you will both work two hours on your off day, organizing the practice shed." Elodie winced. Master Driard bowed again to Elodie. "Good day, Your Highness," he said with a pointed look. Turning sharply, he stalked away from the practice grounds to the warmth of the castle.

Silas sighed. "Well, we do need to clean up and see if there's any lunch left before we get to our lessons, and Master Driard did have a point. You just got off your deathbed from the talk of the servants, you should be in by a fire."

"Yeah, that sounds nice and boring," Elodie said, rolling her eyes. "So, anyways, what are you guys doing tonight?"

"Homework. I had too many wrong answers on my math figures yesterday and got a load more heaped on for tonight." Eyvi widened his eyes and blushed fiercely before ducking his head again.

"Oh great. I can help with that. I'm great at math," Elodie said.

"Well, Eyvi's level is working on calculations and things," Silas said evasively.

"Yeah, that's like algebra right?"

The boys looked stumped.

"Don't worry about it, I bet I can handle it. What time are you guys heading to the library?"

"Probably a half hour after the dinner bell, but Elodie, we do have a lot of work," he said looking at her meaningfully.

"Okay, I get it, I won't distract you too much. Just work. I will meet you guys there."

She tried to jump off the fence gracefully and stumbled with flair. Silas caught her, without skewering her on his sword. When she met his eyes she saw his big sideways grin. "You really haven't changed, have you?" Elodie stuck her tongue out at him.

They said their goodbyes and Elodie returned to the castle while the boys walked to the storage sheds.

Chapter Fourteen

IN THE KITCHENS, Elodie begged a few meat pasties from the chef, wrapping them in a cotton handkerchief. She spent the rest of the afternoon sequestered away in the library.

If she hid well enough and stayed out of the way of anyone official, she could make it through her time in Tross without someone realizing they should put her in lessons.

The library was Elodie's favorite place in the castle.

The main room was large and open, with tall vaulted ceilings and glass windows high on the walls to let in light. The bookcases were made of dark walnut. Walnut trees were a symbol of intelligence and wisdom, magically used to boost knowledge and instill inspiration. The smell of old books and their leather bindings saturated the air and brought a peace onto Elodie she couldn't find anywhere else. This place was safe and familiar.

The librarian curtsied to her from the reference desk. Elodie waved but passed without a word. Librarians were good people, they understood when decorum could be set aside. Elodie knew the layout by heart. She took the path through the bookshelves lining the side of the wall and avoided the bulk of the library and tables where people worked.

Toward the back of the library were the archives, a wonderfully deserted refuge Elodie had spent many days in over the years when she hid from etiquette teachers and overeager stewards. On the way to the archives she picked a random book off a shelf of written tales, then went to her usual corner holding the kingdom's harvest archives for the last three hundred years.

Storytelling was an old tradition in the Twoshy. There were many scholars who made it their mission to record tales so they might not be lost over time and the fading of memory. Written tales whether read aloud or read quietly to oneself didn't hold the same magic as a tale told aloud to a room of waiting people, but she still loved reading them. Sometimes she found recorded tales about people she'd known over the years. Her greatest joy came in finding a tale told by her father or mother.

Elodie spent the next few hours reading tale after tale in the thick book she'd picked. Eventually the light shining in from the tall windows high above the bookshelves began to wane and she knew the dinner hour was approaching. This part of the library, so rarely used, didn't have any of the light globes like those hung over the tables. She debated heading back to the kitchens to sneak another meal, but the kitchens would be hectic with preparations. It was a long walk, and the tale she was reading was quite good. She opted to finish reading the current tale and then when it ended, to read the next, and the next until finally her eyes strained with the lack of light and she could no longer make out the words.

Getting off the ground, Elodie stretched out her sore legs. She vowed to sneak in some cushions like she'd done in the past and make a small nest.

Elodie left the stacks and headed back toward the main room where tables stretched out in between shelves filled with more frequently used books. Here, brightly lit globes cast a gentle glow over each table. The room was still empty, with dinner winding down students and apprentices would trickle in over the next hour.

She wandered past the tables until she spied Silas setting out some books and aligning his paper, inkpot and quill just so. He was joined by Eyvi and a few other pages. She recognized one as the girl who'd almost beat Silas in his second match, and the other was the tall nervous boy Silas first fought. The tall boy sat straight in his chair with a small confident grin, so unlike what he'd worn on the practice field.

Elodie crossed the room toward them, the tall boy first to see her. His eyes went wide, and he nudged Eyvi beside him until they all watched her approach. Silas gave her a wave and they all got to their feet. Elodie motioned for them to sit but they dipped into bows before her. Elodie sighed.

She sat in a chair next to Silas and gave the others pointed looks until they cautiously sat. Silas then launched into the introductions, less formal than at the practice yard. The girl was Page Candessence of Lacanto, Dess for short. The tall boy was Page Timothee from Gliedal. It took a little while for the two new pages to warm up to her and even longer for them to stop using her title. Even Eyvi started using her title again until Elodie gave him a look and he blushed.

Elodie was glad to see a stack of paper in front of Eyvi, Silas the only one with a slate. Paper in the Twoshy became easily accessible after a sorcerer with calxophobia looked for a readily available fiber source and stumbled upon a pile of dung. The digested fiber was cheap and plentiful, and after a bit of magical experimentation, made thin, usable paper.

Having paper created from animal dung opened the way to a number of puns for sleep-deprived scholars of every age.

Elodie asked what the pages were working on, besides a load of crap.

This got a chuckle out of the pages, and she could see Dess and Timothee openly relax toward her. Silas and Timothee were both finishing history reports while Dess was writing a paper for her etiquette class none of the other pages had. When she asked about it, Dess explained.

"I sort of have a problem sometimes with correcting our etiquette teacher Master Bernid. My mom is Ambassador Anatia.

I've been held to a higher standard of etiquette not just of Aluna but following the guidelines of Pundica, Rohop, Leronia, and Eplaria since I was old enough to walk. So when Master Bernid tried to tell us the proper honorific for a counselor of Pundica was Haci instead of Hoca, he didn't appreciate me correcting him and I got stacked with writing a two-page report on the respect to be shown to one's betters." Dess made a face, clearly of differing opinions as to who was whose better.

"I don't think correcting him was the problem, Dess. I think it was you insisting a man who's never even visited a third of the Twoshy shouldn't qualify to be teaching that vexed him," Silas said with a grin.

"Well he isn't," Dess said, crossing her arms.

Elodie laughed with the others and turned to the last boy. "And what are you working on Eyvi?"

"I have to finish some math problems I got wrong from yesterday." He sighed. "Then I have ten more problems assigned today and an additional five problems as punishment for those I got wrong yesterday." The boy looked defeated, staring down at the work before him.

"I told you to copy my problems from today's work," Timothee said, fishing for a page stacked in his folder.

"That's what got me into trouble in the first place," Eyvi said, throwing his arms in the air. "I've been copying you for the last two months, and now I don't know how any of this works. So the one day I can't copy because you had to go and get yourself in trouble with extra cleanup duty, I'm left trying to work it out myself, and I don't know how! I just need to learn this so I can do it for myself."

"Well, I don't have any work of my own I should be doing, so I'm happy to help," Elodie said, ignoring the work waiting for her back in Gedas's rooms. Elodie stood to move around the table to Eyvi. All four pages started to stand. Elodie froze and made exaggerated sitting motions to the pages. Once they sat, she moved around the table and slid into the chair next to Eyvi.

Elodie pulled Eyvi's small pack of papers in front of her and began reading over the crossed-out problems to see what Eyvi had been missing. Then she took to teaching him the tricks she used to remember the steps.

Elodie respected Eyvi. He was quick to pick up what she showed him, and wasn't afraid to ask questions once he got over her being a princess. A common-born page was held to a higher standard than his noble classmates, and even then had to be the best if he wanted a squire position. He wanted to learn and understand what he struggled with.

Facing your own fears and trying to conquer them was the definition of brave, and Elodie couldn't wait to find out where this boy would end up.

While they worked, more academics filtered in. Magic apprentices and students sat segregated from pages or the occasional squire. Several pages made as if to sit at their table, but froze at the sight of Elodie. Each time Silas intercepted them, made introductions and begged them to sit. Elodie promptly ignored the new pages, hoping this would help them relax, and sure enough as they saw her focused on helping Eyvi, they slowly relaxed.

By the time they reached the last of Eyvi's problems, Elodie had talked with every page at the table at least a little, and was glad for the new friends. In the past, Elodie tried to make a friend when they stayed somewhere long enough, but she'd never befriended such a large group. Inwardly her heart fell knowing when she left the Twoshy they would continue to grow and age without her till they, like the friends she'd made in the past, were too distant by age to befriend the Misplaced princess.

"So what do you think, Eyvi?" Elodie asked as the boy started putting away his math and pulled out an unfinished history paper. "Does it make more sense?"

"Yeah it does. It feels like it's starting to come together. But I guess we'll see if I can remember it all tomorrow."

"Math definitely takes repetition," Elodie said, nodding. She cracked the book of tales she'd been reading in the stacks.

Silas asked what she was reading, and she turned the book for him to read sitting across from her.

"The Tale of Curk the Foolish?" Silas read.

"Oh, is that about the other misplaced, Kirk?" Dess asked.

"There are other misplaced?" Eyvi asked.

"Of course there are, you loon." Timothee rolled up his papers and hit Eyvi over the head with them. "Aluna isn't the only kingdom who lost their heir to the illusion."

Dess looked at the book ignoring her friends as they fell into a mock duel with paper swords. "Oh, no I think his name is spelled differently. Also I'm not sure how he would be considered foolish. He's just a kid. Have you met many Misplaced?"

Elodie shook her head. She knew of them only as an idea. When the spell trapping her in the illusion was cast, every ruler of every nation of the Twoshy lost their children below a specific age. Some of the nations' leaders in the Twoshy like the king of Rohap didn't have any children at the time, so no one was lost. Other nations like Pundica, a noocracy ruled by sixteen counselors, had lost many.

Elodie knew there were others, but she'd never *met* any of them. She'd asked Gedas once, but he said they all mostly traveled near their original location. Tross being so far from the other nations of the Twoshy, it wasn't likely their paths would cross. Elodie had asked him then if all the other children had wizards like him looking after them and waiting for them when they traveled.

He'd changed the subject.

"No, I've never met any of them," Elodie replied. "How about you?"

"Let's see, there's Kirk and his twin brother Christopher," Dess said, counting on her fingers. "Then there's Allen, he's really cute, although he was older than me when I met him, now I'm probably older. Oh, and Thomas. He has a younger sister too, but I haven't met her. There are a few more from Pundica as well, but I haven't met them yet."

The librarian emerged from the reference desk to tell them all the library would be closing in fifteen minutes. The pages began stacking up their papers or scribbling fiercely to finish their thoughts.

Silas screwed the lid back on his inkwell. "May I walk you back to your room?" he asked Elodie.

"Are you sure you have enough time before curfew?"

"Sure, it's not far."

Elodie nodded and went to put her book of tales back. She'd borrowed a scrap of paper from Eyvi to mark her page, and left it poking out the top of the book so she could find it again.

She returned to the table to see Silas waiting for her. They left the library in good spirits, Silas doing an impersonation of the stodgy librarian telling the pages to get lost.

"Anyways," Silas said, once their laughter faded. "I wanted to thank you for sitting with us, and making the other pages feel welcome." Elodie gave him a look. "Yes, I know it's not out of the usual for you, but *they* don't know it. I try to tell people you aren't, you know, what everyone expects for a princess. You care about people, enough to sit with a common-born and help him with his numbers. Some of the pages won't even talk to Eyvi or Timothee or the others unless it's an insult."

Elodie had noticed not all the pages at their table had joked as openly with the two, and she'd also noticed another table of pages throwing rude looks at her table from time to time.

"You don't treat them any differently either," Elodie realized.

"No, but you know my father. He wouldn't tolerate any of his sons not giving a person proper respect regardless of rank. Well"— Silas winced—"except for slaves, he turns a blind eye to them since he can't strictly prevent them in Tate. He just adds extra taxes to those who use them to help discourage it. Anyways, I think it does us all good to know you. Builds loyalty, you know? All of us are working every day to go into service for the crown, your crown, and we're the next generation. It's good for us to get to know you."

Elodie blushed. "I don't know if it's so important. You guys may be old men by the time I'm old enough to rule. Not to mention if the spell will ever be broken."

"What does Gedas say to it? Doesn't he have any idea when it will end?"

Elodie told him about the prophecy Oburleck mentioned.

"I always thought the other Misplaced were never talked about because you're the only one from Aluna."

Elodie shrugged. "I just never really thought about it."

"You know, I remember one time Ambassador Teluri came from Rohap and stayed in the castle for a few weeks while they discussed trade agreements. He told a story about a boy from Pundica who came to Rohap for work, started apprenticing as a blacksmith. He said Pundica had so many Misplaced they had a hard time looking after them. He said it like it was a joke, and then made a comment about how the others don't really matter when Aluna's Misplaced was the real prize. I didn't really get it at the time, but maybe that's what he meant."

Elodie shook her head. "I don't get it. If there's some prophecy about me, I should know it."

"Let me see what I can find out. It may take me some time, but I'll learn everything I can."

"Time is the one thing I don't have. Gods only know how long till I travel." She laughed. "Well, gods and Gedas only know."

"So he knows exactly when?"

"Gedas keeps his own counsel. I don't really know what he knows or when he knows it. He told me I would be here long enough to finish a project he set for me, so I figured, maybe if I never work on it I can stay forever."

Silas gave her a sad smile. "Is that why you were around all day and so willing to help in the library? Avoiding the wizard?"

Elodie shoved Silas with her shoulder gently. "Quit being so insightful. It's not very generous to point out all of my flaws, and quite annoying coming from a ten-year-old. I was only partially avoiding him. I did also really wanna hang out with you guys. It's nice to be around kids my age who don't all think I'm crazy."

"What do you mean?"

Elodie briefly, and with as little emotion as possible, explained the people in her life in the illusion, about how the stories she told were seen as far-fetched and made her either a liar or insane.

"It is weird," Silas commented after a silent pause. "It's a spell, an illusion made up by some wizard. But the stories you've told about your life, they seem so real and detailed. It's hard to think of it as not being real."

"And that's the trouble, isn't it? My actions there have consequences I have to live with. I'm surrounded by people I have to establish relationships with, even when later I question if they're real people at all."

When they reached Elodie's rooms, Silas stopped her from going in right away. "You're going to see Gedas tomorrow right?"

Elodie rolled her eyes at him. "Yes, Mom."

They both laughed before Elodie said good night and closed the door.

Chapter Fifteen

ELODIE GOT out of bed with a big sigh when the maid entered her room. She ate everything on the breakfast tray, hungry after skipping meals the night before, and then took her bathing things down to the bath rooms below the castle. After she returned and put away her things, she made her way to the mage hall.

The castle employed a number of mages of differing ranks for various tasks. The first few rooms were taken up by apprentices, the opinion being mages who hadn't yet reached their accreditation would have magical workings less likely disturbed by the foot traffic in the busy end of the hall. Farther down the hall, the rank of mages increased to enchanters, then sorcerers. The end of the hall was reserved for Gedas, the only wizard in Aluna.

No mage below the rank of enchanter was employed by the crown.

Her stomach turned over with anxiety and threatened to toss her large breakfast as she neared the last door.

At the base of the large wooden door was an untouched tea tray. Elodie puzzled over it for a moment and shook her head. Gedas was usually better at letting the maids bring tea. He liked tea. The oddness of it shook her out of her fear, and she raised her hand and knocked loudly.

She was prepared for the roaring thunder this time, and brushed the dust off her dress before knocking again.

The door clicked and opened with a spark of blue.

Elodie picked up the tea tray and walked through to an empty sitting room. She set the tray on its stand, and the door clicked shut behind her automatically. She tiptoed through the room to the open lab door. Peeking through the entrance she saw Gedas crouched over a beaker sitting on a small flame. The gold liquid within the beaker roiled and boiled, letting off a glittering smoke above the glass.

"Good morning," Gedas said in his deep clear voice.

Elodie jumped.

"Good morning," she replied. She took another step forward.

"If you haven't broken your fast yet, there's pastries over on the desk next to the dragon dung." He gestured behind him without taking his eyes off the liquid. He raised a hand over the beaker, and Elodie saw it held a dropper full of black liquid. Gedas waited for a moment and let a single drop fall into the potion. Suddenly it swirled and writhed like a living thing within the glass until all at once it turned a crisp silver and went utterly still atop the flame. Gedas let one more drop fall, and the liquid began to move again, slowly and sluggishly and became a beautiful iridescent cream color. Gedas sighed with pleasure and set down the dropper. He blew out the flame below the liquid.

Feeling the touchy part was over, Elodie dared to speak. "What is it?"

"A new beard oil a friend wrote to me. I have a mind to try it."

"Really?"

Gedas picked up the beaker, with a thick glove and prepared to pour it into a dark blue glass bottle. He stopped and looked at her, raising his eyebrows, his expression serious and grave. "Pick out five ingredients in the bottle I provided you two days ago, and tell me the method you would use to create such a potion, and I will tell you what I am truly making." His eyes went back to the potion, and he began pouring again.

Elodie sighed, thankful Gedas didn't mention their argument, and turned to the table where the mysterious bottle still rest.

"I brought in your tea. The maids left it outside the door." Elodie turned her attention to the potion.

"Would you mind getting me a cup, my Gull?" Gedas slowly drizzled his concoction into the bottle.

Elodie went back to the sitting room and flipped over two cups. The tea was still hot, kept warm in its cozy. She lifted the lid and inhaled.

Black tea, bergamot, orange, lime, grapefruit and lavender.

She tipped the pot toward a cup and stopped. There was something else in the tea. She took a deeper breath over the rising steam.

It was faint, nearly covered by the sharpness of the bergamot. She'd smelled it before. She inhaled again and closed her eyes. She'd first smelled this in a forest. Elodie had been examining a charming moss. Gedas told her to come see a bush and she left the moss with regret to look at a completely unremarkable bush blossoming with small white flowers. Gedas broke a leaf in half and had her smell the sap.

"Ruemort," he said as she memorized the odor. "Steeped in tea it can help to thicken the blood. A great poultice for clotting a wound. Distill it down and ingest with a few specific types of citrus and you will be dead before nightfall."

Elodie blinked and pulled the leaf away from her nose.

"The spells for detecting this are very complex. It has a magicity of zero, the plant rejects magic." He grinned at her then. "Of course you would likely not have the same problem with your talent of recognising plant life outside of your magic. Remember this one, my Gull." He went on to describe the berries that would cover the tree in late spring, and a number of uses for each part of the plant.

Elodie sighed and set down the teapot. "Ruemort," she said to herself. Gedas was testing her.

The tea had several citrus varieties, and she didn't know which one, if any would react with the ruemort to make it deadly. She left the tea where it was and reentered the workshop.

Elodie eyed the shelves of small bottles and jars while Gedas continued to pour a slow trickle of his potion into the bottle. She spotted the small jar on a top shelf and stood on her tippy toes to grab it before returning to the sitting room.

Elodie lifted the lid off the teapot again, and sprinkled in a good bit of arrowroot powder. The arrowroot immediately clumped in the hot liquid, and Elodie stirred slowly. Once it felt right, she strained the tea into the cups, leaving the dregs and the clumps of arrowroot and ruemort behind. She added sugar for Gedas.

Returning to the workshop she set his cup next to his elbow and moved to examine her bottle. She was confident touching the bottle wouldn't harm her, poisons and curses would only be stored in a bottle that could isolate its contents. Elodie stretched out a tentative finger and touched the bottle. She pushed her magic out into the glass and was surprised with the results. It wasn't a poison at all. Instead it was a familiar brew, one she'd drunk recently. This was the potion Gedas fed her while she was ill. She grinned and started listing ingredients she sensed inside.

"Did you add arrowroot to the tea?"

"Yep."

Elodie opened the bottle and tipped some of the thick liquid into a shallow dish. She looked over the texture and consistency and tried to list the proper amounts of each ingredient.

"Why?" he asked.

"It neutralizes ruemort when combined with lavender."

"Ruemort," Gedas muttered. "Where did you say you found the tea?"

Elodie looked up. Gedas was looking at her. He usually didn't ask so many questions when she completed one of his silent tests.

Knocking sounded from the hallway door.

"**Do not disturb me, peasant,**" Gedas bellowed at the door. He turned to Elodie. "Do you still plan to drink the tea?"

Bang. Bang.

They looked at the door.

Elodie shrugged. "The arrowroot neutralized it, so it should be safe to drink. Are you gonna get the door?" Elodie asked.

The knocking continued.

Bang. Bang. Bang.

Gedas sighed. He left the workroom and opened the front door. Elodie moved to the workroom doorway to watch.

"How dare you," the purple-faced man in the doorway raged. The sorcerer paused and took a deep breath. "Do you have any respect for life or your fellow Human? To attempt to frighten any who would knock!"

When Elodie had seen Sorcerer Cosimo in the council room on her first night, he'd been even-tempered and argued with his peers with rational logic. Gone was that calm man, the head sorcerer and elected council representation of the Aluna mage board.

"Do you need something Cosimo, or are you just here to rant?" Gedas asked.

Steam rose from Sorcerer Cosimo's head and his face grew more purple, a great contrast to his white beard braided around his chin. "Wizard Gediminas, are you aware of the duties belonging to you as Wizard of Aluna?"

"Would you like a cup of tea?" Gedas asked. He moved away from the door into the sitting room, leaving the steaming sorcerer behind.

"No, I don't want any of your tea. Gediminas, do you care at all for the state of the realm you are entrusted to protect?"

"Are you here to scold me for anything in particular, or shall this be an overall chastisement for my general existence?"

"How are you voting tomorrow, Gediminas?"

"Is it another vote day already? I hadn't thought to attend this one." Gedas moved to the tea tray and poured a cup.

"Do you understand nothing of your role as wizard? Teaching, apprenticing, and collaborating are the foundations of our society. You isolate yourself from others and it hinders the potential of all.

How are any magical advancements to be made in our lifetime if you will not play your part?"

"Most societies, as you so put it, don't have the benefit of a wizard, and they seem to do just fine." Gedas handed the teacup to Cosimo.

"Yes, but the ones who do attract young and eager magic users to their gates in the hopes of gleaning knowledge from the community of mages."

"Score scavengers, the lot of them."

"That's very uncharitable, Gediminas. We all must scavenge for learning and knowledge if we ever want to better ourselves farther than we can reach in our academy years." Cosimo paused and sipped the tea. "If one's goal is to increase their mage score only, I believe they are one in one hundred at most."

"You are an idealist. I hate idealists."

"Hate me as you will. Teach and collaborate with me not. But find some mage you can tolerate and teach. Maybe an illusionist or charmer, someone who couldn't afford a few more years of education perhaps. If you hate politics so much, then be charitable."

"I don't know, Cosimo. I think I have my hands full with my current apprentice, I'm not sure it would be fair to take on another." He gestured to the workroom.

Elodie would have darted out of view but wasn't thinking quick enough. Cosimo spun around. His eyes grew wide at the sight of her, and he bowed. "Your Highness, I apologize, I did not realize I was interrupting your work."

"Not at all, Sorcerer Cosimo."

Cosimo drained his teacup and set it on the tray. "Gedas, come tomorrow. I don't care how you vote, just participate. Your Highness." Cosimo bowed deeply to her. He turned and frowned at Gedas, then left.

The room was silent for a moment. Gedas returned to the workroom and began labeling his bottle.

Elodie followed him. "You did put the ruemort in the tea, didn't you?"

"Now how could I possibly answer that? If I say yes, you may lower your guard. If I say no, you may have a panic and then we won't get any work done for the rest of the day."

Elodie sighed. "Why is the mage board so mad at you?"

"I try not to pay attention to their politics."

"Maybe you should."

Gedas examined her notes. "These percentages are incorrect, and you are missing three ingredients."

Elodie sighed and got back to work.

ELODIE'S DAYS began to fall into a pattern. She worked with Gedas in the mornings and afternoons, taking lunch and dinner with him before heading to the library to meet Silas and the other pages. Sometime she helped Eyvi or another student with math work. Sometimes she read a book of tales.

On days when the pages all had some mutual history project to research, she whisked them off to Gedas's warm sitting room. After enduring his grumpy protests of being interrupted, he would tell them more of the history they needed than any book in the library.

Reverse engineering the potion Gedas had made for her took weeks and involved countless ruined potions and trips into the city to purchase ingredients in bulk. Eventually, she got it right. Gedas shrugged off her excited glee, asking if she'd documented her steps well enough so she, or another magic user could reproduce her results. Properly documenting the potion took Elodie another week, rebrewing the potion each day until she could do it by memory. It took her time and extensive practicing to figure out and record all the little things she did naturally in making the potion so another person could follow her instructions.

Elodie's daily routine was only interrupted by Oburleck's occasional dinner invitations, or him insisting she attend council meetings. Elodie knew it was petty of her to want to avoid the actual responsibilities of her title, but she didn't enjoy the meetings like

Silas. The council meetings dragged longer than they had her first night, without the fog to escape into.

Her second dinner with Oburleck, Baron Byron joined the dinner party. He was a tall thick man with warm brown skin and sharp brown eyes. He sat on the council, which was surprising as his family's nobility only stretched two generations.

When he lent his opinion to a conversation, people listened.

Gedas had told her he was an illusionist, barely. Many of the upper-class families had magic, and it was common for second or third children to be magically trained. As Byron had been a second son with magical talent, he was tasked with establishing a magical presence in their family and was sent to the University of Pundica to become certified. As Gedas told it, an illusionist ranking was the lowest offered by the university and Byron had barely received it. His true passion was swords. He was a fierce swordsman and was known for a few nasty duels over the years.

After the death of his sister he'd taken her place as head of his family. Byron wasn't very knoble, and he wasn't very magical, but he did have both topped with a large helping of wealth. It made him a powerful player in the castle politics.

Elodie didn't care for him.

As she sat across from the tall man, she couldn't help but feel intimidated as he dissected his lamb roast with his large gleaming belt knife. He cut each piece into a small exact bite and ate with extreme precision. He was silent except for the occasional short and direct comment when Oburleck drew him into the conversation.

Eventually Elodie began to see what Silas had first pointed out. Oburleck did have a skill to control a room or conversation. Once she saw this, conversing with him became more frustrating than she'd found it in the past, even if it did always end with her agreeing with him.

One night after working in the library, Silas was walking her back to her rooms. The study session had ended a bit unproductive as Elodie shared one of the tales in the book she was reading.

The particular tale was of a brave and courageous knight. Sir Fadwin was known in the land for his strength and relentless determination in battle. The man was renowned across all of the Twoshy for his fighting ability, and fought duel after duel, against men and women, Hu, Elv, Dwarv, and Avi alike.

Sir Fadwin became the one to send out when the situation was dire because the knight had never failed to vanquish his enemies. He lived to an old age, after countless battles, eventually dying peacefully in his sleep. It was, his wife told anyone who would listen, a great tragedy.

From a young age, Fadwin had only one wish—to die courageously in battle. The dream of a foolish warrior who believed their worth would be in their death instead of their life, but the knight had believed this with his whole heart. Of course it was impossible for the man's dream to be a reality, for his wife confessed to all who would listen, the man's noble lineage was incorrect and he was a bastard with an albatross birthmark on his rear end telling the secret of his mother's infidelity and of the impossibility of his life's ambition.

The pages found Fadwin's story endlessly funny and kept telling Elodie she could accomplish anything she wanted if only she put her mind to nothing. They joked she could be the greatest swordswoman who ever lived if only she tried her hardest to never pick up a blade.

As Silas walked Elodie back to her rooms that night, they continued the joke, Silas declared Elodie a warrior queen, able to defend them from any attack.

"And then you will be queen, and I will be your brave knight, accompanying you on all your great deeds. Tales will be told all over the Twoshy telling our adventures."

Elodie laughed along with him, the image of her as a warrior too funny to ignore.

A moment later, the ruakh that always existed around her in the Twoshy drew in closer before pulsing back out.

"Maybe you should sign up for page training and be a lady

knight. They say a ruler with a sword always makes for a strong kingdom," Silas continued.

Elodie looked around herself, confused, before the magic drew in again and held her tight. She only had time to meet Silas's eyes before the magic, the ruakh, moved in tight and yanked her to the left. She tumbled through nothing, unable to breathe, unable to think. Just her and a thin blanket of sparkles wrapping around her then pulling away quickly, making her spin like a top.

She landed roughly on the asphalt, skinning the base of her palms.

Chapter Sixteen

ELODIE SUCKED IN A QUICK BREATH, and pressed her skinned palms into her jeans. As the pain subsided she pulled her hands away and looked at them. They weren't really bleeding, no more than a few drops on her jeans. She shook her hands a few times. She closed her eyes tight and pressed her hands to her forehead willing herself to remember where she'd been when she first disappeared. What period was it? She looked around. She was near her Math class. Hopefully that was where she needed to go. She stood up shakily, and braced on the bulletin board beside her, then bent down to retrieve her backpack.

Her backpack wasn't there.

A sinking feeling crept into her stomach. She spun in a circle. It still wasn't there. Her hands started to shake. She looked over her shoulder and tapped her back for good measure, but the backpack was gone.

Lost in the Twoshy.

She checked her clothes next, her shoes, socks, jeans and shirt. They were all normal illusion clothes.

It was a small favor.

She didn't always lose things when she traveled back to the

illusion, but too frequently it missed something like the time her light-up shoes were gone, replaced with silk slippers.

She sighed. It could have been worse, but losing her backpack was bad.

She wasn't quite sure what to do and who to tell. She turned and headed back down the gravel hill toward the school's office.

It wasn't her fault, it was the spell's fault. The office would help her get the books she needed and some paper and pens to be able to finish her day and do homework.

As she walked over the asphalt toward the office, the world continued to solidify around her. She was a different person now from who she had been before her trip. She was carefree, able to work with Gedas and learn her magic, studying and helping Silas and the other pages. She didn't want to go back to the routine of classes and . . .

Her stomach sank thinking about going home. Why didn't she want to go home? She could sleep in her own bed, watch TV. She wouldn't have to dodge Oburleck, or walk several floors to take a bath.

Her mom flashed through her mind wearing the anxious look she would cast upon Elodie when she asked how her day had gone.

And just like that Elodie remembered.

She remembered telling Doctor Abernathy the Twoshy was made up. She remembered lying. Lying to everyone.

Why had she done that? She wasn't a liar.

She stopped walking and paused. There was a reason she couldn't go into the office and tell them she lost her backpack in the Twoshy. They would think she was crazy. They would call her mom and her mom would know she was crazy. Elodie turned around and rushed to her Math class as the tardy bell rang.

The class was passing their homework forward when she slipped in. In the chaos of shifting papers only a few noticed her. Mrs. Davis gave Elodie a warning look, but said nothing. Elodie loved Mrs. Davis. She taught Elodie's favorite subject, and her kindness made the class a refuge. She sank into her chair in the second-to-last seat in the third row, and tried to not look guilty. She hoped no one would notice her lack of paper and books.

The first half of the class, as usual, was spent with Mrs. Davis explaining and demonstrating the next chapter of their algebra book. If she noticed Elodie not taking her usual notes or not following along in her book, Mrs. Davis didn't say anything. Lots of students didn't pay close attention, Elodie just wasn't usually one of them.

Her Math class was dark and cramped with only one window in the temporary module. The fluorescent lighting was yellow and harsh after living with the bright light globes in the castle. Elodie covered a yawn.

Once Mrs. Davis was done teaching, the class broke up. They were assigned all the even problems from the next chapter as class-work, and as homework all the odd problems. Repetition, the key to math, just as she'd told Eyvi weeks ago in the library.

As the class broke into independent work, students moved seats toward their friends and talked quietly as they relaxed at their desks. Elodie crouched lower and lower in her seat.

She usually worked alone in this class, but now it would be obvious she didn't have a backpack. She kept thinking over and over again, be invisible, be invisible, be invisible, but she didn't have enough magic to will herself unseen. To go invisible she'd need a number of plants and herbs to create a barrier around herself and it would only work if someone wasn't looking for her. There were more advanced types of protection circles, but none of them would work in a classroom, and none of them would work in the illusion. The ruakh felt far away and unrealistic.

The thought of using magic made Elodie's fists clench. She relaxed her hands, her scraped palms aching. Magic had got her into this mess in the first place. It wasn't a tool, it only ever used her.

As Elodie worked on willing herself invisible, the teacher said her name from a few paces away and her stomach flipped, threatening to leave her body all together.

"Elodie, why don't you have your math book and paper out? Where's your backpack?" she asked quietly.

Elodie looked up, most of the class was looking at her now. Her heart was beating too fast; she felt her face heating up. All through the first half of the class Elodie thought over and over what would be the most believable lie. In the end she didn't know. She wasn't a very good liar. She didn't have enough practice yet. Elodie took a deep breath and let it out slowly.

"I'm not sure." She looked down at her hands, then flipped them over to hide the scrapes. "I thought I left it in the bathroom but I couldn't find it. I even checked my last class. I think it's gone."

"What do you mean gone?" Mrs. Davis looked at Elodie with soft eyes. Her eyebrows drew together and her jaw clenched. "Did someone take it?"

Elodie winced and looked down. "I don't know."

Mrs. Davis's sigh floated out across the room. "Can someone partner with Elodie to work on today's assignment?" Elodie didn't look up, but something told her no one would be jumping to help her. She was wrong of course.

"I can help, Mrs. Davis."

Elodie looked up to see Jackson with his hand in the air. His face was open and kind, the face of an expert liar who was never up to any good. Elodie's eyes closed and her heart beat even faster as the rest of the world fell away around her. She wanted to flee.

She should just leave. She knew how to survive in a forest on her own. Gedas had taught her enough. She could forage, she could try setting traps. She wouldn't like skinning squirrels, but she knew how. She could do it.

As Jackson thumped into the desk next to her and scooted closer, she was jolted back to her present reality. Even if she could run away, this world of the illusion didn't have any wilds like she knew in the Twoshy. Even in a national park, she would be found eventually, and she couldn't just find a village where no one knew her and start over. That wasn't how things worked here.

"You okay there, Harpy?" Jackson's voice was kind and light as it usually was when he said the most cutting things. "You're not going to faint or anything are you? I mean, yeah, it would probably get you even more attention than pretending to lose your backpack, but just don't hurl on me."

Her eyes opened as Mrs. Davis dropped some paper and a pencil on her desk. "Thanks, Mrs. Davis!" Jackson said for her.

Elodie grabbed the first piece of paper, white lined, three holes on the left. This wasn't the thin sheet paper of the Twoshy. It wouldn't break down into magically strong fertilizer in a few months to be sold back to farmers at a markup. This was regular binder paper made from tree pulp. Trees grown for the purpose of being chopped down.

"What, you aren't even going to talk to me?" Jackson's voice was upbeat with just a hint of hurt. "Jeez, Harpy, why are you always so rude to me when I go out of my way to help you."

Grabbing the pencil she started copying all the even problems onto the paper, leaving enough space between each to show her work. She had to lean closer to Jackson than she liked to see the far page. She grabbed another sheet and started writing the odd problems for her homework. Once all those were copied, Elodie needed to turn the page to see the rest.

"Can you turn the page?" She tried to keep her voice as even as possible.

"Can you say please?" Jackson asked. Elodie refused to look at him, but she could hear the smile.

Anger born of anxiety and dread flooded through her stomach and twisted. She didn't want to deal with this jerk, she couldn't give him what he asked for. "Jackson, just let me see the other page and then I won't need it at all anymore."

He flipped the page for a moment. "See?" he asked, before going back to the first page.

Elodie couldn't think, her face was burning. She was shaking, and her vision kept narrowing. "Jackson," she said sharply. She made herself breathe. "I just need to copy the problems."

"Elodie, be reasonable, I have to finish this work too. I'm still working on the first problem."

She was going to start crying if she didn't distract herself. She didn't say anything, she just looked down at her paper, thankful her hair worked as a shield as she tried her hardest not to cry. It would only make him happier to see her cry.

"Why don't you just work on what you have, then when I get to the next page you will be all set."

"Please, Jackson," she spat out, trying not to grind her teeth.

"And there's the magic word. See, was that so hard?" He flipped the page and scooted the book a little closer to her. "A little politeness is all you needed, Harpy."

Elodie looked at the book, her jaw clenched. She copied out the rest of the problems on each page. She kept making mistakes and had to erase. Once she'd finished, she pushed the book away and started working. Jackson pulled the book back in front of himself and started to write.

"Why are you writing them so weird?" Jackson asked, causing her to look up. He was looking at her paper and pointed to her first equation and the multiplication symbol. She frowned. She'd been copying from the book but using the multiplication symbol from the Twoshy automatically. She bent over the pages and fixed her mistakes.

It was hard to shake herself back to the reality of living in the illusion when she was so mad and could barely think.

She could feel the near silent motions above her head. He was motioning over her, maybe to his friends on the other side of the room. He was making fun of her for sure.

She tried her hardest to ignore Jackson as he scribbled along beside her. The scratches of his pencil became the only thing she could hear. When she made a mistake, he erased his paper along with her.

Elodie turned to glare at Jackson and he looked back, blue eyes bright, a happy smile on his face.

"Stop copying my work." She shifted her hair and arm to shield her paper from his view.

"Jeez, Harpy, I'm not copying. You are always so mean to me when all I want is to be your friend."

Elodie hunched further over her paper. Eventually Jackson gave up. He went back to his own desk and friends laughing quietly. Elodie finished her classwork, and started on her homework until the bell rang. The class filed toward the door, depositing their work on the teacher's desk before leaving.

Elodie waited till most of the class was gone before she scooped up her papers and borrowed pencil and made her way over to the desk.

"Mrs. Davis?"

The teacher looked up at her, expression blank.

"Would you by chance have another math book I could have?"

Mrs. Davis frowned. "You really don't know what happened to your backpack?"

Elodie shook her head.

Mrs. Davis sighed and rubbed a hand over her face. "Elodie, you can talk to me. Did somebody take it, or did you just misplace it?"

Elodie tried not to react to her choice of words. Yes, misplaced it truly was. Just like her.

"I've looked everywhere it could've been. That's why I was late. It's not like there's a lot of places I could lose it between first and second period." She looked at her feet. She had to get used to lying, but she hated doing it with her favorite teacher.

"All right, I believe you, but I don't have another book right now. If I did, I would have given it to you instead of sticking you with Jackson." She grimaced. "You copied the work you need for tonight?"

"Yes."

"Good. I will get another copy from Mr. Smith after school and have it for you tomorrow, all right?"

"Thank you, Mrs. Davis." She meant it.

"Just promise me one thing, Elodie. Promise me if it gets too bad you come and talk to me okay? I can't fight for you if you're not willing to admit people are bullying you. I'm here for you, okay?"

Elodie nodded and handed back her pencil.

"No, you keep it," Mrs. Davis smiled. "I'm sure you'll need it for the rest of the day." Mrs. Davis reached into her desk and pulled out a thin green folder. She added more paper and handed it over to Elodie. "And, maybe this will help."

Elodie nodded and thanked her teacher again as she left. Thankfully her next class was Gym and she wouldn't be under prepared.

She headed to the locker room and input her combination incorrectly a few times. She took a deep breath and wiped her sweaty hands on her pants. She hadn't used the combination in weeks.

She closed her eyes and leaned her head against the cold red metal of the locker. She pushed away thoughts of potion making, the proper number of times to stir or the number of herbs to add.

Her locker combination was something she did automatically, her fingers knew the right numbers to press. After a few more wrong tries she got it right and popped open the lock. She tucked her folder and pencil in and pulled out her gym clothes, sports bra and old sneakers. She changed quickly with the modesty of an awkward insecure girl. Bathing in the Twoshy with Mistress Piera or being fitted by Charmaine was less embarrassing. They would never be cruel.

After tying her shoes and locking her clothes in her locker, she headed out to the field.

Chapter Seventeen

SHE WAS EXHAUSTED by the time the bell rang. Running had sapped the last dregs of energy from her body and she dragged herself to the quad.

"Did you leave your backpack in the gym?" Vanessa asked.

Elodie frowned and looked over Vanessa's shoulder at the group of girls in hearing distance. "No, I'll tell you on the way to class." She pulled Vanessa away and headed toward their art class.

"Okay, okay," Vanessa said as soon as they left the quad and the mass of students. "What's up?"

"I just got back from the Twoshy," Elodie said, relieved to be telling someone the truth at last.

"Are you serious? But I thought you said it was too soon for you to go again. Oh my gosh, how long were you there? Did you disappear straight from gym class? That would be so embarrassing. What actually would happen if you disappeared while running? Would you pop into the Twoshy still running and like, hit a tree? Did anybody see you? Gosh I'm so jealous, I wish I could go. Did you have fun this time? How was Gedas, and did you guys go on any adventures?"

Eventually Vanessa paused in her questions, putting one hand over her mouth with a muffled apology and gestured for Elodie to explain.

"No one saw me, and no it wasn't while I was in gym class. I disappeared and returned all within the bells between first and second period. But Vanessa, I left my backpack there. All my homework, books, paper, binders, it's all gone. You should have seen me in Math class, I was a wreck. Mrs. Davis was nice and gave me this folder with paper and a pencil but guess who was the only one willing to share their book so I could copy the work for tonight?"

"Jackson," they both said at once.

Vanessa grimaced and said a bad word. "Do you have your science homework for sixth period?"

Elodie tried to remember, but couldn't. "If it's due today I don't have it. What was it?"

"It was that big report on rocks. We finished it over the week-end. You really don't remember?"

"Ness, that was like two months ago for me."

"Oh well, Mrs. Brook is so lax, she won't care if you copy my paper during class."

Elodie suppressed a grin. Their old art teacher could barely see halfway down the classroom. She wasn't relaxed, she was just blind, and couldn't see when students weren't working.

One of the few older buildings left in the school, the art room had high ceilings and a cement floor permanently stained with decades of paint. The walls were a collage of posters of famous art and student attempts. Clotheslines stretched around the room with fresh work, hanging to dry.

They slipped past the wet paintings hanging around the room and sat at their normal table in the back corner. Vanessa said separating herself from the negative energies of the other students always helped her make better art, but today it had its advantages as Elodie told Vanessa all about her trip and copied her homework. Her trip to Tross hadn't been very exciting, but Vanessa liked hearing about the pages and their different personalities. Elodie appreciated having someone she could confide in.

Near the end of the class Elodie fell asleep in the middle of her rushed painting of a bowl of fruit.

Vanessa noticed her hair drooping into her wet paint and nudged her. "Honey, what's wrong? Why are you so tired?"

It wasn't even lunch but she was ready for bed. Before returning, Elodie spent the entire day in Tross. Silas had been walking her to her room for the night when she'd been caught up by the ruakh and returned. She tried to calculate how many hours she'd been awake by now but couldn't. She'd just have to manage till she got home.

At lunch Vanessa was gracious enough to go with Elodie to their history class and science class to ask the teachers for spare textbooks. Mr. Silber handed over the most ratty and graffiti-covered science book Elodie had ever seen with little protest. Their history teacher on the other hand didn't understand how Elodie could have lost her backpack in the course of the day and wasn't convinced by her story. Vanessa pointed out even if her backpack did turn up, Elodie wouldn't have it in time for homework and Mr. Eleon relented.

She now had a small stack of books to carry from class to class.

"The real problem is going to be history homework tonight," Elodie said. "I don't have any of my notes from last week and I only vaguely remember the homework. Isn't the quarter summary due soon?"

"Ohhh no." Vanessa's eyes got big and then she winced. "Why don't I come over tonight and we can do homework together. You know your mom loves me." Vanessa grinned.

Elodie's mom did not love Vanessa. She tolerated her because having no friends was worse than her daughter having a slightly weird friend.

"Oh yes, please, Ness."

When the final bell rang, Elodie and Vanessa headed to the front of the gym. When her mom's SUV pulled up Elodie plastered a fake smile on her face and opened the front passenger door. "Hey Mom, is it cool if Vanessa comes over for dinner? We have a history project due Friday and want to compare notes." She was getting better at lying already.

"Hello, cupcake, hi Vanessa, is it okay with your parents if you come over?"

"Yeah, Mrs. Harper, they don't mind."

"Alright then, hop in and buckle up," her mom said through a thick smile. Her mom watched Elodie settle her stack of books at her feet before buckling her seatbelt. "Sweetie, why do you have those books? Where's your backpack?"

Elodie hoped they would get a little farther from school before her mom realized her missing backpack.

"Um." The silence hung.

Vanessa knew better than to jump in and come up with a better excuse for Elodie. When they'd tried that in the past, it never worked out well.

"Elodie?" her mother asked in a sharp voice she usually didn't use in front of company.

"I lost it."

"What do you mean you lost it? Where did you leave it?"

"I'm not sure, I had it during first period, and then when I got to my second class I didn't have it anymore. I checked everywhere, but it's gone."

"Did you check the lost and found, and with the office?"

"Yes, we checked there at lunch." Lies on top of lies.

"Elodie." Her voice wasn't quite as sharp this time, and sounded tired. She turned in her seat until she faced her daughter. "Did someone take it?"

"I don't know," Elodie said, looking down. She couldn't blame someone else when she had no evidence. If she tried she could get caught in an even deeper trap. As much as blaming Jackson and getting him in trouble would be awesome, she didn't think she could pull it off. Jackson was too good at disarming adults. Even Elodie started to question if she was just taking things too personally and seeing offense where he didn't mean it. The doubt mixed with her frustration and made her constantly on edge around him.

Her mother sighed. "What else did you lose."

"All of my schoolbooks and"—Elodie had to think about it —"my binders for every class, my pens and pencils. Oh, also my sketchbook and my book for English class. That was a library book."

"Do you have everything you need for your homework tonight?"

"Yeah, but I need a new English book for the report due Monday."

Her mom took a few deep breaths. There was a long pause as she put the car in gear and pulled away from the sidewalk.

"When we get home you girls can get to work on your homework and I'll head to the store, alright? We'll have to do something simple for dinner but I can pick up what you'll need for tomorrow. And, Elodie honey, I want you to be more careful with your possessions. We can't go out and buy you new school supplies every time you lose something, do you understand? If this happens again I may have to take the cost out of your allowance."

"Yes, Mom."

Elodie spent the afternoon at her desk writing till her hand cramped. They listened to music and talked. Vanessa sketched in her binder while Elodie told her more about the Twoshy. She fought to stay awake as she completed her work and copied way more than she normally would.

When her mom returned with a new backpack and school supplies, Elodie spent some time rearranging things, copying her agenda and upcoming projects from Vanessa. Vanessa lounged on Elodie's bed drawing dragons on each binder with permanent markers. An old wizened dragon on her history binder, a dragon with algebra on her scales for her math binder, and a dragon surrounded by books for English. As she started on the science binder drawing a green dragon among plants and trees, she paused at the wings and looked up at Elodie. "Are there dragons in the Twoshy?"

"There used to be." Elodie leaned back against her headboard, making sure not to lean on the dried tarragon hanging there. "There kind of still are, but not the kind you're thinking of. It's like asking if there are dinosaurs here. Earth used to have cool big impressive ones, but now we just have a few different types of smaller ones, like lizards and alligators."

"And Nessy, the monster of Loch Ness," Vanessa cut in.

"Yep, can't forget about her. In the Twoshy there are little dragons, from the lizard family. Apparently real dragons find it really offensive to be compared to them. Anyways, they're about the size of a blue jay but with really pretty scales, and shiny iridescent wings that fold into their scales like a beetle. They come in all colors and are really stupid. Rich nobles pay a lot of money for trained ones they can carry around. It was a fashion a few years ago for ladies to have a matching dragon on their dress, but I always thought it was gross when they had poop drying on their shoulders." The girls laughed.

"But there are no big dragons? What happened to them?"

Elodie shrugged. "They still exist, just not in the Twoshy. Gedas says they are scarcely seen around Humans, because we suck. When my ancestors invaded the continent and killed all the men living there, the dragons fought on the side of the Elvmen. They weren't all killed off, but the dragons left the Twoshy heading to other lands far away from the folly of Humans. They haven't been seen in the Twoshy since."

"That's really sad."

"Yeah."

"There go my dreams of someday traveling with you to the Twoshy and having a dragon best friend I can ride around." Vanessa returned to her drawing.

Vanessa's mom came to pick her up after dinner, and as soon as the door was closed, Elodie's mom appeared with two little pills, and a glass of water. Elodie took them, not meeting her mom's eyes and returned to her room.

She changed into her pajamas, exhausted from living through two days. It was too early for bed but she lay down anyways.

She needed to think about what had happened. It was strange, she'd traveled two times in a row, only a few weeks apart. She likely wouldn't travel again for a while, maybe even a year or two, but she needed to have a plan for when it did happen. She lay in her bed and tried to think about her time in the Twoshy. She should've written it down, but she was too tired.

She didn't want it to disappear and fade. She needed to write the exact words Oburleck had said when talking about the prophecy. She needed to remember Silas's promise to help her figure out the spell.

Instead Elodie drifted off to sleep, letting not just the Twoshy, but also her anxiety, fears and troubles all fade into nothing.

Chapter Eighteen

THE NEXT DAY started like any other when Elodie wasn't living in the Twoshy, with the bone-deep beeping of her alarm clock. Elodie sat up out of bed and a wave of dizziness caught her. It felt for a moment like the room was spinning and she took a deep breath of air. It passed in a moment and Elodie shrugged it off before she showered and headed to breakfast.

Her mom served up those two little pills and Elodie dutifully took them before eating her provided portion.

Elodie interrupted the song on the radio and asked her mom to drop her off a few blocks from school so she could meet Vanessa. Her mom agreed, without question. Elodie hopped out of the SUV and felt a little dizzy as she brushed her hair out of her face and grabbed her backpack. It passed in a moment and she waved Vanessa's concern away as they started the short walk.

The same students as always waited in the quad for school to start but this time when Jackson decided to start in on Elodie, Vanessa headed him off with a biting insult and led Elodie to their first class.

She had another small dizzy spell on her way up the classroom steps, but Vanessa coming up behind her steadied her. As she turned in her homework, and started taking notes, everything felt like it was returning to normal and Elodie began to relax back into her routine.

ELODIE GREETED Doctor Abernathy and walked past him to her window seat. She settled into the cushions as the doctor sighed and rolled his chair over. He asked about her last few days, and Elodie thought she did a pretty good job saying they were normal and good. She even added in a few details like enjoying the book they were reading in English, hoping it would direct their conversation away from anything she didn't want to talk or lie about.

Of course it didn't work.

"I also heard you lost your backpack this week, do you want to talk about that?"

Elodie shrugged trying not to look guilty. "I mean we can. There's not really a lot to talk about. I must've left it somewhere and someone picked it up. Maybe it'll turn up eventually."

"So you're saying no one took the backpack?"

"Well it's not where I left it, I don't really know. I looked in all the normal places. Maybe somebody took it planning to return it to the office and forgot."

Doctor Abernathy took off his glasses. He took the small square of fabric out of his pocket and began cleaning the lenses. "And that's what you think happened, Elodie?"

"I don't know," Elodie said, spacing out each word. "I really don't. It's just a guess."

Doctor Abernathy sighed. "I don't think you're being truthful with me."

"I mean you can think whatever you want. That's not going to change the fact that I don't know."

Doctor Abernathy's eyebrows went up a little. "Your mother says you've lost things in the past, small things here or there. She said one time in class you lost your shoes and even lost a few books, library books. She said previously you blamed magic as an excuse, and trips to your other world as an explanation."

Elodie knew exactly what he was talking about. The time with the shoes had been when she returned wearing those beautiful slippers. She hadn't lost her shoes strictly speaking, they just stayed in the Twoshy. It had been the truth. She knew her mom never believed her, but the reminder stung.

The books, yes she'd lost a lot of books. She liked books and often had them around her. Was it her fault every time the ruakh surrounded her she ended up holding tightly to the things nearby and braced for the pull? Yes. It was her fault and she probably needed to stop doing that.

Gedas didn't mind. He quite enjoyed the books she took with her.

"I don't know why I lied and blamed it on magic in the past. Maybe I thought the real way I lost things was boring and magic would make a better story. But it doesn't change the fact I don't know what happened to my backpack," Elodie said defensively. "Just because my mom calls to report every little thing that happens doesn't mean any of it's a warning sign of something wrong. Maybe it's just a coincidence and me being absentminded."

"I'm starting to feel a little bit of hostility from you, Elodie. Are you feeling upset today?"

"I'm not mad I'm just tired of coming here three times a week and having you ask me a million questions about every little thing. Maybe I don't know why something happened. Maybe I don't know why I feel a certain way. Why do we have to talk about all of it?"

Doctor Abernathy crossed his legs and shifted in his seat. "You're here, Elodie, because several weeks ago you disappeared. For two weeks, nobody could find you until you turned up downtown. The excuse you gave was you traveled through a spell to a magical land. You're now telling me that wasn't true and you made it up. Would you like to tell me where you really were for those two weeks, Elodie?" He paused and uncrossed his legs leaning forward. "We care about you and we want to make sure you were safe. If you were in danger, if you were somewhere bad, we want to protect you and make sure that never happens again. But it has to start with you being honest with us. Where were you?"

Instead of answering, Elodie stared out the window at the maple tree. She could see the tiniest bits of yellow on some of the outermost leaves as the tree began the change for fall.

She wished she could speed up time. She wished for once time passed here in the illusion like it did in the Twoshy. She wished she'd returned to see several years had passed. She'd be older, maybe old enough to go off to college, get a job, get an apartment with Vanessa and not have to answer to anyone. She hated being a kid. She only had the vaguest idea of what it would be like as an adult, but that future felt nearly as far-fetched as the day the spell would be broken. How old would she be by now if she'd only been living in one world? If she hadn't been traveling to the Twoshy and living years before coming back and having no time at all pass? Surely she'd be over eighteen.

"Elodie, do you plan to answer me?"

Elodie took a deep breath and leaned against the window, feeling the cold glass press up against her skin. She started to feel dizzy and light-headed, her stomach turned but she took a deep breath. She almost thought she might be sick. She turned and pressed her forehead against the cool glass of the window. It passed in a moment.

"I don't remember," she replied, not sparing the doctor a glance.

"You don't remember where you were for two weeks."

"No. I don't remember."

"Well why don't you run me through that day, you were downtown with your mom. What were you doing?"

"I don't remember."

The doctor continued to press and Elodie continued to say she forgot. When she left his office, she headed straight to their car so her mom and Abernathy could talk about her behind her back. She didn't even care what they said. She was almost a teenager.

Weren't teenagers forever being blamed for being moody and distant? Maybe Elodie could start now. Maybe it would help.

As she walked to the parking lot she passed the maple tree and the other trees without sparing them a glance. She could still feel them in the back of her mind, their need for more water, their sluggish growth with the onset of fall, but she ignored it. This was exactly what made her different. This was exactly what started to cause all of her problems. She needed to cut magic out of her life.

Her mother didn't ask her anything on their way home, and Elodie tried to ignore her pinched expression. They rode home in silence.

Once home Elodie slung on her backpack and headed directly upstairs. "Dinner at five, sweetie," her mother called.

She didn't respond but went into her room and closed the door. She started in on her homework, ignoring the occasional dizzy spell. Once finished she flopped back on her bed intending to reread her book for English. It was a very small book, but she was a few chapters in when there was a soft knock on her door. Elodie ignored it. After a pause the door slowly creaked open and her mother walked in tentatively. She sat next to Elodie on the bed and handed her a scrap of paper. Elodie grabbed the paper and saw it was the science fair paper she'd ripped off before being pulled into the Twoshy.

"Are you planning on entering?" her mother asked with her sickly sweet voice. Elodie stared at the paper and didn't respond. "I pulled that paper and quite a few leaves out of your pockets while I was doing the laundry. If you're going to insist on picking up leaves everywhere you go, you need to do something with them before you put your clothes in the laundry basket, sweetie."

"Sorry, Mom."

She'd forgotten to take the leaves out of her pockets. She needed to stop doing that. Filling her pockets with herbs and plants made her weird. She needed to stop being weird.

"Doctor Abernathy spoke to me today." Her mother's voice was softer. Elodie took a deep breath waiting for the gavel to fall.

She'd been rude and she wasn't quite sure she cared. "He said maybe we should take a little break from your sessions, and start meeting twice a week instead. For now we're going to skip Friday's session and start meeting only Mondays and Fridays as of next week. How does that sound?"

Elodie couldn't believe it. Mouthing off had gotten her less time with Abernathy and not more.

"That one's new," her mother said in an unsure voice. Elodie looked up and saw her mom looking at the dried plant hanging from her headboard. "Is that thyme?"

Elodie blushed. Normal girls didn't hang dry plants from their bed unless they were roses or other flowers given by someone they liked. "No, it's tarragon. Some cultures believe it helps prevent bad dreams."

There was a pause, and Elodie didn't look at her mom. "You know you can talk to me right?" Her mom's voice was soft and faint. "I'm your mother. We're here for you."

The silence stretched.

"I'm on your side. I just need you to talk to me, Elodie."

Her mother reached out her hand to take Elodie's as it rested on the bed. Startled, Elodie pulled away. Her mom sighed.

"If you're not ready to talk, that's fine. But know I'm here for you."

Elodie didn't know if she believed it. Wasn't she on the edge of being carted away to some facility so her mom would never have to be faced with a broken child again? Why was this comfort and support coming now? Did her mom decide it was her motherly duty to at least fake it before carting her away? She signed the legal papers to adopt her so now she better start acting like she cared?

Elodie wasn't sure, but she knew she needed to do anything possible to prevent being sent away. Living with her mom and her dad under this awkward tension would be better than being trapped for the rest of her life in a scheduled and sterile prison. She needed to get things figured out and start pretending she was normal, erase her mother's doubt. She'd stop slipping up by leaving plants in her pockets, and get rid of all the dried plants around her room.

"So the science fair, are you thinking of entering?" Her mother's sweetness was back in her voice, and Elodie was glad they were back in known territory.

"Well," she started, unsure how to continue. This was a chance to start undoing some of the damage and pretend like her weirdness was just normal nerdiness. "I like plants. I've always liked plants, I think it's interesting seeing how they grow and all the things they can be used for. I mean, our world can't exist without them, so they seem pretty important. I thought it would be cool to take a look more into the science of plants, you know?" She emphasized the word science hoping her mom would catch on.

Her mom nodded after a moment. "I think given your interests it would be quite productive. And participating in something like this will of course look wonderful on your college record. Do you have an idea for your project yet?"

Elodie wasn't so sure about a science fair from the seventh grade looking good for college but she let her mom have that one.

"I was planning on talking to Mr. Silber tomorrow about possible projects. I saw somewhere plants being grown without soil in just water and thought it would be cool to try. It's supposed to be great for places where the soil has been overworked and is no longer healthy. I thought maybe it'd be cool to see if there's a difference in the type of plants that took to growing in water." She didn't mention it'd been in the Twoshy where she'd seen this, and the aqueducts where the plants grew were fueled by magic, but she thought the overall concepts would be the same.

Her mother's eyebrows rose. "That sounds quite advanced, but like a worthy challenge. Definitely talk to Mr. Silber and get his opinion. Once you have a plan we'll see what supplies we need to get. Alright?"

"Thanks, Mom."

"Anytime, sweetie. Now I'm going to finish dinner. Your father should be home in a minute. Dinner in fifteen, alright?"

"Yes, Mom."

She left, closing the door behind her, and Elodie sighed with relief. She wasn't sure if it was just something Doctor Abernathy had recommended her mom try, or maybe something else was going on, but either way Elodie didn't want to break this tentative peace. Regardless of what her mom said, she was sure she would be walking on thin ice.

The faint sound of the front door opening and closing made its way to Elodie's room. She got off of her bed and quietly opened her door. Her father's soft murmurs as he greeted her mother changed and became more understandable as they moved into the living room. Elodie silently sat down on the stairs out of sight.

"So we had a few new developments today," her mother said.

Her father responded but she couldn't make out the words in his lower tone.

"Doctor Abernathy thinks the stress might be getting to her and they should start meeting only two days a week. I just got finished telling her. Frank, she didn't even give me a response. It's like she's just putting up more walls between us."

Her father's response was low, and only part of it was clear. ". . . say how it happened?"

"No," her mother responded. "I was so sure she was going to use her normal excuse, but she hasn't. Do you think she's being bullied?"

Her father's response was a little longer this time and Elodie couldn't make out much of it.

"I don't know. She won't speak to me. Am I doing something wrong here, Frank? I don't feel like we connect the way a mother and daughter should. She's so different and I don't understand her. It's like living with a stranger."

Her father's low voice sounded again and Elodie stood up and walked quietly back to her room, wiping a tear off her cheek. She needed to make a list of all the weird things she did and stop doing all of them.

She looked around her room at the dried plants hanging from the windows and walls and bookcase. The peace and comfort they radiated reached out to her and she pushed it away. She pulled them down one by one and threw them away. She didn't need the baby's breath or juniper. She took down the rosemary, sage and lavender, and trashed the chamomile. She didn't want to remove the tarragon completely, so she tacked it on the back of her headboard where it was hidden. Waking up her parents with her nightmares wasn't a risk she would take.

Most of the plants she just tossed in her trash can. A few, like her lavender, she tucked into books or journals, not quite ready to part with them. When she was done, her room felt bare. She needed more things to hang on her walls. Maybe she could ask Vanessa for advice. She had a different way of looking at the world but was so very good at being different while seeming completely normal.

When dinner was ready, Elodie headed downstairs and paused. On the landing, another, much stronger wave of dizziness overwhelmed her. She gripped her stomach with one hand and the banister with the other hoping the contents of her stomach wouldn't leave her.

When the dizziness passed a moment later it once again felt like it had never been there. She straightened herself out and walked into the kitchen like nothing happened. She greeted her dad and helped her mom serve up dinner.

Her father asked her the usual questions about her day, and Elodie kept the answers short and upbeat as was expected of her. When her plate was clear she carried it to the sink. She took her pills and started toward the stairs when her father's voice stopped her.

"Elodie, honey, why don't you sit and read with me. You're too young to be hiding in your room all day, and I refuse to admit I already have a teenager living under my roof. Come on, I have another book by that author you're reading for English I think you might like."

Elodie nodded and followed her dad into the room. She took the book he offered and folded herself into the large squishy leather chair to read. She passed the next hour or two in comfortable silence.

This was how she liked to communicate with her father, silently reading in the same room. It was all the bonding she needed.

She could hear her mom in the background while she read, cleaning up the kitchen, then working on a project or finishing up some wedding plans for her coordinating business. Her mom was always in motion, always doing something productive. It wasn't like she didn't read, she just didn't seem to be able to sit in silence without motion the same way her father and Elodie could for hours at a time.

After a while, the dizziness returned to Elodie with force. She felt herself sway in her chair. Her stomach lurched. She didn't want to throw up in the den. She stood, then froze as the dizziness continued.

"Time for bed already?" her father asked.

She didn't respond but rushed to the bathroom in as straight a line as she could manage. She nearly collided with the bathroom door frame and fell to the floor in front of the toilet in a dizzy heap.

Her mother was at her side holding her hair and rubbing her back before Elodie was finished being sick. Her mother said comforting things and helped her upstairs.

Elodie felt exhausted as her mom tucked her in with a bucket.

She was still dizzy but her stomach, now empty, only pulsed and spasmed.

Her mom switched off her alarm clock, turned off the light, and told her to yell if she needed anything. She left the door open a crack behind her.

Elodie wasn't sure what came over her. She hadn't been feeling quite normal all day but nothing like this. Eventually she drifted off to sleep.

ELODIE WOKE to the late morning light trickling in behind her curtains. The dizziness was gone and Elodie's stomach ached, this time with hunger. Getting up she wandered downstairs to see her mom spread out on the kitchen table working on her latest wedding plan.

"Good morning, sweetie, how are you feeling?"

"Hungry."

"Well how about I make you some oatmeal? Hopefully that will go well on your tummy."

Elodie nodded and sat down at the table curling in on herself. She looked over the pages spread out trying to get a sense for the event. "They're getting married at the zoo?"

Her mom chuckled. "Yes, in front of the giraffes."

Elodie made a face. "Isn't that kind of smelly? What if a giraffe, like, poops in the middle of the ceremony or something?"

Her mother shrugged. "They know the risks, but you can't really judge someone for their love story. Ultimately it's up to them how they want to tell it. Apparently they met on a school field trip when they were young while feeding the giraffes, so it's a cute story."

As she waited on the oatmeal, Elodie's mom handed her the two little pills and a large glass of water. Elodie took them without a word and drank the whole glass down. She'd slept longer than normal but still felt tired, the edges of her mind faded when she didn't look too close.

After breakfast Elodie curled up on the couch and read.

It felt good to be babied once in a while even when she didn't feel sick anymore.

Vanessa called to check in and give her the homework assignments for the day and would only hang up when Elodie promised to be at school the next day, and make her mom drop her off at their planned meeting spot. Elodie headed upstairs to work on homework which took longer than normal as her attention kept fading. Her mother tapped on her door when it was time for dinner and Elodie snapped to as the fog cleared. Looking down she hadn't finished her math work. She sighed.

She could work on it after dinner.

The next day at lunch Elodie headed to her science class a little early, promising Vanessa to meet her there. As expected, Mr. Silber was present, preparing for class.

"Mr. Silber, do you have a moment to talk about the science fair?" she asked, poking her head in the door.

"Elodie, yes, come in. The science fair, do you mean the one in the spring for the whole district?"

"Yes, I was thinking about entering."

Mr. Silber's eyebrows went up. "Really? What did you want to do a project on?"

"Well that's what I wanted to talk to you about. I wasn't quite sure what would be a good idea."

"Okay. What are your interests? Anything we've covered recently you want to explore further?"

"Well I've always been interested in plants, and I thought it'd be cool to do something in relation to how they grow. I've heard a little bit about plants being grown in water instead of soil and I thought that would be a fun project."

"Hydroponics? I mean it's a great idea but a little advanced. I know a few plant-based projects that might be better suited for someone at your level."

Elodie shook her head. "I'm up for a challenge."

Mr. Silber tapped his chin. "What's your motivation for doing this?"

"I mean, my mom says it would look good on my college application."

"Yes, but you've never seemed very interested in science. Don't get me wrong, your grades are great, but you don't seem engaged."

Elodie shrugged. In the Twoshy the world evolved with magic instead of technology, and while plenty of science was still true across both worlds, learning both sets of rules and remembering their differences was too much work.

"Well, I'm kind of in the market for a hobby at the moment," Elodie started. "I really like working with plants and I thought the science fair would be a productive way to use my time. And . . . as the world's resources get used up, isn't finding efficient ways to produce crops super important?"

"Elodie, the type of experiment you're talking about, it's something I would expect from a junior or senior in high school. It's much more advanced and involved than something I'd recommend to someone in seventh grade. Now, there are a few other experiments I do think you would be great with. For example there's something I read about with flowers." Mr. Silber turned to his computer and typed for a moment. "Ah, here it is, *Thigmotropism in Morning Glories.*" He looked up at Elodie to gauge her reaction.

"Thigmotropism," she said, thinking. "That's about plants moving when they're touched, right?" Gedas always loved to use big words, and when they were about plants, Elodie listened.

Mr Silber's eyebrows rose in surprise. "Yes, that's correct, very sharp, Elodie. Morning glories are a climbing plant, they grow little hands to hold onto things they touch up against as they get taller." He clicked a few keys and a printer sounded off under his desk. "This is all about experimenting with the type of touch required and studying it."

He handed the printed papers over and Elodie took them nodding. She'd done something similar on a much larger scale with another type of plant in the Twoshy. The flowering preyhold was known for trapping small animals, and occasionally much larger ones with its tendrils. While a morning glory may grow its tendrils slowly over a few weeks, when properly stimulated a preyhold would grow thick strong tendrils in a matter of moments. The pollen of a preyhold was also a great cure for earaches.

"This article covers the basic premise and a few theories you can choose to take. This will also be a lot less expensive in materials than setting up something for hydroponics."

Elodie thanked him and tucked the papers into her science binder. It sounded absolutely boring, but maybe boring was what she needed. The first bell rang and Elodie found her seat. Students filled the classroom and Vanessa popped down in the seat next to Elodie.

"How did it go?" she asked brightly.

Elodie made a face. "He didn't like my idea and offered me a lame middle-school project to try instead."

"That stinks," she sympathized. "But with the project he offered, won't you still have the same end result? You know, convincing your mom you're normal and interested in normal things?" Vanessa asked with a smile. She thought the idea of trying to be normal laughable, but this was of course because she never tried to be anything other than who she was.

"Yeah I guess it will work. I just feel like it's too boring." The second bell rang for class to start and the students quieted as Mr. Silber launched into his newest lecture about shale and how it formed on Earth.

Elodie sighed and started to take notes. Focusing was hard, and when the bell rang ending class, the fog cleared from her mind and she saw she'd only taken half a page of notes.

Vanessa put a hand on her arm. "Are you okay, El? You seem a bit out of it lately."

"Honestly, I'm not sure. When I was in the Twoshy, I felt really good and then I came back and got sick, and now . . . I don't know, I just feel so muddled again." She sighed. "Let's just get to English."

At dinner, Elodie's mom asked about her science project, and Elodie reluctantly told her about the morning glory idea. Her mother and father liked the idea and were happy to supply the project. They ate veggie spaghetti for dinner. Her mom took her plate when she went for seconds and handed her the little pills to take instead.

The weekend was spent going to several hardware stores to track down the equipment Elodie would need. Apparently finding morning glory plants in the fall wasn't a great plan, but an employee at their independent hardware store was able to find some seeds in the back of their shop. Elodie added a sun lamp to their shopping list and promised her mom it would all work out great.

Elodie could always get plants to grow.

She spent her weekend setting up a spot in the garage for her morning glories to germinate. She was tempted to use magic to help ease them along, but she resisted.

Magic was not her friend anymore. Maybe it never had been.

The days passed quickly and without too much tension. Parts went a little fuzzy as Elodie phased in and out of the fog, and the Twoshy and its problems faded into the back of her mind. Forgetting made life easier.

Monday dawned and Elodie fell back into the swing of school. Her therapy session with Doctor Abernathy went well. He didn't comment at all on her outburst the week before and instead seemed quite interested with her new science fair project. He didn't ask any questions such as where her motivation came from, nor did he broach the topic of where she'd been when she disappeared for two weeks.

Elodie was incredibly thankful.

The rest of her week went as smoothly as it began. Friday she went again to see Doctor Abernathy. The change of pace was a relief.

On the way into the office Elodie realized she'd picked up her backpack to bring with her, moving on autopilot. Her mom handed her the keys and went to check in while Elodie went back to the SUV to stow her backpack. Locking the car, she put the keys in her back pocket and turned back to the building.

Elodie noticed the trees in front of the office were a few shades darker as the leaves leaned into the change for fall. Focusing on the seasonal color change, Elodie missed the shimmer hanging over the sidewalk in her path. She walked straight into it without any warning.

The shimmer grabbed her up, wrapping around her, and pulled her tightly to the left. She exhaled sharply in surprise and tumbled through the nothing, spinning and twisting, too preoccupied to think of anything but the motion until she landed hard on her back on a hill covered in wildflowers.

Chapter Nineteen

THE SKY WAS a beautiful blue with thick puffy white clouds. The air was warm and fresh. She lay on her back for a few moments and took slow shaky breaths. She could smell clover, and daisies, and bluebells blooming around her. Her view of the sky was ruined by a face leaning over her. Gedas's long beard hung down close to her face and Elodie laughed and batted it in the air. He stepped back and offered her a hand. Once on her feet Elodie looked around. From the hill she could see a good distance. A few sheep grazed in the fields, the shepherd unseen, and in the distance stood Tross, with the palace rising up out of the cluttered city.

She took a moment, breathing in the air around her before turning to Gedas. "How long have I been gone?"

Gedas leaned against his thick walking stick and peered down at her fondly. "Oh, about a year and a half." He brushed something out of her hair. "How have you been, my Gull?"

Elodie chuckled again. "Gedas, I was only in the spell for about a week. Not much happened for me."

His thick eyebrows rose. "I did notice you didn't seem to be too much older from the last time I enjoyed your company."

"No, again I'm younger than the last time I saw you." She

looked back at the city. "I guess this means we'll be hanging at Tross again. Or do we get to go on a great adventure?"

When his answer didn't immediately come, Elodie looked back at him. He was still leaning against the staff, his eyes on the horizon. "Actually, I wanted to ask you about that. Are you quite steady on your feet yet? I figured we would have a nice stroll to the city." Elodie nodded, and they began their walk down the hill. "I have some errands to run and thought it may be best if I leave you in the care of someone I trust in the city."

"Can't I come with you like normal?"

Gedas's face looked troubled and he shook his head softly. "You know I quite enjoy your company, my Gull, but where I travel I must go alone. I know the timing isn't quite desirable, but I'm afraid that can't be helped."

"Where are you going?"

The older man was silent for a moment. "It's a far boring journey, but would you allow me not to share the details?" He looked down at her with a sad smile.

Elodie shrugged. "You will be safe?"

"Oh heavens yes. I may be in danger of dying of boredom, but I think I will be quite safe. I only think your time may be better spent in the city."

Elodie's heart sank, she felt ready for an adventure, not the boring pace of the castle. "But with you gone, that means I'll have to be even more creative than usual with finding excuses to dodge Oburleck." She tried on a smile for Gedas's benefit.

"Well, actually, I think I have a fair solution for that. What if you didn't stay in the castle on this trip?" Elodie looked at him with confusion. "I have a friend in the lower city, Healer Beathan, she runs the clinic there, and could use some help rebuilding their medical stock after the winter. I was thinking, the castle didn't need to know you were in town, and you could stay incognito if you will, in the lower city as her apprentice for the summer."

Elodie's outlook on the next few weeks or months brightened. "That sounds like it could be fun."

"It will be work, you understand? Healer Beathan does need help which I think you will be quite adequate to provide, but you should also be able to find a good deal of fun if you go looking for it."

"How long will I be here for?" she asked.

"Long enough to do some good for yourself and the lower city I think."

Elodie sighed, she didn't think she would get a real answer from Gedas, but it was worth a try.

They entered the city through the southern gate. Gedas loaned Elodie his cloak to help her pass unnoticed through the streets. In the lower city, with Gedas dressed in well-made but old clothes, the two didn't draw the eye as a wizard and princess. They didn't have far to travel to the clinic as its clientele all lived in the outermost ring of the city, lovingly known as the Odure District. If the castle grounds were less than pristine due to the poor water and sewage system, the lower city suffered thricefold. Long thin trenches ran down the sides of the main roads, carrying water runoff and things Elodie chose not to think about into the few sewer entrances scattered about. When the system backed up, most of the Odure District flooded.

The Odure clinic was a large, two-story building. It was old, with crooked doorways and three kinds of patches on the roof. The walls looked like they'd been whitewashed so many times that the paint was adding to the thickness of the walls. Gedas told her it was originally constructed with high-quality materials, better constructed than the structures surrounding it, or it wouldn't still be standing. Over time and a shortage of funds allowing for little maintenance, the building looked ready to topple over.

Gedas took her through a side door into the clinic. The door creaked ominously. As they stepped inside, Elodie was hit with a draft of fresh crisp air. With the door closed behind them the contrast from the smelly dirty city was severe.

It was spotless. The walls were painted white, and the wooden floorboards were worn smooth and soft from scrubbing. Even in the brightness of the light globes lining the ceiling Elodie couldn't see a single cobweb.

Healer Beathan, as she was introduced, was an older round woman with steel-colored hair and sharp eyes. Her skin was dark, and her face was wrinkled into a perpetual frown. She wore an undyed apron with red trim to show her status as a healer mage.

"Gediminas, you look younger every day," the Healer said in a scolding voice. "Do we need to find you more paramount tasks to put your magic to so you don't have so much excess to waste on vanity spells?"

Gedas leaned down to kiss the older woman on each cheek. "It's good to see you too, Lore."

"Now, this must be Elodie." She turned to Elodie and offered a short bow. "It's a pleasure to meet you, Your Highness." The words came out a little stiffly.

"Thank you, Healer Beathan," Elodie said with a curtsy. "But please call me Elodie."

"Actually," Gedas began, "I was thinking during your time here, she should not call you Elodie. That is, if you wish to stay incognito."

"Yes, about that," Healer Beathan led them into a side room equipped with a high bed-like table, a few stools, and a cupboard and countertop. She headed to the cupboard and pulled out a large basket full of clothes. Elodie moved to help her lift the heavy basket. "Thank you, dear. I have clothes that should serve you well here in the lower city but won't be nearly so fine as what you're used to."

"No worries, I'm not so used to nice clothes. Gedas and I try to not spend a ton of time in the kind of places where we have to act too proper," Elodie assured the woman, smiling.

"I see." Healer Beathan gave Gedas a look. Gedas just shrugged. The healer pulled a simple, worn dress out of the basket, holding it up to Elodie for comparison. She added to it stockings with a few darns, underthings and a pair of boots that looked to have been nice once. The bottom of the basket was filled with clean white cloth folded neatly. The clothes would work great. No one would recognize her in plain clothes. No one from the palace would look twice at a girl in Odure.

"Now, as for your cover, I was thinking we should call you Ellie. It's a common enough name, and close enough to the real thing you should remember. Alright?"

Elodie nodded.

"For your history," Gedas added. "If anyone is to ask, you should say you are from Mysener. Your grandmother was dear friends with Healer Beathan when they were in school before she married a diplomat and moved there."

Elodie thought it over. Mysener was one of the countries across the ocean to the east. It was one of the original kingdoms who'd provided support for the colonists in the great war, but their notable history with the Twoshy ended with the founding. She'd never met anyone from Mysener, and didn't know anyone who had. It'd be a decent cover for her accent and any cultural slipups she had. If people pressed for too many details, she could feign offense over being shucked off by her family.

"I think it will work."

"Excellent," Gedas replied, placing a hand on her shoulder. "Healer Beathan will be the only one to know your origins, so make sure you play the part and stay out of the way of anyone from the castle. Now, why don't you change while I have a chat with the healer?"

Gedas and the older woman moved into the hallway, closing the door behind them. She was thankful to see the clothes were indeed her size. The dress was high collared and short sleeved, perfect for covering her birthmark while still keeping cool. There was a thick clean apron in the pile. An undyed beige material, likely from being washed so many times, but it didn't hold any stains. The healer's symbol was embroidered on the top right corner of the apron, just over Elodie's heart.

Once dressed with the boots laced, Elodie tied the apron over her clothes, sealing in the appearance of a healer's apprentice.

She opened the door to the hallway, and the adults stopped talking abruptly. Healer Beathan gave Gedas a look and gestured Elodie back into the room. She emptied the basket and folded Elodie's jeans and spare clothes up, storing them in the basket before covering it all with the plain white folded cloth. Elodie tried to help when the healer hefted the basket on her hip, but she waved Elodie away.

"I'll just be right back," she said before leaving.

"I trust Healer Beathan," Gedas told Elodie once the door was closed. "I've known her for many years, and I know you will be safe here. Do you think you will manage?"

Elodie nodded. "Will you be back before I'm gone?"

"I'm not sure, my Gull." He reached up and patted her on the cheek. "You will do well here I think. Learn as much as you can from Healer Beathan, she is a wise woman, and can teach you more of the healing arts than any university."

Beathan returned, the basket no longer in her hands. "Well, now that's done, how about a tour?"

Gedas said his goodbyes. Elodie gave him a fierce hug before he strolled out of the clinic.

She'd never spent more than a day or so in the Twoshy without Gedas's presence. She already missed the old man. Healer Beathan allowed Elodie one long sigh before whisking her off on a tour of the clinic.

The first floor of the building was divided up between workrooms and patient consultation rooms. There was a large open laundry room, with three fireplaces heating large vats of water and a dozen large metal basins spread around the room. It smelled like strong soap, vinegar, and an assortment of herbs. Elodie took a deep sniff, it was hard to sort them out under the smell of vinegar, but she detected sage, heather, witch hazel, tea tree, and oregano. All plants known for their antiseptic properties.

There were two rooms dedicated to preparing medicines, both lined with bundles of plants hanging to dry and shelves full of bottles and jars. Entering the rooms, peace overcame her, each plant collected for its healing properties.

She discovered the room she had changed in was a consultation room and there were six identical rooms on the first floor. The main entrance to the clinic had a large foyer with a dozen or so chairs where even now people sat coughing or sleeping, waiting for a healer or their loved ones. Elodie was introduced to everyone they passed as they walked through the building; healers, apprentices and assistants with only the half apron marking their status. She forgot most of their names by the time they were done.

The second floor of the clinic housed a few storage rooms, and the rest were all patient rooms for people who needed to stay overnight or even longer. This was where Healer Beathan and a few others lived, and where Elodie would be staying. Elodie was surprised at the size of the operation, they couldn't have much funding in the lower city.

When she asked, Healer Beathan explained the clinic was founded by Elodie's great great great grand aunt (by marriage), Sulesia, who saw the state of the lower city in her days and wanted to make sure there was a refuge for those who needed it. The clinic was the hub of modern healing and healers came from all over to apprentice. The clinic served not just those of the lower city but people of the villages and farms within a day's ride. Princess Sulesia set aside a large amount of money in one of the banks of Tross to continue to fund the clinic. Sulesia wasn't a blood relative, and didn't have the albatross birthmark, so the clinic was a success in her day. Over the years with inflation and the rising purse healers expected to be paid for their work, the funds didn't go as far as they once did. Now the clinic was short-staffed and manned by a few good healers who didn't care about wealth, and a few not-so-good healers who couldn't get a job anywhere else.

Elodie was surprised at the number of patients staying in the clinic but Healer Beathan explained this with a long sigh.

"It's hard to tell an old woman who's at the end of her days she's recovered enough to head home and live out her final weeks, when you know her home is an alley behind the bathhouses."

Elodie decided the healer had the hardest job in the world, not keeping all the beds so full she didn't have room when people needed it.

"This winter was hard," the healer continued. "We had each room stacked full of as many pallets we could fit. We had a sickness come through as it will every few years, hitting the young and the old the worst. This one was particularly bad. We lost many from the lower city. The few orphanages around the city are nearly empty, and most of the older generation are gone. Even the upper class felt this one with not a few lords and ladies leaving their heirs to inherit."

That was a surprise. The upper classes usually had healers to do away with any sickness they faced. A healer of Beathan's level could heal a dozen people of a flu. Given she worked with many more than a dozen people in a day, she couldn't heal people directly but had to rely on medicine and helping the person's body heal themselves. The upper class didn't catch illness as easily as the lower class given they were in better health to begin with, and had better sanitation and living conditions. When they did grow ill, a healer would be called to heal them outright.

Beathan explained with the most recent illness the sheer number of the upper class who'd grown ill prevented many healers from helping anyone else.

"This illness was waterborne," the healer explained.

Elodie's stomach fell. Tross's water supply left a lot to be desired after the mess her family had made of the city. A waterborne illness meant when the sewers flooded over the winter, everyone would be exposed because of her family's curse.

Toward the end of the tour an older girl in the half apron of an assistant found them. "It's Mrs. Harriot. She ate a spoonful of sappin spice tryin' to get the twins out early."

"Dima defend us from foolish women," the healer prayed before following the assistant. She turned back to Elodie. "Head back to the second preparation room and work on the detoxifying potion you learned last year. Everything you need should be in stock and it will be a good test for me to learn your skill."

The healer disappeared, and Elodie made her way downstairs. She was curious to see what effect sappin spice would have on the woman. It was known to cause muscle spasms in higher quantities, not something that should be effective in inducing labor.

The second preparation room looked exactly like the first and granted the same peace when she entered. The only differences being the two rooms was the type of plants and ingredients present. Nonmagical medicines, tinctures and the like, could have unexpected consequences if magic influenced them unexpectedly, so the first room was dedicated only to works that did not include magical influence. The detoxifying potion had several magical ingredients and needed to be made in the second room.

Elodie wandered around the preparation space. She looked in cupboards and on shelves at the labeled jars, and sniffed the drying herbs hung around. She found a bottle of vanilla extract and uncapped it to inhale the strong smell.

She was reminded sharply of her mother's perfume and recapped the bottle quickly.

Looking around the room she couldn't quite remember what she needed to get started. She thought back to that cold winter in the castle. The memories were far away and surrounded with thick fog, but when she focused, she could remember. The cold stone of the castle floor chilled her feet through her fine slippers and the warmth from Gedas's fire on the side of her face made her cheeks redden while she worked on her notes by the hearth. The fog slowly started to separate, and then all at once cleared from her mind.

Elodie trimmed a few twigs of greyglove and sage off the drying bundles by the window and pulled out a sack of chia seeds from the cabinet. One by one she pulled up the mental list of things she needed for her creation and laid them out in order on the worktable. The steps came back to her after her weeks of repetition.

The last few steps of the potion involved a lot of stirring as the potion cooled, and Elodie's mind wandered until it fell deep into a foggy bank.

A hand fell on Elodie's shoulder and she looked up into the face of Healer Beathan.

"Are you quite well, dear?"

Elodie blinked and the fog cleared from her mind.

"I'm fine. Did you need something?"

Healer Beathan chuckled. "Did you hear a word I said, dear? I've only been talking to you for the last few minutes. Here I am chittering away as you stirred at your potion."

"I'm sorry, what was it you were saying?"

"I was apologizing for leaving you to yourself for so long, but it looks as though you've done all right. Are you hungry? I should have asked someone to grab you for dinner, but I was more than a little distracted."

"How are the twins?" She looked down at her potion and sprinkled in the chia seeds before continuing to stir.

"Oh, they are quite well, despite having a loon bird for a mother. The sappin spice started her contractions alright, they were thirty seconds apart by the time they brought her in. She's still having contractions now, even after the babies are out. Every muscle in her body is contracting."

The healer yawned and looked closer at the bowl in front of Elodie. She stuck in a finger and sniffed, then peered closely at it for a moment. A spark of blue lit her finger as she examined it with her magic. At last she nodded and wiped her finger off on her apron. "That's very nice. The strongest detoxifier I've seen of its type. Gedas created this?"

"Yes, Healer Beathan, I can write out the steps if you would like a copy."

"Do you have much experience with writing out potion recipes?"

Elodie shrugged. She lifted the spoon out of the potion judging the thickness. She grabbed the funnel off the table and placed it in the thick brown glass bottle she'd picked out and started carefully pouring in the potion.

"I've done it often enough and I have lots of experience with this one. That was part of Gedas teaching me. He gave me the finished potion and made me recreate it enough times till I could write it out." She finished pouring and placed the funnel and spoon in the bowl and capped the bottle. "This needs to sit in a dark space for another four hours so everything can bind before it should be used. Gedas didn't give me any dosage, but said it should be treated as an eight for magicity." Elodie pulled a label out of a drawer and began writing the details in clear letters.

"Yes, I would quite appreciate if you could write out the recipe for me. I'm quite impressed. Gedas said you would be more advanced than I expected, and he was of course correct."

When the potion was stored in a bottom cabinet, the two made their way into the clinic's kitchen. An apprentice set to the task would be by the preparation room in the morning to neutralize any remaining magic in the tools and clean up the workroom.

Light globes running along the ceiling cast the only light in the hall, dimmer than they'd been that morning. The kitchen was quiet and dim, a contrast from the chaos of earlier in the day. There was only one baker in the room, kneading a few loaves of bread for the morning.

Healer Beathan pulled a few rolls out of a basket on the counter and a wedge of cheese from the pantry. "I hope you don't mind simple fare tonight, just to tide us over." Elodie didn't mind. She was growing tired, and was ready for bed, although she was hungry.

After they ate the rolls, Healer Beathan led Elodie to her room, and Elodie followed, sinking farther into a fog with each step until at last she fell into her bed and the fog took over completely.

Chapter Twenty

THE DREAMS CAME in full force as she slept, and stayed with her long into the next morning. Gedas was there, his cloak was made of shadows, a bouquet of rue in his hand. He left green footsteps trailing behind as he made his way into a mountain cave.

Her mother, stood in Doctor Abernathy's office signing her in before looking back toward the entrance. Worry and fear covered her mother like a thick choking blanket that seeped into her skin until it became a part of her.

Between each dream the thick roaring fog billowed into her mind, suffocating everything around her.

A large albatross let out a piercing cry that flew out of it and wrapped tightly around Elodie.

Eventually she felt someone wiping her forehead with a cold damp something. The fog wiped against her forehead, her face, then her neck. The fog brought itself to her mouth and tried to shove its way down her throat. It was thick and cold and Elodie fought it before the fog held down her arms, and she fell again back into its clutches.

Chapter Twenty-One

SHE AWOKE SOMETIME LATER. She was confused at first by the small narrow room with no window. The only light came from a globe hanging by the door on the opposite wall. In a chair by the foot of her bed sat a young woman crocheting under the light. She wore a simple brown dress, and an undyed apron tied around her. Seeing Elodie was awake the woman left the room without a word, and Elodie fell back on her pillow. The door opened again and Elodie looked up to see Healer Beathan standing over her.

"Glad to see you're back with us, dear."

"It happened again, didn't it?"

"It did indeed." Feeling for her legs, Healer Beathan sat on the edge of Elodie's thin bed; she looked as tired as Elodie felt. "Gediminas told me about what happened the last time you were at the castle and warned me it may happen again."

"So he told you to get me to make the potion," Elodie said, understanding.

The healer nodded. "He also asked me to examine you if you showed symptoms. I wasn't sure if I should share with you what I found, but given Gediminas won't be returning any time soon, I feel you are the best person to entrust with the knowledge." She worried her hands before continuing. "To be quite honest, I'm not even sure what was wrong, this is something I've never seen before. It was indeed a toxin of some kind, but it reacted to the ruakh in your body, causing chaos and conflict. I've never seen anything quite like it."

Elodie frowned. "But it's gone now?"

"Yes, the potion was effective in isolating and neutralizing it. Gediminas said that was the first time you've had this reaction?"

Elodie yawned. "Yeah, it was weird. But last time I didn't feel this tired when I woke up."

"That was after a few days, was it not?"

"Yeah, it took Gedas a few days to come up with the potion."

Healer Beathan put a hand on her forehead and Elodie felt a tingle of magic. "Well then, I think the best solution is more sleep."

Elodie agreed and tucked back into her blanket. She was asleep in a moment.

ELODIE AWOKE the next morning to the sounds of a house waking up. Movement in the room next to hers thudded through the wall.

She felt great, clear-headed and alive. She looked around viewing the small room in the faint light cast by the glow of the globe over her head. Reaching up she tapped it three times shielding her eyes as it grew brighter with each tap. Once the room was lit she threw off her covers and stretched. Her body had that ache that came from sleeping too long after not sleeping long enough.

After using the chamber pot in the corner, she lifted the pitcher from the short chest of drawers and dumped water into the basin. She cleaned her teeth and scrubbed her face, then washed as much of her body as she could with a rag before digging in the chest of drawers for fresh clothes. She would ask Healer Beathan about a bathhouse later. Likely it was too costly for her to visit daily, but it would take her skin and hair a while to get used to bathing less often and produce less oil.

Elodie felt gross, ready for a real bath.

She struggled to pull a brush through her hair, then braided it back out of her face. Leaving the bedroom, Elodie was surprised to see the hallway still so dark as it, unlike her bedroom, had a window. It was earlier than she thought.

"Oh, you're awake,"

Elodie turned and saw one of the apprentices she'd met on her tour. She was a cute brown-skinned girl a few years older than Elodie, with a dimpled chin and big brown eyes.

"Audrey, right?"

The girl nodded. "Well, if you're feeling well enough, you can come down to breakfast before we start on the chores." She leaned toward Elodie and whispered conspiratorially. "Although, if I was you, I would go back to bed and skip as much as you can."

Elodie's stomach rumbled, loudly announcing her preference. Both girls laughed and headed down the stairs.

"Porridge again," Audrey groaned when they entered the kitchen.

"You don't have to eat at all, missy," the cook told her as she handed Elodie a bowl.

Elodie took the food happily. When Audrey gave her a look, Elodie shrugged. "I eat this at home all the time, we just call it something a little different."

Elodie took a big bite and immediately regretted it. Her mother usually added milk and sugar to her oatmeal, while the glob in her mouth was quite flavorless and nearly glued her mouth shut. Audrey laughed at her stricken expression and got her a cup of water. She patted Elodie on the back as she choked it down.

Healer Beathan entered the kitchen and greeted those she passed. When she reached Elodie and Audrey she stopped in surprise. "Ellie, I didn't expect to see you up so soon, how are you feeling?"

Elodie swallowed at last and coughed twice before taking another drink of water. "Wonderful."

Healer Beathan raised her eyebrows. "Well don't overtax yourself too soon."

"No no, I really do feel great."

Healer Beathan put a hand on her forehead and Elodie felt a tingle of magic. "Alright then. When you're finished eating, why don't you help Audrey with the morning tasks."

The girls finished their porridge with smaller careful bites, as Audrey gave Elodie a rundown of their morning routine. Returning their bowls to the maid scrubbing up, Audrey led Elodie to the patient rooms.

"First things first, emptying the chamber pots for the night from all the patient rooms. Don't make that face, you're the one who said she was ready to get back on her feet. Come on."

They got to work.

Elodie carried the first pail out to dump in the trench lining the road outside the clinic. It took more than a little effort for her to remember mind over matter, and not lose her breakfast so soon. When she opened the door to the street and turned toward the gutter, she jumped in surprise and nearly made a huge mess.

Several kids were sitting up against the wall of the clinic, they stirred as though waking. First one, then the rest, all jumped up with differing reaction times. As the kids moved, several seagulls roosting nearby were startled into flight.

"Mistress, can I help with that?" The boy was maybe a year older than Elodie. His face was streaked with dirt.

"Any tasks for a gentle child like me?" a small dark-haired boy asked. He was so skinny it hurt.

"I'm a quick runner if you need any fetching." This was the girl on the left, who could possibly have fiery red hair if it was clean.

"I'll dump that mess for you, mistress." A boy of maybe six with a dark face and sweet smile took the pail from her before she knew what was happening and dumped it in the gutter.

"She's not a mistress you ninny, she looks younger than me."

"Aw man, did she get here before us an' take all the ration work?"

"Na, she's no street kid, look at her, she's too fat." The kids all talked in a mess, and Elodie wasn't quite sure who to direct her attention to.

"I'm good at brooming the floors!"

"Hasn't missed many meals that one."

"Stuff it, you canker sores, you shouldn't make fun of someone for the way the gods made 'em." This was the redheaded girl again.

They all started to argue whether Elodie was or wasn't someone they should bother with. The young boy was back with the empty pail handing it back to her. "Can I have sommat to eat now?" he asked. Elodie flinched away as he pulled on her sleeve. His hands were disgusting.

"Um, wait here," she said before slipping back inside.

"Aw man, no way is that one givin' us anything to eat."

They argued behind the door whether or not they should wait.

Elodie leaned against the closed door for a moment, a little overwhelmed.

"Ellie, where are you girl?" Healer Beathan rounded the corner. "You don't need to take each bucket down stairs, that will take all morning, just dump it out the upper window into the trench." She peered closer at her. "Are you alright?"

"There's a mess of kids outside," Elodie explained. "One of them emptied the bucket for me."

Healer Beathan sighed. "Were they sleeping out there again?" Elodie nodded. "The poor dears, how many times must I tell them not to sleep out there in the cold. How many are there?"

Elodie hadn't counted. "Maybe a dozen."

Healer Beathan took the pail from her. "Well it looks like you may be getting off easy today, dear. Fetch them inside and have them wash up in the laundry. Make sure those who need it scrub their fingernails. I will be there in a moment." Healer Beathan turned and marched back into the clinic.

Despite their talk, none of the kids had left. In fact, a few more had shown up and joined those waiting. She gestured them inside and led them to the large laundry room. Pointing to one of the large basins she told them to scrub up. The idea of scrubbing was a little foreign to a few and they needed more direction. Others, like the redheaded girl scrubbed her hands till they were cleaner than Elodie's.

When Healer Beathan looked over the children, most of them dropped their faces not meeting her eyes. Behind the healer's steely expression, Elodie saw pity and sympathy.

"Raise a hand if you've helped in the laundry before," the healer asked. Four girls and three boys who all looked tall enough to reach the bottom of the large metal bins raised their hands. "All right, you get to it. You answer to Mistress Bailey, she'll be the one who says if you've worked hard enough for your lunch." The kids headed to the side of the laundry room where Healer Beathan gestured. "Wait, not you." Healer Beathan tapped the redheaded girl as she passed. "If I remember, last time you made a mess of the laundry getting everyone to laughing till there was no work to be done."

The girl lifted her chin. "Please Healer, I promise not to be disruptive this time."

Healer Beathan looked the girl over for a moment, eyeing her closely. "Ellie, what do you think, could you put her to work assisting you?"

She wasn't sure what tasks she would be given, but she nodded to the healer anyway.

"Alright then, I will take another chance on you, girl. You will assist Ellie in making medicines. It's important work, do you think you're up for the challenge?" The girl straightened her back and nodded furiously. "Excellent, Ellie, I left a list of what's needed on the table in the first preparation room."

She dismissed Elodie with a nod and started assigning the remaining children with tasks of scrubbing and cleaning. Elodie nodded at the redheaded girl and led her to the first preparation room.

"I'm Ellie," she said, to break the ice.

The girl chuckled. "I'm Callie. We're a great match. Ellie and Callie."

"That's a pretty name."

"It's short for Calendula, but I think that's too big a name for me. I'm not tall enough for it yet."

"Oh, I love calendula, they're such beautiful flowers." Elodie moved to the table and lifted up the paper waiting. A list of tinctures needing to be made up. It was busy work, but much better than dumping chamber pots. Pulling down a few bundles of echinacea, Elodie found a few sharp knives and laid them out.

"First we need to chop this into fine little bits." She grabbed a few large empty jars from one of the cabinets. "When it's chopped, drop it in here, until it's loosely full."

Callie seperated a few of the dried stems in front of her, and picked up the knife. "Are there any specific ways I need to be doing this?"

"What do you mean?"

"Well aren't there some plants that need to be cut with a silver blade under the full moon?" Callie asked, throwing her arms wide and saying the words with a deep dramatic voice.

Elodie laughed, and moved the girl's knife-wielding arm to a safer distance from her head. "Actually yes, thistle bright needs to be cut under a full moon but only using a copper blade or it loses its potency. There's a few others as well, but that's usually only when harvesting magical ingredients, or sometimes when preparing a magical potion. What we're doing is creating a standard tincture. No magic involved. You could make this one yourself and it would be as effective as someone with magic."

"Do you have magic?"

"Yes, a little, but I don't use it often." Elodie started chopping.

"So you're a witch?"

"No, I haven't been accredited. I guess I'm just a hedgewitch right now."

Callie nodded. "Apprenticing here will be good for you then. If the healer accredits you, you can make good money as a witch. I knew a girl once who got apprenticed. Best thing to ever happen to her. Kids on the street with magic don't stay on the street long."

"Do you have magic?"

The girl laughed. "If I did I wouldn't still be on the street at my age."

Elodie didn't know what to say to that, so she kept chopping.

"So do you like making medicines?" Callie asked.

Elodie shrugged. "My magic works best with plants, so I'm good at it. I like being good at something."

"Magic with plants," the girl said with wonder. "What does that do exactly?"

"Well there's a lot, helping plants grow, or figuring out what's wrong with them if they're sick. When making a tincture like this I could boost the ingredients and make it more powerful, but we're not doing that today."

"Why not? If you can make something more powerful why not do it?"

"Well for one when treating the sick you need to know the exact strength of your potion. If you don't know how the person's body will react to the magic then a stronger potion could kill them. Right now Healer Beathan set me for creating basic tinctures. I'm sure at some point I'll be creating more powerful ones but for now this is it."

"So for this tin-cher, it doesn't matter how I cut this?"

"Nope, it just needs to be cut up into little tiny pieces."

Callie started trying to cut up the plant into very small pieces making tiny precise cuts, one stem at a time. When Elodie realized she wasn't joking she stopped laughing and showed the girl how she could rock the blade back and forth and cut it quicker. "Just make sure you don't cut your fingers," she warned.

"Do I look like a four-year-old who's holding a blade for the first time? I may not know all the fancy ways for cutting but I know which one's the pointy end and how to keep my bits away from it."

"Good."

They chopped for a few minutes, and Elodie tried to think up something to say to break the silence. She was saved the trouble when Callie spoke up.

"Do you like jokes?" the girl asked.

"What kind of jokes?"

"Where does the King of Wulfram keep his armies?" Callie asked.

"I'm not sure?"

"In his sleevies," Callie replied in a squeaky voice, shrugging her shoulders so the worn fabric of her dress sleeves wiggled.

Elodie chuckled at the absurdity of the joke.

"Want to hear a joke about paper?" Elodie asked after a few moments.

"Sure."

"Nevermind," Elodie said, shrugging. "It's terrible shite."

Callie laughed so hard she had to set down the knife for a moment. "Did you hear the rumor about butter?"

"No, what was it?"

"Well, I'm not going to spread it!"

The girls went back and forth as they worked, telling jokes so basic, and at times stupid, they couldn't help but laugh. Once their first jars were full and Elodie's face started hurting from laughing as she grabbed more jars and herbs, Healer Beathan opened the door to the preparation room, her arms crossed.

"You two better be getting work done in here, not just chittering like a group of flighty feather brains."

"Sorry, Healer Beathan, we're laughing while we chop, I promise." Elodie smiled at the healer.

The older woman nodded with a stern look in her eye. "I expect that list to be complete by lunchtime, Ellie."

"Yes, Healer Beathan," Elodie said, with a curtsey.

Once the door was closed Elodie returned to her chopping.

"Don't you sigh at me, girlie, and chop faster or it's back to the streets for you, Ellie!"

Elodie spun around in surprise, she hadn't heard the door open again or Healer Beathan come back in. Turning she saw Callie standing behind her, posture rigid with a scowl on her face. "Well? Back to work Ellie," Callie said in the exact same tone and inflection as Healer Beathan.

Elodie burst out laughing and Callie broke, her posture dropped and a smile crossed her face.

"That was amazing! How did you do that?"

Callie laughed. "I've always been good at copying people."

The girls continued to think up jokes to tell the other, laughing quieter as they worked. After they filled the first few jars with echinacea, Elodie cleared away the remaining herb bits from the table and pulled out fresh bundles of dried marshmallow flowers.

"So where are you from? You don't talk like you're from around here," Callie said, copying Elodie's accent at the end.

"Oh I'm from Mysener. My grandma was good friends with Healer Beathan, and my mom, well she just remarried and thought it would be a good idea for me to go on a long trip," Elodie said with a frown. The lie came easier to Elodie this time, and she made sure to look down and feel as sad as she could about the event, hoping this would cause the other girl not to ask any other questions.

Callie nodded. "I hear that. Same thing happened to Rich. He's one of the boys doing laundry. It sounds like you were lucky enough your parents found a good place for you before dumping you. Rich got dumped in the streets when his ma left with the merchant she married."

"She just left him?" Elodie couldn't believe it. It was so cold and unfeeling. How could someone do that to their kid? Elodie's stomach sank in fear. What would it take for her mom to do that with her? Except instead of leaving her on the streets she would pack her away to some facility to 'help' her. Elodie shook her head trying to make the thoughts go away. "What about you? Where are your parents?" she asked, not thinking.

"My dad died when I was a babe. My mom died four years ago from a fever, which also took my brothers," Callie said casually.

"I'm so sorry, I shouldn't have asked."

"It is what it is. I was helping out at this house over near market street. There's an old woman who converted it into a sort of orphanage. Us older kids helped with the younger, and she provided food and necessities. Some rich old cracked woman thought living in the lower city and helping orphans was her calling from Dima or something. I didn't really care who was telling her to do it. As long as it meant two meals a day and a corner under a roof to sleep."

"It doesn't sound like she was so rich if that was all you got."

Callie raised her eyes at Elodie. "That's more than anyone else has given me since my ma passed. Besides, she had a lot of kids living there, so we took what we got and were happy for it."

"Why aren't you there anymore?"

"She died over the winter. Same as most of the kids in the house. The rest of us moved on, looking for some other place to crash. It's fine, I wasn't there long," she said at Elodie's expression. "I had experience on the streets from before I went to her house, so I know how to handle myself."

They completed their tasks after a few hours. Elodie filled each jar with a strong alcohol before screwing on the lids. She labeled and stored each one in a dark cabinet.

Next it was time for lunch. Elodie waited in line with all the other children. After getting a roll of thick bread stuffed with cheese, she ate alongside Callie. The rest of the children were getting dismissed, and Healer Beathan told Elodie she could take a break for the day as well. Callie waved to Elodie as she prepared to leave, but Elodie followed her.

"Where are you going now?"

Callie shrugged and looked away, then she looked back at Elodie. "Why? Do you want to come?" she asked with a gleam in her eyes.

"Yeah, can I?"

"You'll have to take off that apron, and you have to be quick. Are you quick?"

Elodie knew from many P.E. classes she wasn't in fact quick.

Callie smiled. "Don't worry about it, I'll watch out for you." She gestured for Elodie to follow. Elodie took off the apron and stowed it in the cabinet of an exam room before rejoining Callie on the street.

They wandered the streets that afternoon. Callie didn't seem like someone who grew up on the streets. There was a joy that radiated from her even as she jumped across gutters in her bare feet. She taught Elodie all the secrets and hidden spots of the lower city. Callie knew which shops and pubs threw away the best food scraps at the end of the night, and which sold seagull meat and should be avoided. She could tell you which cart sellers didn't keep a very good eye on their merchandise and what corners and crannies to hide from the city guard with your stolen loot.

Callie's true gift wasn't for thieving and outrunning the slow guards of the lower city, although she did enjoy it on occasion. Her true passion was for playing like other people. Putting on the voice and mannerisms of someone else and talking in their words for whoever would listen. Elodie and Callie spent most of their time together, with Elodie bent over with laughter watching her friend put on pretend shows walking the streets in rags and impersonating the elite of Aluna.

Chapter Twenty-Two

ELODIE'S DAYS followed a similar pattern that summer. Every morning she would bring in the street kids waiting for work, and help sort them into roles they could best help in.

She noticed after some weeks, kids she used to see wouldn't come around anymore. When she asked Callie about this, she shrugged.

"There's a million reasons why they're gone, so there's really no point in worrying over it. Either they got sick and died and are in a better place, somewhere they don't have to fight for food or a place to sleep anymore, or they got snatched up by slavers and are now bound and will get sold off to some master and won't have to fight for food or a place to sleep anymore. Either way they're likely better off."

Elodie's chest ached at the thought.

Each afternoon was spent with Callie running the streets. Elodie wasn't really built for running, and more so, she hated it. But over the last quarter in P.E. she'd built up quite a bit of endurance and now with Callie she began to build up speed, and a bit of coordination, dodging around carriages and horses. She ate less at mealtime since there wasn't a ton to go around, and ran her afternoons away with Callie. As the weeks faded into months, her dress fit less and less snug and Elodie had an easier time dodging the occasional city guard and slipping into hidey-holes.

In the evenings, after her time with Callie, Elodie would return to the clinic and Healer Beathan would teach her advanced potions and medicines. She showed her principles and fundamentals of healing Gedas only ever glazed over. She let Elodie try new things with her magic. At first Elodie was hesitant to use her abilities. She'd decided back in the illusion to stop using magic, but as the days turned to weeks, and the ruakh saturated her life, she was back to her old curiosity.

Callie brought Elodie a bracelet one afternoon. It was a small thing, made with twine and uneven glass beads she found in the trash behind one of the glass makers in Prole. It was beautiful, and Elodie hugged her friend tight before she put it on, trying to hide the tears that fell.

Callie had so little, it hurt to think she was giving something to Elodie, and she hadn't tried to return the favor.

"It's for guidance and peace," Callie had said, pointing out the different colors of the small lopsided beads. "Green and browns for the roads, and blue for the sea, all under Ravid's domain."

Elodie and Callie were hanging out behind the stalls of the Prole District market one afternoon with no plans for the day. Callie was doing an impression of a noble she'd seen once who stepped in horse poop in the lower city and Elodie was laughing along, her sides aching. Callie pronounced some of the most colorful curses Elodie had ever heard when a boy she recognized from the clinic came around the flower seller's cart and nearly crashed into them.

"They're doing a round up!" the boy called before disappearing around the corner. Callie came to life and grabbed Elodie's arm.

"We need to run," her friend said and dragged her away. Shouts and whistles echoed in the distance.

"What's happening?" Elodie asked as she tried to keep up. Callie weaved between people and carts, never moving in a straight direction but always heading toward the east end of the city.

"The guards are rounding up the beggars," Callie gasped out as she darted around a man on horseback.

They climbed down one of the city's many sink holes into a tunnel network below the streets. Elodie had been shocked to learn the natural caverns she'd known caused cave-ins around the city were not natural at all with the tool marks to prove it. Tross's underworld used the underground passages to move between each district and for who knew what else. Callie said it was safe to use as long as you didn't get caught.

As they tiptoed through the dark passage, their path lit by the light stones borrowed from one of the thieves' many hidden caches, Callie explained. Roundups came when the guards were looking for a criminal. They would round up anyone out of place, kids, beggars, homeless, and lock them up. If no one came to claim them in a day or so with the proper fees, it was assumed they were vagrants, and were bound and sold as slaves.

"That's awful." Elodie had never heard anything like this before. She knew criminals were sometimes punished by being bound, but this was so much worse. "Does it happen often?"

Callie shrugged, copying the motion with the same inflection Elodie often used. "Not so often to keep street kids from going into Prole, but I know a few who's been caught and shipped off to who knows where. Aluna's got a lot of farms, and they need someone to work 'em."

Elodie's stomach made uncomfortable turns.

THAT NIGHT A RIOT broke out in Odure.

It started when a well-respected tailor from Odure confronted the guards in Prole for arresting her son. She disputed the illegal soliciting charge saying he'd been making a delivery to a client in Prole on her behalf. The tailor was thrown out of Prole after a beating the guards said was for insubordination. With tempers running high from the round up, and one of their respected members bloody in the street, Odure responded.

Elodie didn't see the fighting as it started, or as it escalated from protests of injustice into an angry mass of hate. She didn't see the destruction of the lower city until long after the fires were out. Instead, Elodie spent the night and the following three days working alongside every able body of the clinic patching and tending the wounded.

She spent hours stewing dandelion greens and water moss, to help with blood loss, adding in a good dose of her magical strength. She made potions to stop infections and poultices to clot wounds. Healer Beathan taught her how to tell if a bone needed setting and how to stitch up a wound. She watched people grieve over loved ones, and saw life leave glassy eyes. She was sick many times when faced with ruined flesh or broken bones. She ate little and slept less.

After the third day those who were worse off died or were starting to mend, and the frantic pace the healers and assistants had worked finally ebbed. Healer Beathan gave Elodie a tonic for deep sleep and sent her to bed.

When she awoke the next afternoon, Beathan sent Elodie out of the clinic for fresh air and to remember what life looked like.

She found Callie at one of her favorite stalls, watching the baker fold bread into unique designs. Somehow Callie knew exactly what her friend needed, and the two spent the afternoon sharing light-hearted laughs, and stayed far away from the parts of the city recently damaged.

They passed a small shrine to Dima, goddess of healing, and Callie stopped and bowed, pausing for a moment before moving on. Elodie did the same.

Each time they passed a shrine or temple for one god or another Callie always stopped to pay her respects, and Elodie copied her so as not to insult any prickly god. She knew it was good manners to be respectful to the gods, but Callie went out of her way to address each shrine they passed.

"Why do you always stop for them?" Elodie asked, after Callie led her to a shrine hidden behind a bakery.

"I think it would be quite nice to be in the service of a god," Callie said.

"You do? Why? They just make life harder, don't they?"

"Well, according to the tales, the gods touched do tend to get into sticky situations, but things usually have a way of working out for the person's benefit. I bet it'd be a great way to get out of the streets."

Elodie could think of a dozen tales off the top of her head where this wasn't the case. "I'm not entirely sure that's true."

"Well o'course there's always those who don't handle the gift or task the god puts them to, like Podrick the Doubting or Kenrick the Flayed."

"Yes, exactly," Elodie cut her off. "Those are great examples. Kenrick the *Flayed*."

"But in those cases, it's always the fault of the gods touched, not the gods themselves that everything went bad," Callie continued, not persuaded for a moment.

"My teacher, Gedas, he always says having a god's attention is one of the last things you want. He says it's better to direct your own destiny."

"Hmm, I bet he's never dug through a trash heap in summer looking for his next meal. I think when it comes to caring about destiny, it matters first if you've got one."

Elodie had nothing to say to that. She was quite sure Gedas had never dug through trash heaps, but she'd also always had the feeling when he warned her of the gods, he spoke of experiences he'd yet to share.

Thinking about destiny made a low pressure born of frustration and impatience build in her chest. She was ready for her destiny to happen to her already.

A week later, Callie was doing a perfect impersonation of the accent of a man from Pundica, near one of the bread sellers. Mr. Bordinsky, a baker who was very kind to the street children, always giving them the old or burned bread, was completely enthralled by Callie, a little girl, talking with the voice of a foreigner.

Callie thanked him with an impersonation of his own voice.

He told them his fiancée worked in the kitchens of a baron's house in the wealthier part of the city and asked Callie to deliver a message and a gift for him, offering the girl a few coppers as payment.

Callie, shocked at the offered job accepted, and then immediately regretted it as soon as the baker was behind them.

"Ellie, I can't go into the Opulent District! They won't let me through the gates!"

Elodie thought about this. She was right. Even dressed better than Callie, the guards wouldn't likely let Elodie into the inner city either.

"Do you know any of the sinkholes that connect to the Opulent District?" Elodie asked.

"Yeah . . . But we can't use it. I've never been that far. We could get caught. And besides. I can't go into Opulent looking like this! I smell Ellie! I know I do!"

"Callie, relax." Elodie grabbed her friend by her shoulders and looked her in the eyes. "You're one of the bravest people I know, you can do anything. Look, once you start talking, no one is going to notice what you're wearing. You can do this. Okay?"

Callie nodded and took a deep breath.

Callie led Elodie to one of the large sinkholes on the east end of town and the two descended into the darkness. They borrowed light stones from the cache in the rock floor, hidden under a large flat rock, but the lights were barely needed once they passed into Opulent. Here the tunnels had light stones perched on small crevices of the walls lighting the way.

They hid from other people walking the tunnels twice, the second time they stayed hidden down a dark smaller tunnel for a half hour while two people argued in an intersection.

The climb out of the Opulent District sinkhole was long and

Elodie's arms ached by the time they reached the top. They emerged on a back road a few streets over from one of Elodie's favorite herb merchants.

Navigating side streets, they kept to the shadows so as not to be stopped and accused of troublemaking. Elodie had grown used to the stink of Odure. She hadn't even realized it until she found herself back in Opulent. She felt dirty and very visible on the back roads, but she kept herself calm and walked with confidence, hoping it would rub off on Callie.

Callie had never ventured past Prole in her life and was torn between nervous energy and excitement and wonder at the finery visible from their path. When they passed servants and maids on the side streets Callie would flinch and look for a place to hide. Elodie stopped her, pulling her back on the path.

"It's just like you always tell me," Elodie told her friend. "Act like you belong and no one will notice."

"But what if we see a noble?" Callie asked.

"Nobles aren't so bad. They probably won't even notice us."

"They won't even notice us," Callie repeated under her breath. She took a deep breath and straightened her back to copy Elodie's stride. It lasted until the next messenger they passed.

Eventually they made it to the large ornate house, the baron's crest of a large black-and-red gloved fist marked it as the right one. The town home of Baron Byron. Lucky for Elodie, a baron wouldn't hang around the kitchens, and would be unlikely to recognize her in her old clothes even if she did encounter him. The girls found their way to the back of the house opening into the kitchen. The door was open wide looking for a breeze to draw out the heat from the ovens.

The household was preparing for the evening meal and everyone was bustling around in a flurry of organized chaos. Elodie had visited many kitchens in country castles and larger city homes like this one. This kitchen was unusually quiet. She was used to cooks yelling at maids, and dish washers muttering curses under their breath as they scrubbed out pots and dishes.

But here, although everyone was bustling around getting their work done, they did so silently as though fearful of attracting attention.

Elodie only had a moment to ponder this before Callie took a deep breath. With that breath Callie dropped the shell of fear and anxiety she had been wearing and transformed into a confident and cordial person. She jumped through the doorway, arms spread wide and announced herself.

"Greetings, fellow exploited peasants and overworked laborers, I come to you today with a message for the beautiful Haddy." Callie announced this with the flourish and confident declaration of one of the best tellers of the city.

Regardless of how she felt or the looks of those glaring at her from the kitchen door, Callie continued to stand her ground, her head high and her chest out to deliver her important message. An old and withered woman with flower on her hands and a deeply lined face came over to them with a stomp.

"Leave now chit, we have no need of you here." The cook had a look of warning in her eyes which Callie promptly ignored.

"Now now, I know you not to be the Haddy I look for, for her beauty has been spoken of with such brilliance of language, I know a shriveled old bag like you cannot be her." A few people deeper in the kitchen stifled a laugh.

A pretty girl of about sixteen wearing a plain gray homespun dress nudged the older woman away and stood before the young girls.

"I'm Haddy, tell me your message quick and be off with you."

At the appearance of the object of her message Callie again transformed. She took on the posture of a larger man, back curved from years of bending low over a work table kneading bread, and her face became hard like a man fighting for his lot in life, but there was softness in her eyes at the sight of the girl Elodie remembered seeing on Bordinsky's face when he gave them the message.

When she opened her mouth it was neither the cant of the lower city nor the aristocratic flare of a teller. She spoke in a deep guttural voice perfectly reflecting the tone and speech patterns of Mr. Bordinsky.

"My dearest Haddy, three days will it be before ye marry me, and me heart can't stand the delay. With yer face like a flower, me love will never sour, and I promise I won't never turn away. So today, my beautiful Haddy, it would make me oh so gladdy, if ye dwelt on me love fer ye all the day."

And with a last flourish Callie took a bow and threw a hand out behind her back. Elodie remembered her cue and rushed forward to put the small handkerchief wrapped parcel in the waiting hand. When Callie straightened up, she unwrapped a small cookie decorated with a beautiful red iced flower.

Through the performance Haddy's face changed from a look of slight fear to one of delight. At the end Haddy scooped up the beautiful flower cookie and held it close to her chest.

"Thank you, that was lovely."

Before she could finish her thanks, someone rose from a corner of the kitchen and everyone rushed back to work in a flurry. Haddy wrapped the cookie back up and stuck it in her apron pocket before disappearing.

As the crowd departed Elodie saw why the kitchen felt off. She crouched out of view of the doorway as a man in clothes finer than anything found in Odure rose from his seat and crossed to the door. Callie shrank in the shadow of Baron Byron but she stood her ground.

"That was very well done, girl. Do you often carry messages for people?" the baron asked. He looked over Callie with a sharp look, and his glance flew over Elodie standing in the shadows before returning to Callie.

"Yes, Your Grace." Callie curtsied properly for a girl of no rank. Elodie recognized the curtsy as identical to one she'd given Healer Beathan as a joke. "I have delivered messages between a few of the guilds in the lower city and twice to the priests of Reza."

The baron nodded. "And does such work pay well?"

"Yes, Your Grace. Usually with payment of food or the occasional copper, but I mostly do it for the fun." Callie smiled then dropped her expression back into a blank respectful gaze.

Byron stroked the edge of his ornate braided beard as he looked Callie over with predatory eyes. "And how would you like to start passing messages for me?"

It was a life-changing question, and Callie hesitated only for a moment before accepting. The baron ordered a maid to find the head housekeeper and sort out the details while he disappeared into the house. With the baron gone, the entire kitchen relaxed as one.

The head housekeeper was a stern graying woman who made Mistress Piera look like a sweet maiden. She gave Callie a once over before grimacing, and then listed rules. A uniform was ordered and a maid was assigned to escort Callie to the baths before she would be allowed into the house.

Elodie said goodbye to a very shell-shocked Callie and made her way back to the sinkhole. She was nervous on her way back. Climbing down the deep sinkhole was harder without Callie's direction, and she got lost once while trying to decipher the direction marks on the tunnels as Callie taught her.

Everything had happened so fast Elodie didn't know what to think. She would miss Callie and the time they spent together, but she was so happy Callie now had someplace to live, a way to make a life for herself.

The next afternoon, after the morning's work was complete, Elodie exited the clinic not sure what to do with herself. To her surprise, a messenger in a crisp new uniform made in the red and black of the baron's house was waiting for her. Callie glowed. She was cleaner than Elodie had ever seen her, but more so, inner joy shined from the girl, brighter than ever before.

"Wanna help me deliver a message?" Callie asked, holding up a rolled note with a red seal.

Elodie laughed and hugged her friend.

Things between Elodie and Callie didn't change. Callie lived in a small shared room in the baron's home, and spent the morning passing messages while Elodie worked by herself in the clinic workrooms. In the afternoon Elodie would join Callie in delivering messages, usually in the form of sealed scrolls but occasionally in verbal messages he would have her repeat for his business partners' amusement. Callie delivered each message with her usual flair. She was well paid by the standards of Odure, but it would take a while for her to make up the cost of her new clothes and uniform.

The baron ordered Callie to keep secret everything he ever told her or she overheard. He was intensely private, she told Elodie, and all the servants were scared of him, although Callie couldn't yet figure out why. Elodie wasn't sure either but told her the stories she knew of the baron's sword skills and past duels.

Elodie found Callie's dedication to secrecy hilarious and was always trying to get her friend to slip up and tell her something about the baron. "What's the name of his favorite horse?" she asked with a smile. But Callie sternly closed her lips and shook her head in refusal.

Even if Elodie asked over and over, she wouldn't tell her any of the baron's secrets. Elodie didn't really care, but enjoyed trying to get it out of her friend.

It wasn't long before many of the men Callie delivered messages to were asking her to carry messages of their own. Before the summer was up Callie had a route she would travel, gathering messages from wealthy men and nobles and delivering them. It was funny for Elodie, how in plain simple clothes tailing behind a message carrier, even nobles she'd met before in social settings didn't recognize the princess and heir to their throne.

Chapter Twenty-Three

WHILE LIFE DIDN'T CHANGE COMPLETELY for the friends, the journeys they took together were no longer full of mischief as Callie, wearing the baron's colors, couldn't get into any trouble and risk her position in the house. Instead Callie found other ways to have fun that didn't involve trouble. One afternoon they were in the Opulent District delivering a message to the silver guild. They took the long way back to the baron's house, wandering through the markets. Callie never tired of looking at all of the beautiful and fine things hanging in the market where anyone could steal them. In Odure anything fine was hidden, and the markets only openly sold low-quality merchandise to low-quality people.

The Opulent market was rich. Rich in color, scents, sounds, people. Elodie had spent a good amount of time in this market, purchasing herbs and supplies for her work with Gedas, venturing out on the pages' days off to buy treats and be free of the castle, but now Elodie had spent more time on the outer edges of the city she saw the Opulent market with new eyes. Strong stable stalls lined the cobblestone paved streets, scarves dyed with a million colors, their fabric so fine and light they billowed out in the air created by people passing by, tunics and jackets with fine embroidery, worked in gold thread, others with symbols for health and life worked into the patterns. Even the seagulls in the Opulent District were cleaner and better fed than those that flocked in Odure. It was baffling how one city could hold such different worlds, separated by only a few streets and walls.

They wandered down the fabric sellers' road, Callie talking in the accent of someone from Skuna as she told Elodie in extreme detail of the beautiful gown she planned to wear to the next palace function. Elodie had to cover her mouth to try not to burst out laughing as she saw a woman hanging dresses in her shop stare at Callie in absolute confusion at the girl's words. Callie did in fact sound like she was some great princess or courtier from Skuna in the market looking for accessories to purchase. She carried herself with her head high and shoulders back with a posture Elodie's etiquette teachers had drilled into her. But most of all, the look in Callie's eyes was not of one who had ever lived in a gutter, it was of a girl who would someday be a woman and who knew with absolute confidence who she was and who she was meant to be. Elodie wished she could fake confidence like that for even a second.

When they reached the end of the street, Callie let her façade drop.

"Oo, do you smell that? Let's get sweet rolls!" Callie darted away, once again a little girl still adjusting to having pocket money for the first time in her life.

Elodie chased after Callie as she followed her nose to a baker's stand. It was the same baker who Elodie had visited a few times on her last trip to the Twoshy when she went out to the market. As Callie approached the stand her posture again changed, she shouldered her way in between a boy and a maid waiting to make purchases.

"Excuse me, peasants, but I have important business with this baker," Callie said to the boy using a voice nearly identical to the baron's.

The boy turned to her, a look of utter confusion on his face as Elodie came up beside her friend. The boy's eyes went wide as he saw her. "Elodie?" he asked in shock.

Elodie turned surprised to hear her name and examined the boy closer. Well dressed in finely made clothes, every tight curl of hair in perfect shape, green clever eyes shocked and baffled in his dark face.

She gasped. Silas began to bow and Elodie rushed forward stopping him arms on his shoulders. "Stop, stop. I'm supposed to be incognito," she whispered.

He looked at her perplexed. "What?"

"I don't want anyone to know who I am," she said. "Call me Ellie and treat me like a commoner."

Silas's eyebrows drew closer together. "I don't understand the joke."

"I'm not joking. I've been helping out in the clinic in Odure, and this is the best way for me to do it without having to deal with any of the boring stuff at the castle," she said with a smile and a wink.

He seemed taken aback. "Well I did hear Wizard Gediminas was traveling. He left the palace a few months ago, I assumed to meet you. Is he also in the city trying not to be recognized?" he asked with a small smile.

"No, he did go off on some trip. I arrived just before he left, and he left me in the hands of the healer in Odure."

"Why didn't he take you with him?" Silas asked.

"I don't know. He said it was too dangerous or too boring for me and I didn't pry."

"That's strange," Silas said, his eyes narrowing. "Has he ever not taken you with him before?"

"No. He's left me for others to teach before, but he was always around. But enough about me how is your page training going? What are you doing in the city? I thought you guys didn't get freedom?"

Silas noticed Callie standing next to Elodie listening to their conversation and turned to the girl. "I'm so sorry, I'm being rude. Elodie, will you introduce me to your friend?"

"Elodie." Callie's eyes went wide. "Who's Elodie and how do you know a money pants?" she asked in a fake whisper Silas could hear.

He frowned.

Elodie eyed the other patrons of the pastry cart and turned back to her friends. "Callie, Silas. Silas, Callie. Okay, can we talk somewhere more private? I don't want to do this where we might be overheard."

"Wait, let me buy our buns first." Callie turned back to the cart.

"Allow me," Silas said before ordering them each two buns stuffed with fruit and spices.

Callie's eyes went big as the baker filled Silas's handkerchief. Elodie had a feeling Callie only meant to buy the cheaper rolls.

"Alright where to, my lady? I am yours to command," Silas said, not at all joking.

"Ooh, do that little bow again," Callie said, trying to copy the casual motion Silas made. It wasn't a full bow more so just a movement of his head shoulder and arm to show respect. Silas gave her a look of confusion and didn't repeat the motion.

"Oh fine, I know a place we can talk all quiet like." Callie led them a few streets over, back behind a tanner. The smell was enough to keep plenty of people away. Behind the building was a small shrine to Ravid god of travelers and wanderers, in charge of transitions, change, and mischief. They all paid short respect and then sat on the steps around the shrine to talk.

Elodie turned to Callie. "Can I trust you with a secret?"

Callie, sensing this was a serious moment, lowered the roll she was about to bite into and thought before nodding. "If it's important to you I promise I won't tell."

Elodie nodded. She trusted Callie. She'd shown her some of her secrets around the city and trusted her with her past and her pain.

"My name isn't really Ellie. It's Elodie. You know, as in the Misplaced princess." Elodie didn't meet Callie's eyes. "I'm sorry I lied. My mentor told me I should so I would be safe at the clinic." As the silence stretched, she glanced at her friend, hoping she wasn't mad.

Callie was chewing thoughtfully, a look of mild delight on her face as she ate her bun. She swallowed. "I thought it would be something like that," she said. "I saw someone from Mysener one time when I was really little. It's before I got good at accents so I can't really remember it, but it was much different from yours. And how you never wanted to meet at the baron's house or go on runs with me to the castle. Even after you were always so brave around nobles. I figured there was something you were hiding from." Callie shrugged. "It's not my world, and I've always known you weren't totally a part of my world. But I sure had a lot of fun sharing it with you." She nudged Elodie and grinned.

"Thank you," she told her friend, and meant it. "So anyways, this is Silas or more properly Page Silas of Tate. He's a good friend."

"Actually prin—uhh, Ellie? I'm not a page anymore. Now I'm a squire," he said with a smile. "I think I've finally managed to catch up to you in age too. I turned twelve last month."

Elodie sighed looking down. "I guess more time has passed than I realized. Who are you squired to?"

"Sir Jesper. He has some business in the city this summer so I'm not officially starting my service for another month."

Jesper was the knight commander in charge of Aluna's army. There was no real war between the nations of the Twoshy, but bandits were a real threat. The position was very prestigious. She was proud of her friend.

"How is everyone else? Eyvi, Timothee, Dess and all the rest?"

Silas's face grew dark, a shadow crossing his eyes. "Eyvi died over the winter. We had a bad sickness hit the city."

"Oh I'm so sorry, Silas," she gasped. Eyvi, how could the shy honorable boy she'd known be gone? He'd been Silas's best friend growing up. She couldn't imagine the loss he felt. Elodie couldn't imagine losing Vanessa, or Gedas, the ones who'd always been there for her from world to world.

Silas was quiet for a moment. "I just wish I could have seen him have his chance to be a squire. He would have been great."

Elodie didn't know what to say, her own emotions overwhelmed her and she didn't know the right way to comfort Silas. She hadn't known Eyvi long, but the boy she had known was smart and honorable and dying for a chance to prove himself. He would have made a great knight if his birth had given him a chance.

It was her fault he was dead. Her and her family's fault the broken sewers bred illness and death through her city.

Callie placed her hand on Silas's shoulder and he looked up at her, surprised. His eyes glittered.

"He's gone to the Bright One now. He has him in his kingdom where he won't know suffering or pain any longer. Isn't that the best we can hope for? Maybe the Bright god will let him be his squire," Callie said.

Elodie pulled out one of her rough handkerchiefs and dabbed at Silas's cheek. He took the cloth and wiped at his own face. "Thank you," he said to Callie. "I think I like the idea of him squiring for the Bright One." He smiled weakly and was silent. On impulse Elodie took his hand and held it. He squeezed and didn't let go.

They sat in silence, grief heavy in the air.

A seagull broke the bubble of peace as it swooped through the air for Callie's fruit bun.

"Not on your life, feather brain," she said, swatting at the bird to defend her roll. Silas and Elodie chuckled as Callie defended her snack.

Silas wiped his face one last time and cleared his throat. "Dess has been a squire to the lady knight, Sir Dohesi, for the last year. She's loving it of course. They've been having border duty up in the north, and she's fought against raiders. Timothee didn't make the squire cut again this year, so he has another year of being a page before him. He says if he doesn't make it next year he'll give it up and be a clerk."

The three of them left the shrine to walk a while. Silas went on to tell her about the rest of their group, the pages Elodie had met and got to know over her last visit, but who she hadn't grown as close to.

"So are you two a thing?" Callie asked making motions between Elodie and Silas.

"No!" they both said, blushing.

"That would be a good tale, The Princess and the Page." Callie chuckled. She ran over and jumped onto the edge of a trough startling a horse at the far end. "Gather in close and I'll tell you their tale," Callie started to say in a deep strong voice that would put many grown men to shame. Elodie chased after her and pulled her off of the trough before any magic formed over the watching crowd.

"You know, you could make a killing as a wandering teller," Silas told her as they fled the crowd.

"I've tried." Callie sighed dramatically. "I'm too young. Maybe when I'm older and I'm either really pretty or really ugly I will try again. But just as I am people only see a street chit trying to beggar a meal. They don't give you a chance to even start talking."

A few minutes later, a bell rang signaling the hour and Callie groaned. "Ellie, I have to get back, will you be alright getting back to Odure?"

"Of course, don't worry about me. I'll see you tomorrow?"

"Always," her friend said before running away.

"I like her," Silas said once she was out of sight. "She seems like a good person." He looked back at Elodie with a small smile. "I like that you have good people around you, even when I'm not."

"I like her too. I'm so glad she got on with the baron's household. Even if he is . . . whatever he is, it's good she has a place." Elodie had never particularly liked Byron, he set off a totally unfounded warning in her head when he was around.

"Maybe I'll tell my father about her. He's always looking for good people."

"Oh, yes, you definitely should."

"It's settled then."

"Did you know there are tunnels under the city?" Elodie asked, remembering the discovery.

"You mean the caverns that caused the sinkholes?"

"No, Silas. These are real tunnels that stretch all over the city. They had to have been made by people. You can reach them by climbing down into some of the sinkholes."

"Oh please tell me you didn't," Silas said, an amused expression on his face.

"Oh yes I did. They're the only way I can get into Opulent dressed like this." Elodie gestured to her old and patched dress. "Although the first time I used them, Callie and I were running from some guards, and we had to hide from the thieves who run the tunnels," she said with a wicked smile.

Silas laughed and they joked about Elodie running from her own guards.

"I also have news about the Prophecy." Silas said. "I don't have a direct transcript yet, no one I've asked seems to know the exact wording, which you know, is important for prophecies. But I was looking around for any clues, and last summer it occured to me. What has the spell and the prophecy hurt the most?"

Elodie thought this over, then shrugged. "I don't know, the families of those Misplaced?"

Silas nodded slowly. "Definitely the families felt the most acute pain from the loss, but most of the rulers who lost their children are long gone. But still, decades later the effect of your loss is felt. Politically we're weaker without a queen, domestically we're falling apart without a ruler who can make absolute choices. The steward doesn't have absolute control over the kingdom, a fact Oburleck likely dwells on daily. He can't create or abolish any laws, and can only make small changes to existing laws with the approval of the council. Sir Jesper says Oburleck tried to pass a few laws in his council meetings lately, and keeps getting shot down because the guidelines for a steward set by your father before he died. Oburleck doesn't have the authority. The point is, when the heirs of the Twoshy went missing"—he nodded at Elodie —"the ruling parties added an amendment to the Constitution of Sixteen saying the Misplaced would return as told by Gediminas."

Elodie blinked. "Is that the twenty-seventh amendment? I've never actually read it before."

"Yes, exactly. I can't remember the exact wording now, I read it last winter, but it implied the spell would be broken."

"Well I need to read it then, it should give us the clues we need!"

"It's copied out in a book in the library, I can show you where it is," he said gesturing back toward the castle.

"No, I can't go into the castle, I'm supposed to be incognito."

They pondered the predicament for a few moments. "Why do you think Gediminas didn't want you in the castle?" Silas asked.

Elodie shrugged. "He said he knew I would prefer not having to deal with Oburleck."

"Do you ever get the sense something more may be going on with Gediminas?"

"Well, I know there's a lot he doesn't tell me, but I trust him. He's always been there for me," Elodie said defensively.

"I guess you're right."

Seeing his closed expression, Elodie nudged him. "Why do you ask?"

"Well, it's like with this whole prophecy, the Twoshy isn't doing very well at the moment, and it can all be traced back to the twenty-seventh amendment holding the inheritance and titles of the Misplaced for their return, crippling the nations. The amendment makes it sound like the heirs would return in a matter of months or years, but it's been decades and so many of the kingdoms have been without proper rulers for generations."

"What do you mean the Twoshy is in bad shape?" she asked, a sinking feeling growing in her stomach.

"We've done all right here in Aluna, we're the largest of the nations so of course we have the cornerstone of trade from farming. But there's a few nations like Oskela who are all but falling apart. There's been rumors they're planning on breaking the treaty by electing a new ruler. They need it in order to get the kingdom back in shape. There's other rumors Vasniydor, the empire that borders them, has been building up their military for an invasion, which would be an even bigger breach of the treaty. We've even been having a lot more issues with bandits on our northwest border than we have in the past. There are some who say this is because we're losing power, and that if we had a king this wouldn't be happening." Silas shrugged. "I don't know how much of it's true and how much of it is scared men talking where I can overhear. But if I can hear them, others can too. As far as I'm concerned there's a number of reasons why our top priority should be breaking the spell."

Elodie shook her head. She knew Aluna was flawed, but thought it was unpreventable. Tross and its sinkholes and wood-patched castle was ugly, but this was the fault of her family's curse. The rest of Aluna was in better shape. Tate, the lands Silas would one day inherit, was thriving and clean.

Thoughts of golden-plated dinnerware and pearl-trimmed dresses conflicted in her mind with the sludge and hunger of Odure.

Elodie pushed away the contradictions.

She thought Aluna's problems were because of her family's curse, and ultimately the kingdom may be better off without her. If Silas was right, her absence, and that of the other Misplaced children were the problem.

They entered a courtyard with a large fountain. Unlike the lower city, no one washed laundry in this fountain. Ladies in fine clothes passed merchants without a care in the world. city guards walked by casually, their presence a deterrent for any shady characters to linger. The statue in the middle of the fountain showed a king standing straight and strong. The statue was quite a good likeness. Carved from marble, it was just larger than lifesize, and looking up, Elodie could imagine the statue was alive. The hair would be black, spattered through with gray, his eyes would be as blue as the summer sky. His strong face, showing a proud wise expression would turn to her and soften, the corner of the eyes crinkling with wrinkles. His clothes were finer in the stone than they had been in the forest, and when she met him he hadn't worn a crown.

"I met my father once," she said, turning from the statue and sitting on the rim of the fountain.

"You did?" Silas sat next to her.

"Yeah, it was the first time I traveled, I was only five, and the whole thing seemed too magical. Sometimes I forget it even happened, more than I do normally. I didn't know he was my father at the time. Sometimes I wonder why he didn't say it back then, but now I think it's because he didn't want me to lose him a second time. If I'd known it was him, maybe leaving would have been that much harder."

She trailed a hand through the water of the fountain not meeting Silas's eyes as she talked. She shook the water off her hand and turned back to him, wiping her hand on her skirts. "Anyways, I remember he told me when I arrived that this was my home, and I would travel back and forth. He said"—she screwed up her face trying to remember—"he said there was an evil wizard who was mad at a lot of people, and came up with a spell to trap his enemies in an illusion, but adults take a lot of energy to trap so instead he trapped their children." She met Silas's eyes this time. "He said I traveled from the spell because the spell was weak, and would continue to weaken as we grew older until I broke the spell, and freed all the children who were trapped."

Silas was nodding. "That makes sense in a way with what I read in the amendment."

"I need to read it, I think it will help."

"But you said you aren't able to go into the castle."

"No, but you could sneak the book out of the library."

"Elodie, that's against the rules, I can't do that."

"It's technically my library, isn't it? If I give you permission shouldn't that be enough?"

Silas groaned and stood up, his back as straight as his honor.

"Come onnnn. Please, please, please?" Elodie pulled on his arm till he bent. "You can do it! It'll be super quick!"

He protested a few more times before eventually giving in.

Chapter Twenty-Four

ELODIE KNEW in the end he wouldn't say no to his princess and she stomped on any potential guilt at the manipulation. Silas headed back to the castle, leaving Elodie in a quiet place by the inner gate to the palace grounds. She was just out of sight of anyone standing guard at the gate so she wouldn't be told off for loitering.

Silas was gone for over an hour, and she was bored by the time he returned, a thick book under his cloak.

"Sorry," he said as way of greeting. "I had to wait for the librarian to wander off, and then Oburleck stopped me and asked me to send a message to Sir Jesper." He pulled out the book and sat next to Elodie while he flipped through it. "Here it is." He tapped the page.

Amendment Twenty-Seven.
The titles and inheritance of all Misplaced Children, legally specified before this event, will be held until the Misplaced return as foretold in the prophecy spoken by Wizard Gediminas of the heir to Aluna's termination of the spell.

Elodie reread it three times. "So it says the heir of Aluna would terminate the spell. That's me since my parents never had any other kids."

Silas nodded and opened his mouth to speak. Suddenly he slammed the book closed and slipped it behind Elodie.

"Silas?" Elodie started.

Silas jumped to his feet and stood in front of Elodie blocking her view. Silas bowed and a moment later Elodie realized why.

"Ah, Squire Silas, I thought I saw you come this way," the voice made Elodie's stomach drop. "Did Sir Jesper have a reply for me?"

"No, Steward Oburleck," Silas replied rising from his bow. "He thanked me for passing along the message that you appreciated his opinion in the last council meeting."

Elodie frowned. That wasn't anything that would need a reply. Why would Oburleck follow Silas off the palace grounds for that? Why would he follow Silas at all?

"Thank you, dear child, sorry to interrupt you and your friend." Silas leaned to the side and Elodie suspected he was blocking Oburleck from peering around him. "Will you introduce us?"

Silas slumped slightly. There wasn't a proper way he could rebuff the request. He stepped out of the way and reached out a hand to pull Elodie to her feet.

"Princess Elodie, what a surprise." He bowed, although his features didn't show any surprise. "I wasn't aware Gediminas had returned to the castle."

"Oh, he's not. He's still traveling," Elodie said.

Elodie saw a man over Oburleck's shoulder. He was a tall thin man with nearly white blond hair, and very pale skin. Something about him caught and held Elodie's attention. He waved at her and winked before moving out of sight, almost as if he'd never been there. She looked at Silas, but the squire didn't seem to have noticed.

Oburleck looked puzzled. "Was our Wizard not present when you arrived from the spell?"

Elodie blinked and looked back at the steward. "Oh yes, he

was, he just left me in the care of some friends." She swallowed. She needed to find a way to end this conversation without getting dragged back to the castle.

Oburleck frowned as he looked her over, his eyebrows creasing in concern. "Well, you must come back to the castle with me, Princess. The castle offers you the best protection and care. I don't mean to understand Wizard Gediminas's intentions with abandoning you before journeying to such an unreputable location, but I think we can all agree you would be much better suited by returning to the castle."

Elodie frowned. Did Gedas tell Oburleck and not her where he was going?

The confusion on Elodie's face must have shown for Oburleck continued. "Did Gediminas not inform you as to where he was headed? Oh it's the strangest thing, I heard from a trusted source, that he was seen entering the Tokke mountain range."

This news wasn't as strange as Oburleck seemed to find it. Gedas was likely after some plant or herb that only grew in the higher elevation. Of course, that would be a trip Elodie would have enjoyed, and Gedas said he was going somewhere Elodie would find boring. She dismissed the thought.

"Thank you for your concern, but really I should be going." Elodie bent down and picked up the book, trying to keep it somewhat covered with her skirts. "It was good seeing you, Silas." She moved to dart around Oburleck.

"Just a moment, Princess." Oburleck turned with her. "That wouldn't be a book from the palace library, would it? I would hate to see anything happen to it in the city." He looked to Silas. "Especially if Squire Silas checked this out from the library under his name, we wouldn't want anything to happen to it." He grabbed the thick heavy book out of Elodie's hand and flipped it over. "*An Archival History of the Kingdoms of Sixteen.* Archive books usually aren't permissible to be taken from the library. I would hate to see anyone in trouble over removing this one. Why don't we all return this to the library together and you can continue reading in comfort."

"Actually, I think I'm all done with it, I should really be getting back."

"My lady, it isn't proper for you to walk the city without an escort, I insist—"

"Oh, don't worry, Silas can escort me back. Thanks, Steward Oburleck, for your concern, and for offering to return the book." Elodie grabbed Silas's hand and pulled him away.

Oburleck didn't protest further.

As soon as they were clear of the alley Elodie looked around for the man she'd seen. She wanted to see him again and figure out what it was about him that caught and held her attention. When she didn't see him she started running, pulling Silas along. Thanks to Callie she'd learned well how to lose someone in the city, and while she didn't think Oburleck would send someone after them, it was better safe than sorry.

When they reached the Prole District, they slowed and caught their breath walking toward the edges of the city.

"You won't get in trouble for any of that will you?" Elodie asked.

Silas shrugged. "I think Oburleck has plans for me."

"What do you mean?"

"Nothing specific, but ever since your last trip, he knows we're friends, and seems to go out of his way to notice me. When I passed my page exams he congratulated me and asked if I had made any decisions on my knight master. I told him I had a few offers and was still thinking it over, and he told me I should Squire for Duke Devoss."

Elodie frowned. Devoss was one of Oburleck's big supporters, while Sir Jesper, Silas's current knight master, was known for his occasional opposition of Oburleck. "I think now he's thinking if he can get me on his side, I may give him information or something. He's always asking me questions about Sir Jesper."

"I thought you reveled in Oburleck's leadership," Elodie said, smiling. "Didn't you say once he was amazing?

"I don't think he's a god or anything. He has his own agenda, like every other man on Eres."

When they reached the Odure District Silas was visibly uncomfortable, jumping a little too high over the muck-filled gutters and watching the people around them.

"Do you ever get tired of following orders? Doing what everyone else says to do, and never getting to live your own life?" Elodie asked him.

"Not really."

"Oh, well, then never mind."

"Oh, don't be like that, Elodie. I know what you mean, but I think I handle it differently."

"What do you mean?"

Silas tipped his head back while he walked, gathering his thoughts before he turned to her. "It's about duty and honor. Orders are an integral part of that. You can't escape the orders without losing your honor."

"You know, you would make a pretty good king when you get tired of knighthood," Elodie said.

Silas started laughing. "Well if you're offering."

"Oh," Elodie blushed. "I didn't mean like that."

"My father did say as the eldest of his children I would be expected to make a strategic match, but I'm sure he won't say no if I asked his blessing," Silas said seriously. The edge of his mouth turned up in a smirk.

"Silas!" Elodie exclaimed.

"Yes, obviously we are too young to make things official quite yet, my lady, but don't worry, I will wait for you." Silas lost it then, laughing hard and strong. When the bulk of his laughter was gone, he still had a gleam of mischief in his eyes.

"You are ridiculous." She shoved him with her shoulder.

"Yes, ridiculously in love, Your Highness," he said in a high-pitched voice before shoving her back, not quite as hard.

"Marriage plans aside," he said, his voice serious again. "Here's how I feel about it. I made a vow to start my page training, with the hopes of becoming a knight one day. I say hopes, because it's always possible I could fail, but I know I won't. I can't. It's what I've always wanted to be, and as the some-day Lord of Tate, it's my duty to invest as much as I can into that future. My father won his knight's shield before he gained the title, as did my grandmother before him. It's expected of me, but it's also what I want. To gain a title and to earn respect that has nothing to do with my family, and everything to do with my own accomplishments." He paused as he jumped over unidentified brown sludge in the street. "In order to get to this envisioned future, I have to live the page life, and the squire life, first. That means fetching and bowing and serving, and showing I know what it means to work for something. Yes, I get tired of it. But when I am so sick of it I just want to quit, I stop myself. I take a deep breath, and I remember what I'm working for."

"But don't you ever wish you could skip all the work and *be* a knight already?"

"Sure, if it was possible. But even if it was . . ." He trailed off, trying to pick his words. "Anything worth living for, is also worth sacrificing for. How will I ever be deserving of the title of a knight of your crown, if I can't first spend a few years toiling for it?"

His words made Elodie feel a little guilty, and she thought again that Silas would likely make a much better ruler than she ever could.

"You know what I do?" he said, startling her out of thought. "When I start to wish I could skip a task or a day I don't want to live? I take a deep breath, and I just do whatever is in front of me. I forget about the things I really want, and I just pretend like that task, or class or practice where I don't want to be is the only thing left in the whole world. And then I throw everything I have into it. I don't try to separate myself from the thing I don't want to do, I embrace it."

"It's so hard to do that when I'm in the illusion. It's so hard to commit myself to something I don't even know is real or not."

"But does it matter if it's real? It's real when you're there, right?"

Elodie nodded. "Yes, and then the Twoshy starts to feel like it's the dream." She looked Silas in the eyes. It was hard to imagine thinking he wasn't real when she was standing in front of him.

"We need to break the spell," he said, meeting her eyes with a fierce look.

"Yes, but that's easier said than done. We can't even find out about the prophecy." Elodie threw her hands in the air as they walked, startling seagulls into flight.

"I asked my father and a few other people when it came up. All of them said basically the same thing when pressed. They didn't know the original prophecy, only that the spell would end because of you. I think we probably won't get the specific wording of the prophecy unless we ask someone who was alive back then, like Gediminas."

"But he told me in very clear terms he wouldn't tell me."

"Maybe knowing the wording of the prophecy isn't as important. Maybe we just need to learn more about the spell."

"But neither one of us are mages." Having a bit of magic and being good with plants didn't qualify her to learn about complex spellworking. Gedas never even broached the topic when teaching her since it was so beyond her skills. She may be able to classify as a witch, if Gedas accredited her, but spellcraft was way beyond her reach.

Elodie thought back to the few mages she'd got to know over the years. Gedas said Sorcerer Cosimo was a good man, even if they did always argue.

"Do you think Sorcerer Cosimo would talk to me if I asked? He always goes on about how the sharing of knowledge is the mage's top responsibility."

Silas looked uncomfortable. "He died last winter."

"What?" Elodie's stomach dropped.

"They said he burned up too much power healing during the sickness this winter, so when he caught it himself, he didn't have enough strength to fight."

Elodie covered her face with her hands for a moment, guilt eating away at her chest. Silas put a hand on her shoulder and she shoved away the emotion. She couldn't fix anything until she was no longer trapped by the spell.

"You know, Dess's brother is in Pundica in his fourth year. Maybe I will write him."

"But aren't you going to be busy with your squire training? Roaming the country and rescuing damsels in distress?"

"Fetching things, polishing armor, looking after the horses. Setting up camp and digging latrines? Yes, I will be so busy with the exciting life I'm sure I will forget you the moment you leave, princess." He smirked at her. "Elodie, you're the proper ruler of Aluna, the land I'm dedicating my life to protect. Writing a few letters is the least I can do if it'll help make this kingdom a better place."

They reached the clinic, and Silas asked her three times if she was telling the truth that Gedas had intentionally left her there. "Are you sure you don't want to come back to the castle? Oburleck's breath smells better than this place."

She hit him in the arm as hard as she could. He grinned at her.

"I've been here all summer, it's not that bad, and I get to help people."

Silas nodded, his face serious again. "You're right, I'm sorry. These people probably need your help more than anyone in the castle."

"Will you come by again if you have time?"

"Of course. I will come tomorrow if I can get away."

"Deal."

"I will see you then, Princess." Silas laughed when she shushed him and tried to push him out of his bow. He waited and watched as she went inside and closed the door.

The next afternoon, Elodie went with Callie to the gold

merchant in the Opulent District to drop off some papers from the baron. As they walked, Callie asked Elodie about the illusion and what it was like living there. She told Callie about her home and family, and about Vanessa and going to school every day. She spent a lot of time talking about TV and movies and electricity and cars. She told her what it was like, bouncing between two worlds and always having to forget one so she could live in the other.

"Will you forget me when you go back?" Callie asked softly.

"No. I won't forget you ever, Callie, how could I?" She gave the girl a quick hug. Callie froze when she hugged her, but then hugged Elodie back fiercely before she could pull away. When they broke apart Callie continued walking as though nothing happened.

"Next time I come back to Tross I'll find you at the baron's house and we can have even more adventures. You can even come see what life is really like in the castle if Gedas doesn't try to hide me away again."

"I think I'd like to go there someday," Callie said dreamily.

Elodie frowned. "But you've been to the castle—"

"No, not there. I want to go to your world. In the illusion. I mean, obviously I've been to the castle to deliver messages."

Elodie smiled. "I could see you becoming famous for sure, you would be some great comedian and be on all the comedy shows. Then someday you'd land a spot on a popular TV show and everyone would love you and would know your name. Then you'd start acting in movies and you'd make so much money you'd never have to work another day in your life, but of course you still would, because you love acting so much."

Callie laughed and then made Elodie explain more about movies and acting. Elodie attempted to explain sketch comedies to the girl, as they sat side by side on the edge of a fountain. Women washed laundry on the other side of them, the water splashing up causing a mist around them that caught the light. The mist shining and glittering around her caught her attention for a moment and

Elodie stood up suddenly. It wasn't just the water she saw glinting in the air.

"Ellie, what's wrong?"

Elodie tried to get out a word as the ruakh gripped her up. "Callie—" she started, but then she was pulled to the side, and tumbled, falling through the nothing.

Chapter Twenty-Five

HER KNEES HIT cement and she threw out her hands to brace her fall. It hurt. She shifted till she was sitting on her butt, and sat blinking in the afternoon sun. To her left were the maples and crabapple trees, slowly yellowing for fall. The doors at the end of the walkway opened, and her mother stepped out. "Elodie, are you alright? Did you fall down?"

"Um," She turned her head to look over her shoulder for Callie, but she wasn't there. Elodie was back in the illusion again, where Callie didn't exist. She shook her head to clear it.

Her mom was there in a moment helping her off the ground. She dusted off her clothes, and muttered over her ripped jeans.

"Come on, let's see if Doctor Abernathy has any bandages."

Her knee was bleeding. As soon as she saw it, her nerve endings remembered to do their job, and it stung. Her mother peered at her face, and didn't seem to see what she was looking for. "Did you hit your head, sweetie?"

She started to respond in the common language of the Twoshy, then stopped herself. "I don't think so," Elodie replied, rubbing her head.

Doctor Abernathy did have a first-aid kit and Elodie's mom spent the next few minutes fussing over her daughter and patching up her knee and a few scrapes on her hands. "This is new," her mother commented on the bracelet she wore. Elodie looked down, and smiled, peace and relief washing over her. She hadn't lost Callie's bracelet in the trip back.

Her mother stopped cleaning her hand and Elodie looked up confused. Both Doctor Abernathy and her mother were looking at her.

"Sorry, what?"

"I was asking where you got it, sweetie."

"Oh," Elodie thought for a moment. "Vanessa made it for me." Once she said it, it felt like a good lie, it was the kind of thing Vanessa would make. Lumpy and uneven, in a way that looked totally intentional.

"Elodie, have you been having any coordination issues lately?" Doctor Abernathy asked.

"Last week she had a few dizzy spells, but then she got sick, and it just seemed like maybe it was a twenty-four-hour thing." Her mother sighed and stood up, turning to the doctor. "She's also had some trouble focusing lately." She spoke quietly, not looking at Elodie. "I thought maybe she was just ignoring us, but sometimes she snaps out of it, and it was like she was gone for a moment."

Elodie blinked in surprise. Had she been having so many issues her mom had noticed? She'd felt great in the Twoshy, but her last week of school now felt like forever ago. She tried to think back.

Doctor Abernathy turned to Elodie. "Let's schedule some blood work for tomorrow. If you're still up for it, Elodie, we can still talk for a bit." Elodie nodded and rose from the chair in the lobby. She followed Abernathy into the office on autopilot and sat in the chair in front of his desk. Abernathy paused beside her. "Not taking your usual seat in the window today?"

Elodie looked up and remembered the window seat with the view of the trees, and moved to it. Abernathy rolled his chair over before sitting.

"How has your week been, Elodie?" He asked.

"Um." She really couldn't remember. What day of the week

was it anyways? It was a Tuesday in the Twoshy. Elodie and Callie were going to get sweet rolls after the goldsmiths' guild.

"It was fine," she said at last.

"Would you like to elaborate?"

"Not really," she said with a sigh.

Doctor Abernathy examined her, his eyebrows knit together and she started to remember why she was here, in his office. He was the one who decided if a kid was crazy enough to be sent away. She could kick herself for entering the office. She could have just said she didn't feel well and got out of the session all together. Her stomach sank and she shifted in her seat. She needed a better response.

"Sorry, it was just a boring day. Math, English, just the usual."

"How is your science project doing?"

Elodie couldn't remember what he was talking about, she didn't remember any science homework. She hadn't sat through a science class in months. Her face must have shown the confusion for Abernathy tried to be helpful. "Your magnolia flowers I believe? Have you started testing their tendrils for movement?"

Elodie frowned harder. Magnolia flowers didn't have tendrils and Magnolia trees didn't even grow in this part of the country. The only one she could think of was one Mrs. Franklin planted in her front yard a few houses up from Elodie. It was small and didn't have any blooms on it yet. Tendrils were on climbing plants like sweet peas and morning glories.

"Oh! The morning glories!" Elodie said, remembering the science fair project all at once. "They are good I think, I should probably check on them, they must have gotten tall over the summer," she said mostly to herself. No, that wasn't quite right, as far as the plants knew she'd been gone a day, the plants wouldn't have even sprouted. She looked up at Doctor Abernathy realizing her mistake, and saw him examining her closely.

"Didn't you start your science fair project last week?"

"Yeah, sorry," Elodie covered her face with her hands. "I'm not thinking right, and my knee hurts."

"Do you have trouble thinking right often?"

"Sometimes. Sometimes the fog rolls into my head and I can't think of anything."

"Fog?"

"Yeah, it's like fog when you can't see anything, but I can see, I just can't think."

"And do you feel the fog right now?"

"No." Elodie needed to stop talking. She really really needed to.

"Why don't we call it a day and you can get some rest?"

When they got to the car her mom rooted around in her purse. "Oh, Elodie, do you still have my keys?"

Elodie's stomach shrank and chills ran over her body. She clearly remembered her mom handing them to her so she could put away her backpack. She'd had them when she went to the Twoshy. Where were they now? Had she dropped them? She ran back over to the cement walkway and began looking around.

Please, please, please.

She looked over the ground. Her mother went with her, looking in the gravel on the sides of the path.

After a few minutes of unsuccessful searching, her mom sighed. "Did you double check your pockets?"

Elodie, hands now shaking reached into her front pockets, pulled out a few leaves and a small pinecone. She saw her mother shaking her head as she dropped the plants on the ground. Once the front pockets were empty she stuck her hands in her back pockets, and felt the clink of metal. She sighed with relief and pulled the keys out of her pocket. Her mother sighed as well and took the keys from her daughter.

"Oh good, I was hoping they weren't locked in the car."

Elodie was going to say she was glad they weren't lost in a magical world, but she held her tongue and climbed into her seat. They rode home in silence, Elodie too lost in thought to realize her mother was in the same state.

Healer Beathan was going to teach her a poultice for venomous bites later that night. Would she worry when Elodie didn't come back to the clinic? There was still more work to do. There were always more potions and medicines that needed to be made, and Beathan was shorthanded.

When they got home Elodie fled for her bedroom and pulled out the old beat-up journal she wrote her trips to the Twoshy in. The last time she'd written in it, she'd forgotten some details, like the prophecy and her plans with Silas to break the spell. Now she added in everything she could remember from her conversations with Silas in the market, and then started writing about her days spent with Callie and working in the clinic.

The memories faded faster each moment, like a dream fading where all dreams go, but writing helped. She could read back over her words and then small memories would bloom back into her mind and she could keep writing. She wrote until the memories faded to soft comfortable fuzzy feelings in the back of her mind, and then she closed the journal, hooked her pen in its binding and slid it back into its place on its shelf.

She wanted to curl up on the bed with her journal, flip back to the first few pages she'd started years ago and read through her memories of the Twoshy, but dinner would be soon and that wouldn't put her in the frame of mind she needed for the interview with her parents. Instead, she flopped back onto her bed and closed her eyes, and attempted to take in her surroundings.

The feel of her spring mattress, so different from the low thin straw mattress in the clinic she'd been sleeping on. The smell of her bedding. Fabric softener and that light floral detergent her mother had been trying. It was an artificial smell, not comprised of any real plants. The clean and herby smell of the witch hazel and oregano, mixing with the strong soap used on all bedding in the clinic faded into her memory.

When she'd first entered her room she'd stopped in shock seeing all of the dried leaves and flowers that had covered her walls and hung from her bookshelf were gone. The wave of peace she usually felt was a heavy absence. It took her a while to remember why she'd thrown most of them away, and hidden the rest. She was trying to convince her mom, and her dad, and her doctor that she was normal.

She didn't like remembering her mother's and father's worry, the mocking words of the boys at school. The tight ball that made its home in her gut, and left for a time while she was in the Twoshy, returned with a hard plunk into her stomach.

ON SATURDAY MORNING after breakfast and pills Elodie and her mom went to the doctor's office. She had a brief dizzy spell getting out of the car, and her mom watched her closely with a pinched expression. After Elodie's mom signed a few papers they drew a few vials of blood and Elodie and her mom were free to head to the ice-cream shop to get ice cream in the shape of a clown. It was a long-standing tradition, the sting of needles must be forgotten with clown-shaped ice cream. She might be too old for such things but she didn't protest because the ice cream was sweet and reminded her of memories long ago, back before she started noticing the broken-adopted-kid look in her mom's eyes.

"Mom can I spend the night at Vanessa's house tonight?" Elodie asked as she ate the frosting pom pom off of the clown's cone hat. She wasn't quite sure why but something inside of her told her she missed her friend. Whether the friend she missed was Vanessa or a redhead too far away for her to visit didn't really matter, Elodie didn't want to be alone that night.

"Are you sure you're feeling up to it?"

"Yeah I feel great." Elodie smiled. "Clown cones fix everything."

"Alright, I'm fine with it as long as her parents are, as well."

"Thanks, Mom." She didn't have to call Vanessa's parents to know they would be okay with it, but when they got home she did anyway. Once she had the official approval, Elodie went to her room to pack her things. She emptied her schoolbooks from her backpack and filled it with a change of clothes, pajamas, and the things she would need. As a last thought she tucked her journal into the top of the bag so she would remember what to tell Vanessa when she asked about her trip.

Once downstairs, her mother put a plastic sandwich bag with her pills and a folded piece of paper into her backpack, and they headed to the car.

Vanessa lived on the other side of their small town. Out on the edges where people had large houses on large pieces of land bordered by trees so you couldn't see the neighbors or hear any sounds from the road.

Vanessa's house was big. It had five bedrooms not counting the living room, library and den. One of the bedrooms served as her mother's office, while they had a detached granny unit her father turned into his studio, equipped with a large kiln. Vanessa also had a huge backyard with a lot of unused fields left mostly to their chickens. Elodie and Vanessa would spend hours in the trees around their property building forts or pretending they were adventurers or Elvs living in the trees, and in the summer they would take sleeping bags and sleep on her large trampoline under the stars.

Vanessa's parents believed raising a kid with dirt under her fingernails and twigs in her hair would only add to being a healthy adult.

When they pulled up to the house Vanessa ran out the front door to meet Elodie. "Bye, Mom!" Elodie yelled as the two girls ran inside. They passed Vanessa's mom who was on the way to greet Elodie's mom.

Elodie stopped Vanessa in the hallway. "I traveled again yesterday," she whispered to her friend, trying not to be overheard by her mom.

Vanessa's eyes lit up. "You have to tell me everything! Come on!" The girls ran upstairs to Vanessa's bedroom, laughing as they went. Vanessa's room was large with high ceilings and a loft bed. Her parents let her paint the ceiling over her bed, a bright blue with big clouds swirling through the sky. Dragons of every color flew through the clouds performing aerial acrobatics.

Elodie threw her backpack onto Vanessa's large beanbag, and pulled out her journal before following Vanessa up the ladder onto the bed.

"It's weird you've traveled so much recently, isn't it?" Vanessa asked.

"It definitely feels weird to me."

"What does Gedas think?"

"He hasn't really said anything. I'll ask next time. Although next time will likely be in a few years since I've been gone so much recently."

Vanessa frowned. "That's sad. It's been fun getting so many stories. If you stop traveling for a while I'll have to find something else to entertain myself," she said dramatically, throwing an arm across her forehead as she flopped back on the bed. Elodie laughed and flopped beside her.

"So where did you and Gedas go this time?" Vanessa asked.

"That's the part that was different. This time when Gedas met me, we were just outside of Tross on this big hill overlooking the city. It was early summer and the hill was covered in wildflowers that I fell into."

"Oooooh," Vanessa said and got up. She grabbed a big black book and a cloth bag of colored pencils off the small shelf by the foot of her bed. She sat with her back against the wall and the sketchbook in her lap.

Elodie closed her eyes and continued telling Vanessa everything she remembered about the field and Gedas standing there, the flowers blooming and the look of concern in Gedas's eyes when he told her he was leaving and she would be staying in the city. Vanessa asked questions about the flowers or the sky, and Elodie filled in the details.

She told Vanessa all about the Odure District and the clinic and Healer Beathan, and about Callie and the adventures and time they spent together, even showing Vanessa the bracelet she'd managed to keep. Vanessa asked questions here and there but was quiet when she asked about Callie. The faint scratches of her pencil filled the air. When she got to the part where she'd met Silas in the market Vanessa burst out.

"Silas? Oh I like that one. Is he still a cute annoying little kid?"

Elodie huffed. "I never said he was cute. And no. Now he's our age. He's only an inch shorter than me. Soon he's gonna be taller, and then he'll be an adult and then an old man and die, and I'll still be trapped in this stupid spell." Elodie was silent for a moment, her emotions flooding through and around her, and the looming dread of a future hope that may never be hers.

"Like what happened with Pippa?" Vanessa said after a moment. Her pencil had stilled for a moment in the memory before it continued its scratching.

"Yeah, like Pippa," Elodie said in agreement.

Pippa had been one of the first friends Elodie made when she traveled to the Twoshy the second time. Elodie had been young, six or seven, and Pippa, the granddaughter of the first steward, had been only a year or so older than her. They'd been the best of friends and spent a year running all over the castle. The steward had been old and kind and gave the two girls sweets when they snuck into his office. The next time Elodie saw Pippa, she was a teenager and the coolest person Elodie had ever met. She let Elodie tag along wherever she went, and pretended it was completely normal for Elodie to still be a little girl while she'd aged.

In the way only a little girl can, she believed Pippa was perfect and wanted to be just like her when she grew up. The next time they met, Elodie was a little older, maybe nine, and Pippa had been grown and married. She was probably only seventeen or nineteen but it felt like a world away from Elodie, and the cool maturity Pippa wore made Elodie feel worthless when she'd ridiculed Elodie's youth and childishness.

When she was ten and traveled back again, she found out Pippa had died during childbirth the year before. She remembered looking around her, at a few people she'd known for years who'd all aged, and noted others who should have been there, but had passed on. And then Elodie started to realize the pattern her life would meet as every connection and friendship she made would inevitably outgrow her and leave her behind. Everyone except Gedas, who still looked the same age as the day she'd met him.

She clung to Gedas as the roots that kept her grounded through the chaos her life was becoming.

From then on, Elodie had striven to only make casual friends with the people around her in the Twoshy. She didn't realize it until now she'd failed at this, letting Silas and Callie, and even Eyvi get too close to her.

"So how was Silas?" Vanessa asked trying to bring Elodie back to the present.

"He's a squire now, under Sir Jesper. They'll be leaving in the fall to the northern border, I guess there have been a lot of raiders recently. Did I tell you about the prophecy after I came back last time?"

"No, what prophecy?" Vanessa asked, clearly interested.

Elodie sighed. "I didn't think so, it was one of the first things I forgot." Elodie went on to tell Vanessa all about the prophecy, or the little they knew of it, and the urgency Silas had in feeling like they needed to figure out how to break the spell.

Vanessa's questions got fewer, then stopped all together as Elodie talked of breaking the spell. When Elodie was talking about their run in with Oburleck there were a few soft knocks on Vanessa's door before it swung open and her mom entered.

"Hey girls," her mom said, smiling. Elodie sat up and greeted Vanessa's mom. Rhonda climbed onto the first rung of the ladder so she could see them better and set a platter with a few sandwiches and sliced veggies on the foot of the bed. "I thought you may be getting hungry." She turned and reached down, pulling two juice pouches out of a pocket and set them on the bed by the sandwiches. "What are you two up to today?"

Vanessa flipped back a page, and turned the sketchbook

around and showed her mom her picture. "Elodie traveled to the Twoshy again yesterday and she's been telling me all about it."

"Oh honey that's beautiful. Is that Elodie?" she asked, pointing at the paper.

Vanessa nodded. "Yeah, and that's the wizard Gediminas, and that's the city of Tross. It's the capital of the kingdom Elodie is going to rule someday."

"I love it. It looks magical and lovely. Did you have a good adventure?" she asked Elodie.

Elodie nodded. "I got to spend the summer working in a clinic making medicines."

Rhonda smiled. "That's quite a peculiar adventure, but I'm glad you liked it. You will have to tell us more at dinner." She stepped off the ladder and turned toward the door. "Make sure you two don't stay cooped up in here all day and go enjoy the sunshine," she said before leaving.

"Thanks, Mom!"

"Thanks, Rhonda!"

Elodie grabbed the sketchbook from Vanessa so she could see the drawing. Vanessa was a great artist. Her sketch still looked like a twelve-year-old had done it, but a really talented twelve-year-old with an eye for detail. In it were the backs of a girl who looked like Elodie, and a tall man who looked like a proper wizard with a pointy hat.

"Oh I love it!" Elodie announced. "But Gedas stopped wearing the pointy hat unless it rains," she informed her friend. The two people in the picture were standing on a meadow looking out on a beautiful castle with spires and turrets. Birds flew in the clouds over the castle. It looked nothing like Tross, there was no wooden side of the castle and no uneven patches to the wall that hemed it in, but Elodie liked it all the same. It was what she envisioned a perfect castle to be.

"Yours looks better than the real thing," she told Vanessa before returning the sketchbook. Vanessa flipped back to the next page showing the beginnings of a street and an old lopsided building in the middle of smaller shacks.

"So did Oburleck end up dragging you back to the castle?" Vanessa asked as she continued sketching.

Elodie laughed. "No, he tried but I escaped, and then I traveled back the next day, so he won't even get a chance to find me."

They talked for a while longer, until their sandwiches were gone and Vanessa finished her second sketch. She closed the book with a thump and they climbed down the bunk bed. Once on the ground, another bit of dizzy washed over Elodie, but it passed quickly. The two girls took their lunch leftovers downstairs and went to jump on the trampoline and then play in the woods till dinner.

Vanessa's dad, William, was setting the table when they came in. His arms were damp and clean and he smelled strongly of apple soap. "Hey, Elodie, how's it going?" he asked, giving Vanessa a kiss on the forehead. Elodie saw he had bits of dried brown streaks on his cheek and forehead, and spattered on the sleeves of his shirt. The girls grabbed the silverware and finished setting the table with him.

"I'm good. Did you make anything cool today?" Elodie asked.

William chuckled. "Probably not anything you would see as cool, no. I'm finishing up a sculpture for the museum exhibition opening next month."

Rhonda brought a steaming bowl of rice to the table and set it in the middle before turning to her husband. She laughed in his face and licked her finger before trying to wipe off a few spots of clay. "I thought you said you washed up?" she asked with a smile.

He held up his hands to show her. "Nothing under my finger-nails this time," he said with a grin. He grabbed her head and kissed her.

Elodie looked away and Vanessa mimed throwing up.

When they were finished, Rhonda turned to go back into the kitchen, but stopped. "Elodie, your mom said she put your pills in your backpack for after you eat, can you go grab them for me?"

Elodie nodded and headed up the stairs. She returned and handed the plastic bag to Rhonda before sitting next to Vanessa at the table. They ate Rhonda's chicken curry, chatting about their day. Vanessa told them all about the adventure they had in the trees, and Vanessa's parents asked Elodie questions about her recent travel to the Twoshy, genuinely interested in what she had to say.

Elodie loved Vanessa's parents. They always made her feel wanted and accepted, just like Vanessa.

Elodie stood up from her chair to reach for a napkin in the center of the table and the world took a little spin around her. She sat down hard in her chair.

Vanessa's mom came around the table and was by her side as Elodie's head stopped spinning. "Are you all right Elodie? Are you feeling dizzy? Cynthia did mention she's been having some issues lately," she said to her husband. "Here maybe you should take your pills."

"Right because pills are gonna help."

"Will!" she said sharply.

"She's twelve and just has an active ima—"

"Will!" Rhonda said, even sharper.

"What? All I'm saying is this isn't the kind of thing you should just throw pills at. Cynthia and Frank—"

"Yes," she said cutting off her husband again. "Cynthia and Frank trust us with Elodie and asked us to make sure she gets her pills after dinner."

"I'm okay," Elodie said, hoping they would stop arguing. Her stomach felt sick, but for a different reason. "I was just dizzy for a minute."

Rhonda patted her hand. "If it gets worse let me know and I can call your mom, alright?"

"Thank you, but I'm fine really." Elodie took another bite of her rice to convince them. The table fell into silence as they ate.

"So Elodie," William said trying to continue the conversation after a long awkward silence. "What was your favorite part of your trip to the tushi?"

"It's Twoshy, Dad," Vanessa said, shaking her head at her father.

"I don't know," Elodie said and then paused thinking. "I made a friend when I was there. Callie. She grew up on the streets and she taught me a lot about the city and we had a lot of fun. She's really cool. She has a thing she can do where she can copy the way somebody sounds. Then she almost sounds exactly like them. If she lived here, she would totally be a famous actress someday."

"Too bad she can't live here," Vanessa said in a sarcastic voice that surprised Elodie in its sharpness. She looked at her friend but Vanessa's face looked expressionless as she took a big bite of food and chewed intently.

"So tell me more about this prophecy again?" Rhonda asked.

"Well, I don't know what the prophecy says exactly, but basically it says I will be the one to break the spell keeping me and all of the other Misplaced children stuck here."

Vanessa let out a huff and Elodie excused herself to the bathroom. The tension at the dining table was thick. With Vanessa's parents having argued, and now trying to pretend they hadn't, even Vanessa seemed upset, but Elodie wasn't sure why.

Instead of heading into the bathroom, Elodie walked through the hall to the back door and stepped outside into the cooling evening air. She leaned against the wall of the house, closed her eyes and breathed. She wanted to come to Vanessa's house and escape a little of the tension and frustration she had at home, but now that tension had followed her. Maybe it was all her to begin with.

When she opened her eyes she thought for a moment she saw a firefly. She loved fireflies. They felt like magic, flying through the air, shining bright and looking for love through the darkness. She took a step forward to get a better look.

She should have known better. It was too cold here for fireflies, even in the summer. Instead, the glimmer she'd mistakenly seen came up around her, grabbed her up and pitched her to the side, into the swirling nothing.

Chapter Twenty-Six

THE AIR RUSHED out of her lungs as she collided with something hard and everything went still. It was dark. She panicked she'd gone blind.

Something sharp dug into her shoulder and she rolled over.

Her hands landed in a cold crunchy mix of snow and leaves. She coughed getting air back into her lungs. Faint light glinted around her, firelight reflecting on damp leaves and ice. A soft glow filled the air and a hand grabbed her shoulder helping her sit up. The hand rubbed her back as air returned to her lungs.

"There, slow breaths." Gedas's rich voice comforted her. She looked up into his face, lit by the soft glow of a mage light hanging over his shoulder. She knew she was safe. Gedas threw a cloak over her back wrapping it tightly around her arms. It fought off the chill. When her breathing had slowed Gedas patted her shoulder. "Feel ready to try standing up? I have a nice fire just beyond those trees."

Elodie nodded and accepted Gedas's strong grip to help her stand. Once on her feet, she looked closely at her surroundings. It was true night, the glow of the snow broken up by the dark trunks of trees all around them.

"How long have I been gone?"

"A few months," Gedas said lightly. "It's April."

"April?" Elodie looked above herself to the trees and their leaves, a bright mix of shades of purple with large maroon fruit hanging heavy in the branches. She would have guessed it was harvest season experiencing an early winter. Her sneakers crunched through the thin layer of snow as Gedas led her.

Just beyond a few trees was the glow of a fire. The warmth reached out to Elodie with soft fingers as they approached. The fire was in the middle of a small clearing, free of underbrush with thick branches above keeping it mostly clear of snow. The pit was dug well, lined with rocks embedded in the soil and soot showing years of use. A familiar tent was pitched under a particularly thick-branched tree holding off the snow. Two horses were tied nearby with feed bags, covered in warm blankets. The fire was large and hot.

Elodie sat on the cleared ground in front of a log and moved as close as she could to the flames without wincing.

"It feels way too cold for April." She snapped a long thin twig off of a branch and held it in the fire, allowing it to burn.

"A last-minute winter storm coming up from the mountains." Gedas pulled a glass bottle out of his bag and uncorked it, handing it over to Elodie. Elodie took the bottle and sniffed. It was the detoxing potion.

Elodie drank half the bottle and handed it back to Gedas. "Where are we?"

"In the Variant Forest." He recorked and wrapped the bottle, and stored it in his bag. Next, he pulled out a sturdy clay mug, and began dropping in a few dried herbs from a leather pouch.

"Where?"

"It is a small wood near the village of Lottsin."

"Where?" she asked again, this time starting to get a little impatient. She held the burning stick low in the fire so a cindix resting among the glowing coals could lick the ash off the end.

Gedas took his time. He unhooked the water kettle hung over

the fire and filled the mug with steaming water. "We're about a week's ride south of Tross."

"Oh." There wasn't much south of Tross except for farmlands and small villages before the Tokke mountains. She'd never been quite so far south. "How long will we be here?"

"A few days I think," he replied, handing over the mug.

Elodie wrapped her hands around the warm ceramic. She leaned over the mug and inhaled the steam. Black tea leaves, dried ginger and cinnamon bark. Perfect for a cold night.

"Are you hungry?" he asked.

"No, I just ate dinner."

Gedas nodded and refilled the mug sitting next to his log. "And how long has it been since your time with Healer Beathan in the clinic?"

Elodie paused blowing on her tea and looked at her teacher. "Gedas, that was yesterday for me. I was in the illusion barely a day."

The old man said nothing, blowing to cool his own tea.

"What's happening to me?" She couldn't hide the fear in her voice.

"Nothing has changed, my Gull. The spell you are trapped in is continually in flux. While these recent travels may be unusual for what you've experienced previously, they are not unexpected. There isn't a set pattern. Your travels are, after all, a resulting reverberation of the inevitable breaking of the spell."

"Does that mean the spell might break soon, if the pace is increasing?" Excitement pulsed through her.

Gedas frowned, a sad look on his face. "I do not believe so, child. Your travels are both unpredictable and unprecedented and is not something we can set strict rules against with only the data we have collected. The other Misplaced Children for example do not all travel at the same time as you. Each one of you experiences traveling anomalies on an independent schedule as the ruakh and the spell fluctuate around you."

"But you're saying you don't know. You don't know why I'm

traveling so much, so it's totally possible it's because we are going to break the spell soon, right?"

"You know I cannot make an absolute statement without the necessary data, but I do not believe this is a result pointing to the near ending of the spell."

Elodie's face fell, and disappointment crept over her. She didn't want to let go of the spark of hope she'd seen.

"Why don't you set the wards for us tonight," Gedas asked. "You do remember how?"

"No."

"No? You've forgotten?" His voice was touched with disappointment. "Then maybe this trip will be good practice."

"No, Gedas. I don't want to set the wards." It was something she'd been thinking about in the illusion. It got hard to remember what was acceptable weird and what wasn't. She needed to draw clearer lines for herself in the Twoshy so it wasn't so hard going back and forth. Magic felt too far on the crazy side of things. Knowing about plants was one thing, and knowing their medicinal uses could also be explained away, but using magic, using plants to create a ward . . . It felt like it crossed a line she needed to set for herself.

Magic had proven enough times it wasn't her friend.

Gedas was silent and Elodie kept her eyes on her tea. The cinnamon and ginger warmed her, and the fire was making her face tight with its heat.

"Well we can hold off for tonight then, you should get some rest. Your pack is in the tent with some warmer clothes."

She was relieved he didn't argue. Standing up she resettled on the stump, a more reasonable distance from the flames. "Aren't you going to tell me about the trees first?"

"What about the trees?"

"Everything about the trees. What are they? Why are they in harvest in April when they should still be dormant this far south."

Gedas adjusted in his seat and collected himself. Elodie relaxed. The campfire's glow reflected off sparkling snow and ice to keep the darkness at bay. The purple leaves and trunks of the trees were eerie.

The sounds of the forest were muffled by the snow. It was silent except for the soft pattering of snowfall and the occasional crack and snap of a tree limb under the weight of snow.

It was spooky and peaceful.

"These are variant trees, a magicity of sixteen." Gedas set down his mug and stood, walking to a nearby branch hanging low with the weight of ripened fruit. He twisted one of the purple fruit off the branch and walked back to his place by the fire.

"A variant tree is one of the most magically potent plants in the Twoshy. It relies on ruakh for nourishment more than it does the sun." The old wizard held the fruit up before him and brushed off ice and snow. "Being that the winter solstice is the point of peak energy in the world, this tree experiences its renewed growth in the dead of winter. Come the end of spring its leaves will begin to fall off, and in summer it will appear dead in hibernation. Next fall, the tree will spring to life and begin blooming again."

Gedas took his eating knife out of his pack and cut the fruit into slices like an apple. Taking care to cut out the core, he handed a piece to Elodie.

She took it hesitantly, afraid it would unleash some magical event inside of her.

"Don't worry yourself, the fruit has no extra properties other than being delicious and filling your stomach."

Elodie took a small bite and looked at Gedas, shocked. For the temperature of the air, Elodie expected the fruit to be frozen, but it was cold and crisp and very refreshing. "It tastes like pineapple! Only, creamier like a banana."

Gedas chuckled. He continued carving the fruit, handing pieces to Elodie and eating slices himself. He set the core carefully on his stump. "We will stay in this forest for the next week or so, long enough to let the storm pass, and harvest some seeds. They are very valuable for boosting the potency of potions and spells."

"Why have I never heard of it before? If it's a sixteen on the magic scale I would think it would come up at some point. Is it native to the Tokke mountains?"

"Indeed it is not. It's not native to this continent at all, but instead grows in the forests of Pecraetho far to the west across the Mimor sea." Gedas took a moment to refill their mugs and Elodie settled in feeling a story approaching.

"This region was once home to a great wizard named Cymberlin. He traveled all over Eres in his long life, but eventually came to rest here. With him he carried twelve seeds from a variant tree he encountered in his travels. He planted the seeds so he would be able to harvest the fruit for his own purposes. The trees took to the region better than planned and expanded into a forest that stretches like an arm twenty leagues to the coast.

"Cymberlin was renowned for his strong and powerful potions throughout the land, but the secret to his success or why the same recipe did not prove as potent for another maker was never discovered."

Elodie decided not to mention that if no one ever found out the secret then Gedas wouldn't be telling her this now. She ate another piece of fruit instead of commenting.

"Today, this grove is thought to have sweet fruit and little else to offer. In truth, incorrect knowledge passed down from under-qualified mages, to hedgewitches, to uneducated peasants has given these trees a bit of superstition that keeps people away and leaves the uneaten fruit to waste." Gedas paused to eat another piece of fruit and scratched his thick beard before continuing.

"It is even commonly believed a magical creature guards these trees from intruders. If someone were to take the fruit unworthily, it would pounce and take retribution from their flesh."

Elodie set down the piece of fruit she was eating.

"Completely preposterous of course. As we well-educated know, there are several breeds of animals that respond more sensitively to ruakh, but they are not all-powerful sentient guardians of a magical tree."

"But there are parts of this world even you don't know everything about. How can you say there isn't some creature guarding this tree?"

She looked around the brightly colored leaves, the growing darkness made the purple look black. A small point of fear grew in the back of her head, but Gedas laughed.

"Because, my Gull, as you can see we are now eating this fruit and our flesh is still very much intact." The wizard continued eating.

The trees overhead began to rustle softly and Elodie jumped as snow trickled down from the trees around them. Gedas laughed loudly. A small breeze had picked up, nothing was about to pounce from above.

"And on that note, I think it's time for bed."

ELODIE AWOKE EARLY the next morning. She lay in her bedroll running her finger through the chilly condensation collecting on the wall of the tent. After a few minutes of timing her movements to Gedas's loud snores, Elodie tucked her arm back under her blanket. The air was cold, but not as cold as it would be outside the canvas. She had to pee, but she didn't want to get up and brave the cold. She closed her eyes and tried to will herself back to sleep but Gedas's snores and the pressure on her bladder worked against her.

Frustrated, Elodie tore open her bedroll and flinched at the shock of cold. She pulled her jeans on over the thick leggings she'd worn to bed and added a second set of socks before pulling on the boots Gedas brought. She added a second shirt and a thick sweater before pulling on the fur-lined cloak and gloves and moved to the entrance of the tent. She opened the flap and dug her face into the collar of the cloak as the cold air bit into her.

She made sure the flap was closed behind her so as not to freeze Gedas out, and wasted no time heading over to the far side of the clearing where Gedas had dug the latrine. She felt the small tingle of the wards Gedas had set as she exited them.

Peeing outside in winter was not an experience Elodie enjoyed, and by the time she was done she was very much awake. Instead of retreating back into the tent, she built the fire and wandered the edge of the clearing. In the daylight the trees were startlingly vibrant and every shade of purple. The bark was nearly black and the overripe fruit falling onto the snow around the trees left a gruesome mess of vibrant burgundy. Purple tracks showed some forest animals had enjoyed the fruit overnight. Even Elodie's fingertips had been stained purple.

Elodie walked around the clearing, enjoying the muffled peace only a snow cover could provide. The distant creaks of the trees contrasted to the light *fwump* of snow falling off branches onto more snow. She felt peace here in this strange forest. She didn't mind the dusting of snow that covered her as it fell from the trees above.

The cooling fall night and the tension with Vanessa's family felt a lifetime away.

Something reached out to her in the morning air. Goosebumps that had nothing to do with the cold raced up her arms as she felt a presence move past and around her. It was warmth and life and joy and love, and it called to a deep part of her.

She pulled away from the strangeness and moved quickly back to the fire.

Gedas was stirring in the tent. Elodie hooked the kettle over the fire and let the familiar warmth of the flames wash over her. She watched the cindix sleeping in the embers.

By the time Gedas emerged from the tent and finished complaining about stiff joints and cold weather, Elodie was sipping her mug of tea and had convinced herself the strangeness had been imagined.

Chapter Twenty-Seven

THEY SPENT a little over a week in the Variant Forest harvesting seeds. Snow and ice coated some of the fruit, causing a hard layer that had to be cracked before it could be sliced. Elodie's fingers were stained purple and frozen solid.

Every meal they ate included fruit, and Elodie didn't grow tired of it. Gedas surprised her when he explained the flat and wide contraption leaning against the stones of the fire pit was a dehydrator. They kept it full all week, rotating frequently to preserve as much fruit as they could manage.

Elodie liked the fruit dry nearly as much as she liked it fresh.

While they worked, Gedas explained the different preparations for the seeds, when they were best used fresh or dried, whole or ground. Each day they took turns caring for the horses or cooking the meals, falling into the comfortable rhythm they'd developed over years of traveling.

When they left the forest, saddlebags filled with dehydrated and fresh fruit, they traveled east with no clear destination in mind. The Tokke mountains stayed in view to their right but they didn't approach the foothills.

Elodie started to wonder more about Gedas's trip into the mountains as mentioned by Oburleck. In the past she'd never hesitated to ask her teacher a question, but the dread of his refusal was enough to keep her quiet.

Gedas set the direction but was hedgie and vague in answers of his destination or how long they'd be on the road. Each night Gedas asked Elodie to set the wards, and each night Elodie refused. They stayed in every village they passed, and as usual, Gedas was known everywhere they went. He wasn't known as the wizard Gediminas, but instead was greeted as a familiar traveler, fellow researcher or mage. He helped hedgewitches with their work or traded news with farmers, and every day he taught Elodie something new about the world. Sometimes they would stop for a day to help an illusionist stock up on cures, a farmer with a sick animal, or a charmer perfect a spell.

Aside from the daily tension when she refused to set the wards, this trip was just like many others they'd taken over the years and she figured it would end with their arrival at some old rich man's house pursuing an ancient library.

They entered a trading post several weeks into their journey. It was a small village like any other with travelers taking a moment to stop among others for an afternoon or night of trade and community.

To Elodie's shock and delight, they encountered two Avimen passing through the region. Elodie knew stories of the birdlike people who lived high in the mountains, but they were well known for their distrust of Hu. She'd never seen one outside a tale.

After her ancestors slaughtered the Elvmen, took their land, and drove the Dwarvmen away to the lands south of the mountains, it was natural for the fourth race of man to keep their distance.

The male and female Avi were beautiful and Elodie tried not to get caught staring. While it warmed up after the storm passed, the weather was still seasonally cold but the two Avi seemed impervious. The woman had light pale skin and brilliant blue feathers that gleamed iridescent in the sun. The feathers covered her as would a Human's hair, small feathers brushing out high on her cheekbones and long feathers cascading down from the crown of her head. Her forearms were mostly pale skin with feathers starting near her elbows traveling up her arms and disappearing into the light airy tunic she wore under a few pieces of armor. Her breeches ended at the calves to reveal feathered legs ending in talon-tipped feet built for climbing. She had two large swords strapped to her back and a dagger at her waist.

There was a calm peace about her as she walked through the trading post, ignoring the gaze of every Hu. The man who walked with her had soft brown skin and orange-yellow feathers. He was clad similarly in a mix of light clothes and scattered armor and had a large bow peeking over his shoulder. He seemed more aware than the woman, looking around himself constantly.

Gedas didn't openly acknowledge the Avi. Elodie tried to keep them in the corner of her eye but got distracted looking over an herb seller's stock. When she looked up again, the Avi had made their way to the same booth. Gedas greeted them in a language the translation spell Elodie had been given years ago clearly didn't contain. The woman's eyes rose in surprise at Gedas and she returned a greeting.

After they exchanged a few words the woman switched to the common language.

"I feel rude conversing so your companion cannot understand," she said, nodding to Elodie before returning back to Gedas. Her accent was subtle, only a slight clipping of her vowels. "We have several beautiful finds to share with those trading at the right price."

Gedas rooted in his shoulder bag and startled Elodie when he removed one of the small leather pouches of variant seeds they collected. They harvested many plants over their journey and Gedas frequently traded these for supplies as they went, but he told her the seeds were too valuable to be sold.

He opened the pack and removed one seed, handing it over to the woman. She took it with careful fingers, her expression neutral. Her companions' face however revealed recognition and shock over the seed. The woman sniffed the seed carefully before handing it back. "We would be delighted to bargain."

As if on cue, the man pulled a thick piece of folded leather out of his bag and unfolded it to reveal a collection of stones held to the leather with small straps. Most of the stones looked like large crystals with a few opals of varying kinds mixed in. Each stone was raw and unpolished, cut just enough to hint at their treasure. Elodie knew only the basics of stones and their magical uses, losing interest in things that had never been alive. The cutting and shaping of the stone was crucial for the effectiveness of the magic. High-quality stones were sold uncut.

Gedas looked over the stones with mild interest. "A very fine collection, although I am looking for something a little rarer." The man refolded the leather and put it back into his bag. The woman instead removed a smaller leather pouch and opened it to reveal brilliant opals and some rarer precious stones. One looked like a large ruby and another maybe an emerald.

Gedas leaned back on his heels crossing his arms. "I am willing to part with more than a few seeds for a unique piece if you have it."

The woman nodded to the man and he reached into the edge of his armor and pulled out a pouch. Opening it he slid a large boring stone onto his hand. When he turned it over the face was a vibrant and brilliant opal running through the veins of what looked like—

"Wood! That looks like wood," Elodie said.

"Very sharp, young one." The woman looked her over. "This is opalized wood. A very rare type of fossilized wood." The woman took the stone from her companion and held it lower for Elodie to get a good look. "Touch it. You can feel the power of such a stone forged through time and pressure."

Elodie reached out and ran her finger lightly over the opal outlining the growth rings. Strength pulsed within the forgotten wood. A spark of the Aviwoman's yellow magic jumped from the rock to Elodie's finger. When she lifted her hand away she looked up and saw the woman examining her closely. The woman lifted the stone away and turned to Gedas.

They spoke in the Aviwoman's language, the woman gesturing to Elodie. After a few tense moments the argument ended. The woman presented the stone to Gedas for a closer inspection, and then the bargaining resumed in the common language as though nothing happened.

Gedas traded a pouch and a half of seeds for the stone, and when they were finished with the trade, the woman turned to Elodie and handed her a small stone nearly the size of her thumbnail. It was a polished piece of opalized wood, small and streaked through with blue fire.

"It is too small a piece to be of much value, but perhaps it will bring you good luck."

Elodie doubted the stone was worthless but thanked the woman for the beautiful gift, giving her a deep bow of respect. With the trade complete, Gedas bowed to the two Avi. It was a strange but elegant bow with arms stretched out to either side, and the Avi returned the bow with beautiful grace.

That night they shared a campfire with some of the other travelers and the Avi. As was customary at such gatherings, each party told a tale. Gedas, who frequently enjoyed putting Elodie in 'growth opportunities' left the tale to her, and she retold a story from one of her favorite books about a girl who could talk to animals and whose father was a god.

When everyone but the Avi had spoken, most of the travelers turned toward their campsites, but the woman spoke. "We thank you all for sharing your fire and your stories with us, and feel it would only be right for us to share as well."

She paused while the travelers shook off their surprise and refocused. None would expect an Avi, an outsider, to trust Hu with one of their tales. Excitement raced through Elodie. She knew how rare a moment this would be.

The Avi woman started with the traditional words. "Gather in close while I tell you the tale of the mountains." As always, when the words were spoken, Elodie felt the ruakh rise up around the collective group and catch them into the tale.

"The mountains are older than those who walk above them, and those who live beneath. They were here before us, and they will be here long after we are gone." Memories of the mountains began to flow through Elodie's mind, carried from the mind of the Aviwoman.

Crisp air burned in her lungs as she approached the foothills. The mountains filled the skyline, and looked artificial, as though painted onto the sky. Blue, purple, and gray through the hazy mist.

The hard stone of the mountain was a comforting weight under her talons as she perched on a rock face. Looking out on a village below, peace flooded her as the Avi went about their day, raising their children and caring for the animals they shared the mountains with.

She traveled through the memories down to a valley with a fortress set into the side of a cliff. She led a mountain goat loaded with rare supplies past the guards at the gate, down into the mountain passing Dwarvmen and women.

"While now they are called Tokke by the Hu of the land, for generations they have been known as Home, Domicile, Roost and Sanctuary. The mountains are sacred for their ability to isolate and protect."

The mountain rose around them, strength and safety in the stone.

Elodie felt the Aviwoman's gaze shift. Her focus narrowed in on her through the magic, yellow fire surrounding her. The memories flowing through all those entwined in the tale seemed to shift away from Elodie until she was alone, isolated in a memory only for her.

"Many have found sanctuary and peace in the mountains when the rest of the world has threatened or shunned them."

Elodie saw the face of a dark-haired man, pain and hurt in his gray eyes, replaced by hate and rage as he left a room full of people.

"In much the way of my own people, the derelict have flocked to the mountains to live out a separate life from their fears, their enemies, and even their own fate."

The man climbed a mountain path, cloak pulled tightly around him and a bulging pack on his back. His walking staff was a gnarled wooden rod.

"While one may hide from their destiny in the mountains, another may find it and break the chains that keep them separate from the world."

Elodie saw a cliff face shaped like the outstretched wing of a bat, and far to the base of the cliff was a cave with a glowing energy radiating out. The light stretched far from the cave, reaching its fingers across the country. One long tendril found its way to Elodie and wrapped tightly around her, pulling her into darkness.

Elodie felt the focus and attention of the Aviwoman shift away from her, and like a release of pressure the memories that flowed through her shifted again until she could feel the collective group in the tale again. The cave and the face of the stranger faded.

Men and women of every race flashed before her, each one making a home in the mountains for themselves.

"Do not enter the mountains unprepared for only trouble and harsh elements will be found. They are home to many who will protect them unto death."

The Avi woman finished her tale, and the magic left the gathering, dissipating into the night air.

LATER, in their own tent, warded from the other travelers, Elodie thought back to the Avi tale. It wasn't a story in the traditional sense, but it carried a warning on its edges Elodie couldn't place. She wanted to ask Gedas about what she'd felt when the woman's focus was only on her but telling anyone felt like a betrayal of trust.

The next morning as they readied the horses to continue their journey Elodie handed Gedas the small piece of opalized wood.

He looked at her, eyebrows raised in surprise. "Do you not like it? The chief was very gracious in her gift. That type of generosity is rarely shown to one outside their flock."

"She was a chief?"

"Yes, the leader of her flock. The embroidery in their tunics tell the stories of their accomplishments if you can read them."

Elodie wished she'd known that when she could have studied the two Avi's tunics. She sighed at the missed opportunity.

"I love it. The stone is beautiful, and I can feel the magic in it, so it must be valuable. But that's the problem isn't it? I don't want to lose it the next time I travel back into the spell."

He took the stone from her and tucked it into an inside pocket. "Fine, I will hang onto it until you can keep it safely."

"When will that be?" She didn't expect an answer, but after she said it a fire lit in her heart. "Do you even know?"

"No, my Gull, no one can know the future."

"Yes they can, isn't that the whole point of a prophecy? And weren't you the one who told my father it would happen?"

"I told you that was not something you should think on. It will do no good to dwell on words from the past."

"Why Gedas? You've told people before. It's in the freaking Constitution of Sixteen so clearly the council thought it important enough to be remembered. You told my father, you told the council of sixteen, but you won't tell me? I don't even know anything about the spell. I don't know who cast it and I don't know how it was made. You teach me about plants and trees but nothing that will let me free myself!"

"Now you would like me to teach you advanced magic? After weeks of refusing to practice the most basic of protection spells? How shall I teach you advanced magical theory when you are too immature to practice the skills you have?"

"If I'm so immature, why do you even bother with me?"

"Sometimes I'm not entirely sure, Princess."

That stung. Gedas always treated titles as a thing to mock, or a tool to keep distance. Elodie tightened the saddle on her horse and walked away to get the last of her bags.

It was the last words spoken between them for two weeks when they camped on the edge of a plateau filled with flowering bear grass. The tall stalks topped with an explosion of tiny white flowers dotted the view as far as she could see.

Her anger burned hot for a while before dying down to a deep ache that went with her everywhere.

She was building a fire, adding sticks to the growing flames when the ruakh grabbed her up. Gedas turned to her as the world started to fade away, a sad look in his gray eyes.

"Go in peace, my Gull," he said, just before Elodie was thrown to the left and tumbled through an infinite nothing, the pain in those eyes radiating through her chest.

Chapter Twenty-Eight

ELODIE LANDED on all fours on the boards. The wood below her made a *thunk* as she hit and her hands and knees burned with the force. Her hands were covered in the bandage her mother put on weeks ago when she'd last returned from the Twoshy. She was back in the illusion.

Elodie rolled onto her butt and scooted till the rough siding of the house was against her back. She rubbed her sore knee and leaned her head against the wall. She felt a sharp sense of injustice she'd been spat back into the illusion and the spell had reopened the wounds on her hands.

She took a moment to let the world stop spinning. It was dark, and the air smelled like decomposing leaves. It had been spring just a moment ago, the scent of wildflowers and pollen on the air.

She was sitting on the back deck of Vanessa's house. They'd been having dinner and Vanessa's parents had been arguing. She leaned her head against the wall and just breathed. Her mind was a jumble, but she needed to get back before she was missed.

When she felt ready, she stood up using the wall for balance. The wood of the deck was cold, and the rough spots caught on her socks. Elodie looked down. She didn't have any shoes on. She didn't even have her boots from the Twoshy. She was wearing her normal shirt and pants, but her socks were the thick wool ones she'd worn with her boots.

Elodie sighed. Just another day stuck in an illusion.

There was nothing she could do. She opened the back door and walked inside.

"Dad is that you?" Vanessa turned down the hall toward Elodie. She stopped and crossed her arms in front of her chest. "Where were you?"

"I was in the Twoshy. I never disappear this often, it's so weird," Elodie said, a hand rubbing her face.

"My parents are so upset." Vanessa's voice was sharp and angry. "They thought you ran away from them! They had to call your mom. Do you know how much trouble they could get in if something happened to you while you're here?"

"It's not my fault, I didn't do it on purpose," Elodie said, confused with Vanessa's anger.

"No, it's never your fault, is it? You just get to go off on adventures and leave everyone behind to pick up the pieces. You think we're just some spell you're stuck in, but we don't stop existing when you leave."

Elodie shook her head, her friend had it all wrong. "You don't know what it's like, Vanessa. You're not a part of this. I'm the one getting my life ripped in half every few days. You can't understand what that's like."

A look of pain crossed Vanessa's face. "You said it yourself, you never disappear this often, Elodie," she said quietly.

"Are you saying you don't believe me?"

"I'm just saying it sounds a little convenient." The anger was back in her voice and it hurt.

"It's not convenient," Elodie said, rubbing her head. "It's really annoying."

"So you don't like the attention then? Everyone worried about you when you get back, everyone listening to your stories? Elodie, you said it yourself. You've never traveled this many times in such a short time."

Elodie didn't know what to say. Vanessa always believed her, why was she saying this now?

Vanessa turned toward the inside of the house. "Found her!" Vanessa yelled. She turned back to Elodie. "Better get your lies together quick," she said in a soft whisper before turning her back on her friend. A moment later Rhonda entered the room trailed by Elodie's mom. Vanessa walked out the back door of the house, yelling for her dad.

The two women surrounded Elodie looking her over and asking her question after question. She started to say exactly where she'd been, but then stopped herself and said nothing at all.

Vanessa was sent to retrieve Elodie's backpack and things from her room as Elodie ignored questions about where her shoes went.

"I don't know," was all Elodie would say. Vanessa didn't say goodbye as her mom loaded her up in the car.

As soon as they pulled out of the long driveway Elodie's mom turned her head and looked at Elodie. "What happened, honey? I promise you won't be in trouble if you tell me."

Elodie let the silence stretch between them. She wouldn't respond, she couldn't. If she tried to make the lie too complicated her mom would know. So she fought the need to fill the silence and looked out the window.

She wanted to hide until she felt more grounded. She needed to think, get back into the swing of the lies.

"Did anyone touch you, honey?" her mom asked softly.

"No! Mom, no. Nothing like that."

Her mom sighed. "You can tell me. Whatever it is, sweetie. I'm here for you."

Elodie shook her head and turned back to the window. Her mom asked a few more questions which Elodie ignored as they drove.

When they got home, Elodie shouldered her backpack and

headed straight for the stairs. The phone rang and Elodie paused on the first step to hear who it was.

"Rhonda, yes, did you find her shoes?" Silence as her mom listened. "Her pills. Right. No you can just toss them. Yes, her results came back. The doctor thinks they may have been causing her dizzy spells. Thank you, Rhonda. Have a good night."

Her mom hung up the phone and Elodie climbed the stairs quietly.

Something inside of her broke as she took each step toward her room. With the door closed behind her she set down her bag, and lay down on her bed and cried.

She wasn't sure what she was crying for at first. Anger, guilt, frustration and confusion at both Gedas and Vanessa? The two people she trusted the most in any world.

It felt like nothing Elodie did was enough, like her life would never be whole. No matter what she did or how hard she worked, she would never make any progress, or get any older. She would always be alone.

When the tears stopped falling and she was left with a sad calmness, she got up from her bed and grabbed her journal from her backpack. She started writing down everything she could remember from her trip. The variant trees, the sweetness of the fruit. The direction they'd traveled and the meeting with the Avi. She wrote about the tale the Avi chief told, and the strangeness in the memories shared. She wrote about her argument with Gedas.

When she finished, she wished again for someone to talk to. She turned to a new page and wrote.

Dear no one,

I remember what you told me, about just doing what's in front of me, and putting my all into it, but I think that's the problem. Here I can only sit on my hands, and my heart, and my tongue. How can I put my all into doing nothing? I feel like I'm waiting for my life to start while everyone else is moving around me.

Will I ever be free to live in just one world? And if I do finally get free of this illusion, will I have to say goodbye to my life here? These people feel real, how can they not be real? Does anything I do here matter if it isn't real?

I just want to close my eyes and wake up ten years from now with everything figured out. I just want to sleep and not wake up for three months. Maybe I can work on putting my all into sleeping.

Chapter Twenty-Nine

A LARGE PART of her hoped Gedas was wrong when he said he believed her travels happening so frequently was not due to the spell being broken soon. She hoped and hoped she would keep traveling even more frequently until she was finally free.

She was sad, a part of her knowing this would mean she would never see Vanessa and her family again. She didn't hate her mom and dad. She wasn't quite sure how to show it, but she loved them.

Another part of her that she tried to forget was still mad and bitter with the injustice of being thought a liar and would be happy never to see any of them again.

As the first few days after her return passed without any travels, the hope inside of Elodie began to shrink. After the first few weeks it grew even smaller, and after a month passed, a month of not talking to Vanessa, a month of avoiding her therapist's questions, a month of silence between her and her parents, she started to lose hope all together.

When she wasn't at school she was at home, in her room or in the garage taking care of her plants. The morning glories sprouted and grew long enough with a sun lamp that she could start the next step in her experiment. This involved touching the vines of the morning glory in the same spot with a pencil at the same time each day, each plant on a slightly different schedule.

The project required specific planning and a very regimented schedule. In the end it was good that she and Vanessa weren't talking, so she didn't have any distractions making her miss the scheduled times for her experiment.

She found the days went by easier when she didn't think about the Twoshy or write letters in her journal to no one. Some days she went the entire day without speaking a word until she was home from school and forced to say something to her mom or dad to keep them quiet and happy. She found her silence at the end of her trip with Gedas had been good practice for her silent months back in the spell.

Doctor Abernathy's line of questioning shifted subtly from questions asking her about being anxious or nervous. Now he asked her about her energy level, her sleep and her happiness. Elodie found she had an easier time shrugging his questions off. Everyone was sad sometimes, it was normal. Especially normal for a teenager, as everyone was so frequently saying out of her ear shot.

She was just getting started early.

Being labeled a moody antisocial teenager was a lot easier than coming up with lies, and she found the longer she evaded her parents' questioning the less they asked. Eventually dinners were spent with neither one addressing her directly, talking as if she wasn't even there. It was so much easier than the alternative. The lying and pretending everything was fine, everything was normal.

She'd redefined her normal, and everyone was accepting it in stride.

When you're in seventh grade, and your best friend isn't talking to you, two months of silence feel like the end of hope in your world. Elodie didn't even have the fog her pills had caused to escape into and pass her day. Vanessa was never rude to Elodie when they encountered each other in their day, they just didn't talk. There were still a few times when other kids started picking on Elodie, Vanessa would step in and make the kid back down. She never spoke to Elodie directly, but sometimes they made eye contact.

Vanessa's gaze showed pain and regret and sadness. Elodie wished she knew how to fix things. Her loneliness would smother her anger long enough for her to want to apologize, but then when she thought about doing it, she wouldn't know what to say and what exactly to apologize for. Then her anger at Vanessa for not believing her would return, and she wouldn't say anything, letting the moment pass.

Elodie entered her Math class, head down, and made her way to her desk.

"Elodie, note for you," Mrs. Davis called from the front of the room.

She looked up and saw the teacher holding a small note out.

Elodie turned, halfway down the aisle. The small confined spaces between the desks, mixed with oncoming students made Elodie feel like she took up too much room.

Jackson stood at his desk, blocking her way with his backpack perched on his seat as he rifled through it. She stood there patiently, eyes down waiting for him to sit so she could get by. After too many seconds he turned and acted shocked and surprised to see her.

"Sorry, Harpy, go ahead and squeeze by." He leaned in with a wicked smile on his face.

Jackson was thin, and Elodie was not. Even without her backpack she wouldn't have tried to move past him in the narrow aisle of the desks. She sighed heavily and waited, her face getting hot. The teacher, noticing an issue, picked the note back up off her desk and handed it to Elodie in the aisle before turning to another student.

"Oh no, have an emergency crazy appointment you have to get to?" Jackson asked as Elodie was about to open the note. She kept it folded and turned back to her desk instead. "How much longer till they cart you off to crazyville anyways?" he asked loudly as she stepped over backpacks and jackets. Only a few kids snickered.

The second bell rang as she slid into her seat. Everyone who wasn't already doing so sat down and pulled out their books and binders as the teacher started talking.

Elodie unfolded the note, it was from one of the office secretaries just letting her know her mom had a work emergency and she needed to walk home. Elodie tucked the note into her backpack and pulled out her work. She walked home often enough when her mom had appointments. Lately she enjoyed the peace of the trip.

AFTER SCHOOL ELODIE WALKED HOME, opting for the slightly longer route that would take her out of the path of the school buses and most kids driving home. She'd learned kids could be just as mean driving past with their parents as they were at school.

It was a few miles from school to home, mostly downhill. She walked along the main road, a two-lane road where people drove faster than the posted signs and kicked exhaust and dust into the air.

The walk gave her time to clear her head or escape into a daydream after a long day at school, but today she couldn't find escape from her mind.

She felt heavy and tired. So many thoughts ran through that she couldn't put them together or sort them out. Everything was too much. She was out in the open, but she felt stuck in a closet or a cave and the air was stale and dead, and the walls were closing in.

No imaginary world could offer an escape from the life she was stuck in. Other fantasy worlds were so picturesque in movies and books. They had their dangers, but the excitement and adventure always outweighed the bad. In contrast, Elodie's magical world was smelly and falling apart, both literally and metaphorically.

There was nothing idealistic about Tross.

Her path took her down the sidewalk across the street from the ice-cream parlor. The brightly colored building reminded Elodie of the Twoshy, and her first trip through the glitter under the table. She pushed the bittersweet memories away.

A teenage girl wearing jeans and a hoodie stood outside the shop looking bored. The door swung open and a man emerged carrying two clown cones.

Elodie blinked.

It was Doctor Abernathy.

Elodie could hardly believe it. If she thought about it, he must eat food, and go to stores like a normal person, but it was weird to see Abernathy out of the office. Like seeing a dog walk on its hind legs.

He attempted to hand one clown cone to the girl who rolled her eyes hands on her hips. He said something with a big grin, lifting his arms and the clowns into the air before dropping them down and waving them before the girl. The girl cracked a smile and grabbed the ice cream. Abernathy, smiling wide, threw his arm around the girl and walked down the sidewalk licking his blue ice-cream clown.

Something ached inside of Elodie, and she turned away from her doctor and his daughter. She knew Abernathy had a daughter. She'd seen a picture on his desk once, but for some reason she always imagined he would be stiff and questioning with her like he was in Elodie's appointments. It was weird to think of him as a normal person, a normal dad. Well, he wasn't a dad like her dad. Her dad would never eat blue ice cream, or make a scene on the sidewalk, but Vanessa's dad was like that. Playful and maybe a little goofy just to put a smile on his daughter's face. Sometimes Gedas was like that too.

When she got home she grabbed a snack from the kitchen and headed to her room to work on her homework. Ten minutes before she needed to check her plants, Elodie closed her math book and made her way downstairs. Her mom was in the kitchen working on dinner.

"Hi cupcake, how was school?" her mom asked in a chipper voice.

"Fine." It was the first thing she'd said all day. She shrugged off the thought and closed the garage door behind her.

On the side of the room, next to the two large windows letting in the daytime sun, her dad had set up a long folding table, covered in a vinyl tablecloth. On it she had a drain pan and twelve morning glory plants growing in two rows. Clotheslines stretched above to hold the stems without any external pressure where she was trying to grow the tendrils. A sunlamp was perched on the windowsill above the plants to help them grow indoors.

If their growth was doing better than a girl with no plant magic could have managed, Elodie didn't know. In moments when the ruakh was close, glinting in the air, she may have enough magic to influence the plants, but mostly, Elodie was magically benign in this world. She attributed the morning glories' growth success to the sunlamp.

Elodie looked at the clock above the table. Eight minutes. She opened her notebook and turned to the chart where she tracked what plants needed to be tapped on what days.

The theory said if the same spot on a stem had pressure applied to it over a long enough period, the stem would grow a tendril to climb the object applying pressure. Elodie's experiment was to see if changing the frequency of the pressure had any effect in the rate of growth. She had six sets of two flowers, each labeled with a letter so she couldn't get them confused. The first set was never touched, to act as a control, while the second set was tapped daily, the third tapped every other day, and so on. She'd worked out a calendar in her book so she knew which ones were due each day. Today would be pairs B, D and E.

She looked up at the clock again. Six minutes to go.

She was determined to be scientific and precise on this. Magic wasn't normal and wasn't healthy, but science was natural.

Elodie could feel the flowers around her, growing out of season but content in the warm light. They radiated a feeling of peace and contentment, mixed with the innate gift of joy and brightness they possessed. She pushed the feeling away. Feeling a plant wasn't normal. She looked at the clock again.

Three minutes.

She closed her eyes and took a deep breath and let it out sharply as the ruakh caught her up and shoved her to the left. She lost her connection completely with the morning glories and the trees outside the garage, and everything else as she spun through an infinite nothing.

Chapter Thirty

"NO!" Elodie cried out as she landed, her knees sank into cold mud under the grass. "No no no no no no no no no no." She covered her eyes with her hands and tried to will herself back to her garage.

She needed to tap her plants in three minutes!

"Am I interrupting something?" Gedas asked, a light chuckle in his voice.

"Yes, as a matter of fact you are." Elodie dropped her hands and stood on shaky legs. "Send me back, Gedas! You have to know how! Send me back. I have things to do and I don't have time for magic to get in the way."

"You know I cannot influence the magic of the spell holding you."

"Then how do you always know where I'll be?"

"If I look for it, I can see the ruakh shifting through the world, and I travel to meet you, my Gull. I've come a very far way to meet you today." His eyes were sad and the corners of his mouth dropped.

"I don't care about that. You travel for a living. What's one more journey?"

"One more journey is a small price to pay for a chance to spend an hour with you, child."

"Yeah right." Elodie crossed her arms and rolled her eyes. "Like I've been such a pleasure to be around."

"No, you've been obstinate and not a little bit prickly, but that doesn't change anything."

"What do you even get out of it? Why not just leave me wherever I land and let me deal with it?"

Gedas waited, leaning against his staff and examining her. "I promised your father long ago."

"My father, right, my father. Some random man who I've met once in my life, who didn't even bother to tell me we were related. Tell me again why a promise to an old dead man is so important?"

Gedas sighed and straightened. "I did not wish to fight with you today, my Gull. I don't like how we left our last meeting and hoped we could talk in peace."

Gedas's eyes were honest and open and Elodie felt a pang of guilt, followed by the loneliness she'd lived with for the last few months of her social isolation. She should apologize for her rudeness.

"So how long has it been since last we met? Hopefully more than a day?"

Elodie shrugged. "A few months, how about you?"

"Two months," Gedas replied lightly.

Elodie frowned. "It's been about the same for me. That's weird."

"One cannot define weird when one has no rules to follow or standard in which to set normal," Gedas replied automatically.

"Right, whatever. You don't have to tell me a thing." Elodie turned away from him to look at her surroundings, the guilt evaporating almost immediately among her anger. She was standing in a small meadow with hills stretching in every direction. Fresh clover covered the ground. It could be nearly anywhere in Aluna, being wholly unremarkable.

"Where are we?"

"Finchearst."

Elodie looked up. "On the coast?"

Gedas nodded and when Elodie looked for it, she could see the evidence. The sweet pepperbush, and a red cedar. The slight scent of brine in the air. They must have been a few miles off, but close enough for a detour. Finchearst was the east coast of Aluna, Gedas had been serious when he commented on his long journey.

"Can we go? I haven't seen the Backirk ocean since that time when I was seven." She didn't remember much more than hunting for shells and the warm water on her feet. A warm ocean, so much a contrast between the chilly ocean on the west of Aluna, and the ocean she knew in the Twoshy.

"I don't believe we have time to make the trip," Gedas said, an odd expression on his face.

"Where could we possibly have to be that we can't take a few hours detour to the ocean?"

Gedas sighed, and it was his turn to look away. "I wanted to apologize for the things I said the last time we met. I've grown quite fond of you over the years, and I have no desire to stop bothering with you, as you put it, for as long as I can manage."

"It doesn't matter. You're allowed not to like me. Everyone else does, so why not you, too."

"Now I don't believe that's true."

"It is. I haven't spoken to my best friend in weeks, and I've almost convinced my parents to stop talking to me too." Elodie dropped and sat on the ground. The mud soaked into her pants. "You might as well join them."

Gedas crouched next to her. He lifted her chin with a gentle hand. "I will never get tired of you, my Gull, and I will never stop talking to you."

"Never stop talking without really saying something you mean. You never really tell me anything, Gedas."

"Well then, what have I been doing teaching you all these years? You mean none of my lessons have stuck?" he asked with a slight smile on his face, but Elodie wasn't ready to forgive. Instead the anger brewing under the loneliness began to rise once more.

"Why don't you tell me about the prophecy then?"

Gedas sighed and straightened up with a groan, his knees cracked. "Why do you care so much to know about a prophecy?"

"Life would be easier if I had a prophecy telling me exactly what to do next. Something to hold onto when I start to doubt everything around me."

"That's not how things really work," he said carefully. "Even if someone does have a prophecy spoken over them, a prophecy should never be directional, only confirmational. A prophecy doesn't tell you what to do, or even what you will do, and if it does, it probably isn't a very good one."

"So then why won't you tell me what it says?"

Gedas shook his head and leaned forward on his staff again, a sad look in his eyes. He looked up as an albatross flew over their heads toward the ocean, and then his eyes fell back on her. "Someday you may actually believe me when I say it is for your own good you do not know."

The anger in Elodie ruptured to the surface and her vision wavered for a moment in rage. Then all at once the wavering was no longer just in her vision, but was all around her as a shimmer wrapped itself around her and pulled her back into its depths.

Chapter Thirty-One

THE CEMENT FLOOR was hard and smooth and cold against her skin. She inhaled deeply and let it out with a growl. She pushed all of her rage and anger and frustration, her sadness and loneliness and guilt into that one breath. She put her hands over her face and hesitated to take in a new breath, trying to push out more and more.

There was so much pain inside, it needed to come out.

After a long shaking moment she inhaled and sat panting on the cold ground. She shook her head trying to snap herself back from the edge of the abyss growing inside.

"What was even the point of that?" she said out loud. She'd been gone for just a few minutes.

She looked around for something to focus on, something tangible and real. The morning glories sat on the table. She ran a hand over her face and stood, steadying herself on the edge of the table. She needed to do something with the plants. She needed to tap them for her experiment.

She looked to her book then looked up at the clock. She stared at the clock for nearly a minute trying to understand what she was seeing. She was thirty-four minutes passed the time she needed to tap the plants.

She's lost more time than she'd spent in the Twoshy. That had never happened to her before.

The morning glories radiated peace in response to the anger coming off her.

All her hard work for the last few weeks for nothing. Tapping the plants now would make her results trash. Gedas taught her precision was everything when experimenting. Scientific experimentation, whether Earth or Eres based, followed the same rules.

She leaned over the morning glories with so much anger inside of herself and braced her hands on the table. She'd wasted so much time on these stupid flowers. The anger flared inside her and she pushed it out, pushed it away from her and toward the flowers as the last shimmers of the ruakh faded from the spell.

She turned and stormed inside.

Her mother's sharp voice emerged from the kitchen. "Elodie, sweetie, why are you covered in mud?"

"I fell," she said a little too sharply as she took the stairs. She stomped hard on the way to her room.

"Bring down your muddy things after you change, sweetie! Don't put them in your hamper! Dinner in fifteen!"

The voice was sweet again at the end as Elodie slammed her bedroom door.

Elodie looked down at herself, covered in mud. Why hadn't her mother been furious with her for the mess? Elodie kicked off her muddy shoes and changed into pajamas, carefully folding her clothes to trap the mud and set them with her shoes. By the time she was finished, Elodie sat on her bed feeling empty and tired.

Gedas had told her something this trip. He told her how he knew when she would travel. It was the most direct answer she'd ever got from him about the spell. He could see the ruakh moving through the world. If he could see it, maybe someone else more willing to help could also find it.

BEFORE SCHOOL, Elodie headed to the garage to water her plants and turn on their sun lamp. When she entered the garage, she saw each of the twelve morning glories laying brown and dead in their pots.

Her mother found her there, crying on the floor. The tears racked Elodie's body, making it difficult to breathe.

She couldn't get the words out to answer her mom when she asked what was wrong. Instead she pointed at the dead plants, the plants she'd put so much of herself into so she could be normal. Missing a day tapping the plants wouldn't have been the end of the experiment. No one but herself would have even noticed. Now each plant was limp and brown, the few blossoms turned to mush and fell to the table like a drop of mud, and a rotten decaying odor seeped from the ruined plants.

Her experiment was worthless.

Her mom sat on the ground next to her and held her while she cried, getting her nice dress slacks dirty on the hard floor. Elodie tried to stop her tears, to say she was fine and get her mom to leave. She was embarrassed to be caught crying and mad she couldn't stop. It was too much. The emotions stacked up as fuel to power her river of tears, no end in sight.

After a time, her mom began to rock her back and forth, as though understanding Elodie wasn't just upset about the death of her flowers. Her mother's whispers began to penetrate the cloud of sadness that cut Elodie off from anything else.

"I wish you would tell me what's wrong. I just want to help. Tell me how to help, please."

After a few minutes the sobs subsided and Elodie pulled away from her mom. She wiped her face on her own shirt and apologized.

"I'll go change." Elodie stood and headed for the garage door.

"Honey, why don't you stay home today, I'll write you a note for tomorrow."

Elodie nodded before escaping to her room. She didn't want to look back at her mom and see the disgust as her mom examined the gooey mess her tears and snot left on her shoulder.

Elodie stayed home and read. She decided to pick a book she knew and loved to reread. The familiar story wrapped around her like a comfortable friend. Her mom also didn't go into work. Elodie was a bit surprised since she had a wedding coming up, but her mom spent her day being busy around the first floor of the house, making phone calls and checking on Elodie whenever she emerged from her room for food. Elodie didn't have it in her to talk about what happened, and her mom only asked what she wanted to eat.

Walking into school the next day, Elodie saw Vanessa and wanted to stop and talk to her, but when she made eye contact with Vanessa across the quad Vanessa's cheerful face fell with a look of sadness.

On their lunch break Elodie took her food to sit by the trees on the edge of the school property.

She walked behind the science class on the way to her spot when they cornered her. Jackson, Greg, Mitchell and the rest of her biggest fans.

"Hey Harpy, where you going?"

"Going to go sit by yourself and cry some more?"

"Even your loser friend doesn't like you anymore."

"You should just leave."

Elodie just stood there, with her lunch in her hands, head down, eyes on her feet and hair falling in front of her eyes. She went numb and her eyes stopped seeing as the boys yelled and mocked and jeered.

Someone touched her shoulder and she shied away, so afraid the abuse would turn physical, but the person grabbed her shoulder and held on, turning her.

"Look at me," the voice said, finally cutting through the anger and hurt around her. She looked up into Vanessa's angry eyes. "Stand up. Look at them. They're nothing, do you understand? They are worthless people." Vanessa turned from Elodie to Jackson. "Shut up before I make you."

"Oh right, what's a little hippy girl like you gonna do about it?" He ended the sentence with a slur Elodie was shocked to hear. Vanessa's stance shifted and then she pulled back her arm and threw her fist forward until it collided with Jackson's chin. He went down with one hit and Elodie gasped along with everyone else.

Jackson cried out and held his chin, tears gathered in his eyes. "That's it you're going to get in so much trouble now." His friends helped him stand. They traded a few more insults before they made their way back toward school. Vanessa turned to Elodie.

"I can't believe you just did that. Oh man, I'm going to replay that memory for the rest of my life." Elodie looked at her friend as anger cooled in Vanessa's face. "Vanessa, won't you get in trouble?"

"After what he just called me?" Vanessa asked, an amused look on her face. "I doubt he'll even go to the principal's office. The school says it has a zero-tolerance policy for racist garbage. He'll totally get suspended."

She was silent for a moment and then they both started to talk at once. They paused and Elodie tried again. "Vanessa, I'm so sorry."

"Elodie, do you even know why I'm upset?"

"Because I almost got your parents in trouble disappearing to the Twoshy?"

"No, Elodie, I'm not mad about that. Well, maybe I was when my mom started panicking, but I know it's not your fault." Vanessa sighed. "When you go to the Twoshy, you leave me behind. If I'm just another part of the illusion . . . I don't know. The world doesn't stop for me when you leave."

Elodie frowned and looked down. She hadn't ever thought of it like that.

"Someday you'll break the spell and leave me forever. It hurts knowing you're trying to do it soon, and sometimes I get a little angry that you don't seem to care. I'm sorry for that Elodie, and I promise I'll try to work on it." Vanessa sighed again and left Elodie there, standing on the grass with her lunch, as her friend walked toward the office.

After school Elodie's mom picked her up, and they drove to Doctor Abernathy's office. She walked down the stone pathway keeping out an eye for stray shimmers, and tried to ignore the crab apple and maple trees beside her as they gave up their leaves and sunk within themselves for their winter hibernation.

"I heard you had a hard day yesterday. Do you want to talk about it?" Abernathy asked from his rollie chair beside Elodie's window seat.

Elodie sighed and looked out the window at the falling leaves. "Not really. My plants died for my science experiment and I cried about it. It was stupid."

"What about it was stupid? The sunlamp was left on overnight, right?"

The lie was ready made, when her mom had asked about the light. Yes, she'd forgotten to turn it off, but she'd done it before, and it didn't kill the plants. But her mom and Doctor Abernathy didn't need to know that.

"Yeah, the light. It was stupid I cried. They're just plants and I can start again or not. It doesn't really matter. It's not like the science fair counts for my grade beyond extra credit."

"And you're a good student. You don't need extra credit. Why did you want to do the science fair in the first place?"

"I don't know, it was stupid," she said again. "I just wanted something to do."

"If you just wanted something to do then why did you get so upset when it stopped working?"

Elodie just shook her head. She didn't know how to explain the feelings raging inside her and why the science experiment seemed so important. She didn't know how to say all of it without giving off any warning signs she might be crazy. She didn't want to go back on pills that made the world foggy. She was living such a careful balance.

Instead she said nothing. Abernathy tried a few more times to get her to speak. But long silences had become a routine between them.

"Have you talked with Vanessa recently?"

"Yes actually," Elodie said, startling herself.

"You have? That's great." He shifted forward in his seat as though grade-school friendship counseling was the top of his interest list. "What did you talk about?"

"We didn't talk, she helped me with something."

"And how did it make you feel? I know you've been upset since you had your falling out."

Elodie shrugged. "I know why she's mad at me now, I just don't really know what I can say to make it better."

"Is it something you can fix? Something you can change or do differently?"

"No, she said she knows that, but it doesn't change the fact it makes her mad."

"And what about you? Are you still mad at her?"

"No. I get why she was mad, but I don't know how to make it better."

Abernathy thumbed the spiral of his notebook. "That can be a really hard place to be. As we get older, we change. Who we are as children isn't always who we are as a teenager and then we just keep changing every few years. Some friendships can withstand this. You both grow and change, and the friendship changes too. Some friendships do die over time, and that's perfectly okay. You might get back in touch ten years after you graduate and be better friends than ever, or you might never speak again. Regardless of how your friendship changed you and Vanessa will always be important to each other for the time you did have."

Elodie decided to forgo homework since it was Friday. Instead she went in the backyard to the old oak tree in the corner of the garden and sat under it, thinking about Vanessa and what Abernathy had said.

She noticed some mushrooms growing along the fence, and after a very close and thorough examination realized they were a familiar type she knew were edible. She took them inside knowing her mother loved mushrooms and they would be a great addition to the spaghetti sauce she was making for dinner.

Elodie was nearly to the entrance of the kitchen when she stopped walking.

She wasn't in the Twoshy, and her mom would never cook mushrooms she found outside. Her mother would likely screech and make her drop them and wash her hands with strong soap while she called poison control.

Elodie turned toward the backyard to put the mushrooms back where they would do some good, adding to the nutrients in the grass. As she walked, the shimmer came again and caught her up. She held the mushrooms close to her chest as she was picked up and tossed aside and tumbled through nothing.

Chapter Thirty-Two

HER HEAD SPUN. She lay still for a moment, taking in the air around her filled with the scent of damp soil and decomposing plants. The ground was wet and the sky was dark with a bright full moon shining between the trees.

"Hello? Who's there?" a deep voice called out of the darkness.

As a dark shape emerged from the trees, Elodie wasn't quite sure what to say in reply.

"Uhhh, hi. Have you seen the wizard Gediminas by chance?" she asked the stranger.

"Elodie?"

Moonlight glinted off metal and the sound of a sword sliding in a sheath reached her. Elodie froze. The figure crouched down before her, sword sheathed at their side. "Your Highness, I didn't expect to find you out here."

"Uh." Her head was spinning from her travel and her eyes slowly adjusted to the dark. She tried to sit up and the mushrooms in her arms fell around her. "Crap." She felt around trying to find the fallen mushrooms without squishing them.

"Here, allow me, my lady." He came closer and pulled a bright light from his pocket.

Elodie shielded her eyes at the sudden brightness from his light stone.

"Sorry," he said, covering most of the light. He bent down to pick up the fallen mushrooms and the light illuminated his dark face and bright green eyes.

"Silas?" she asked, unsure. This boy was several years older, and several inches taller than her. His features were strong, his chin and cheekbones defined in his face. No softness of childhood remained. His eyes were the same, sharp and soft at once with long lashes. She would assume he was an older brother if she hadn't known Silas was the eldest of his siblings.

"At your service, Your Highness." He attempted a bow from his crouched position. "Why are your shoes green?" he asked suddenly, breaking his reverence.

"Because the spell ate my last pair."

"Oh." Silas paused. "I quite like them actually." He let show the smallest of smiles before bowing his head again, his face returned to a neutral mask she'd seen so many times on the faces of nobility who didn't have the time for a ruler who never aged. Had his training removed all his spirit?

Silas took off his cloak and draped it across Elodie's back. He fastened the collar and pulled the cloak over her head. His hands dropped nervously a moment later and he fumbled for the mushrooms before standing.

"How long have I been gone?" Elodie asked.

"I'm not sure, have you traveled at all since the last time I saw you?"

"Yeah, a couple of times."

"I'm not sure how long it's been since then, but it's been nearly two years since I saw you last."

"Two years!"

"Yes, how long has it been for you?"

"About two months," she said softly.

"Well then, I guess this means I'm finally older than you," he said with a small smile before dropping his head.

Silas reached down a hand and when she grasped it, pulled her from the ground as though she were half his size. When she was standing next to him, she wondered if maybe she was. He towered over her with broad strong shoulders. He clearly didn't slack off with page training.

"May I carry these for you, my lady?" He held her fallen mushrooms in one large muscled arm.

"I thought I finally taught you to call me Elodie?"

"That wouldn't be proper, my lady." He dropped his gaze.

"Please don't tell me squiredom has driven the fun out of you?"

"Squiredom is helping me to be a noble and chivalrous man so one day I can be worthy as a knight under your rule." His posture was straight, not an ounce of joke in his words.

"You say noble, I say stodgy," Elodie said under her breath.

"Allow me take you back to the others." He gave her his light stone.

She followed his lead for a few minutes trying to think up something to say, hoping to spark the old friendship they once had, but nothing came to mind and soon Elodie could see the glow of fires and the sounds of horses and a large camp.

"Wizard Gediminas sent me in this direction five minutes ago and said he'd seen some wild strawberries I should pick and bring back. I didn't find any strawberries but I guess he was trying to be funny."

That sounded like Gedas.

"Where are we?"

"The great highway, near Chalkworth. We're on Progress," he said lightly.

"Progress?" Elodie asked, not quite believing it.

The King's Progress was a tradition for the king and queen alone. They would take annual trips into their lands to hear from the people and see what needs there were for the coming year. She'd heard tales of Progresses in the past. Knights and lords joined the king looking for opportunities to show support or make a name for themselves. Some Progresses carried tournaments bringing excitement and commerce across the country.

A Progress wasn't something that fell into the rights or duties of a steward.

"Yes, Steward Oburleck thought it would be a good idea, help boost the kingdom's morale." Silas's voice was light and even, and it surprised Elodie, although she wasn't quite sure why. Hadn't Silas always said Oburleck was a good leader, even if he didn't agree with his politics? Maybe Silas's worry about the kingdom's state and the prolonged absence of a proper ruler had shifted his ideas for a solution.

"But . . . He's not king," Elodie replied as though it explained everything.

"No, he's not," Silas said stiffly. "But he did manage to sell the idea to the council and the most influential nobles. He says the King's Progress was originally designed to be a link between the people and the ruling party, and as the council is the ruling party, they all could act as substitute, so they felt obliged to attend."

"Wait, all of them?"

"Yes, my lady," Silas replied.

"But Riyan is eighty."

"Eighty-six. He's not with us anymore."

"He died?" Elodie asked, shocked at Silas as he kept such a blank tone and manner.

"Oh, no. Just left the Progress, my lady. Over half the council dropped out within the first week. Lord Riyan made it four days before saying he was too—uh, old for such nonsense and said he trusted Oburleck to represent his interests on the road."

Elodie smiled. She could imagine the colorful language the oldest lord on the council may have used. Then she frowned. "But Riyan doesn't like Oburleck. Like, he hates him." Letting Oburleck represent his interests was a big deal. That meant the nobles who looked to Riyan for how they should move politically would shift to Oburleck.

"Oh yes, but apparently he hated sleeping in a tent in the mud more, my lady."

"They had him in a tent?" Elodie asked, incredulous.

A Progress was always mapped out to stop by inns or villages with large towns so the nobility didn't have to rough it. The goal was to make income for the people without inconveniencing the nobility.

"Yes. It would seem we've had a bit of bad luck the first week or two of the Progress. A bad storm the mages didn't predict coming, some flooding, a fire at an inn."

"Wow. That seems like a bit more than bad luck, what are people saying about it?"

"Nothing at all. Usually there would be a few people saying Steward Oburleck's plan was folly or cursed by the gods. But he's assured people it's a pot of bad luck, and everyone is either going with it and keeping on, or leaving the party in the hands of Steward Oburleck." Silas's voice dropped as they approached the closest camp. "After Lord Riyan called it quits half the council decided they didn't need to stick around either and gave Steward Oburleck their vote of confidence."

Elodie's eyebrows rose.

"We've been out for just under a month and nearly everyone who votes against Obulrleck regularly is gone. Lord Gregor left last night after the inn we stayed at had a little issue with bugs. Sir Jesper and I slept in the stables."

"Sir Jesper, yes. How are you liking your knight master? Is he teaching you to be a good knight?" Jesper was the knight commander, in charge of Aluna's army. Silas would learn more than the average squire at his side.

Silas looked as if he would reply, but they reached the first of the campfires and he closed his mouth. They wove through tents and camps until they came to a familiar-looking large tent.

Gedas sat in the opening, a small fire before him with a stew pot hanging over the flames.

Silas dropped the mushrooms next to the fire and swept a bow to Gedas. "Wizard Gediminas. I found no strawberries in the forest, only mushrooms and a princess." He turned and bowed to Elodie, keeping his head low as he spoke. "Thank you for the privilege of your company, my lady. I look forward to conversing with you more on our journey ahead." He rose from his bow and Elodie handed back his cloak. He held it close to his chest and nodded to her softly before he turned into the night and was gone a moment later.

"I'm not sure what Jesper is feeding him, but if he doesn't stop, soon that boy will be taller than me," the old wizard said lightly. Elodie turned to her mentor and saw he'd picked the mushrooms off the ground. He gave them a sniff and began cleaning them.

"You sent him after strawberries in the dark?" Elodie asked, a smile on her face.

"I thought you might prefer a more youthful and friendlier face to greet you," Gedas said casually, although she heard a slight hesitation in his voice. "How are you, my Gull?"

"Fine," she said, then cringed at the fake answer.

She'd been using that word so much with her parents and with Doctor Abernathy, but she didn't want to be fake with Gedas. Their fight was still so fresh in her mind.

"I'm sorry for . . ." She trailed off, not quite sure what to apologize for.

Gedas smiled kindly at her. "As am I."

They were quiet for a few moments as Gedas cut the mushrooms with his belt knife and added them to the pot over his fire.

"So how did you get roped into this Progress?" Elodie asked, breaking the silence at last.

"Ahh, a Progress is a very old tradition, a ruler taking to their land, being in touch with their people. As head magical proficient of Aluna, it is tradition to join such a Progress."

"Right, a title you only ever pull out when it suits your plans. You don't have to tell me if you don't want to." Elodie pushed down on that twinge in her stomach.

Gedas patted the bedroll next to him. "Have a seat, my Gull. Will you join me for dinner?"

"Yes please, it was almost dinner time when the ruakh grabbed me up." Elodie sat next to the old man in the entrance of the tent.

"These are nice mushrooms. I assume they are from you?"

"Yeah, I picked them in the illusion, they came with me."

"Really?" Gedas's eyebrows rose as he stirred the stew pot. "Then I will be delighted to eat them."

Gedas was silent and Elodie closed her eyes. She took in the world around her. The smell of burning pine and the aroma of the stew pot. The scent of horses, and the other one she only ever associated with Gedas that smelled like a mix of herbs even she couldn't decipher. She listened to the crackle of the fire, the horse noises, and the low conversations around her. She took it all in on a deep breath, and tried to let out the anxious tightness she'd built around herself in the last weeks.

"Do you wish to stay with me during the Progress, or would you prefer to stay with the nobility? I can even provide you with a charm against bugs for the next inn if you wish."

Elodie opened her eyes and looked at the old wizard who'd always been there for her, teaching her and watching over her. He was carefully preparing tea and not looking at her. She shrugged as if it didn't matter, when she knew it mattered a great deal.

"I'll stick with you. I fit better here anyways. Not with all the stuffed shirts. Do you have my bag?"

"Of course." Gedas handed her a mug of tea. "There is also a trunk beside the tent for you, filled with fine clothes courtesy of Mistress Piera."

"You told her you were expecting me?"

"I told her I wanted to be prepared. And she obliged by providing a wardrobe fit for a princess on Progress."

Elodie rolled her eyes as she blew on her tea before taking a deep breath of the steam. Black tea with nutmeg. A simple campfire tea. "So that means I have fine fabrics and embroidery to stain and dirty that cost more than the people I will be meeting will ever see in a year. Fun."

"I convinced her to stick a few of your older things into the trunk as well."

Gedas handed her an amber glass bottle. She set down the tea and accepted it. She screwed off the lid and the familiar scent of dandelion and greyglove hit her nose. She put the lid back on the detoxifying potion and handed it back. "I don't need that anymore. I figured out what was causing my sickness."

"Oh?" Gedas took the bottle and tucked it back in his pack. "That's quite the discovery, do tell."

"It was the crazy pills they had me on, I think they were making me sick and causing the fog." Elodie pulled her knees to her chest and wrapped her arms around them. Her mom had never discussed it with her, and the silent dismissal of her medication somehow made her feel more broken than she had when they were prescribed.

"Ah, I see. It's not surprising your doctors would have a hard time treating you."

"I know. I mean I'm not crazy, so it's not like I needed them anyways." Elodie rested her chin on her knees.

A thoughtful look crossed Gedas's face. "Tell me, is that what they said these pills were for? They said they would resolve the crazy within you? I didn't think crazy was so easily diagnosed in any world."

"No, of course it's not what they call it. It was just to make me more normal."

She shrugged and tried to think back to the weeks after she'd returned from the Twoshy when this mess started. She returned in the middle of the mall bathroom, exactly where she'd disappeared, but the mall had been dark and empty, and she set off security alarms when she tried to leave. More time had passed while she was in the Twoshy than ever before.

The police took her to the hospital and called her parents. She'd been missing for two weeks and no one would believe her when she said she had been fine. Gedas had been with her, and they'd gone on adventures.

She got so mad when they didn't believe her. She'd yelled at the fourth doctor who asked her leading questions about being hurt, and she kept yelling when anyone told her to tell the truth.

She was telling the truth, they just wouldn't listen. It made her mad and then it made her sad.

"They said it would help me feel more normal. They thought I was lying about the Twoshy and said it would help so I wouldn't think I needed a reason to lie. But I'm fine on my own."

"Hmmmm."

Gedas sat for a while looking into the flames of the fire, and Elodie decided their conversation was over. She watched a few cindix crawl out of the leaves of the forest floor and make their way into the embers. They shook out their fur in the flames the same way someone would shake off cold rain after reaching shelter.

"If you had a patient suffering from depression what would you suggest?"

The question startled her. So far from their previous conversation.

"Two cheer leaves steeped once a day. Taken morning or night depending on the patient's needs while they sought heart or mind healing." It was a simple, common cure.

"So you wouldn't recommend the patient tough it out or deal with it on their own?"

"No." Elodie shook her head confused by his question. "It's pointless to suffer when we have something that can help. And taking the edge off is a good tool while you work on real healing."

"Indeed." Gedas frowned and tapped his chin. "Tell me, if we know cheer leaves will dampen the symptoms, why not suggest the patient take up chewing cheer sticks or leaves as a permanent solution? It's much more powerful and much easier. It will completely remove the depressed feelings, not just mute them to a manageable level."

"Right, but chewing on a stick or leaf is too potent. It causes people to start separating from their emotions which can be addictive. Instead of resolving the imbalance in their brain and working with a mind healer for a permanent solution for their feelings, we would be removing their ability to cope with their own emotions altogether."

"So the dosage needs to be intentional then?" Gedas asked.

"Yes definitely."

"And would you prescribe cheer leaves to anybody with issues of depression or anxiety?"

"Not necessarily."

"Explain."

Elodie sighed. "I wouldn't give it to anybody with an allergy to frog grass. Cheer can cause panic attacks or night terrors."

"So you're saying cheer isn't a solution for everyone?"

"Right, sometimes you need to go by trial and error, what works for one person doesn't always work for another. There are other options that can help."

"Yes exactly," Gedas said as though proving something.

"I don't get your point." Elodie frowned and picked up her tea again. She sipped the cooling liquid. "We're not talking about a magical plant here are we? My pills aren't like that. They weren't made using magic."

"No, in the illusion medicines have been developed through nonmagical research but that doesn't make them any less real or effective."

"So you're saying I am crazy and do need the pills?"

"I am saying that most of us are a little crazy and do need something of some kind to help us now and again. Thinking you're invincible, thinking you don't need help, is a great way to get yourself unhealthy. I don't know what your pills were for or what they were trying to help, but I do know your doctors weren't trying to hurt you. Those pills were created to help people with very real issues, and probably work great for most people. But not all people are the same, and you, my Gull, with ruakh flowing through your veins are not the same. Given time I have no doubt your doctors could resolve the issue and find something that works for you, but for now I'm happy to know you are well and won't have any fainting spells on me. This Progress has been hard enough as it is."

The stew contained a rabbit and two squirrels caught by Silas on the road. It was gamey but Gedas had cooked it till the meat was chewable. They shared the meal with some of the holsters who'd been short rations that night. Gedas casually mentioned the food shortages of the Progress. A few wagons carrying supplies had been lost in a mudslide. He alluded to the attempt of a few of those present, like Sir Jesper, Silas's knight commander, to forage for as much food as they could along the way to lighten the load they put on the local people. Elodie ate her stew and didn't complain.

Once the pot was empty, Gedas banked their fire and they turned in for the night. It took Elodie some time to fall asleep among the noises of a large party. Everyone tried to be quiet, but with so many bodies, horse and Human, the Progress made much noise. She took a deep breath, and felt a small ache in her throat. With a start she realized she'd spoken more that night around the fire than she had in weeks.

Her heart was heavy with longing for comfortable friendships with Gedas and Silas. She wanted to peel back the isolation she'd been trapped in and go back to normal, but she wasn't sure how to start.

She rolled over in her bedroll and closed her eyes, focusing on the familiar and comforting sounds of Gedas's soft snores.

Chapter Thirty-Three

THE MORNING CAME EARLIER than she felt ready for as the noises of people tearing down tents and packing campsites woke her. Elodie rolled over with a groan and covered her head with a blanket as Gedas patted her back firmly.

"Come. Help me build up the fire so we can make breakfast for those with hard jobs."

Elodie sighed and threw off her blanket to the chill of the morning.

As much as Elodie would have loved keeping her green sneakers so Silas would be shocked at how bright they were in the daylight, riding would be easier in the fine leather boots Mistress Piera had packed for her. She dug until she found the more casual clothes in the trunk, well-made breeches of good cloth, worn from the last time she'd been in the palace. A tunic of a light blue color with the least embroidery she could find. Instead of the deep blue cloak with silver trim, Elodie pulled out an old fading olive green cloak she'd worn for years on her travels with Gedas. It was a little short for her, but she would be on horseback, and the familiarity was comforting.

They cooked a large pot of porridge and Elodie helped by serving it up to anyone who stopped working long enough to eat.

After they cleaned the cooking things in a nearby river Gedas and Elodie saddled their horses and helped the men stow their belongings on one of the many wagons.

Elodie quickly realized Gedas made his campsite near the end of the progression among the people who made the Progress work. These workers spent the early and late hours, building and tearing down the camps for any of the upper class who didn't find lodging in the inn they'd stayed near. They took care of the horses for the nobles and supply wagons and did all the little tedious things needed when traveling.

They'd camped along the great highway, trailing off from one of the many inns that happened along the way. Once their horses were ready, Elodie and Gedas traveled along the chaos of camps till they reached the front of the Progress in front of the inn. Hostlers readied horses for the nobles who'd spent the night in the inn, and Elodie recognized a few sleepy-eyed courtiers sitting atop beautiful horses, waiting for things to start.

Sir Jesper and Silas camped along the road closer to the inn, according to Gedas, to help make sure the men at arms and scouts were well fed. Now Jesper could be seen directing and organizing the progression before they set off. He shouted commands at a man attempting to put a small saddle on a warhorse it would never fit and helped a maid repack a crate so it stacked properly in a wagon.

Elodie had heard tales of Progresses from the past, caravans three times this size moving like a well-oiled machine. The teardown process should be smooth and simple. Instead she saw men and women frantically packing tents and cooking equipment. Several bed rolls fell off a badly packed wagon into the mud and were stepped on by several people carrying bundles before someone picked them up.

Sir Jesper spotted Gedas with a nod. He finished helping a man load a large trunk and made his way over.

He swept a deep bow to Elodie, and held it for a moment before straightening. He was tall and broad shouldered. Larger than Silas, but Elodie wondered if that would be the case for long. His face was round and pale with soft laugh lines around his wide-set eyes. His armor was light leather over a deep blue tunic, and every inch of him was speckled with mud. In her memories of tales, knights wore their finer plate armor or chain mail on Progress. It was a time to show your best and flaunt your wealth.

"Your Highness, I'm very glad you could join us on this expedition," Jesper said before nodding to Gedas. "Wizard Gediminas, my squire tells me you find the best surprises in the woods at night."

"Just attempting to teach the young squire the merits of foraging," Gedas said with a smile. "Has the Steward awakened yet or should we send someone in for the job?" He gestured to the inn.

"I believe I heard his man servant drawing him a bath a moment ago," the knight said, his straight face not betraying the mirth in his sparkling eyes. They continued to talk for a few moments about the distance they would travel that day. While some of the nobility who'd slept in the inn started to make their way to their horses, it was clear there was no sense of urgency or a timetable in mind as the rest of the Progress finished lining up and organizing themselves into pre-arranged riding positions.

Silas came up on her side patting her horse's neck, a bay mare named Apple. "We've been slow to start each morning and tend to take long breaks for lunch. At this rate we'll finish the Progress this time next year," the squire said quietly as if talking to the horse. Elodie looked down at him, and saw he was examining the horse's tack very carefully, not making eye contact with her.

"Well at least we can keep each other company," Elodie said.

Silas looked up and met her eyes for just a moment, his expression unreadable before looking away. "Of course, Your Highness," he said before stepping around her horse and approaching his knight. "Shall I fetch the horses, Sir Jesper?"

"Yes, thank you, Silas."

"Who is the Master of Progress?" Elodie asked. She hoped it wasn't Jesper. The title was an honor, marking the leader and organizer of the Progress. Whoever was in charge of this mess would be seen as a failure.

"Duke Devoss is our Master of Progress," Jesper said with a careful expression. I believe he is still in his rooms as well."

Elodie frowned. The Master of Progress should be out here making sure everyone was in their place. No wonder everything was a mess with a missing leader.

"You speak and the gods deliver," Gedas said with a sigh.

Elodie turned in her saddle to see Duke Devoss and Baron Byron emerge from the inn. Devoss looked tired and half awake as he mounted the horse being held for him. Once in his seat he pulled a flask from his belt and took a quick drink. Byron in contrast looked bored but sharp. When he turned Elodie saw he had a long scar running down one side of his face.

Seeing the baron made Elodie remember Callie. She would have to ask Silas if he knew what became of her friend in the last two years. Silas returned with two large horses, a bay and a piebald. He held the bay stallion while the knight mounted, and then climbed into his own saddle.

"Come, our places are a little further up on the Progress I believe." Jesper led Elodie and Gedas to the front of the column. Elodie felt a few eyes on her and tried not to duck her head as they made their way just behind the lead horses.

Oburleck came out of the inn a few moments later with a gaggle of nobles and courtiers in fine clothes, rumpled and mudstained. Elodie was surprised to see so many had endured the conditions just for the opportunity to rub elbows with the steward.

Oburleck made his way to his horse, greeting those he passed as he went. He stopped mid stride catching sight of Elodie. The look of shock on his face flashed to something else. Frustration? It was quickly wiped away with an even smile and he approached them.

The steward gave Elodie a lavish bow before straightening. "Princess Elodie, what a surprise to see you." His eyes flicked to Gedas before returning to her. "When Wizard Gediminas recommended we stop at this inn last night, I expected he'd seen something in our path to be avoided, but it turns out we had nothing to fear but the overwhelming joy of your presence."

"Thank you, Steward Oburleck," she said, trying to choose her words properly. "I'm excited for the opportunity to join the Progress you set up."

"Yes, the council thought it would be good to resurrect the tradition." He bowed to her again and took a few steps closer to grab her hand and kiss the back of it. "This Progress has felt like it was missing something, and dare I say it, I believe you were it." Elodie tried not to grimace as he spoke, breathing slowly and through her mouth. The smell of his breath was unavoidable and nearly overwhelmed her.

Elodie waited a beat longer than was likely proper then replied with a nod of her head. "Happy to be here." Oburleck wasn't bad, even if she didn't understand why he was running the Progress.

"Shall we commence then?" Oburleck turned from her and mounted his own horse, turning it toward the road. The party followed.

While Elodie was at the front end of the column and started riding straight away behind a few lords and dukes, she wondered how long it would take the people in back to reach the same pace.

Each of the nobles seemed to have their own servants or a few of their house men at arms along on the Progress, but as they rode out, Elodie was surprised to realize nearly all of the soldiers and guards who rode to either side of the column, or scouted in front, bore the crest of Oburleck's house. She expected to see the men Jesper commanded, men of Aluna's army protecting the Progress.

Throughout the day Elodie noticed Silas disappear off into the trees sometimes lining the road. He returned from one such trip with a few rabbits and a fowl hanging from a stick tied to the back of his saddle. When Elodie gave him a curious look he just shrugged and found a place to ride farther behind her on the column.

They stopped for lunch in a small town, Chalkworth, apparently the location they'd planned to stop the night before. The town was small with the highway running through it. A large old inn and tavern sat close to the road with a large square on the south side surrounded by a market. The town started as a waystation on the highway long ago before turning into a trading post and slowly growing into a village. Men, women and children lined the road and waved small yellow flags as they rode past.

When they reached the inn, Oburleck dismounted and handed his horse off to a manservant in purple and gold before he approached the village leaders with arms wide. Elodie dismounted when Gedas did and looked around, curious for where she could tie off her horse for some lunch of her own and a good brushing. Sir Jesper was at her side a moment later taking the reins.

"Leave that for Silas or one of the spare hostlers. Come, you should meet the Mayor."

"Uhhh," Elodie stammered as Silas took the reins. Sir Jesper led her away from Gedas to the men who'd gathered around the village leaders. Elodie felt awkward standing there among the tall men. The village head man glanced down and away while he greeted Oburleck and the rest of the party.

"We have refreshments waiting if you'd like to rest from your journey, I also have our census and tax records waiting," the mayor said. He had an awkward way of standing and kept bowing his head to Oburleck before straightening as though torn on the best way to greet a man who was over him in both rank and status.

"Yes, let us adjourn somewhere more comfortable, shall we?" Oburleck asked. Before he could lead the mayor away, Sir Jesper cut in on the conversation.

"My lord, Mayor Isat, I would also like to introduce you to Her Royal Highness, Princess Elodie of Aluna."

The mayor took another longer look at Elodie as though connecting pieces in his head before he dropped to a knee. The men at his back followed likewise. Elodie's stomach turned. Everyone was looking at her. She spent so much energy back in the illusion to keep people from looking at her because the looking was always followed by snide comments and whispered insults.

She took a deep breath. This wasn't the illusion. She was safe here.

"Your Highness, I didn't realize we had the pleasure, I apologize for my rudeness, I meant no disrespect," the mayor said to the ground.

Elodie tried not to grimace at the adult men kneeling in the dirt before her. "You honor me, Lord Mayor," she said slowly. "Please, rise. I'm glad we could come to your town and see how we can help make it better."

The mayor rose bowing as he went. "Thank you, Your Highness, for your patronage. King Kristo, may he rest in peace, your father visited our town on his last Progress when I was just a boy. I remember his strong countenance. It's such an honor to have you here." His face paled a moment later and he turned to one of his council. "Prepare refreshments for the princess at once. I apologize to keep you waiting in the elements, Your Highness, just this way, please."

At the mention of her father Elodie straightened her posture and tried to smooth her expression. This man had seen her father. She didn't want to be a poor representation of his legacy. She trailed after the mayor and tried to look confident, the nobles of her own council and Oburleck following behind.

"We're so thankful the princess could join us," Oburleck said, matching his pace with the mayor. "So last minute of course, due to her affliction, we had no way to send word ahead, but we appreciate your understanding in working with us."

The mayor looked almost startled at Oburleck's words. "It's no problem at all, truly. What is a Progress for but for a monarch to be introduced to her people? We are very honored of course."

"Indeed," Oburleck replied evenly.

They entered a large room with a hodgepodge of tables and chairs lining the perimeter as if the furniture was recently rearranged. In the center was a large wooden table with a few dozen chairs surrounding it. The town must not have had word so many of their party abandoned the Progress. They didn't need nearly so many chairs.

Elodie was directed by the mayor to the most ornate chair at the head of the table, Oburleck was directed to her right and the mayor sat on her left. Members of the town leadership sat interspersed with the council from Aluna, the end of the table was left mostly empty.

Sir Jesper winked at her as he found a seat halfway down the table. Elodie wasn't sure why the knight dragged her along. She felt insignificant and in the way as servants came out with platters of food and served each person at the table. She wanted to sink into the floor.

Elodie caught the eye of the girl pouring her drink, the metal band at her neck glinting in the light. They both dropped their eyes at the same time. Not servants then, slaves. Elodie wondered if she belonged to the mayor specifically, or to someone else present. Looking around every server wore the same thin metal ring around their neck, each one a girl, years older than Elodie. They wore fine pretty dresses Mistress Piera would be scandalized if Elodie ever attempted to wear, and there was an odd tension from the men around the table as they received their food and drinks from the servers.

The mayor talked more about the state of the town and spoke his thanks repeatedly for the honor of the Progress stopping with them.

"I know you don't have much time after the delays you've already faced, but we appreciate your assistance."

"Anything we can do to help, we are here for. Baron Reginald, our master of the bank, is happy to help your treasury officer with any concerns they have," Oburleck began. "Sir Jesper our knight commander will talk with your guard about any of the bandit issues you've seen. Thank you, my lovely," Oburleck said that last part with a wide shining smile to the slave girl who offered him a sweet roll. She blushed and returned to the kitchen.

"And what of our royal guest?" Mayor Isat asked, turning to Elodie, an uncomfortable look on his face. "Is there anything of interest for you I can have our people provide?"

"If Chalkworth has a clinic, I could help out there." Mayor Isat looked confused at her words, and the table went mostly silent. Oburleck let out a deep laugh, and the rest of the table joined in.

Elodie wanted to disappear.

"Our Princess likes to be of whatever use she can when she is able to visit us. She has a bit of magic and an affinity for plants you know." Oburleck changed the subject back to one of taxes and tax breaks for specific business types.

Elodie rolled her eyes before standing from her seat. All the men in the room stopped talking and rose from their chairs respectfully.

"If you'll excuse me," she said before turning from the table and walking toward the door to the outside.

When she reached the hallway she heard the scraping of chairs as the men sat back down.

A few menservants and squires stood against the walls of the hallway waiting for their masters. Their eyes followed her as she took slow steps toward the outside door.

She just wanted to find somewhere she wouldn't be watched.

Elodie turned as footsteps approached. "May I escort you, Your Highness?" Sir Jesper came up beside her. She nodded and made her way to the door. Silas left his place along the wall and followed.

A weight lifted from her as they reached the fresh air of daylight. Elodie paused in the middle of the square a few paces away from Jesper and breathed in the air. Something heavy rested over the atmosphere back in the large room and Elodie was happy to be free of it. "Did you need something, sir?"

"I would feel safer were you to travel with an escort while on Progress." The knight bowed his head.

"Isn't the whole Progress technically an escort?"

"Where are you headed, my lady?" the knight asked.

"To find Gedas."

"Then may my squire escort you?"

Elodie sighed. "I go places on my own when I'm with Gedas all the time."

Jesper took a step closer to Elodie, speaking in a softer voice. "You don't usually travel as the princess when with Gediminas. While on Progress I would appreciate it if you wouldn't go anywhere without myself, Gedas, or Silas. Do you understand?" His voice wasn't commanding but instead hinted at something he was trying to convey. Elodie didn't understand but nodded anyways.

"Thank you, my lady. You did well today meeting the Mayor," Jesper said with a grin.

"I just sat there and ate." She'd felt completely useless, but the knight shrugged and smiled.

"Sometimes a person's presence is enough to make a difference," he said. "Which is one reason why Squire Silas's presence will lend both to your importance and safety while on Progress."

She nodded, and Jesper, taking this as acceptance, bowed to her before returning to the building they'd left.

"My lady," Silas said, dropping into a low bow. Elodie sighed and walked down the street into the town, heading in the direction that felt the most busy and cluttered. "Where are we headed?" Silas asked, catching up to her.

"To find Gedas," she said again.

"And where is he?"

"Probably at an apothecary or clinic," she said before turning between a cloth seller and a tanner. The shops in this part of town all sold things of good quality. Gedas would be somewhere a little more shabby. She crossed a few streets till she saw a baker with a sign selling day-old bread, and turned down that longer road checking the shops on either side. "You really don't have to come with me, you know."

"Yes, I really do."

"Why, because your knight commander ordered it?"

"I could give you a list of reasons if you would prefer, my lady."

"Don't you ever get tired of following your orders?"

"If I did then I would be in the wrong line of work, my lady."

"What about when you're a knight and have to give the orders?"

"I will still have orders given to me by the Kingdom, the realm, and my own honor." Silas stopped walking and after a few paces Elodie stopped and turned to look at him. She crossed her arms in frustration. Silas just stood with his arms folded behind his back, posture straight.

"What?" she asked, impatient.

Silas gestured to the building he'd stopped in front of. Elodie sighed, seeing the symbol for the apothecary above the door. She stomped up the steps, leaving him to follow behind.

When the apprentice learned who she was and why she was there, she curtsied repeatedly as she led them to the workroom where Gedas and a healer were going over potions.

"Good, just in time," Gedas said, as though they'd been expected. "The village had an increase in influenza this year and is running low on cough suppressants." He passed a few bundles over to Elodie. "See if you can make up a few quarts before it's time to leave." Gedas eyed Silas up for a moment before nodding. "He can help with the chopping. Now Healer Myila, show me that tonic you confiscated from that patient you mentioned."

The healer led Gedas away from the workroom and, with a sigh, Elodie began organizing the ingredients before her. She found two large blades among the tools and instruments on an organized table and passed one with a bundle of echinacea to Silas.

"These need to be chopped very fine."

The squire nodded wordlessly and set to work while Elodie picked the blooms off an elder branch.

A time later Elodie began to wonder how long they should keep at it before heading back to the Progress. She didn't mind getting left behind, but not if it meant more work for those sent to find her. While she heated the elder flower, a messenger came to the apothecary sent from Sir Jesper.

Oburleck had decided they would be staying in town for the night.

When the messenger was gone and Elodie and Silas were alone he sighed in what sounded a lot like frustration.

"Tell me what's wrong," she said in a playful voice trying to draw Silas out.

He was silent.

"Look, I know helping me isn't as glamorous as a squire's regular duty. Gedas is here so really, you don't have to stay. I'm sure you have armor to polish."

"I'm happy to help."

"Then why are you so glum about it?"

"I'm not."

"Then what are you glum about."

Silas was quiet for a few more minutes. And then he wasn't.

"The palace sent people out weeks before the Progress to the villages and towns we planned to stop in to make sure each one would be prepared for the company, but then we do something like this, and call the day early. We're two weeks behind schedule, Elodie," he said looking her in the eyes for the first time that day. He realized it too and dropped his gaze. "This whole thing feels like an unholy laid plan, my lady." He applied his pestle once again to the peppermintsteel she'd set him to grinding.

Relief came over her and a small smile crept onto her face. She wasn't sure at first why his anger made her smile. Then she realized it was because she wasn't the source of his anger after all. He wasn't mad at her.

"I keep forgetting to ask. Have you heard anything from Callie when you were last in Tross?"

Silas grew even more rigid at the question, Elodie was surprised to see his posture was capable of being any more straight.

"I sent a letter to my father about her shortly after you left," he started, speaking slowly until the words flowed from him. "He said he's always looking for bright young people to fill his city with, so if she could make it to Tate she was welcome. He knew of a few businesses in the city where a bright creative person might do well. I was on the border when I got his message, it was delayed a few months as they rerouted it to me from the castle. When I returned I was going to take a trip, and escort her. I thought it would be better if I waited and did it myself. I thought she was in a good enough position with the baron."

He paused and took a deep breath. A pang started in Elodie's chest.

"We were delayed in heading back to Tross several times that year. When I finally did arrive, I went to the baron's to check on her and she wasn't there. It took a while to get the story of what happened. No one in the household will talk about it but I tracked down a baker's wife who worked for the baron at the time and she told me the story."

Elodie stopped her work to listen, but Silas continued grinding the herbs with precise careful movements. Each steady even grind felt like a warning of what was to come.

"The baker's wife said she didn't know what truly happened, but the story told afterwards said Callie attacked the baron unprovoked. He invited her to his study to give her a private message and sometime later they emerged, Callie screaming and the baron raging. He threw her down the stairs. He had a large deep scratch on his face. You can still see the outline of it now if you look. The baron said she'd gone crazy and attacked him unprovoked. That type of attack on a noble, her life was forfeit to him. He sold her to the bound services."

Elodie waited for him to continue, but he grounded the peppermintsteel in silence not looking up to meet Elodie's eyes.

"Do you know where she is?"

"From what I understand she's in Comak but none of my letters have been successful in reaching her."

Comak was not along the great highway. It wasn't a stop they would be making on their Progress, a few days out of the way. Elodie wondered if maybe she could detour when they got close enough. Sneak off from the Progress and find her.

"What type of bound services was she sold into?"

"I believe in a bound bordello in the city, but I haven't been able to receive confirmation as to which one. I'm sorry, my lady, I know you asked me to help keep her safe and I failed." His hands stilled at last, and his head dropped toward the table.

"You couldn't have known what would happen, Silas. And you have responsibilities of your own. It's not your fault," Elodie said, her mind already gone as she thought through the calculations in her head, how much buying someone's bond would cost, how she could get together the money.

Money had never been an issue for her, but it wasn't like she actually had pocket money to spend unless Gedas gave her what she needed to purchase specific herbs or supplies. She could ask Gedas how she could get the money. Maybe all she needed to do was ask and the palace's coffers would be open to her.

She got back to work on making medicines while she thought.

Chapter Thirty-Four

ELODIE STAYED WITH GEDAS, sleeping with the hostlers and off-duty guards of the Progress. They camped to the north of the town along a river that ran parallel to the great highway for miles. The mosquitos were unbearable until Gedas remembered he knew a quick spell to ward them away and gave it to the working men and women, and to Elodie.

When their evening meal was over and everything had been cleaned and stowed for the night, Elodie went to give Apple another brushing. She hoped a soothing task would help ground her in the present while her mind dreamed and schemed with ways to help Callie. After she was at the task for several minutes, Gedas came up beside her, giving the mare a gentle pat on her neck.

"Now, I've been thinking. Since we will likely have much downtime in the afternoon, we could work on your natural magical skills. Do you remember how to make a soundproof barrier within a warding circle? I believe you have everything in these woods you may need."

"No, Gedas, I don't want to do any magic," she said calmly as she ran the brush down the horse's side.

"Then what shall you do to grow yourself during your time here?" he asked patiently.

"Isn't being here enough?" Anxiety began to fight its way into her stomach, breaking her peace.

"Oh, I know," Gedas said, continuing as though he hadn't heard her. "Perhaps I can ask Sir Jesper to borrow his squire for archery lessons. It has been some time since you've had regular practice."

"Uuuggg. Isn't riding all day exhausting enough?" she whined.

"Nonsense. There is much more exhaustion to be had. It's decided. I will talk to Sir Jesper at once." He disappeared toward the camp at the head of the Progress before Elodie could argue further.

She buried her face in the side of her horse and groaned. There was no arguing with Gedas when he was like this, unless she wanted to pick a huge fight. She sighed. She wanted to keep their tentative peace. She was so tired of fighting with her friends.

He'd been gone five minutes before Elodie realized she'd forgotten to ask the old man about finding money for Callie.

Sir Jesper agreed to loaning out Silas in the evenings, and the next morning Gedas found a practice bow from one of the shops in the village before they left. He showed it to her with a smile like a doting uncle providing his favorite niece with a present and Elodie tried not to grind her teeth. She wondered if maybe this was his way to punish her for slacking with her magical talent. He'd give her an exhausting and boring task so she'd crawl back to her magic lessons with weak arms.

Traveling back and forth between the illusion and the Twoshy it was nearly impossible to keep up the muscle needed to draw one of the longbows or even one of the smaller bent bows some of the archers preferred. So now she would start again with one of the practice bows, building up her strength.

Over the nights of the Progress, as they traveled painfully slow across Aluna, Silas gave her pointers in hitting whatever target he picked for the night. During these practices Elodie tried to draw him out and joke with him, but the boy she'd known who'd been excited to be in the castle and willing to share a laugh at every turn faded into this tall stoic stranger who ducked his head when she tried to rile him up.

She was mostly sure he wasn't mad at her, but worried his distance was partially caused by an annoyance in having to train her. She was absolute rubbish with the bow, having forgotten nearly all of her old lessons. It was embarrassing and his calm stiff patience made her frustrated. She wanted to laugh off her mistakes, but this new Silas was incapable of laughing, and it made her feel like a little kid, too immature for the world he lived in.

In the end Elodie decided not to ask Gedas about the money and freeing her friend. The wizard had been so elusive when she asked him direct questions, she didn't want to add one more thing to the pot of conflict between them. Instead she decided to wait. To plan an opportunity to ditch the Progress and ride to Comak. She was familiar enough with how to travel. She knew she would be fine, and she doubted she'd be missed by more than Gedas, Silas and Sir Jesper.

Regardless of how many meetings the knight dragged her to when they stopped in a town or village on the Progress, Elodie knew her presence was mostly a novelty.

Three days after they left Chalkworth it started to rain and didn't stop. The first night they reached a town with two inns and everyone on Progress managed to find a dry spot to sleep. No one wanted to set out the next day as nothing had dried out overnight, but Oburleck spurred them on ensuring everyone the weather would stop soon, being so unseasonable for this time of year.

Another courtier, the fourth-born son of a lord, decided to call it quits and stay behind. Apparently the favor he could win on the road wasn't worth riding in the rain.

Elodie didn't understand why Oburleck insisted on setting out when they were already so far behind schedule. When she mentioned it to Silas he just cryptically replied "That's the point, isn't it?" before walking into the rain to help push a stuck supply wagon through the mud.

That day the wagons got so bogged down in mud they didn't make it to the next inn before Oburleck called them to a halt. Oburleck assured the party they would do fine in tents for the night. The steward and several of the lords stood under a tree to supervise while the rest set up tents. No wood dry enough to start a fire was found and everyone ate cold meat with bread and hard cheese for dinner.

After the camp was set up, Silas came to Elodie as he had each evening to practice archery. She looked up at him over Apple's back while she brushed out the mare. He held up her bow and she slumped.

"Silas. I feel like I'm starting to mold. Let's just skip tonight."

"You won't get good unless you practice, come on, Your Highness."

"I won't get good regardless. As soon as I return to the illusion all my muscles will be gone. Come on, I'm sure you don't want to be out here."

"There are things you can learn shooting in the rain. You can't plan when you'll need to use these skills. Come."

Elodie sighed exaggeratedly and trudged after the squire.

Baron Reginald and his men were up at first light packing their things to head back to the last town. They prayed for the favor of Ravid and Cooric, the gods of travelers and fools over Oburleck for his bravery and sacrifice for the kingdom as they went. The baron left his interests in the hands of Oburleck for the remainder of the Progress.

They pressed on.

Every time the Progress passed a shrine to Ravid the god of travels, nearly every member of the party took a moment to pause and pray or leave a favor. They prayed for a break in the rain and relief from their travel woes.

In the rain the caravan didn't stop for long lunches or breaks that turned into early campsites, but even without the delays, their pace did not pick up. Instead they got bogged down in mud constantly. Each time they stopped, the caravan collectively prayed they would stay till the rain ended and their supplies dried out. Unfortunately Oburleck was cheerful as ever and ushered them forward into the elements.

In the mornings, when everyone emerged from the tents or inns their clothes were just as rain-soaked and muddy as they'd been the night before. This was true of everyone except for Oburleck and a handful of the courtiers still enduring the Progress. Elodie recognized a few of them from the mage wing, and wondered why enchanters and sorcerers would endure the Progress. They had their own places on the mage board and didn't need any favor from the council or Oburleck.

Elodie pulled on her wet boots the fourth morning in a row and begged Gedas to use a spell to dry them out. "I just want to not squelch for a few moments," she pleaded.

"Not even I have the magic to dry the boots of everyone on the Progress, my Gull," he said as he patted her head and pulled on his own damp cloak. Elodie truly doubted his statement for a wizard's rank was nothing to scoff at, but she bit back the retort not wanting to sound selfish. She didn't want him to dry everyone's boots, just hers. It was true she was miserable, but compared to those in charge of setting up and tearing down the camps each day, being responsible only for herself was a luxury.

Silas still disappeared each day, riding ahead and into the woods looking for anything to supplement their diet as their grain and bread stores were ruined by poor planning. When asked, the villagers were happy to provide Oburleck with any supplies they needed, but Elodie saw worried looks on thin faces.

After a week of rain three more of the council left wishing Oburleck luck on the journey and giving him their confidence for their affairs. During their practice, Silas pointed out the only council members left were Duke Devoss, Baron Byron, and Knight Commander Jesper.

"Why haven't Devoss and Byron left yet? They can't possibly care enough about Oburleck's favor to stay," she asked.

"Duke Devoss is Master of Progress. He's honor bound to stay till the end. Even he isn't willing to compromise his honor so far. Keep both eyes open when you aim," Silas commented as she raised the bow to shoot.

"My other eye has rain in it." Elodie relaxed the arrow on her bowstring and wiped at her face.

Silas pulled her hood down so it covered her face completely. "Better?"

She turned till she was facing him, unable to see with the hood over her eyes.

"At least this way you can't tell if my eyes are open or not," she said. She turned back to the direction she assumed the tree she was using as a target was located and drew back the bowstring in the correct stance and pretended to sight, then released the arrow.

"Interesting. You're almost a better shot with your eyes covered," Silas said.

Elodie pulled back her hood and looked for her arrow. She could just see the feathers through the rain sticking out of the grass at the base of the tree. Silas was grinning slightly but dropped the expression back into his neutral mask when she smiled back.

"Try it for real this time, my lady."

"What about Byron?" she asked as she fixed her hood and grabbed another arrow. "Why is he still here?"

"That one is a mystery. He sides with Oburleck on all votes, so giving his power to Oburleck wouldn't matter. I personally think it's because he's enjoying himself."

Elodie looked at Silas to see if he was joking, but his face and spine were as straight as ever. Elodie thought about the barron, she'd never seen him smile. He did everything with a hawkish manner. It was true he didn't seem particularly bothered by the rain and just sat stoic on his horse while Devoss refilled his flask from the bottle kept in his saddlebags.

Elodie's next arrow fell a little to the right of her last one.

"And the courtiers? What could they possibly get out of staying at this point? Most of the influential members of court are gone."

She could almost see the old Silas when he talked about politics and the inner workings of the court. Topics she usually hated, but when Silas explained them, she started to see all the moving pieces on the game board. Even if he didn't make it interesting, Elodie would still prompt him to keep talking. She felt less alone when she saw those glimpses of her old friend.

"You mean the gaggle of younger siblings and mages? They're all looking for council positions," Silas said. "Get your elbow back up."

Elodie raised her elbow. "What positions are open?"

"The Aluna mage board has an open position for their representative explaining the presence of the mages. They know a backing from Oburleck will all but guarantee them elected. As for the younger sons and daughters, Lord Riyan is getting up there in age."

"Wait, the mage board hasn't elected a representative yet? Cosimo died over two years ago, right?"

"Yes, and Sorcerer Alena was elected his replacement. She died three months ago under suspicious circumstances still under investigation."

Elodie's arrow shot wide of the target. She turned to Silas and stared at him, her eyes wide. The squire wiped the rain off his face and sighed; he gave her a knowing look.

"What could kill a sorcerer?"

"That's the question best left unasked, I think." Silas handed her a new arrow.

"Doesn't Riyan get to name his own successor on the council?"

"Only if he steps down before he dies. And now he's given his power to Oburleck for the remainder of the Progress, so reasonably Oburleck could name his successor before we get back to the castle."

"Riyan would hate that." Elodie released her last arrow and it sunk into the base of the tree, still below the knot she was aiming for, but she did a fist pump in victory.

"Yes, he would, but he knew the risk when he left the Progress."

Elodie looked up at the cloudy sky spitting on her. "He never would have survived this."

"In which case Oburleck could still appoint his successor."

Elodie frowned. "Do you think he will use it? The council has been giving him their confidence, but it's just a formality. He wouldn't really make any big decisions." It didn't come out as a question, and Silas pretended it wasn't one.

"Come, let's collect the arrows and start again."

Elodie followed him across the muddy field and hunted beside Silas in the rain for her arrows.

TWO WEEKS into the rain Elodie knew they were nearing Comak. She'd been planning out her approach, how to make sure a tent was tied to her pack instead of onto the supply wagons when the time came, and what food she would need to bring that wouldn't weigh too heavily on the party she left behind. Elodie began to grow anxious with the planning. What she would say if Gedas tracked her down and accused her of leaving. She rehearsed the words over and over about how it wasn't a big deal, just something that needed to be done. She worried her plans were obvious. Silas looked at her strangely when she asked Sir Jesper about their distance from one of the lesser roads branching off toward Comak.

The morning she planned to set off Silas didn't head off into the woods to hunt as he usually did. Instead he stuck close to the caravan. Elodie tried to think up excuses to separate herself from Gedas. She let her horse's pace slow till she drifted back in the column. The rain picked up into a thick curtain of water soaking every inch of her, and she tried to get lost in the downpour. She couldn't make out Silas's or Gedas's horses any longer, and hoped they couldn't see her. She slowed Apple further and moved to the side so the Progress passed her horse by horse. She would wait under the trees till the last wagons passed, then she could find the road for Comak.

A cry went up from the riders at the front of the Progress. Elodie's heart raced and she turned Apple toward the trees. There was a blinding flash and a crack of thunder so loud her heart nearly stopped. Apple lurched forward ready to break for the trees and a hand came out of the downpour to grab her reins.

Chapter Thirty-Five

ELODIE GASPED and tried to pull her reins back from the stranger, but Apple steadied against the piebald mare and her rider as if comforted by the presence of a friend.

Horses not as even-tempered as Apple rushed past in the rain. Lightning flashed and lit Silas's face under his hood.

"Stay close to me," he yelled.

Another clap of thunder and a stallion screamed in the distance.

Silas held tight to her reins and led them toward the trees. She clutched at her saddle and patted Apple's neck whispering soothing things only she could hear.

Shouts from all directions reached them, but Elodie couldn't make them out through the rain and rolling thunder. Horses with empty saddles crashed past them in every direction and a horse, eyes wide in terror, passed dragging a turned cart.

Under the trees they could at least see a few feet in every direction. Elodie felt useless cowering with the horses.

"Should we go and help?" Elodie asked. People and horses had to be hurt trapped out in the open, clear targets for the lightning.

Silas's mouth was a grim line, his jaw set. "No. You'll do no one good if you die in this."

"My life isn't more important than anyone else's, Silas."

"Yes it is, my lady." He looked at her now, eyes shimmering with anger and fear. She'd never seen so much fear in his eyes before. "You need to learn that now if you haven't already." He looked back toward the rain as if he wanted to leave the trees as much as she did.

"What's wrong?" she asked.

"That stallion scream was Sunburst. Sir Jesper's mount. I've been with him in thunderstorms before. He doesn't panic."

Elodie's heart raced. She liked Jesper. He dragged her to every meeting in every village, but he always encouraged her and insisted she brought value. Silas tore his eyes away from the rain and observed their surroundings. He positioned them with trees to their back and a clear path out of the small forest and kept a hand on his sword while the storm raged.

Guards, servants and holsters found places around them in the trees to tie off horses and shelter from the rain. A few men ventured back into the rain and brought back horses. Silas watched it all with clear, alert eyes.

After a short time Elodie started shaking. The rain wasn't freezing yet she couldn't stop shivering. Silas took off his soaked cloak and draped it over her. He handed her his flask and told her to drink before he returned to watching.

She didn't argue.

The flask was filled with strong mint tea. It was still hot. She looked at the flask impressed. The charm to keep the contents hot was well done. She drank the tea and it warmed her.

She'd been a ways behind Jesper and Gedas when the storm struck, so it made sense she wouldn't see them in this stretch of the woods, but she worried. The storm raged for an hour before the lightning and thunder moved into the distance, and the rain lessened.

When the rain was thin enough they could see the road Elodie nudged Silas. "Let's go."

He nodded and they emerged from the trees. As if waiting for the prompt, the Progress crew followed and began picking up supplies scattered across the road and sunk in the mud. Elodie and Silas rode through the chaos toward the front of the Progress. Elodie met the wide eyes of men and women wandering through the rain to collect supplies. They passed one cart scorched and partially exploded from a lightning strike, but didn't see any fallen horses or people. It was a small miracle.

Silas spotted Gedas's mount first through the trees on the side of the road. Gedas appeared as they approached.

"Enjoying the summer rain, my Gull?" he asked casually, though his eyes betrayed a relief anything but casual. She nodded.

"Sir Jesper?" Silas asked.

"Still with us," Gedas said, and gestured into the trees.

Silas dismounted in a quick graceful movement and moved past the wizard. Elodie tried to dismount and stumbled in the mud. A heavy weight rested on her and she realized she still had Silas's soaked cloak in addition to her own. She peeled off the cloak and dropped it over Apple's back to keep it from the mud. A hostler she recognized from Gedas's evening meals smiled and took their reins.

Gedas threw an arm around her in a tight hug and led her into the trees. Sir Jesper leaned against the base of a tree, his face pale. His pants leg was torn and bloody, but the leg beneath looked whole.

"I'm fine, Silas, really. Just healer's fatigue."

"What happened, my lord?" Silas asked quietly.

Jesper glanced to his left, then winced and straightened his back. A few drowsy-eyed mage courtiers leaned against trees as though resting in the shade after a long day in the sun.

"Nothing major. Sunburst startled in the storm and tossed me. I broke the leg, but Gedas was kind enough to mend the fracture."

"It was nothing serious," Gedas replied. "Just a small break that would have healed quick enough, I only helped it along."

By the amount of blood she saw, that was not likely to be true, but Gedas usually played down his magic use.

People were moving now, leading horses back to the road and lining up carts. Two men approached and gestured to Sir Jesper.

"We have a cart for the commander."

Silas nodded and helped Jesper stand. He was wobbly on his feet and winced with the first few steps but insisted walking on his own. Silas helped him into the cart.

"Mind he doesn't fall asleep on the journey," Gedas told the squire. "He bumped his head and shouldn't sleep for a few hours yet. I will brew him something to help when we reach the castle."

"The castle?" Elodie asked.

"Oh yes, we have lost too many carts and supplies to continue on schedule. Oburleck has called a temporary pause to the Progress and invited us back to his holdings to recoup before we continue."

Silas sighed and left to fetch their horses.

"To Comak?" Elodie asked.

Gedas frowned and nodded.

Elodie almost laughed, but stopped herself afraid the laughter would be followed by tears. All her planning and preparations to escape the Progress, and now they were headed to Comak as if it was nothing. If she started laughing she would definitely cry.

Gedas was looking at her funny, so she found something to say.

"You should be happy then, another lord's personal library to raid."

Gedas did laugh, but it was a short sharp thing. "Yes. Oh joy. Staying a few weeks in one of the worst libraries in Aluna. Oburleck's collection was bought to look pretty. All new books with the most lavish bindings. Picks them out for how much gold lettering the covers possess. Harump."

Elodie knew Gedas's opinions on decorational libraries and decided not to interrupt her mentor's rant. It would make him feel better if he got on a good roll.

"A ludicrous and cockamamy belief the appearance of a library shows more wealth than an authentic storehouse of the world's knowledge. Witless feebleminded planning to buy books and scrolls just to have an excuse to hire a librarian."

Silas returned to them leading Gedas and her mounts.

"Harebrained, fatuous men who wouldn't value proper knowledge if it fell on their small heads."

"What is he on about?" Silas asked.

"Libraries that are full of books but empty of knowledge."

"What?" Silas asked again.

Elodie laughed at the confused look on his face. The laugh felt a little hysterical, but she hoped no one else noticed.

"Gedas is mad because we will be stuck in Comak and the library only has newer books."

"New, my lady?"

"All written in the last century or so I think."

Silas shook his head.

THEY STAYED in an inn at the crossroads of the great highway and the road to Comak. Some of the party stayed with the ruined wagons while spares could be fetched to carry the salvageable supplies. Oburleck insisted Jesper stay in a proper room in the inn, but the knight refused insisting he was fine. Instead they stayed in an empty stall in the stables, and Gedas and Elodie joined them in an adjacent stall. When they were finally in shelter Gedas magically dried Jesper's clothes showing his worry for the man's condition. He sent Elodie and Silas to the inn's kitchens to brew the simple tonic that would heal shock and the sickness caused by a head wound.

When Elodie told the inn's cook she was there on orders of Wizard Gediminas, the cook gave her the tools and space she needed.

Gedas placed a sleeping spell on the tonic before making the knight drink it, and Elodie decided to curl up under her own dry blanket from the stables. With the soft voices of Silas and Gedas near her, she was asleep in moments.

When Duke Devoss emerged from the inn the next morning, he blanched as he saw Sir Jesper mounted and waiting with Elodie and Gedas for the Progress to begin.

"My lord," he addressed Jesper. "Should you be riding so soon after your injury?"

Jesper nodded to the Duke. "I appreciate your concern, but I'm quite well this morning."

In truth he'd woken, shaky on his feet until Gedas handed him a flask Elodie didn't think held tea. When the flask was empty Jesper ventured out into the rain and started organizing the caravan.

"After such a tumble, wouldn't it be best to rest here a few days before continuing?" Devoss asked.

"I wouldn't dream of leaving the Progress for something so minor as a few scratches, my good man. No, once the steward is ready we should be all set to ride."

Devoss frowned and nodded. "I will check on him," he mumbled before returning to the inn.

As though the promise of a resting place was all the storm waited for, the rain stopped the next afternoon. The lack of rain meant instead of being soaked and muddy, now they were muddy with no chance of washing clean. Soon the mud created a thick crust, covering the lower half of everything.

"At least our skin will be feather soft by the end of this," Gedas remarked to Elodie after a lunch break while she tried to scrape the inches of mud off her boots with a stick before mounting Apple.

It took them three days to reach Comak, turning off the great highway the first day and traveling south.

As they approached the castle the weather-worn mud-crusted travelers picked up. Even the horses had an extra bounce in their step as though knowing sanctuary was close at hoof.

Elodie had spent time at many of the castles around Aluna. Gedas very much enjoyed exploring the personal libraries of the old families. In her travels she'd never been to Comack. The city was bright and clean, such a contrast to Tross. With all of the rain from the last weeks, Elodie didn't doubt the sewers of Tross would have flooded into the Odure District.

In Comack, the streets were even and well paved, and even after all the rain, no mud or trash lined the streets.

The gutters glistened.

From the road leading to the castle Elodie could see merchant shops lining the way with brightly colored fabrics flapping in the breeze. No shoeless kids darted between the riders, no beggars sat in the street or leaned against buildings.

It all felt almost artificial in its idealistic beauty.

When they arrived in the castle courtyard the hostlers and stablemen of Comak lent a hand to the party, getting the horses dry and stowed in record time. Elodie was shown to her own room in the guest wing, a floor above Gedas's assigned room, and a floor below Sir Jesper and Silas.

Comak had proper plumbing and Elodie took a hot shower, steaming off the mud and reveling in the warmth.

Once properly pruny, she changed into some of the fine clothes from her trunk she hadn't bothered wearing on the road while a maid picked up her wet and dirty things for the castle laundry.

Elodie flopped on her bed after the maid left, delighting in the feeling of being clean and dry. A knock on her door sounded and she questioned whether she was better off ignoring it and taking a nap, but the knock persisted.

It was Silas of course, in dry borrowed clothes short in the legs and baggy in the tunic.

"Squire Silas, it's so good to see you! I feel as though I haven't seen you in ages what with all the mud previously obscuring my view," she said in her sweetest voice.

"Uhh," Silas stammered before he caught himself and dropped his gaze. "You look . . . nice."

Elodie flounced to show off her many ruffles in the most ridiculous way. "Thank you, my lord." She dropped her posture and looked back to him still standing in the doorway. "So what's up?"

"We are to meet Steward Oburleck for a formal dinner."

Elodie scrunched up her face. "That sounds like so much fun." She grimaced, but took the arm Silas offered anyways.

The floor of the corridors reflected the soft light from the light globes lining the walls. Elodie frowned remembering walking down this same corridor with very muddy boots quite recently.

The walls were lined with tapestries and paintings in gold frames, and the molding along the ceiling was free of any dust or cobwebs. Similarly the great hall was large and grand with ornate golden candelabras lining the walls and tapestries depicting beautiful scenes. Gold and silver threads wove through the tapestries with precious stones that glinted in the candlelight.

Silas escorted her closer to the table until the head footman scooped her up and guided her to her chair on the left of the head position.

Once the whole party was present Oburleck walked in escorting his wife. Everyone at the table stood, except for Elodie, following protocol.

"Thank you all for joining us. I'm so glad we could come together and enjoy some of the comforts of home." Several of the party gave small cheers. "Your Highness, may I make you known to my lovely wife Lady Madelina, Duchess of Comak?" Oburleck asked.

He escorted his wife to Elodie's side and the lady curtsied with a vague smile.

"Madelina, darling, you remember Her Highness, Princess Elodie, don't you?"

Oburleck's wife was an elegant willowy woman who swayed slightly as though life weighed on her in ways not entirely visible to the eye. Her hair was elegantly arranged, every piece set to perfection in an updo with ringlets hanging down on either side. Her dress was beautiful and in fashion, small pearls lining the bodice and the neckline scooped low in a way that was both elegant and beautiful for her age. She smiled kindly, and held herself well, but the blue rimming her mouth and lips made Elodie's stomach sour when she looked at the woman.

Most cheer stick chewers with blue lips came from the lower class. The sticks being cheap and having a lower concentration of the chemical causing happiness were also quicker to stain your skin. Most of the upper class could afford the more potent leaves of the cheer tree to chew instead. Chewing leaves was less likely to dye your lips and teeth the telltale blue color.

Lady Madelina wore red lip paint to help cover the blueness, but Elodie had seen many people with that look. For someone of Lady Madelina's wealth to have lips so tinted blue indicated she had a very major addiction to the leaf.

"Oh yes, little Elodie girl, all grown up," Lady Madelina said, in a sweet soft voice, her eyes meeting Elodie's just for a moment before floating away. As she spoke, Elodie could see her teeth and tongue were equally stained. After the couple took their seats, the rest of the table followed suit.

Elodie was definitely the best dressed among the party, aside from Oburleck and his wife, Lady Madelina. Everyone else on Progress didn't have anything clean left to wear and the other lords, and duke, and courtiers wore partially dried clothes speckled with mud, or like Silas, borrowed clothes with a bad fit.

The table was arranged for a formal feast, Oburleck at the head of the table, with his wife on the right. Elodie sat across from her on the left. Duke Devoss sat next to her. Gedas had been given a place farther down the table, nearer to Sir Jesper, and Silas had not been given a place at all, only serving as her escort. She believed he was standing somewhere along the wall behind her, like some of the other squires and manservants present, but she hadn't turned her head to look, as it would be considered rude.

Elodie sighed. She wished she could have taken a nap.

Although Elodie's rank was technically higher than Oburleck, as the Lord of Comak, he was the highest rank in his castle. Elodie didn't care, but the fact that her chair was the same height as his, a few inches above the others, just made her feet hang off the chair when she sat back properly. She felt like a child.

Servers came and went, in the purple and gold of Comak's

colors, filling glasses with watered-down dinner wine. Soup was laid out as a first course. It was a rich broccoli cheddar bisque and she ate all of it using the slow and careful spoon movements she'd been taught.

When the second course was brought out, braised brussels sprouts and roast duck, Duke Devoss decided talking over Elodie for the entire meal may be a bit rude and asked her what plans she may have while they relaxed in the castle.

"I have a friend in the city I was thinking of looking up, actually," she said aloud not really thinking.

"Really?" Duke Devoss asked, almost interested. "You do travel so much, it's good to know you have contacts."

"I had a friend in the city once," Lady Madelina said absently, startling their end of the table into silence. She looked around, as though surprised to see them, but upon finding their attention she continued.

"Her father was a tailor, and we played together when he came to make clothes for us. The most beautiful garments made by the father of the most beautiful girl. We were friends for years, years longer than my mother knew, but when she found out she forbade me from ever seeing her again saying I would never catch a good husband associating with those lower than me." She trailed off, as though she forgot she was talking.

Duke Devoss asked Elodie another question, but she only half heard it, unable to take her eyes off of Lady Madelina who had skewered a brussels sprout on her fork and examined it like it was a lost treasure.

"Her eyes were such a lovely shade of brown," she said softly to herself before she bit into the sprout, some of her lip paint coming off on the green food.

"My beloved," Oburleck addressed his wife. She turned her glazed look to her husband, a small smile on her face. "Your hair is a mess, please retire and fix it."

"Okay," she said cheerfully before flipping her head back as though her hair had been down. She rose from the table and sauntered from the room. She did not return.

When the meal was over, Elodie made to rise from her chair. Silas was at her side and offered an arm. She took it.

Once they were out of the grand room in a hallway apart from the others, she dropped his arm. "I'll be fine walking back on my own, Silas, you must be starving. Go eat," she ordered. He stood there stoically and patiently, that blank mask on his face. "What?" she asked.

"Archery practice, my lady."

"Silas, no. You must be starving."

"I ate beforehand."

Elodie groaned. "We just got clean and dry, can't I stay that way for five minutes? You've been on wall duty the last hour. You have to be tired."

"Come on," he said, turning and walking away.

"Silas, do I look dressed for archery?"

"That's an advantage to archery my lady, you can do it even in a dress," he called back.

"Look at these shoes!" Elodie called, sticking a foot out from under the pink floating ruffles of the dress. "They don't deserve mud!"

"It hasn't rained for three days, my lady, The ground is dry."

"The archery pit in Tross stays muddy for a week after a rain," she called back down the hall.

Silas turned around. He walked with direct and even steps, not rushing to her side. "The Archery range here drains much better, as does the rest of the city. The pathways there are stone. Your dress and shoes will remain dry."

Silas walked away and Elodie sighed and followed.

Didn't every city drain better than Tross?

Back in her rooms once more that evening, Elodie went through the chest of drawers and found some older clothes inside, breeches, and tunics too big for her. She donned them anyways, rolling up the legs before stuffing her feet into her still damp boots.

It was nearing twilight. It was too late for her to get started on her real plan, but she couldn't sit in her rooms. She needed to be doing something or she would go crazy.

She rummaged through her old pack and pulled out the satchel she used for harvesting plants, her clippers already inside. She tossed in the light rock Silas had given her, and waited till it was nearly dark before heading out.

She made it to the side of the castle, just past the kitchens before she was stopped.

Chapter Thirty-Six

"YOUR HIGHNESS, WHERE ARE YOU GOING?"

"Sorry, no highnesses here, please try again later," she called over her shoulder.

"Elodie, wait," he tried again. When she heard her name, she paused, letting him catch up. "It's going to be dark soon, you shouldn't be out by yourself."

"Well then, I guess you should come with."

"Where are we heading, my lady?" Silas asked, matching her stride.

"Into the woods."

"It isn't proper."

Was that the excuse he would use? That wasn't an issue, and it definitely wouldn't be enough to keep her inside the castle walls. She needed to be outside so she could think, or not think. After weeks on Progress, being in the stone walls was too much.

Elodie looked at him blankly for a moment, then shook her head. "Then stay here and let me go into the dark woods alone." She turned and kept walking to the tree line, suppressing the smile as Silas caught up and followed behind. "I don't see how it's a big deal anyways," she said, hoping to rile him up and break that stoic mask of duty he insisted on wearing. "I thought we were going to get married eventually anyways?"

"Uhhhhhh."

Elodie made sure to turn so she could see the look of shock, confusion and fear on his face. The fear was unexpected and had an equal chance of making Elodie laugh as it did to offend her. She chose to laugh and hurried into the forest forcing him to catch up.

"Where are we going?"

"There's a flower that grows in this part of the country, fairies' breath. It blooms at twilight and is said to be very pretty."

"What is it used for, my lady?"

"Nothing."

"Then why are we looking for it?"

"People say it's really pretty."

A sigh came from behind her. "It's not even twilight yet."

"I know, I'm trying to find it before twilight. It only blooms for a few minutes. If you cut it at twilight, while it's in full bloom, then it will stay that way."

"So how will you find it if it hasn't bloomed yet?"

"The leaf and stem pattern is very unique."

"So we are looking for a random plant somewhere in the forest?"

"You didn't have to come."

"Yes, I did."

"You know for someone so nervous about being caught out alone with me, you sure are being loud."

"I'm talking quieter than you're walking, my lady."

"You're making noise too."

"No I'm not."

Elodie stopped, pausing in the leaves and twigs to prove her point. Silas kept walking till he was even with her side. His last few steps making less noise than the trees blowing in the soft wind above them.

"How do you do that?" she asked.

"Practice."

"That's not very helpful."

Silas seemed to think on it for a moment, tapping his chin in thought. "Try not stepping on every branch and twig you see, my lady."

Elodie gave him a dirty look and Silas grinned back at her, that sly look she'd missed back in his eyes.

Elodie huffed, pretending offense and tried to take a few quiet steps, moving her feet as slowly as she could. The first few steps were marginally quieter, but her fourth step landed on a dry branch hidden by some dry leaves, and the loud snap made her wince.

"Whatever," she said, resuming her quicker and much noisier pace.

"Remind me not to take you hunting."

"I'm better at foraging anyways."

"So what are we looking for?" Silas asked. They were nearly five minutes into the forest and the light was growing dark. Silas pulled a light stone out of his belt purse and Elodie, realizing her eyes had been straining in the dim light, pulled her own stone out as well.

"The fairies' breath grows near other magically potent plants, so look for something you know uses magic."

"Like cheer trees?" Silas asked.

"Yes!"

Silas pointed to their left and Elodie could just make out the glow from the lighter trunks. She rushed over and started looking around the ashy white trunks circling out a few steps at a time.

"The plant should be a light green color, the stems grow in a corkscrew pattern, and the leaves may look all rolled up," she called to Silas, on the other side of the cheer trees.

"Elodie, look here," Silas called. Elodie followed the glow of his light stone. He was on the other side of an older thick-trunked cheer tree. "Have you ever seen anything like it?" He gestured to the red growth spiraling up the trunk of the cheer tree.

Elodie bent closer to look. It was a fungus of some type, the many wavy discs of the fungus sporocarp stacked together and branched off, growing up the trunk in a strange spiral pattern. It was beautiful, the red and orange vibrant colors contrasted against the white of the tree. She'd never seen anything like it.

"What is it?" Silas asked again.

"I don't know." Elodie passed the light stone up the trunk following the pattern. "Look here." She stopped at a point in the growth where some of the fungus hadn't grown as long as the pieces around it. "See how the base of this section is wide, but then it's short growing here? This has been cut off and is regrowing, like someone has been harvesting it. Look." She pointed to more such scars in the pattern around the front of the tree. "It looks like it's been harvested over years."

Elodie pulled out her belt knife and Silas stopped her. "What if it's poisonous?"

"Oh it's likely poisonous based on its color, or possibly just magically potent. But don't worry, I won't touch it."

She pulled a cloth out of her foraging bag and held it under a section of the fungus, cutting carefully along the base of the sporocarp making sure to get as much of the intact fungus as she could to make identification easier. She cut off a few sections letting the pieces fall into the cloth and folded the cloth around it gently before tucking it into her bag with her blade.

"There, now I can ask Gedas about it. Let's keep looking for the fairies' breath." She looked overhead at the sky visible through the trees. "It looks too close to twilight."

Elodie wandered around the trunk of the tree. She spied something glowing just behind another tree a short distance away and tried to hurry to it, nearly stumbling on a tree branch in the process. Silas caught her and steadied her as she rounded the tree just in time to see a pale gray purple flower emitting a soft glow before the bud closed.

"Are you going to pick it?" Silas asked, a small hint of awe in his voice.

"No, you have to cut the stem while it's in full bloom. We were too late." She sighed.

"We can try again tomorrow night."

"It's not that big of a deal, let's just get back," Elodie said before she set off between the trees.

"Where are you going?" Silas asked, the sound of a smile in his voice.

"Back to the castle," Elodie said, now a little annoyed at her failed plans. What a great diversion this had turned out to be.

Silas pointed in another direction. Elodie sighed and stomped off the direction he indicated. She ignored the chuckle that came from behind her, but it lightened her spirit all the same.

Silas walked Elodie to Gedas's room so she could show him the fungus she'd found. She told Silas not to wait around for her, as Gedas would likely go on for hours about the plant, and once she was at Gedas's door, he simply bowed and waited for her to enter.

Elodie greeted the old wizard, accepting a cup of spiced tea. She showed him the fungus and explained the pattern it had made growing up the trunk. Gedas had to think on this for a few moments, taking a long sip of his tea.

"It isn't something I've seen personally, but it does sound like something I read about once." He closed his eyes tight and tapped his forehead a few times, as though trying to tap the memory to the surface. "Dragon's breath, if I remember correctly. Named so for the fire pattern it makes up the tree."

The fungus did resemble fire dancing and winding up the tree trunk. It was a fitting name.

"I didn't think it grew in this part of the world naturally. It is more commonly associated with the continent far to the east. It's the national plant for Risonia, I believe. Checking a book by region will likely be your best bet for more information, but I don't think you'll find a book on Risonia in this puerile library," he finished, the distaste clear on his face.

"Maybe I will look anyways," Elodie said, thinking out loud.

"If you are looking for a project, you could use that spell I taught you back in Tate, using other plant essences to identify any like characteristics or uses from the dragon's breath."

"No Gedas, I don't want to do any spells while I'm here. It's too hard to keep my head on straight when I use magic like it's normal and then return to the illusion. Magic only causes trouble," she said softly, thinking back to her dead morning glory plants.

Gedas didn't say anything in reply, but Elodie could feel the words left unspoken between them, and finished her tea before excusing herself for bed.

The next morning one of the maids who was seeing to her needs delivered her breakfast and tea along with her clean and dry clothes. They were silent and efficient and didn't make eye contact when Elodie thanked them.

Elodie was shocked to see her clothes ready so soon. Everyone from the Progress would have dropped their clothes off with the castle laundry all at once. It was surprising to see they'd gone through all that laundry in one night. Elodie wondered if her clothes had taken some priority or if the palace had called in extra help and every magic wielder able to generate heat to help dry.

With the lavish comfort Oburleck draped over those of the Progress, she wouldn't be completely surprised. Regardless, it would be a big weight on his staff. She hoped Oburleck's people got some sleep last night.

Elodie picked out the nicest of the dresses packed in her trunk and folded them up gently, tucking them into her shoulder pack. After she ate and dressed in simple clothes she swung on her favorite faded green cloak. All her shirts and dresses were low enough to show the albatross at her collar, but the cloak covered it perfectly. She shouldered her pack under the cloak and escaped the castle.

Elodie looked for the most respectable section of the market first. The city was polished around her. No trash littered the streets, and animal droppings seemed to be frequently swept into the gutters lining the road. The gutters themselves flowed well, emptying into grates in the city streets, such a contrast to Tross. The people of the city looked well off. Even when she passed through a part of the city not showing the same wealth, she didn't see any pickpockets roaming about and saw a high number of guardsmen for a city of this size.

The Progress was never meant to detour to Comak but if it wasn't for that fact Elodie would suspect the city had been prepared for the nobles' arrival knowing in advance their lord and the highest of the court of Aluna would be there with scrutinizing eyes.

Elodie wandered the streets for a short time observing the flow of people, and got more than one scathing look as though people wondered if she was up to no good.

Elodie thought she'd picked her nicer tunic and breeches for the trip, not wanting to stick out as someone worthy of a pickpocket but well enough off she'd be taken seriously at her business. It was just the sort of look Gedas taught her to master over so many years.

Elodie opened the door to the tailor shop and entered. The room was bright with racks hung about showing fine fabrics and sample garments. The air smelled slightly of lavender, fresh and clean. It wasn't the best tailor in the city, but the second-best. She'd asked a few people in the streets which one was the best and made sure to avoid it.

After a moment of looking at racks an assistant approached and asked what she needed. "May I speak with the master tailor please?" Elodie asked.

"I am perfectly happy to help you with anything you may need." The apprentice was a short girl with sharp eyes.

"Thank you, I have business specifically with the master tailor," Elodie said, firmly.

"He only sees people by appointments."

Elodie reached into her bag and pulled out one of the fine garments, the gold embroidery of a sleeve gleaming in the light. "I wish to sell. I would like to talk to the master tailor please."

"And who did you steal these from, girl? Should I call the guard?"

"If you call the master tailor, he will be able to see they were clearly made to fit me precisely. They are my gowns, and the latest fashion in Tross. I wish to sell them."

The master tailor was retrieved and after an examination of a few of the gowns Elodie laid out, he didn't ask her who she was or why she was selling. Instead, he bartered.

His eyes lit with a fire of possibility as he looked over the fabric and stitch work. The gowns could be taken apart, the fabric used and the patterns copied and reworked before being sold.

Tross was many things; dirty, smelly, unsanitary, but it was still the capital of Aluna and the palace seamstresses were still renowned for setting fashion in the kingdom.

They bartered. Elodie hated doing it. She just wanted a flat price and to be done with it, but she knew that wasn't how things worked. She felt both selfish for trying to get a higher price and desperate for getting as much gold as she could get. Eventually the tailor handed her over a sack of coins.

Elodie tucked the sack into her shoulder bag and left the shop.

She walked down the short steps of the shop over the gutters and back onto the street. She looked around herself a few times trying to decide which way she should go first. Callie wouldn't be at one of the wealthiest bordello houses in this part of the city but she also didn't want to start by walking into the lowest bordello house and working her way up. She sighed and turned down the road planning on stopping at the first one she found and going from there. Hopefully someone would recognize Callie's name or her description and would be able to point Elodie in the right direction.

"Is this really your plan?" a voice asked from behind making her jump. "Getting a bag of gold and then walking around the city going to every dive asking after some bound girl?"

"Silas, you scared me!"

"Exactly, Princess. I could have been anyone come up behind

you to slit your throat and steal your gold." He met her gaze for once, eyes wide and serious. "You know I'd have come with you if you'd asked."

Elodie looked down at her feet. She knew Silas probably would have come with her, but he also might have tried to talk her out of it or tell her why it was such a bad idea. It also felt so much like something she needed to do on her own. She'd abandoned Callie, she'd left her behind. The thought made her feel sick in her stomach. She didn't want to leave anyone behind anymore. Thoughts of Vanessa and what she'd told her rang through Elodie's mind. Why did she always leave her friends behind?

Elodie took a deep breath and pushed those feelings away. "What happened to all of your talk about rule-following?"

"You know this is different."

Elodie nodded. She did know it was different.

"Besides," he continued. "It's my fault she's here. You asked me to watch out for her and I didn't."

She looked up and saw something in his eyes she knew well. Guilt. He felt guilt over Callie, even though she already told him it wasn't his fault. She'd seen that look so many times the last few weeks but hadn't realized what it was. Was this why he wouldn't meet her eyes?

She grabbed his hand and squeezed it till he looked at her.

"I don't blame you," she said. "And I shouldn't blame myself either. We thought she was somewhat safe, safer than she'd been on the streets. I was pulled away by the spell, and you by your duty. Two forces so strong nothing could break them." Elodie smiled and Silas smiled back. "So let's forgive ourselves, and make sure we right this in the end. Deal?"

"Deal."

Elodie dropped his hand and looked around.

"So, my lord. Do you have any idea where we should start looking?"

Silas frowned. "I've asked around about a few bordello houses specifically owned by Baron Byron. I figured we should start there."

The first bordello house they went to was a bust. It was still early in the day and few patrons sat around the quiet dark room sipping drinks and chatting. Silver rings glinted at the necks of their companions. The blue lipped girl at the counter didn't know any girls matching Callie's name or description.

At the third house, they were lucky. The young boy serving drinks, bronze ring around his neck, recognized Callie's description although he said her name was Calendula. He told them which house to go to.

This bordello was nearly deserted, a few women with bronze rings sitting in a corner with no one to talk to. One of them rose when Elodie and Silas came in. She said she knew who Elodie and Silas were looking for but said she wasn't available. The woman offered to help them instead. Elodie shook her head trying to keep her disgust at bay.

"We aren't here to pay for her, we're here to talk to her. She's my friend."

"Honey, people like me don't have friends like you unless they pay for us," she said pointedly.

Silas pulled a coin out of his bag, a small silver one. "Then we'll pay. Let us see her."

"It's double for the both of you," she said, giving Silas a weird look that made him blanch, breaking his stoic manner. Elodie fished a coin out of her bag and the girl snatched them both up.

A man came in, shaggy dark hair and a light complexion with intense blue eyes. Elodie thought he looked vaguely familiar. He nearly bumped into her as another girl came to greet him, taking him to a table in the corner. Elodie decided he looked like every man she'd seen in any of the bordellos that day and followed the woman upstairs to an empty room with Silas. The furnishings were garrish and overdone. The lighting was bad, but everything looked faded and old and worn out. If the castle had felt stuffy the night before, this building was suffocating.

She knew what went on in places like this, and had tried to ignore it before now. The room below had been dark and crowded, but felt like a tavern. In this room the ugly truth was unavoidable.

"Don't touch anything," Silas said, a look of disgust on his face when the door closed behind them. Elodie agreed standing to the side of a large lounge chair. The air was stale with old incense and spilled beer.

They waited long enough for Silas to get stir crazy. He checked the window in the room three times. His hand didn't leave the sword under his cloak.

Eventually the door opened and a redheaded girl of about fourteen walked in wearing flowing robes of a glittery fabric. Her face was aloof with something like resigned apprehension as she looked to Silas.

"What may I do for you, master," she asked in a willowy voice before her eyes landed on Elodie growing wide with shock.

"Callie, it's me," Elodie said at last rushing to her friend. Callie pulled back, her face showing both fear and mistrust.

"You shouldn't be here, why are you here?" Callie asked, backing up till her back was at the door. Her face was hard, the light and joy she'd always had, even when she lived in a gutter was gone.

"I came to get you, Callie."

"Came to get me?" she said with a sad laugh. "Do you see the silver around my neck? Don't you know where you are, Princess?" She pulled the fine fabric down lower, showing the gleaming metal.

The title stung when Callie said it, but Elodie didn't back down. "I have gold, I can pay for your bond."

"And then I'll be indebted to you. No thank you. Just switching one collar for another." Callie crossed her arms.

It felt like Callie slapped her.

"It's not like that, Callie, you're my friend. I would burn the papers."

"My name's not Callie anymore, I go by Calendula now."

"Why won't you let me help?" Elodie asked softly. Her throat was tight.

"I'm not the same girl I used to be, Ellie. This place changes you, and you can't help me." Callie opened the door to the room and stepped out. "Don't come back here, Ellie, it's not a place for a princess to be." The look when she said 'princess' was filled with disgust and loathing. Callie closed the door, leaving Elodie and Silas standing there.

Elodie stared at the door. After a moment a hand fell on her shoulder and she looked up at Silas.

"Let's go," he said softly.

He handed her a handkerchief and Elodie stared at it. He took it from her and wiped at her eyes. Elodie blushed. She didn't realize she'd been crying.

She wanted to do so many things besides go, she wanted to chase after Callie, to ask what was wrong and why she couldn't help. She wanted to make Callie understand she was there for her, and would always be. But the hate in Callie's eyes caused her to deflate. Her vision of how this meeting would go faded away into the useless cloud of hopes and dreams.

Chapter Thirty-Seven

THEY RETURNED to the castle in silence. Silas escorted Elodie back to her rooms. She entered and leaned against the closed door. Should she go back and see Callie again in the morning? And then again the next day? Each day until she finally agreed to let Elodie help her?

Once Silas's footsteps had faded into the distance, Elodie lifted herself from where she leaned, opened her door, and walked down the hall. She wasn't quite sure where she was headed, but knew the general direction. The castle was spotless, yet she hadn't seen maids outside of her rooms. They must be very good at hiding.

She was stopped by a guard on the second floor of the east wing and told the man what she needed. He led her to a parlor and told her to wait. The room was ornate and beautiful. It had a rich gray-blue wallpaper with a beautiful design, and dark walnut furnishings. After a moment Lady Madelina entered the room with a vase of yellow lilies and set them on a corner table. She spent a moment looking at them from different angles before turning the vase a few ways. She picked it up again, and looked around the room.

She spotted Elodie standing awkwardly by the entrance and her eyes lit up. She rushed over to Elodie, flowers in hand.

"Princess! What a delight to see you. I didn't know we had a date scheduled." She looked around herself for a moment, and then handed Elodie the flower vase. Once her hands were free she curtsied with an elegant sweep of her purple satin gown, and then took the flowers back.

"Marry for money dear, it's much more sensible than marrying for something foolish like love," Lady Madelina said with a smile. She made intense eye contact before breaking it and putting the flower vase on another table. She stepped back to look at it from a wider angle, as if forgetting Elodie was in the room. Lady Madelina pulled something blue out of her pocket and stuck it in her mouth, chewing slowly as she observed the vase.

"Did you marry for love, my lady?" Elodie asked politely, and Lady Madelina jumped and turned to look at her, blue leaf hanging from her lip.

She examined Elodie, and then turned back to the flowers. "No dear, I married for prestige. A man who could walk through any door and win any friends was sure to be something someday." She stood straight and stared at the ceiling for a time then picked up the vase and walked to the small table by the door and placed it.

The door opened and Oburleck came in nearly colliding with his wife.

"Try in the sitting room dear," he said to her, an arm on her shoulder to steady her.

"Oh, yes, by the big window. Perfect!" Madelina said with cheer. She scooped up the vase one more time and held it tight to her chest as she left the room.

"Your Highness, so good to see you," Oburleck said, bowing smoothly. "To what do I owe the honor of your summons?"

Elodie took a deep breath, nearly wincing at the overwhelming smell that hit her.

This was the hard part. She'd been trying to plan what to say, and now every word was flying from her mind.

"I want to end slavery," she said all at once.

Oburleck stood calmly, his expression unchanging and even as though waiting for her to continue. When she didn't, he blinked and he donned a concerned look.

"That would be a very large undertaking, what specifically would you like to accomplish with removing such a pivotal part of our kingdom's economy?"

"A better life for the people of Aluna," she said. Wasn't it obvious?

Oburleck looked her over with an expression she'd seen from many adults when she provided her opinion. "I know, it is a dark and gruesome industry. The economy of Aluna does rely on the bound industry to function. To take away the bound would be to cripple our economy."

"Within the Kingdom of Sixteen only Aluna, Vasniydor and Skuna are known for having a slave industry," Elodie said. "In eight of the nations, slavery is completely outlawed and in three others there are strict regulations against all but serfdom or indenturement. Aluna has both the largest market and the highest number of our own people in slavery."

"That's true, Aluna does have more bound than any of the other kingdoms, but Aluna is also the largest," Oburleck continued. His voice was kind if not a little condescending. "We have the most farmlands and are the largest producers of industry. The rest of the kingdoms do not have the same bound servants because their economies do not need them to function like Aluna. Vasniydor and Skuna both have larger bound numbers due to their sea trade. Take the bound from Aluna and you would cripple our economy and prevent us from producing the food our people rely on to stay alive."

"So what of the bordello? Why does our economy rely on young girls and boys being sold to houses?"

Oburleck's eyes were heavy with sadness. "It is unfortunate for the young involved, and I do agree the system may not be perfect, but bordellos are a large industry. It's complex to explain the intricacies of economy to one who has not received a proper education, but to be simplistic, by allowing a darker business to thrive in their land, a lord can collect taxes to provide resources to fix roads and businesses, all things to benefit the city overall."

"I understand the basics, Steward Oburleck. People spend money which creates jobs and industry for more to spend money," Elodie began before Oburleck cut her off.

"Ah, exactly. So you understand then why a bordello house can help benefit a land," he said, a relieved look on his face.

"No I'm . . ."

He'd turned her words around on her, and she felt frustrated over not being able to express her thoughts clearly.

"The cost can never be worth the gain," she said. "Anyone being forced against their will into a life they didn't choose . . ."

"Ah yes, choice," he said, again cutting her off. "Such a rare thing. A beautiful dream. So many people in the world are left without choice. The farmer's son wants to be a knight, but must take over for his father and learn the trade. The first-born child of a lord wishes to become an academic, but must inherit her father's titles and be leader to her people. The princess who is controlled by magical forces outside of anyone's control and isn't even able to choose when or where she travels." Oburleck paused for a moment and looked down on Elodie with a sad smile, his breath clogging her nose. "I do understand the draw of wishing we all had the ability of choice, but this isn't the world we live in. Not all are gifted with such a great blessing."

He was right of course, he had a very clear way of viewing the world. Not everyone could choose what they wanted, as Elodie was very aware. She'd never been able to choose when the ruakh would take her. She couldn't even break the spell.

She thought of Callie in that faded room, the sadness she'd seen in her friend's eyes. It wasn't enough. Elodie didn't have control over her own destiny, but it didn't mean Callie had to be forced into that non life. It didn't mean she couldn't prevent others from meeting the same fate Callie had.

"I'm going to end it," she said to Oburleck at last. He had bad breath, and Silas and Sir Jesper didn't agree with all his politics, but he was a good man. He would help her if she made her views known.

"End what?" he asked, his expression puzzled.

"Slavery."

"Oh, I see," he said as if remembering. "And how specifically do you plan to end it? As I've mentioned this is a very complex matter, Your Highness, and all due respect, as specified by the laws put in place by your father, while you are victim to the spell of the Misplaced, you are not able to make or change the laws of Aluna."

"No, I can't, but you can. You're my steward, so my interests are yours, isn't that what you said?"

Oburleck's expression grew solemn once again. "My lady, ending the bound industry would require the types of laws I as Steward am not able to make. By the same laws created by your father I have little power."

Silas had mentioned this to her. He'd said Aluna was in a hard state because some changes the land needed couldn't be made while the throne didn't have a proper ruler. Ending slavery seemed the obvious answer to help her friend and everyone like her, but if Oburleck believed it impossible, maybe it was.

"What about small policy changes? Could we set age limits to people who are bound?"

"Hmmmm." Oburleck, stroked his braided beard. "It would require a majority vote from the council, which may be difficult."

"But you have a controlling share of the council while the Progress continues. Duke Devoss and Baron Byron wouldn't vote against you, and Sir Jesper would agree to the changes."

Oburleck looked surprised, then frowned. "My lady, the council members who left us gave me their confidence and their trust. To use their absence in such an underhanded way would be wrong under the circumstances. No, I could not make a change like this in their absence, but I could see a place for a small change once we return to Tross after the Progress. Perhaps limiting the age someone can sell their children into a bound service."

"My friend wasn't sold by a parent, she was sold by her employer," Elodie said carefully.

"That's quite unusual, did she owe a debt to the employer and create the bond to pay it? I'm not sure preventing such transactions would be beneficial to the people, taking away someone's ability to better their life by paying a debt."

"No, she didn't owe a debt, he accused her of an offense and claimed her life for it."

"For her to be sold for such an offense, the crime would have been worthy of a life debt. Was her master a member of the nobility?"

A look came over Oburleck's face as though he understood, and then he tapped the side of his face where Baron Byron's scar was. "This is about the young street girl who attacked Baron Byron, is it?" Oburleck nodded and exhaled a sigh that overwhelmed Elodie with the odor. "For one of common birth to attack a member of the nobility, the penalty is death. I know it seems extreme, but laws such as these were put into place long ago to allow the nobility and the royalty, your family, to keep their power. For one who commits such a crime, she could have been executed. But the baron was merciful. Such a fate is a gift for one so young when the alternative is death."

It made sense, of course it did. But Elodie wasn't so sure Callie did attack the baron unprovoked. She wouldn't do something like that without a reason. But to argue such things with the steward, without any facts, would be pointless.

"So you're saying you won't help me?"

"I am your servant, as always, Your Highness," he said with a bow. "But I'm not sure how I can help when this is not a power you or I have while the spell is active. Perhaps Wizard Gediminas, if he really was as powerful and knowledgeable as people claim, could lend assistance in reaching those ends, but, well, I know he has been less than helpful in the past with such requests. I know I am one of many who have made pleas to him on your behalf, to break the spell, my lady. Perhaps he does not have the knowledge or power. I'm sure he isn't being intentionally malicious in ignoring such requests," Oburleck said, his eyebrows drawing together in worry.

Elodie felt that familiar twinge in her stomach at the thought of Gedas, and the task of breaking the spell looming over her. She took a deep breath and pushed the feeling away. "I will just have to work harder at breaking the spell then. Thank you, Steward, you're right. My first priority needs to be the spell." Elodie turned away.

"If only that task was a simple matter," Oburleck said sadly.

"I think I can do it," Elodie said, more to herself. "There's just a few things I need answers for." She thought back to Silas and what she'd asked him to learn the summer she'd met Callie.

"Do you really think you can do it?" Oburleck asked, his voice high in surprise, startling Elodie out of thought.

"Yes," she said confidently. "Thank you for the encouragement, Steward Oburleck." She left his rooms. She didn't feel capable of breaking the spell, but she had to believe it was possible, as the prophecy said.

In the meantime, she would still have to find a way to help Callie.

Chapter Thirty-Eight

BREAKFAST WAS LEFT by one of the silent maids. Elodie ate quickly and set off for the library, the cloth containing her fungus in one hand as she wandered through the gleaming halls. She made it ten steps inside before a sharp voice called out to her.

"You there, what do you think you're doing, child?"

Elodie turned and saw an older man, lips lined in blue and eyes much angrier and accusing than she would expect from a stick chewer.

"I'm hoping to do some research," she said to the librarian.

"These books are not for causal *research*," he said again, his voice harsh and clipped.

"Then what are they for?"

"Out." He pointed one finger toward the door.

Elodie took a deep breath. Librarians were usually helpful, but this man seemed more like the old stories of dragons protecting a hoard.

"Can I have someone send to Steward Oburleck so he may tell you personally I'm allowed here?"

"And who are you that his lordship would bother letting near his precious books?"

"I'm Princess Elodie." She crossed her arms. She hated pulling the title card, but this guy was frustrating her more than she could believe.

The librarian didn't look impressed.

He rang a bell on his desk and a tall skinny boy emerged from the shelves of books, an iron ring bent slightly and glinting at his neck.

"Go to his lordship's manservant and let him know there is a girl here claiming to be the princess and requesting access to the library." The librarian didn't spare a glance for the boy.

They waited in silence, the librarian staring her down as though waiting for his judgment to be proven right, until finally the slave returned, short of breath and bowed.

"The steward's manservant said the princess is to be allowed the utmost access to the library, and anything she needs."

The librarian scowled. "Fine." He rummaged through his desk until he came up with a white chalky twig and stuck it in his mouth. "You have access," he said with a flap of his hand as though confused why she was still waiting around.

Elodie turned to the closest shelf of books and walked behind it, out of sight of the librarian as soon as possible. She started looking over the titles, trying to get a sense of their organization. Her mouth fell open in surprise. Nearly every spine really was decorated with bits of gold leaf. She looked around shocked at the value of this collection. They were quite beautiful, the detail and designs in the leather, the ornate lettering, but it was so much finery she started to lose appreciation after looking at just a few.

After wandering the shelves helplessly lost, Elodie noticed the slave standing bowed at the end of an aisle.

"Can I help you?" she asked hesitantly.

He rose slightly and bowed again. "Is there anything I can help you find?" he asked softly.

"I'm looking for books about plants, identification, medicinal uses, that sort of thing," she said.

The boy rose from his bow and gestured with his arm. "This way, please." He led her down several bookshelves and gestured to a shelf on the right moving his hand down the bottom half of the shelves. "Agriculture." He moved to a second shelf and gestured to one row. "Healing and cures." He bowed again before disappearing between the shelves.

"Thank you!" Elodie whispered after him. She went to the agriculture section and pulled down every book that might contain something other than farming wheat, and stacked them on one of the tables she'd passed. It took several trips.

When the books with potential were stacked around her, she tapped the light globe hovering over the table till it glowed and selected the first book. Silver studs glinted on the cover. She opened it to the first section, the spine creaked and the pages lined up perfectly.

The book had never even been opened before.

She read, skimming pages and made two piles, one for books that definitely wouldn't be useful, and the second for those that probably wouldn't be useful, but she would read over more carefully.

"Is it alright I leave books at a table while I go get lunch? I should be back soon," Elodie asked the librarian a few hours later.

"Anything for you, dear," the librarian said with a kind smile as he chewed lightly on the white stick. Elodie tried not to wince at the glazed look in the man's eyes as she rushed past him. She liked him more with a personality even if he was mean.

Once her stomach was full, she returned to her work.

Sometime later as she was reading about fungal anomalies, an arm appeared in her peripheral and picked up one of the books from her useless stack. "So garish all this gold leaf. How can you even focus with the ghastly glare it's generating?" Gedas asked from her side.

"Not as bad as the glare from a mage light," Elodie said, glancing to the ball of magic hanging over Gedas's shoulder.

"Fair enough," the wizard commented before setting the book back down. "Have you had any luck?"

"No," Elodie said. She sighed and leaned back in her chair

before gesturing to another small stack of books. "I have a few books left but I'm not very hopeful. Do you know the magicity of dragon's breath?" It would save her some time cutting out books on ruakh-based life.

"It would barely register a two. Nonmagical and nonpoisonous. It's pretty when growing from the drawings I've seen, but usefully benign."

Elodie sighed again; usefully benign, just like her. Nonmagical meant it wouldn't be in the other three books. She sighed and closed the book she was reading.

"If you grow tired of sighing, I have a project you can help with. Healer Magge, Comak's healer, has a medical student with a peculiar rash. She believes it was caused by testing their own cures, but I thought you might have fun running the magical screen to decipher what may have been the cause. I'm sure you remember the spell for such things."

It was a trap and she wasn't going to fall for it. "Sounds interesting, but I still want to read over these last few books." She gestured to the pile she knew would be useless.

Gedas nodded and turned back to the shelves. "You know where to find me if you change your mind." There was something in his voice that almost made her change her mind and join him.

He sounded sad.

But Elodie had made a choice not to use magic, and she was going to stick to it.

When Gedas was gone, Elodie flipped through the few remaining books, then took them back to their shelves, a small stack at a time. While she was fitting books back in the gaps of the agriculture shelves, a book on the very top shelf caught her eye. It sat at the end of a shelf on animal rearing. It was a small thin book, the spine newer like the books around it but unmarked. The blank spine was such a contrast to the artfully decorated books, it caught her attention.

Climbing up on the first level of shelf she could just pull it down. Immediately she noted the pages were much older than the leather spine indicated. The book must have been rebound some-time in the last decade. Gedas would be interested to know not all the books in this library were as young as he believed. He would be delighted over an ancient tomb on pig farming.

She opened the book to a beautiful illustration of a flower. The page was yellowing and the artwork was fading, but it still held sharp lines and detailed shading. The flower was valo's peace as the book explained, so toxic inhaling the scent would kill a man. Cooked it was sweet and created a death-like paralysis in small quantities, full death in larger doses. It had a scent like blueberries on the breath of those who ate it.

She marveled over the drawing and took it back to her desk.

She started at the beginning, reading through each page and examining every drawing, each one more detailed and beautiful than she'd ever seen in a book not guarded like treasure. When she reached it, she didn't even realize what she was looking at, just stared at the beautiful drawing of the red fungus, growing up a tree like fire. She read the details twice before she realized it was dragon's breath. Excitement raced through her.

The dragon's breath, so named twice over, was magically benign on its own, but when grown on a magically potent host, the fungus gained new properties not fully researched or understood. It was believed the plant increased what it only referred to as charisma, to win and charm, but in exchange for the gift, the user would gain the breath of the dragon.

The book mostly sounded like nonsense to Elodie, it's language was an older form of the common tongue and took a bit of deci-phering, but she read over the passage a few more times before finishing the book and putting it back on the shelf.

When she left the library at last, the castle windows were dark, letting her know another opportunity to pick fairies' breath had passed. She returned to her room and flopped on her bed. She'd found dragon's breath growing on a cheer tree. Cheer trees were magically potent, meaning this dragon's breath wasn't magically benign after all.

She wondered if something like this could be a coincidence, that a fungus not native to this area would sprout on just the right trees in the same town where a book on the subject existed.

Probably not, but what would be the benefit of charisma? Oburleck was charming, but maybe he needed all the help he could get with such rank breath. He was a good man at heart, charisma couldn't change that.

Sitting up, she reached for the adventure book Gedas had loaned her, and noticed a crystal vase sitting atop it, filled with three perfect blooms of fairies' breath. Their petals were a soft gray color, a faint lilac light coming from the glow of the stamen in the center of the bloom. She tapped the light globe beside her bed, throwing the room into darkness except for the gentle moonglow of the flower. Useless they may be, but was something so beautiful ever truly useless?

In the morning Elodie rose and dressed in plain clothes. She left her room and headed for the stairs. She heard footsteps behind her and looked over her shoulder to see Silas following behind. He bowed to her, graceful even on stairs. "My lady. May I ask what your plans are for the day?" Elodie stopped on the landing of the floor just below hers.

"Um, just going to see Gedas," she lied. "Seeing if he is working on anything interesting."

"Allow me to escort you."

Elodie sighed and nodded. They took the stairs and walked to the room in silence. "Thanks, Silas, I got it from here," she said when they reached his door.

"Are you going to knock?"

Elodie bit back a sigh and knocked on the door.

"Yes, yes, what do you want?" Gedas said as he swung open the door.

"I came to see if you're doing anything interesting today," Elodie said.

Gedas looked from her to Silas skeptically. "Yes, well, you

know me and interesting. We are one and the same. Come in, come in. Silas, will you be joining us on our interesting?"

"Uh, he probably has more important things to be doing," Elodie said, giving the squire a smile as she entered and closed the door. "Thanks!"

Elodie turned to Gedas, he was looking at her with one eyebrow raised. "And what kind of interesting are you looking for, my Gull?" He turned to the table next to the fire to fiddle with tea things.

"I don't know, what are you working on?"

"Oh, just this or that. How did your perusal of the library go yesterday? Find anything useful in those pretty books?"

"Actually yes. I found an *old* book."

"Old?" Gedas asked, skeptical. "How old?"

"Old, old. It was rebound, so the cover was plain unmarked leather, but the pages were proper old. It was all about rare plants from around Risonia, and actually had dragon's breath in it."

"Truly?" He handed her a cup of tea.

"Yes, the book was written more like folklore than a research guide, and had the most beautiful images. It said dragon's breath on its own isn't magical, but when it grows on a magical tree it gains characteristics, it said something like granting increased charisma and making them more dragon like."

"Do you still have the fungi? There are a few experiments we can perform to suss out any magical traits."

"What kind of experiments?" Elodie asked skeptically.

"A few small spells I think would be quite at your skill level."

"Gedas, no. I told you, I don't want to do magic while I'm here. Magic messes everything up in my life. If I'm going to be normal in the illusion I need to start here."

"Now that doesn't make any kind of sense. Magic here is normal, especially for you. The ruakh is part of who you are, and there is no escaping that."

"It's only a part of who I am when I'm here."

"Yes, and this is your home."

"Is it really? I spend more time in the illusion. How can I call Aluna my home when the spell has me?" Gedas didn't immediately answer and Elodie pressed on. "Please, Gedas. Just tell me what you know of the spell. If you don't want to help me break it, then that's fine, you don't have to. I'll try to find someone who will, but please, just tell me where to start."

Gedas did not respond, and the silence stretched between them as he examined his tea. The expression was one she'd seen before on his face, but she couldn't name it. Close to sadness or guilt, but not quite either.

That twinge returned in Elodie's stomach and she pushed it away, set down her cup and left his rooms.

Thankfully Silas wasn't in the hallway. Instead of heading to the main staircase, Elodie headed toward the servant staircase and left through the kitchens, no squires in sight.

Now she knew the location, the trip to the bordello house Callie worked in was much shorter, perched on the end of the town near the forest where they'd found the dragon's breath. Elodie tried to enjoy the fresh air and morning bustle of the town waking up, but her stomach felt tight.

She entered the quiet and deserted house, and a brown-haired boy rose from a table near the bar.

"I've got this one." The woman they'd met before waved the boy away and approached Elodie. "What do you want?"

"I would like to see Calendula."

"She doesn't wanna see you." The woman crossed her arms.

"I can pay." Elodie reached into her belt purse hanging under her cloak. She felt for a few smaller coins, hands shaking, and when she withdrew them saw she'd pulled a small silver and a small gold coin. The woman's eyes grew and she shoved Elodie's hand down.

"Put that away," she hissed. She sighed and shook her head. "Come with me."

She looked around with fear, and led Elodie out a back door to the alley behind the house. This small alley was cramped and isolated from the noise and movement of the city.

"Are you daft showing coin like that in a place like this?" She wiped a hand over her face. "This city may seem all safe on the outside, but show gold like that an' yer neck will be cut before you know it."

Elodie was shocked. She'd begun to think this city was the safest in Aluna.

The woman sighed and lowered her voice. "Look, I understand you knew Calendula in her last life, but you need to understand a few things." The woman paused and paced a few feet away before returning to Elodie, a heavy look in her eyes. "I was sold to a house when I was sixteen. My man had gambling debts, and used me to break even. My life, that life, it's over. It's as if it never existed. Even if I somehow managed to pay off my bond, what place would I have in the world when all I have to my name is this? All anyone knows me for is what I do here. Do you understand?"

Elodie didn't, and said nothing.

The older woman sighed. "Your friend is gone. The life she had and any possible future is gone. Her bond is all that remains. It's a hard thing to deal with for someone so young and so fresh sold as her. When you come here, askin' for your friend, and waving around gold, all it does is remind her how far she's come from her old life, and how she can never go back. You are torturin' her with your visits, and believe me when I say her life is hard enough."

Elodie dropped her head, shame made her cheeks heat. The woman turned to leave, but Elodie stopped her.

"Will you give her a message for me?" A small movement from an upper window caught her attention, a silver glint and red hair moving behind the frame of an open window.

"What's the message?" The woman tapped her foot impatient to go.

"Tell her that calendula is another name for a marigold," Elodie said. The woman frowned, but Elodie took a deep breath and kept going. "In some cultures it's a sign of the sun: bright, vibrant, and energetic. Providing life to those it's light touches. In other cultures it's used to adorn homes, welcoming its inhabitants and guests. Medically it has a million uses. Magically it grants protection. But just by itself, growing wherever it's planted, in mud, sand, clay or shit, calendula brings peace, life, and beauty." She paused and her eyes flicked again to the empty window. "Will you tell her that no matter who she is, what she does, or what is done to her, she always has been and will be that beautiful and bright calendula?"

The woman gave Elodie a long look before she nodded and headed back inside.

Elodie stood there, asking herself if the woman was right and if there was anything she could do to make it better for Callie. She didn't want to make anything harder on her friend. She looked to the window again, but there was no movement.

Elodie pulled her hood up over her face and turned down the alley, walking and thinking. She walked back to the castle the long way, following the perimeter of the town, hoping for just a little longer in the open air, near the trees and far away from everyone who would look on her with expectations or unspoken secrets.

After a short distance she became aware of someone following her and sighed. She couldn't hide from Silas in a snowstorm. She pulled down her hood and turned to look at him. Instead of his large green eyes she was met with the hard face of a man, greasy brown hair and piercing blue eyes.

She inhaled to let out a scream when the man hit her hard on the head and she fell to the ground. The world spun as she reached out to steady herself.

She tried to stand up, but the man was on her, grabbing her arms while something was draped over her head. She tried to scream but her voice caught in her throat and she coughed.

"Ha! It works!" a second man said, tapping something at her neck.

"Told ye it was a proper mage. I've bought silencing spells

from him before." The first man pulled Elodie's arms together. "Grab her feet."

Elodie's heart jumped and she fought. She pulled away as hard as she could and tried to break the man's grip. He held on tight and her wrists ached. She didn't care. The pain was nothing compared to the fear.

The other man grabbed her ankle and she kicked and twisted, desperate to break free. The man held her foot hard in his armpit and tried to grab the second foot. Elodie felt something pop in her ankle and a sharp pain stabbed up her leg.

She tried to cry out but no sound came from her mouth, the silence was a pressure building in her chest as if she couldn't breathe. She twisted and tried to bite and kick, but the pressure built and built. She couldn't pull in a breath. She gasped for air, but it didn't come. She saw lights in front of her eyes and her arms and legs got heavy, and then everything went dark.

Chapter Thirty-Nine

SHE WAS COLD.

The chill radiated from her back and butt. She tried to move and grab for blankets, but something sharp cut into her wrists.

She opened her eyes. It was dark, the only light coming from the flickering glow of a torch just out of view. The cold hardness at her back was stone. Everything around her was cold, hard stone. There was a large wooden something to her right, blocking the glow of the torch. She tried to move her hands, but the pain was back at her wrists. Metal clinked above her from the manacles wrapping her wrists. She pulled against the metal, it rattled but held firm.

Panic rose in her chest. She was trapped. She opened her mouth to scream but stopped herself. That wasn't how Gedas taught her to act in a crisis.

She took a slow shaky breath to clear her head. Gedas taught her to use what was around to accomplish her task. She wasn't helpless, she needed to think.

She shook her head, still trying to clear it. She didn't make complex spells to accomplish a specific goal like the academics looking for their magical ranking. She shaped magic along the natural path of her tools like a hedgewitch. She needed tools. There was nothing here for her magic to use.

The last few months, or was it a year now? Gedas tried to teach her magic, but she'd refused. If only she hadn't refused, maybe now it wouldn't be too late.

She pushed away that thought. She wasn't going to dwell on regrets. She closed her eyes again and took another deep breath and examined her surroundings. There was barely any life nearby, at least not any big enough to be of any use. The moss and mushrooms couldn't help.

She felt further. There was plenty of potential life around. The ground below her was mostly hard stone, but there was dirt, decomposing leaves and other bits of nature's trash creating a thin layer along the bottom of the cave floor. Hidden in this small bit of soil were seeds. Seeds carried in by the wind or by the droppings of an animal sheltering from the winter. The seeds were small points of potential life in the back of her mind.

The soil was thin, but maybe it would be enough. She closed her eyes and tried to focus. The fear and anxiety made it hard. She had to push away the thoughts and fears several times. How long until her kidnappers came back?

She focused on a few of the small seeds and reached out with the ruakh within her. Small roots of deep blue light stretched out in her mind's eye and into the soil around her. The thin root of her magic reached the seeds and she nudged the ruakh around them, pushed to awaken the dormant life inside.

She felt the sprouts expand suddenly and rapidly and burst from the thin layer of soil around her. She kept going. She kept pushing. The sprouts were an inch then two then three. Each expanded, searching for a sun that wasn't there and the first points of light winked out.

Elodie sucked in a deep breath at the sudden loss of life. Her gasp was silent as the spell on her chest cut off the sound. She'd never been so connected to a plant when it died. The tiny ferns and ivy needed water and sun.

Plants could grow from magic alone, she'd compensated before for the lack of sunlight or water or nutrients in the soil, but never all three. If she tried to keep growing the dozen or so sprouts they would all die. She took a deep breath and picked one. Wild strawberry. It was a natural climbing plant, she could direct it up the wall and onto the shackles around her hands.

She'd never done anything like this, but she had to try. She pushed her desperation into the plant and prompted it to grow and grow. Slowly, so unbearably slowly, it snaked carefully up the side of the stone. When the strawberry tried to put out a leaf or a bud, she stopped it, asking it to focus instead on reaching farther. She kept her eyes closed but she could feel its progress. It snaked around her arm and up her wrist. At last the edge of the climber reached the shackle. Now what?

She didn't know any plant spells to unlock something, the thought was absolutely absurd. Plants protected. They didn't unlock.

But they did sometimes destroy.

A plant could break and erode over time. Ivy cracked mortar between stones, roots tore up cement. The shackles were made of iron. Even if she had the resources to grow the strawberry stronger and farther, she doubted she could grow it fast enough to save her.

She had to try.

She grew the strawberry over the shackle and threaded it through the keyhole, then wrapped it around the lock, and back through the keyhole. Around and around she grew it till the keyhole was filled with the vine. She asked the vine to strengthen itself, to grow thicker and push against the metal. It hurt. The metal cut into the soft plant, but it pushed back. She didn't know how long she sat there, fighting in the war between the metal and the strawberry. She shook, and sweat dripped from her forehead.

There was a scraping sound in front of her and her concentration broke. She opened her eyes as a blond man came into view.

"Awake at last?" he asked, a sick smile on his face. "Don't

worry, the chains are fastened well. You ain't going anywhere, flower."

He moved closer to Elodie and crouched before her. She tried to scoot back against the rock, but her ankle throbbed.

"How about we have a little fun before the boss comes back?" he asked.

She flinched away and tried to scream again, but the pressure on her chest was back. She couldn't breathe. She stopped screaming, gasping for breath, but kept kicking as much as she could, ignoring the stabbing pain in her ankle.

"Easy girl, easy, easy."

"Oi! I said hands off, Calub," another voice said. The blue-eyed man grabbed the blond man. "Don't hurt the merchandise." He shoved Calub away.

Elodie remembered then, why those eyes had been so familiar. She'd seen that man in the bordello house when she'd first gone to find Callie.

"Orders were to kill her. What does it matter if we have a little fun first?" Calub straightened moving away from Elodie.

"I don't care what the orders were. Do you see who that is? That's the princess. We can ransom her for double what they're paying us to kill her. You go tell Leu I want her keeping a lookout and you are to play scout. I'm going to town to set up the ransom."

"Shouldn't one of us stay in here?" Calub asked, his eyes landing on Elodie again.

"Na, she's chained to the wall, she's not going anywhere."

The two men walked out of her line of sight. She waited till she couldn't hear them any longer before she pulled against the chains around her wrist, the strawberry clinging to her arm, forgotten in her panic.

She could escape, she could slip her wrist out. It wouldn't be too hard, her hands were small. She was just a little girl. She pulled and pulled, and the metal cut into her hand more and more, it cut into her vine, severing it.

She could do this, she could do this, she could do this.

She fought against the chains trying to make her hands smaller and smaller.

She could do this, she could do this, she could do this.

The tears fell down her face soaking into her shirt and the sobs tried to come out, but the pressure was at her chest again, she could barely breathe.

Slowly the light died within the plant without magic to sustain it.

Her breaths came in harder and faster.

She couldn't do this.

Her hands hurt. Her thumbs felt like they were going to pop out of their sockets. Her hands felt numb and warm liquid trickled down her arm as she fought against the metal.

She wasn't sure how long she'd been struggling, how long she'd been fighting against the chains.

She couldn't do this, she couldn't do this, she couldn't do this.

She cried silently. She was tired and exhausted. Every muscle hurt and still she cried.

Movement.

A person came into view, a woman. Her light brown hair pulled back to show an angular face and uncaring eyes. She looked down on Elodie, her face blank as she lifted the bow in her hand and brought it down hard on Elodie's head.

Chapter Forty

THERE WAS A LOUD BANG, and a muffled cry that brought Elodie to consciousness. When she opened her eyes it was lighter. The stone of the cave was lit with a pale glow of daylight.

"Go see what that was," came the voice of the blue-eyed man.

The second man, Calub, walked past her view toward the daylight.

A dull light flashed and something large came flying back into the tunnel past the corner where she lay.

It was Calub. His legs lay bent oddly. The other man cursed and came into view, ax in hand. He rushed toward the entrance of the cave, releasing a war cry as he went.

She heard a clash of metal, and another, followed by a scuffling. The man with the ax fell just in front of her, a pained expression on his face. He choked and blood came out of his mouth, and then he stopped moving. Elodie inhaled, a scream in her throat that caught and couldn't escape.

The pressure built in her chest again, and she forced herself to breathe slowly.

Another face came around the crates, and the breath turned into a silent sob as she looked up into the fierce, angry eyes of

Gedas. Blue sparks flared in his cold gray eyes as he crouched before her and placed a gentle hand on the cut on her head.

Sir Jesper appeared next, blood splattered on his face. He looked Elodie over then called over his shoulder. "Check their pockets for keys."

"No need," Gedas's voice was hard and icy.

He pulled the pendant over her head and dropped it to the ground. Free of the silencing charm, Elodie let out half a sob. The pressure on her chest was gone.

Gedas reached above her head to her wrists. She felt his warm hands cover the metal. His eyes glowed before there was a crunch and bits of dust fell over her head. He lowered her hands and picked the flaking metal and rust off her skin before meeting her eyes.

"I caught one trying to escape," Silas called from the entrance.

"Oh goodie," Gedas replied, a scary smile on his face. Another spark jumped in his eye before he stood and turned from Elodie. "Drop him there."

"Silas, get her out of here," Sir Jesper called.

Silas appeared, an intense look on his face.

"Can you stand?" he asked.

She nodded and he helped her to her feet. Pain shot up her leg, but she gritted her teeth.

Elodie looked at the dead man on the ground and froze. Silas nudged her chin making her look him in the eyes. She'd stopped moving. "Hey, don't look there, focus on me, alright?"

She nodded and he led her around the body.

"Please, let me go, I don't know anything I promise," came the voice of the man who'd wanted to play. Elodie looked over her shoulder in time to see the wall of the cave reach out and wrap around his arms, pulling him into the stone.

The man started to scream.

Silas pulled her faster toward the cave entrance.

"What do you think, Jesper? Think he truly knows nothing?"

Gedas asked, his voice had his usual tone of quizzical inquiry to it, but she felt that icy hardness just under the surface.

"Not likely. How far can you make the wall eat him?" the knight asked calmly.

"Let's find out."

Terrified screams followed them as they cleared the cave entrance. Silas led Elodie into the woods.

"Don't worry, they won't kill him, they're just looking for information."

Elodie thought she wouldn't mind if they did kill him, then regretted it. She didn't want to be a bad person.

They passed the woman, laying at the foot of a tree. She looked unhurt except for the faint blood at her nose and the blank look in her eyes.

Elodie started to limp badly before they'd gone much farther, slowing their pace to a crawl. Sharp cries echoed behind them.

Her face was wet and she lifted a dirty rust-covered hand to wipe away the tears. Silas paused and bent down, picking Elodie up into his strong arms. She tried to protest but he shushed her, and she buried her face in his tunic, embarrassed at how heavy she must be and ashamed of her weakness.

"Almost there," Silas reassured her. A few moments later he set her down on a low flat rock on the edge of an outcropping. A few horses tied to a tree beside them nosed through the leaves looking for grass.

Silas dug around in a saddlebag and came back with a blanket and waterskin. He made her drink and draped the blanket around her shoulders before he set to cleaning her wrists. He washed away the rust and blood and pulled out a small jar from one of his packs. The smell of witch hazel, comfrey and calendula in the ointment calmed her with its familiarity.

The dead eyes of the man appeared in her mind again, the woman laying blank and still. Elodie tried to rise and Silas helped her up.

"What? Tell me what you need?"

Elodie turned away from him and threw up on a peppermintsteel bush nearby. She heaved until there was nothing left and the spasms left her body, then she let Silas lead her back to the rock. She kept her eyes on her hands while Silas cleaned the blood and the dirt from her face.

"I threw up afterwards. The first time I killed someone." Silas rubbed the ointment into her wrists. The scent of the herbs wrapped around her.

"When?"

"Over the winter. I was in Haxbie, doing border duty with Sir Jesper. A group of bandits attacked a village we'd been at the week before. They killed a few of the villagers, this boy who worked at a tavern, Adin. Anyways. We found them hiding in some caves, kind of like this. They were mostly drunk on what they'd stolen. I was to watch for anyone escaping, Sir Jesper didn't want me in combat yet. This huge man, maybe seven feet tall, came at me with a blacksmith hammer, and I just reacted. Sir Jesper says that's what the training is for, so your body knows what to do even when your mind forgets or panics. I gutted him then got sick all over myself and the man. I felt like a joke knowing the soldiers and Sir Jesper would come back from the cave and see the mess, me being the boy who couldn't even keep it together to do his duty. When Sir Jesper came back, after they had dealt with the bandits, he said I'd done a good job." He paused. "One of the men, this gruff old soldier who's been married three times and swears he will marry his sword next time, he said that's what it is. Combat. It's messy and we can't always control how we react to it. It doesn't make you weak as long as you try to do what's right."

It made some kind of sense why Silas had been so focused on his duty. She hated that word when she looked at him and only saw the stoic squire. Older than her and distant, not the friend she'd made. She felt duty was a shield he put between them as an excuse not to be friends as he outgrew her in so many ways, but maybe he needed that shield to help get through all he'd seen and to become all he would be someday.

Elodie nodded in response to his words, he looked relieved as though he'd been worried she wouldn't understand.

Silas wrapped a clean cloth around her wrists sealing in the ointment.

"Gedas will need to clean these better, but this will keep it clean while we head back to the castle."

"How far are we?" Her voice was a croak.

"Only a few hours' ride."

Silas handed her the waterskin and she rinsed out her mouth before drinking.

"How did you find me?"

"The man who left the ransom note. A guard recognized him and Gedas gave him something to make him tell everything he knew. He didn't know what caves you were in, but when we were close Gedas sensed your magic. Did you know Gedas could do that?"

"Yeah, it's an easy potion to make if you have the right ingredients."

"No, not the truth potion, the thing he did with your manacles. They just dissolved. He also blasted that woman, and the man who first came out of the cave. It was some type of energy like an explosion under water." Silas looked into the distance. "The mages in the castle, their magic is always so flashy. Shocking to look at, but not impressive. Gedas is usually like that with his magic. Trying to scare away visitors or remind people he has magic, but never anything big. This was big. There was no flash, no excitement or fear, just direct calculated magic meant to destroy."

Elodie had seen Gedas do big magic before, when he stopped a burst dam, holding the water back long enough for the people to escape. But he always acted like it had been a one time thing, not something he could repeat. Possible due to the positioning of the sun that specific day. A fluke.

He did other things sometimes, cushioning the fall of a boy who fell off of a bridge, nearly unnoticeable except for the slight blurring of the air. Healing the wound of a pregnant woman stabbed by farming equipment, saying the wound hadn't been so bad after all, on closer examination. He always downplayed his power and his abilities, the scope of his magic. And as Elodie watched the awe and fear play through Silas's eyes, she thought she might understand why he always came up with one excuse or another when she asked him to do anything more than barely useful.

Before she could answer, Silas's eyes widened in alert focus.

"Stay down," he ordered. He stepped away and drew his sword moving around the rock outcropping. Elodie crouched down among the rocks until Silas returned a moment later, sheathing his sword.

"It's just Sir Jesper and Gediminas."

Gedas came around the rocks and crouched down in front of her again. Elodie was relieved to see the lightning was gone from his eyes.

"How are you feeling, my Gull?"

"Fine," she said with a weak smile.

"Her ankle is hurt I think," Silas announced. Elodie gave him a dirty look, but saw he was helping Sir Jesper drop a lifeless body over the knight's large war horse.

"Is he—"

"Just knocked out," Gedas replied as he wrapped a hand around her ankle. She felt a slight tingle. "We figured the trip back would be easier for all parties involved if he was unconscious. Just sprained." He gripped her ankle tighter. The tingling increased and a warm pressure surged over her ankle and up her leg. It burned for a split second and was then gone. Her ankle felt loose and didn't have any pain when Gedas rotated her foot. "Hands next." Elodie placed her hands in his and he peeled back the bandages on one of her wrists. "A fine job our squire did."

Gedas pressed the bandage back onto the small inflamed cuts and held it in place. Again the tingling and the warmth and the searing heat before he pulled off the bandage and wiped the puss and dirt away from the healed skin. Her wrist wasn't even red anymore.

"I thought it was better to let the body heal itself, and only use magic to help aid the process?" Elodie asked, repeating words he'd said many times before.

"That may be true when I am a little less angry."

"I'm sorry," Elodie started, but Gedas cut her off.

"I'm not mad at you, my Gull, I'm mad at the filth that thought to hold you ransom for gold," he said, disgust clear on his face even as he kept the anger from his eyes. He started on her other wrist.

"They were supposed to kill me, not ransom me," Elodie muttered.

Gedas's hands stilled, as still as the man dead in the cave had been.

"What do you mean 'supposed to'," Sir Jesper asked as Gedas resumed his work.

"That's what he said," she gestured to the man, unconscious and tied to the saddle like a sack of grain. "He said they had orders to kill me, but the other one knew I was a princess, and said they would get more if they ransomed me." Elodie looked down so she didn't have to see the anger flaring in the eyes of the three people before her. Gedas moved to her head next, making her raise her chin so he could see it. The cut on her head was tender to the touch and pulsed through her head. The tingles started again when he put his hand over it, but this time when the heat flashed over her, everything went dark, and then Gedas was helping her sit up.

"Just a minor concussion," he said. "Nothing to worry about. Shall we mount up?"

Jesper frowned and crouched beside Elodie. "I know you've been through an ordeal, my lady, but it's best we talk now while the thoughts are fresh."

Gedas sighed loudly but Elodie nodded and tried to answer Jesper's questions in detail. How she was taken, where she'd seen the man before, everything she overheard. She'd been unconscious for most of it, and didn't think her words helped, but Jesper thanked her and they mounted the horses.

Elodie rode double with Silas so someone could hold her up when she passed out, as Gedas predicted she would. His magic used her body's resources to heal itself, and coupled with the stress of the ordeal, she was asleep before the warmth of Silas at her back had fully seeped through her blanket. She awoke frequently in a drowsy mess of panic only to be reassured by Silas, and drift back to sleep. She didn't remember much of the journey back, Gedas riding in the lead and Sir Jesper walking on foot, leading the prisoner tied to the horse. When they reached the castle there were shouts and cries of outrage. They sent guards to the cave to fetch the dead.

Someone carried Elodie to her rooms, and she slept.

Elodie's dreams were filled with caves and chains and glowing eyes. She awoke, sweaty, her heart racing.

She didn't want to stay alone in her room any longer as the walls narrowed like a dark cave. She wrapped a robe around herself and stepped into her boots. Even if she just sat in a chair by the fire of Gedas's room, she knew she'd sleep better.

Elodie opened her door and almost screamed as someone moved in the hallway.

"What's wrong?" Silas whispered. He approached the gap of her door.

"What are you doing out here?" Elodie's heart raced.

"Standing guard."

"All night?"

"There are a few of us taking shifts. What's wrong?" he asked again.

"Nothing."

"Why aren't you asleep?"

Elodie shrugged looking down.

"Bad dreams?" he asked before sighing. "It is normal you know. Nothing to be ashamed of."

"I was going to see if maybe Gedas was awake or something."

"I haven't heard him stirring in a while. He's just next door now." He gestured to the room on Elodie's left.

"What? His room was on the floor below mine."

"With everything that happened we wanted to make sure you were more secure. Sir Jesper and I are on your other side." He gestured to the right.

A ball formed in her throat and pressure started behind her eyes. They'd changed rooms, and Silas was losing sleep, standing guard. It made her feel safe in a way she'd started to doubt she ever would again.

"Aren't you tired out here? It's the middle of the night."

"I could say the same about you, you know." He smiled. "I have a few hours left and then Sir Jesper will take over." His eyes were warm and caring, meeting hers for once, no shield of duty or pang of guilt making him drop his gaze. Elodie looked away and silence fell between them.

"Do you know I write letters to you sometimes?" she asked.

"When?"

"When I'm in the spell. I keep this journal where I write down everything I remember from the Twoshy so it's harder to forget this place is real. And when I start to question it, I can go back and read about my last trip. Anyways, I started writing letters to you in that journal," she said in a rush, unsure why she was telling him. "It's stupid because I know I can't send them, but I think about what you would say and it helps."

They fell into silence again.

"Will you come to my knighting?" Silas asked. "It's not for a few years, and I know you don't have control over when you travel or not, but if you're here, will you come?"

His eyes held hope, and Elodie's stomach grew tight.

"Yes, I'd love to be there." She knew it wasn't a promise she could make, and the tightness doubled. She had no control over such things, no control at all. But she wished she could keep it. "Did you ever hear from Dess's brother about the spell?"

Silas grimaced. "I did but I don't know what help Jinis will be."

He rubbed a hand over his face. "Dess was supposed to be on this Progress you know, but her knight master was told her services were needed elsewhere." Silas grimaced. "Anyways, Jinis went on a lot about magical theory in his letter. It's the kind of thing we'd need a mage degree just to understand. I ran over it a few dozen times and I think it comes down to two points. He said that there are a few different structures to the implementation of spells, most commonly Surrogate and Ethereal. Ethereal magic is cast directly on the ruakh within or around the object to complete a spell. In contrast, Surrogate magic is cast on the ruakh of another object as a stand in for the real thing."

Elodie nodded, Gedas had taught her basic magical theory. "You can create wards using both. Walking the perimeter of a place and dropping charmed leaves as I do to anchor the ruakh of the ward is Ethereal magic. But if I wanted to place a ward around a whole city, and had the strength for it, I couldn't easily walk the distance. Instead I could create a physical representation of the city and place the ward around that object, then my magic would be projected onto the intended target creating a Surrogate spell."

Silas smiled. "I'm glad you're familiar with the concepts, I was sure I'd butcher the explanation." Silas took a deep breath. "Jinis said it's a long-standing debate among magical users what type of spell yours is. There are some who believe the magic is tied to each of the Misplaced children independently, while others believe it's a spell construct. He also went on to say investigation of the spell is heavily discouraged in the university. Students who make it their mastery projects for example, are shut down. It's sort of become an urban legend, something every student thinks on, knowing in the end no one's going to know what happened or how it was created."

"So in the end he knew nothing?" Elodie asked.

"In the end he explained why he knows nothing," Silas said, agreeing with her. "He did say the first step in breaking the spell would be to determine if it's a Surrogate or Ethereal spell." Silas shrugged. "It's something at least."

"And if it was easy to figure out, someone would have already picked up on the magic around me or one of the other Misplaced."

"Most likely."

"So maybe that means it's a Surrogate spell? They can be harder to trace."

Silas shrugged. "Your guess is better than mine. He also said one of the Misplaced in Pundica has been trying to find out everything they could about the spell. They're secretive and wouldn't tell Jinis anything, but I gave him a letter to pass on to this Allen. Maybe it will help."

They fell into silence again. The fear of her dream had long passed, and Elodie began to grow tired. She leaned against the doorframe and yawned.

"Why don't you go back to bed now. I promise you'll be safe. If anyone tries to get through me, I will at least be able to wake up Gediminas and Sir Jesper so they can save you," he said with a smile.

"I think you can take out anyone who tried to get through."

"I would try."

Those words hung between them for a moment as their meaning sunk into Elodie. She didn't want this boy to ever be put in a place where he could die for her. How could her life ever be worth more than his when his heart and courage and honor shone so bright?

"Thank you, Silas," she whispered. She headed back into her room and closed the door. She wasn't sure she would sleep, but she didn't want to burden Silas with anything more if she could help it.

She'd never come face to face with so much danger. She'd never felt such extreme terror. It was life-changing. It was shattering. The silencing spell had been so real and so smothering. Magic had always played such a consequential role in her life. It had trapped her and controlled her since she was a baby.

Every part of her cried for freedom from magic, but now a small part of her wondered if she'd neglected that side of herself to her own detriment. Magic trapped every moment of her life, even when she couldn't feel the chains around her wrists. She didn't think she could trust it long enough to use it.

And now according to Silas the only way to break the spell would be to learn more magic.

Everything inside of her wanted to hide, to curl up under her blanket and hide from the world.

The Twoshy really was falling apart if someone could kidnap her out of a city as clean and respectable as Comak.

For the first time she could ever remember, Elodie wished she could leave the Twoshy and sink back into the mundane safety of the illusion. Suddenly being sent away from her family didn't seem as dangerous as what waited for her in the Twoshy.

Maybe she shouldn't try so hard to break the spell.

Chapter Forty-One

WHEN PRESSED WITH A TRUTH SERUM, the man, Calub, didn't know who'd paid them to capture and kill Elodie. He only saw the man once, and remembered several large scars running down the left of his face. No one knew the man by description, but Sir Jesper told Elodie he wouldn't stop investigating.

Calub was executed later that week.

Sir Jesper suggested attempted regicide and an execution should call the end of the Progress. Duke Devoss and the few courtiers left jumped at the excuse to call an end to their torture. Oburleck was sad to see things come to an end, but Elodie had a suspicion no one would have continued if the Progress had started back on the road.

Elodie left a week later with Silas, Sir Jesper, and Gedas. The small abbreviated party headed east to Tate.

Before they left Silas came to her with a letter. He said the envelope had been addressed to him and left with a guard, but the letter inside was for her.

She opened the thick paper addressed to Ellie. The writing was elegant and beautiful with little flourishes in all the right places.

Whatever you think of me, I am not sunshine and I am not light. Maybe that's what I could have been had I not been born in a gutter then bound in silver, but that isn't who I am now. I know a lot about pretending to be something I'm not. Trust me on this, Ellie, I'm an expert in masks, pretty lies and playing pretend. I may not be all the nice pretty things you said, but I'm good at surviving and I'm a good judge of character.

Do you know who else is good at hiding behind pretty smiles, my dear Ellie? I'll give you a hint. Pin a rose to your nose or you'll perish before the conversation has ended. The baron asked me to pass messages to Him a few times. The messages asked when they would deal with their big problem and if they could use their little problem to help pave the way. I may not know much that can be put in books or used to make magic potions, but I know what danger smells like, and, my dear, you need to watch who you trust.

Forget me, Ellie, I'm not some houseplant you'll be able to save. Worry about yourself instead.

There was no signature, and Elodie pressed the letter close to her heart before she read it again and passed it to Silas.

She tried to align the good man she knew Oburleck to be with the warning and failed. With the Progress ending there was nothing Oburleck could do to help or hurt her. She would let Silas worry about the danger while she handled her grief. She refused to believe her and Callie's story was finished. She would save her friend one way or another.

Elodie wasn't quite sure why Sir Jesper insisted he and Silas would be better for a few weeks' rest before heading back to the border to resume their duties, but Elodie was thankful for the familiar faces.

They spent two months in Tate, surrounded by Silas's family and the welcoming atmosphere his parents built in their castle. Silas's fourteenth birthday came and Elodie baked him a cake. It was lopsided and the frosting was lumpy, but it made him smile. The shield of duty he'd kept between them had broken when she was kidnapped, and their days were filled with the joy and laughter of their old friendship.

She didn't want to think about the someday he would be old enough to realize she wasn't some shining princess he could put his hope of the future in. She didn't want him to see her for the benign, useless, misplaced scrap she was.

It was a few days after his birthday that Elodie saw that familiar shimmer. She dropped the bow in her hands and turned to Silas on the practice range. She opened her mouth to say goodbye, her eyes connecting to his clear green ones before the ruakh grabbed her up, and pulled her hard to the left.

ELODIE FELL THROUGH NOTHING, spinning head over heels until she landed hard on the carpet. When the spinning ended she sat up and took a deep breath.

Silas was nowhere to be seen, of course, and the dusty archery range with the smell of leather and dirt was long gone.

"Sweetie! It's time for dinner," her mother called. Elodie jumped. She stood up swaying on her feet. It wouldn't do for her mother to come around the hallway to see her on the floor. She wasn't sure why at first, but she knew it was something she needed to prevent.

Elodie steadied herself with a hand on the smooth beige wall and stared at her hand in the fading light from the window. It looked wrong somehow, out of place.

She was wearing her archery glove.

Archery gloves weren't something you were supposed to wear in the illusion, and Elodie was trying to be normal.

She frantically undid the strap of the glove and ripped the leather off her hand. She balled up the glove and tried to stuff it in her jeans pocket before her mother saw, but her dress was in the way and she couldn't reach her pocket. She picked up the skirt of the light seafoam green dress Silas had complimented that morning and stuffed the glove in her pocket. She dropped the skirt and tried to smooth out the bunches of the dress around the waist of her jeans.

Her stomach dropped. She was still wearing her dress from the Twoshy.

Elodie panicked and started to take off the dress but stoped. That would never do, walking around the house with no shirt would be more noticeable than the dress.

She forced herself to take a deep breath and tried to carefully walk down the hall on silent feet like Silas tried teaching her. When she reached the entrance to the kitchen, Elodie listened closely. The sound of a pot on the stove being shuffled, the clink of a glass cup. When she heard the faucet turn on Elodie ran for it, darting past the kitchen and the big bay window.

Elodie ran up the stairs.

When she reached her room she closed and locked the door. She stripped off the green linen dress and stuffed it under her pillow, cramming the leather archery glove with it. She headed to her closet to get a new shirt. She couldn't remember what she'd been wearing before the ruakh had sucked her into the Twoshy all those weeks ago, but she hoped her mother wouldn't either.

Moving her arms felt weird until she realized it was because the muscle she'd built from her bow practice was gone. She knew it would happen, but the realization still hurt. So much work for nothing.

After she changed, Elodie went to her bookcase and pulled down her old journal, trying to write down everything she could remember, starting with Callie. She would not forget her friend.

She wrote about the spell, and what Silas hadn't learned from Jinis. There were clues she would need to break the spell. Maybe this weekend she would sit down and read back through the journal and write out all the pieces.

She'd started writing about her frustrating conversation with Oburleck, the dragon's breath and Callie's warning when her mom called her again.

Setting down her pen, she took a deep breath and headed to dinner. She was setting the table when her mom stopped next to her.

"Did you change clothes, sweetie?"

Elodie froze, silverware poised over a napkin. "No?" she said, trying to infuse as much confusion in the word as possible.

Her mom didn't ask again.

Elodie spent the weekend thinking over the last few months, in the Twoshy as well as in the spell. Between all the traveling and conflict it felt like her worlds had been falling far apart in a storm of chaos. The quiet weeks spent with Gedas and Sir Jesper and Silas at Tate had let a peace settle over her. Coming back, that peace had been broken and Elodie began to feel the fear lingering in the bottom of her stomach, waiting for something to slip and for her to be found out for her lies, and her delusions.

Monday came, and Elodie went to school, her dress and archery glove crammed into the side of her backpack.

In art class, Elodie forged the chasm between her and her best friend and sat in her old seat next to Vanessa. Her friend looked up with a tentative smile before gathering her supplies for the class activity. They didn't talk that period, but there was a momentary peace between them. When class was over, Vanessa asked Elodie if she wanted to eat lunch together.

Elodie smiled and hugged her friend. "I'm sorry," she said into Vanessa's hair. "I think I get it now."

"Come on, kid," Vanessa said, taking her friend's arm in hers and leading her out.

As they headed to their old lunch spot, Elodie told Vanessa about her trip, in the briefest terms, and told her about what happened to Callie. "I think I get what you mean by getting left behind. I've always felt like everyone in the Twoshy is passing me by. I visit them a few times a year, and their lives keep moving without me. They get older and outgrow me while I'm back here. I was so focused on how much I hate that and want it to end, I didn't realize I was doing the same thing to you."

"I know it's not your fault," Vanessa began.

"But it's my fault for how I handle it. We may not have our whole lives to be friends and I don't want to miss the time we have right now. You're my best friend, Vanessa, and life sucks without you."

"I hated it too." Vanessa gave Elodie another tight hug. "But Elodie, do you think you could just remember one thing for me?"

"Anything."

Vanessa sighed. "I'm a real person. I believe you about the Twoshy, I always have, and I always will, but . . . I'm real."

Elodie nodded. "You are."

They were silent.

"Oh, I almost forgot." Elodie told her friend about the dress and glove. "Can you get rid of them for me? I didn't want to throw them away at home or here and have someone get the wrong idea."

Elodie pulled out the dress and glove and handed them over to her friend.

"Ooh, can I keep them?" Vanessa asked, holding the dress up to her thinner frame.

"As long as my mom doesn't find out where you got them, they're yours." She showed her how the archery glove was worn.

"Maybe I'll ask my dad for a bow for my birthday." Vanessa stood, arms up as though she was pulling back a bow. Elodie laughed and corrected her friend's stance as Silas often did for her.

Vanessa would fit in the Twoshy. She would maybe fit better than Elodie herself. She would become a great craftswoman, creating the most unique and beautiful jewelry designs, or maybe a famous painter, doing portraits or frescoes for the wealthy across the Twoshy.

"I don't know how the spell works," Elodie told her friend while they ate. "And the more I look, the more I think I may never know. But, a part of me doesn't want to find out, because I don't want to leave you."

"Being left behind is something I have to deal with, El. That's not up to you to solve. I mean, don't you have enough on your plate as it is? Besides, maybe when you figure out a way to break the spell, you'll find a way to bring me with you." A sad but wistful smile crossed her face.

"Silas says Aluna isn't stable without a permanent ruler. And here I'm just running the risk every day of saying the wrong thing and having my mom and dad send me off to some institute."

Vanessa was quiet for a few minutes as she ate her fruit snacks. Finally she turned to Elodie, a resolved expression on her face.

"Look, El, I know your mom can be . . . your mom, with how she reacts to things, but have you thought of just talking to her? Telling her what you're scared of and what you're working on? Maybe she'll understand. I mean, leave out the stuff about the Twoshy, but talk about the rest and see if that helps."

"I can't talk to her like you talk to your parents. She just gives me the broken-adopted-kid look."

"But what if that's the problem? What if she doesn't think *you're* broken, just your relationship? Maybe she's as worried as you are. My mom says she worries about me a million times a day, and my dad says adults don't have all the answers, they just pretend to so there isn't anarchy."

Elodie shrugged. "What's the worst that can happen? If you're wrong at least I won't stay locked up when the ruakh comes for me."

"Trust me. I know these things," Vanessa said smugly, patting her friend on the back.

"I know," Elodie said evenly. "You're the smartest person I know after all."

"I love you too."

AFTER THEY RETURNED from visiting Doctor Abernathy, Elodie followed her mom into the kitchen and sat in one of the tall stools by the bar while her mom made dinner.

She fiddled with her hands, with the vase holding the fake flowers on the bar, and with the hem of her shirt while her mom moved around cooking and chopping.

"Mom, can I talk to you?"

Her mom froze, knife over the broccoli.

"Of course, honey." She resumed her chopping but now with a more intentional rhythm.

Elodie took a breath and it came out shaky. "I just wanted to say that I'm trying." The tears started falling nearly as soon as the first word came out, and Elodie started shaking in anger and fear at her emotions. She tried to stop herself but it kept coming. "I'm trying, mom. I'm trying so hard to be normal but it's so difficult. Just give me more time, I promise I'll get it eventually. I'll figure out how to be normal." The tears came faster and harder and Elodie couldn't stop them, regardless of how hard she pinched her leg, trying to distract herself. "You don't have to get rid of me or, or ship me off to any facility. I promise I'll get it. Just give me time. I need more time."

Her mom came around the bar and put her hands on Elodie's shoulders, looking her daughter over, confusion and pain on her face.

"Honey, what are you talking about? We aren't going to get rid of you. What would ever make you think that?"

"I heard you and Dad talking about how we couldn't keep going on like this, and a boy at school said he knew someone who visited Doctor Abernathy and got sent away to a facility. You guys put me on crazy pills but they made me more crazy, and now try as hard as I can I still can't be normal!" She nearly shouted her frustration.

"Honey, no. Stop and listen to me." Her mother put her hand on Elodie's face, trying to wipe away a few tears. "Those pills were never because we thought you were crazy. We don't think you're crazy. Don't ever think that word again. Sometimes you have a hard time dealing with things and we thought the pills might help level things out for you, make things a bit easier for you to handle. But you didn't have the best reaction to them. Doctor Abernathy thinks we should give it a few more years and then if you're still having trouble balancing things we can try again after you hit puberty."

"But what if it doesn't work?" Elodie asked, choking on a sob. "I can't keep going on like this, trying and trying and trying to be normal, and failing. Waiting for the moment when I'm going to be too much. For one more thing to go wrong till I'm too broken to function and then you guys send me off somewhere to get fixed."

"Sweetie, we are never going to get rid of you," her mother said, each word pointed and firm. "We adopted you because we love you, and we wanted you. That has not changed, nor will it ever change." She pulled Elodie tight to her chest and held her. "You are ours, and that is never going to change. Biological child or not, I love you with every part of me. It doesn't mean I always understand you, honey, but I honestly think that's pretty normal for a mother and daughter at our ages." She chuckled. "There is nothing wrong with you."

Elodie sobbed a little harder, burying her face in her mom's shoulder.

"You're not broken." She kissed the top of Elodie's head. "But I know sometimes we haven't been very good at communicating and I'm sorry. I'm so sorry, honey. You scared us when you disappeared and we didn't know where you were. We didn't know what happened to you. We still don't know and that terrifies me. I lie awake sometimes thinking about you being gone and what could have happened."

She paused and Elodie felt guilt creep into her stomach. She could never tell her mom where she went. Even if her mom said she wouldn't get rid of her, telling the truth was still a line Elodie didn't think she could get back over.

"I know you may or may not want to tell me what happened," her mom continued. "I just want you to know when you are ready to talk, I'm here. I won't judge you and you won't be in trouble. We will never love you any less, and there's nothing you can ever do to make me get rid of you. I just want to make sure that you're safe. That you're always safe."

"Do you promise?" Elodie asked, choking back her tears.

"Yes, I promise," her mom said, holding her tight.

A knot in her stomach loosened. It was a tightness she'd been living with for a while. She was hopeful that maybe soon, the fear, the anxiousness, the uncertainty, and that knot, would be gone. She prayed it wouldn't be a part of her normal forever.

Acknowledgments

After having written an entire book needing to write something meaningful at the end is kind of the worst torture in the world.

This book has been a long time coming, overcoming self-doubt and pushing through my own laziness and life's many distractions. It has taken a long time to get here, but we did it! Thank you to everyone who had a part with this book, either with its creation or with supporting me through the process. While this in no way details the full list, special shoutout to the following people:

My mom (yeah obviously you're first). The Gaspards, we'll have our castle one day. My Moon and Stars: Kristina, HM Quanstrom, Adele, Michelle, and Cecile, for reading it first. Julie, Krystal, Kody and Karlye, for all your support. Thank you Kat and Rachel, for Making Elodie look and sound good.

Lastly, but most importantly, thank you to the real Elodie Harper and Silas Tate. Thank you for lending your names to these characters and I hope that you will always find your place in this world and know how truly loved you are.

About the Author

Heather Michelle is an emerging author of young adult fantasy. She lives in Acworth, GA with her cat Mister Bingley and a slew of unique roommates.

Growing up, Heather Michelle spent more time living in her imagination than outside of it. Small town life sandwiched between the redwood forests and the Pacific ocean provided a rich scope for the imagination. Before the age of twelve, Heather Michelle was not a reader, but a chance encounter with a rented audiobook launched her into the vast world of the printed word, and she never looked back.

Elodie's story doesn't end here. Keep an eye out for the next book in The Misplaced Children series: A Misplaced Hope, coming soon.

www.hmwrites.com

 instagram.com/heathermichely

Lightning Source UK Ltd.
Milton Keynes UK
UKHW010815280620
365679UK00001B/8/J